"It gave me enormous pleasure."

—*Paul Theroux*

"Anya is a new kind of heroine; Mac is a new kind of hero. . . . He wants to know Anya as he might know a wild river. Her fury attracts him but it is not in him to tame her nor does he wish to. . . . John Casey has nearly made them breathe; the pages of this romance wrinkle with their energy." —*Philadelphia Inquirer*

"A novel that blazes with feeling and intelligence."

—*Brendan Gill*

"Anya is a remarkable picture of what has come to be known as 'modern woman.' While she may be more appealing—because she *knows* what she is doing—she is also more ruthless than most feminist heroines. . . . Yet Mac is an admirable character, a new kind of hero. He is secure enough in his masculinity to support Anya."

—*The New York Times*

AN AMERICAN ROMANCE

JOHN CASEY

A KANGAROO BOOK
PUBLISHED BY POCKET BOOKS NEW YORK

POCKET BOOKS, a Simon & Schuster division of
GULF & WESTERN CORPORATION
1230 Avenue of the Americas, New York, N.Y. 10020

CONTENTS

Part One

A BUTTER-
AND-EGG MAN

CHAPTER

‖‖‖‖‖‖‖‖‖‖‖‖‖‖‖‖‖‖‖‖‖‖‖‖‖‖‖‖‖

1

Anya studied Mac for almost a day before she had a conversation with him.

The two of them were the only nonmembers of the University of Chicago Outing Club on the trip, except for the rock-climbing instructor the club had hired.

Anya was attracted to Mac, although he wasn't any of the types she was used to. In fact he seemed likable, and she was used to not liking the people she was attracted to. Before she even spoke to him she found herself trying to edit out either his sexual appeal or his likability.

She thought he was studying her. At least watching her. This interest was somewhat novel to her too—she was used to people becoming interested in her manner, her talent, her nerve, her thought, and only later in her looks. She sometimes thought it was as if she had to give lessons in the theory of herself before anyone was ready to use the equipment.

No one had ever told her she was beautiful. Her foster father, Henry Sewall, once told her she looked like a picture of a Cretan bull dancer. He showed her photographs of the paintings at Knossos. She saw it was true. He said that the paintings were beautiful. The syllogism didn't close.

Her roommate in college, Tassie, had told her she could be prettier, and showed her how. Tassie was also right. After she did what Tassie told her, she was prettier.

A recent lover, Henniker, had told her she was wickedly handsome. That was his idea of one good way for women

3

to look. His other idea was fragile and elegant. She no longer minded not being fragile and elegant.

But Mac looked at her with what she was sure was admiration. It reminded her of a look she'd seen on the face of a dance instructor, or a theater director, or a costume mistress. A look that said, Now *that's* not bad.

Later she learned how unapt her comparison was. Later she learned that it was true he'd looked at her with admiration, but neither what he'd admired nor the way his admiration composed itself had anything to do with dance or theater or costume. It was raw.

Anya woke up early. Mac was up and had started a small fire. He'd also opened the door to the cabin. Very gray outside. The others had retreated deep into their sleeping bags, a lot of them entirely out of sight. The cabin wasn't too stuffy, probably because so many of them had zippered their fumes out of general circulation.

Mac rather shyly turned to the fire while she put her shirt on. She slid out of her bag, admired the blue shimmer her fishnet long-underwear pants gave her legs and decided to let it go at that. Mac watched her comb her hair. Watched her blue haunch under the net.

He said, "Do these things work?"

"I guess. I can't stand wool ones."

"Don't the strings cut into your skin?"

"The wrinkles come out. Isn't that a punch line to something?"

They drank some coffee. She followed him outside. The pond was steaming. He said it would be nice to be here alone. He was trying to be friendly. She said "Yes" but she didn't want to be friendly.

She thought the group wasn't very vital. Timidly waiting for something to happen. Some outdoor sacrament evoked by diligent outdoors ritual. Dull smart brains. No bright lazy ones. Very serious about safety. Well, that was okay.

She answered, "Yes, but I don't expect much. I went on their bicycle trip, they arrange everything. Like all this climbing gear. That rope with the king's thread . . ." He didn't seem to get it. Or to miss it. She thought quickly how bad she'd sound saying Billy Budd? Melville? scarlet thread braided?—to hell with it. He was certainly attracted to her, but he'd be awfully difficult. She could tell. She thought of

4

asking him to go off, just the two of them, right now. It looked like rain. They'd have to ask for a share of the food. This guy wouldn't like being asked, maybe not being asked, being asked for less reason than—than for no more reason than sensation. Piss on him, the prig.

She was at that moment put off by the way his jaw worked as he surveyed the pond. His jaw muscles looked as though he worked them out in the gym too, along with his pecs, his lats.

At the same time she thought it would be nice if she stopped playing with a smooth man who was light, articulate, Easy. French coffee, small apartment with nice things, maybe a joint, but smoothly self-conscious, always an implied "Why not?" *Cinq à sept.* The unstated assumption of how much we know, how pleasant this is because of what we know. The prevailing response to most of the afternoon, shaded laughter. No one caught out. Orgasm a little crackle, brrrp on the KLH speaker and then the music went on, *da di da,* like boys humming in her ear at dances back in those days.

Mac was still studying the pond. He mentioned beavers seriously. It often took her like this, Anya thought, how many models of experience she could set spinning at once. She never missed an allusion even unintended. A good ear for cross-referencing. She riffled through her file cards on nature, people who talked about nature.

A bad habit she enjoyed, like some parlor fortune telling, Freudian or—not serious in itself, just to see. There were a lot of people who enjoyed it, like the little smart of paper-edge cuts.

She thought she wanted a change of medium, a lot more clay here.

She saw the thought as slightly unpleasant.

She thought about her real ambitions. Not cleverly. To want to be someone, or to want to do something? N/A. To see. To feel what something felt like. Deeper curiosity than her old light voyeur impulse. Proteus. A step up. Her substance adopting the form necessary to experience, necessary to grasp the feeling that attracted her. A step deeper. To adopt completely, so that her vulnerability could not be avoided simply by dropping a mask. "You're nothing but a pack of cards." The only way to escape should be metamorphosis to rearrange, possibly destroy something in her

5

center. That was the only way to find the center. Not that that was the center of anything important—observation. But at least observation with deep nerves.

She had only begun to formalize the notion a few weeks ago. It seemed that way. Violent reaction. Back to a complicated but lower-risk pose—had a friend show to Henniker some fervent despairing verse she'd done up.

Henniker dying to meet her. Drawn to flailing neurosis not like a shark, it turned out, like a tick to mammal heat. She came all innocence. But tough innocence. "It *is* my *poems* you're—"

Henniker: "Oh, the writing and the writer." Later, "You have more talent as a thinker than as a poet. You don't mind . . ."

She got into the part. She was all (everything was all about this girl she was playing) open and breathless. An invented pious Catholic past up to the invented present swirl. He kept his distance. Got bored. She woke him up with veiled Rasputinism—her idea that timid innocence was worthless. That her old faith had to be completely uprooted for her to return to it—oh, she wasn't sure *what* she was saying, her face in her hands. She began to laugh. "I don't know where my thoughts are coming from. Communion in two kinds means communion and anticommunion." She'd laughed shrilly. "But you think my poems are worthless." More meetings. She'd bravely admitted, "I'm only *curious* about you, you know." He'd laughed. *"Only.* Dear girl, you thrill me."

In the stairwell by herself she'd savored that. She could feel the thick preening he'd enjoyed. All his feelings moving at once. There was a deep hunger there. By the time she'd reached the bottom of the stairs she was irritated at herself for her cheap tricks. And he'd been honest on one front, he'd said he didn't like her verse. She'd gone back again; he'd made a move. She'd said, "What will this be like?"

Henniker pulled up short. "Huh?" She said that she hadn't really felt her body since the last time she prayed, that what she felt now was almost entirely—spiritual. Mmm, a kind of sweet decay of spirit. He'd faltered a bit more, wondering about her powers, wondering about the power of religious hysteria, confronted not just by one mad girl but *folie à* God-knows-how-many. Just for a flicker she'd seen him wonder. Everything go cold. He'd fallen

6

back into ridicule, she bore it seraphically. And of course after a few days she'd called him back, he'd regrouped.

Yes—that was where she'd seen Mac before. At the bottom of that stairwell. He hadn't looked at her. Buttoned up to his chin in a rain slicker. She recognized the thick layers of hair, parted near the middle, then curled by the rain. The breadth of the face. She'd leaned against the bar to open the door with her hip, saw it was raining. He, coming in, had pulled the door open, gestured, she'd obeyed, stepping into the rain before she'd got her scarf over her hair. As the door had swung slowly shut on its hydraulic hinge she'd heard him chugging up the stairs. She didn't think he'd noticed her.

He was still talking about beavers.

". . . stick green shoots in the mud under water, they keep all winter. The most successful nonpredator. In America, I mean."

Anya said, "They're just rodents. Overgrown rats."

Mac said, "I'll tell you an odd thing, there used to be beavers in America seven feet long. I mean long before man."

Anya said, " 'I met a traveler from an antique land who said—' there used to be beavers seven feet long."

Mac looked puzzled.

Anya said, " 'O best beloved, the elephant child lived by the banks of the great greasy gray green Limpopo river all set about with fever trees . . .' "

Mac grunted. Cut her off.

For an instant Anya thought she'd been foxed, now had to apologize, then she thought that he was simply bored, didn't take her play as sexual interest. Or wasn't sexually interested? No, he'd looked at her with interest. Interest, well . . .

Someone shouted down from the cabin, "Breakfast!"

Mac left. Anya followed after a bit. She was right in guessing that breakfast wasn't ready or even begun, that whoever called had just had the thick group feeling that everyone should be gathered around for the whole process.

On the hike to the rock face she struck up with him again. He was particularly irritated by her set of amused detachment. Fine, Mac let it irritate him, let him think that what interested her most was the spectrum between amusing

7

and boring. He wouldn't attack full out, lost interest instead. But he picked up when she would start up again pleasantly. What increased her pleasure was that of the other eight people four were too tired to talk. She would cheerily jog up alongside him and start chatting. When she got around to sounding snotty again, he would speed up and leave her behind.

She talked about Chicago, appreciating the variety of class antagonisms, the crystallized minutiae that alarmed or offended this or that section of the population. She said, "I was talking to a man the other day (Henniker—he gives a course in the English department. He's a critic, was a poet, Jewish.) when he suddenly got very excited about the sports news. He was delighted to learn that Notre Dame lost a football game. I thought, Odd, he doesn't care about sports in any other way. He explained he liked thinking about how bad all the Poles on the subway would feel— have you ever heard the phrase 'subway alumni'?—I must say I was puzzled at this—for him—simple-minded malice. He's extremely malicious but usually more sophisticated. But that's an effect of Chicago, you get down to grittier feelings. I imagine the way New York was, oh, in the twenties. Or nineties . . ."

Mac said, "You're above it all, I suppose. With your semiaristocratic view."

Anya laughed. "Semi" would have been a cheap shot from anyone else. She thought it was spontaneous from Mac. He may have even been trying to soften the pejorative—from him—"aristocratic." It was easy, but she liked the bite—as in semiclassical, semivirgin. Semitruthful.

They reached the rock face.

*   *   *

Mac thought everything was fine, was glad he'd got interested in rock climbing, until he got halfway up the cliff face. Seventy, eighty feet.

He felt a small bubble of fear escape up into his chest. He could tell there was a great deal more fear trapped inside. An unstable, surprisingly complex fear. It was a long way down, *that* part was simple. But strength was not the answer. The answer eluded him. He'd watched the group leader go up. Springingly, rhythmically. Mac had thought, I can do *that*.

Caught in such a simple trap.

He couldn't make his mind work. He heard the leader's calm, meant-to-be-calming voice from above. "Put your left foot where your right foot is."

His right toes were on an outcrop the size of a hockey puck. His left foot was dangling. His hands and head were pressed against the rock face. He reached to his right with his right hand. The rim of his helmet seemed to be pushing all of him out into space. He found a knob, a bump really, nothing to get a grip on. He closed his eyes. It made him giddier. He thought, When I count to three . . . No. Wait. He traced the line his left foot should follow to land on the toehold. But the right foot? What message for the right foot? It seemed very hard to plan all this.

He said "Shut up" to the voice from above. He made sure the belay wasn't in the way.

One, two, three.

He wasn't sure he'd done it. He thought, I must have. My weight, my left leg feels the weight.

He said, "Yes. Yes, I see it." The voice was telling him about a handhold up and to the right, a mantel just out of reach, just swing toward it, no need to jump, just push off your left toes, just a little springy swing. Mac thought, You cute bastard.

Oh, Christ.

He was hanging by both hands. His boots rattling below, he could hear them. He didn't dare look down.

His right foot found a hold. Three points now. He tried to relax, ease into rest, but his mind began to cartwheel— to circumscribe a circle counterclockwise—hand, hand, foot, hand, hand, foot.

He stopped it. Moved again. He heard the voice, not the words, just the drone. But he had some memory of what he'd seen the leader do. He was ashamed of imitating. He began to hum to himself. It sounded very nervous.

The voice said, "—overhang—"

That was obvious. It was pressing his helmet down over his eyes. He reached away and up from his crouch with his left hand. No hold.

The voice said, "You're almost at the top."

You idiot.

The voice explained something. He didn't get it. He heard, "—right hand—" That was wrong, his right hand was holding on.

"—stand up—" He realized the man was dangerous.

He threw his left hand out and around the overhang as far as it would go. They didn't know how strong his hands were. But there was nothing but minutely wrinkled rock.

"—feet flat against the rock. Get your weight—your weight onto your feet. Your feet will hold if your weight is *on* them. To get your weight on them you have to stand up."

No.

The voice called down. Another voice called up.

"Oh. Listen. You're turned around. You've got to face the rock."

His heels were in a crack. He turned so that the right edge of his right foot was in the crack. He thought, If I do what they say and show them how wrong they are, I can still grab the crack with my hand, they don't know how strong my hands are.

"—feet *flat* against the rock."

He let his foot dangle, got his toes against the rock. Began to scrabble with them, felt his left foot catch. Ran his hands up. Lunged up from inside. Like swimming in air. Caught at the top of the overhang. No hold. Pressed with his palms. Saw the face of the voice at the top.

It was impossible. He reached out with his right fingers. His left hand began to slide back. He stuck his head forward, his shoulders forward.

"—foot against the rock."

No. He hauled his left knee up. It wouldn't go over the overhang. He grabbed with his right fingertips. He reached forward with his chin. He frogged his right knee up. Everything at once.

His weight came back on his left hand now under his heart.

He saw the leader tighten his grip on the belay before he knew he was falling. He felt his right fingertips being sanded down by the rock as they slowly scraped toward him. He felt a wedge of air puff up between his heart and the rock.

He looked deep into the sky. Deep sky all through him.

Deep cracks in the clouds. Weightless caverns. He floated toward them.

The belay took his weight. He felt the jerk around his waist but it didn't seem to have any connection to his floating body.

Then his emptiness was refilled suddenly with his weight, then with anger as he realized he was being lowered down. Halfway down he felt humiliated as well as angry.

He restrained himself from kicking the faces of the people who gathered him in at the bottom, who guided his dangling legs away from the base of the cliff. To earth.

He unscrewed the carabinier and pulled the belay loose.

He wished he had spoken to no one that day.

A moonfaced girl said, "You were almost there."

He walked over to a rock and sat down. Curled up over his knees. He didn't understand. He thought he should get up and walk around. He wasn't hurt, he should try it again, there was no wound they could see, he should get up and walk around.

Anya told him to put his head between his knees.

Mac said, "I'm all right," without looking at her.

She said, "A little wobbly is all." She laughed. "The belay nearly took off his shirt when you took your dive. I must say, just before you fell was exciting. You looked like a salmon trying to slither up a waterfall."

Mac felt his anger form, but without any force. His feelings had no compression.

Anya said, "When you go up again, don't use so much muscle."

A moment later she instructed him not to go right up under the overhang, to keep his body weight over his feet, not to flop his chest forward (it just pulls your feet away from the rock), to use his hands primarily to keep his weight in the right place. . . .

What is she doing?

Mac watched her climb.

She was good. Was she showing off? He couldn't see anything unessential. But by telling him how to do it she'd certainly made sure he'd watch her.

Something of a tease at the overhang. She climbed very slowly. Not nimble anymore. No sense of muscle. Straight light balanced limbs. He let whatever it was she'd done

11

pass. She was a good athlete. Her sting was another question.

When he began to climb again he was calm to the point of anesthesia. Her sharpness and the way she'd climbed seemed to balance at far ends of a pole. He himself wasn't much, just dull concentration. He noticed that he entered another medium. It seemed as sluggish as water.

When he pressed his foot carefully against the rock face approaching the overhang, he knew he'd been there before but so long ago that it caused no fear. His forearms and palms now on the top of the overhang as though he were speaking from behind a lectern.

And now what? He held still. Let a soundless whinny of panic pass through. Drawn upward again by the same sluggish lightness. It seemed a trick of his nerves, as though he'd pressed the backs of his wrists against doorjambs. It was only his nervous ghost who climbed; he was still in shock.

He reached the top, crawled away from the rim on all fours before he undid the belay.

They rappelled down. Mac found it easy, secure, pleasant, like walking backward on the moon.

They all went over to a smaller rock face, only twenty or thirty feet high with a single crack from top to bottom. The moonfaced girl said to Mac, "I'm just terrible at laybacks—"

Anya laughed. "But you're great in every other position."

The moonfaced girl said, "Huh?" but several other people laughed. The group leader eased into his official remarks after chuckling to show he knew what was funny. "That's right, we're going to learn some layback technique. Now, to do this right you've really got to stop fighting. Climbing isn't fighting. When I climb a mountain I never say 'I've conquered.' I say, 'Thank you for letting me coexist with you.'"

He looked meaningfully at Mac. Mac wished mournfully that the man had not revealed himself as such an asshole. It was a mournful wish because Mac himself had no standing anymore to criticize him.

The group leader climbed up halfway, his toes pressing

against one lip of the crack, his fingers tugging against the other. His ass jutted back to one side, his torso scissored forward, his shoulders hunched to grab the edge of the crack. He alternated hands now to put in the piton, ran his belay through a carabinier attached to it, and continued to spider up, his hands and feet creeping along in close formation. Mac thought it was a very clever technique.

The group leader said, "See, your hands and feet are a little donkey just riding you up. You don't have to tear the crack apart to keep from falling."

Mac let his hands fall between his knees. Listened to his pulse.

He looked up to watch Anya do it. She was long-legged but limber, really very trim piked over her legs, her firm butt waggling through the seat of her pants. She stopped to shake the hair out of her eyes. When she got near the top she gathered herself to reach for the edge. One arm shot up—he thought that she surely couldn't hold herself with one hand—she let her legs swing. He didn't see her other hand go up, but when her legs reached the bottom of their swing she was holding with both hands. Her body kept on in its arc. Just before she reached the horizontal she sent her top leg up over the edge. Her body suddenly established itself over her feet standing on the top.

Mac thought she had a clear idea of how she looked. She slowly undid the belay from her waistband and lowered it down. He thought, Well, this is her game. But he couldn't shrug it off.

When it came his turn he struggled up, heaving with his arms, overshooting the balance point. He had trouble moving his feet.

"Lay *back!*"

He had to look at his feet to see which one was jammed. He got it moving again. Began to rush. He felt stuffed with his own breath. He saw the rim within reach. He said, "All right, you fucker" and grabbed it. Hung one-handed, apelike for an instant. Grabbed his own wrist and pulled. Lurched his head over the edge and grabbed some more ground with both hands. Shot himself up and forward, leapfrogging. Landed hard on his knees.

Again his anger drained suddenly. He wished again that he had not talked to anyone that day, the evening before, had not implied he was—anything. Not that those tricks had anything to do with what he *could* do. No, he was ashamed she had taken him aside with her, invited him to share her superior position, which she had maintained and he had not.

* * *

On the way to the shelter the second night the group leader began to check the map more and more frequently.

Anya said to Mac, "I think we're semilost."

Mac nodded, either not getting it or continuing not to hold up his end of the conversation. Anya was disappointed he was being so serious about what he took to be a defeat. She'd actually rather admired his styleless raw pride, a thick-set knar hammering his way up the rock face. Some rich pod of feeling had burst: she'd caught a whiff of it. Not quite what she'd called it at first—lion piss—the problem being that the only lion piss she knew was stale zoo. She thought, Overheated metal, bearings seizing, yes, boiled metal. Maybe more vegetable, a tree blown over, split, exuding the distress of naked wood fiber, fresh sap. Lion piss.

But she wished he would pass on to a new stage. Even active unpleasantness. Of course, best of all would be if he began to admire her after all, a feeling for which there seemed to be no room in his present mood.

She thought of prodding him again, of telling him with disarming frankness there was no one else worth talking to. Telling him she craved some fresh, primitive elegance—some Elizabethan bawdiness.

He marched on, carrying his sulk. All right then, to hell with him. Only one to a customer, buddy.

But shortly after that, at another map-reading break, Anya suddenly felt compact, distinct, and peaceful. The sky had filled to a single cloud and lowered. The air was thick and electric. She noticed that the group leader was trying to appear cheerful and therefore—somehow—guiltless. She knew they would all be miserably wet, but for the moment she didn't care, it all seemed part of a benign and interesting pattern.

Back down the trail a few grayish green leaves stirred, showed their bright undersides. Around Anya they hung quietly. The air seemed luminous for all the darkening of

14

the sky. She thought it might be a warm rain, it was a
warm day for October. But her strongest thought was of
the welling up, the promise of a promise that she would
feel parts of her inner life lifted mysteriously. She didn't
know why. She could tell only that the sensation was beyond her control, and the hint of danger that it was out of
control intensified it. It was all promise, and the promise
was that the messy, uneasy, cumbersome parts of her
would boil up, and rise like vapor to be distilled in a higher
form.

It started. As always she thought the exhilaration was
going to be permanent. That from now on everything
would fit. Better than that, that she would feel easy, clear,
and serenely entertained—everything, forever.

She was familiar enough with the pattern so that there
was a simultaneous trickle of footnotes (Fabrizio del Dongo
riveted by view of mountains, Stephen Dedalus by wading
girl, Virgin-Mary-blue skirt hiked up, slender ivory thighs;
Flaubert, Faulkner, Woolf, Koestler, new one there, *Arrow
in the Blue?*—but all in miniature, as they should be, not
directly reduced so much as distanced by the enormous
hollow of space. Located—behind her breastbone? behind
her eyes? between herself and what she saw? The questions
embered out as she tried to see where they came from.

It ended. The aura of promise was over. The moment
reduced itself to the size of a file card. Under *E,* for epipha-
nies.

Everyone was unlacing, unpacking, getting out ponchos
or hooded parkas. She couldn't tell if it was going to
graduate school or going up to see Henniker that made her
regard her feelings as short and small.

Of course she'd made them both part of her life. She
didn't *blame* them. It was some acid quality in her that she
should modify, that she should feed some sweetness before
she became too self-corroding.

She used to think her moments of exhilaration would
make her gentler. She wasn't gentler. It was of course difficult, she thought, to acquire a quality she didn't really
admire, only prescribed for herself.

Gentleness—a virtue, a disposition, even a mood she
could not find. Perhaps, she thought, because she did not
believe in innocence. Certainly not as a state to be prized.
She believed in ardor. In deep hunger. Austere purposeful-

ness. In fanaticism. She was willing to find those qualities guiltless in some way, pure. Purity a modifying quality. And what else was innocence? What was it all by itself? What was the allure of a blank page? Balder killed by Loki's sprig. Fine, quite right. The glow of mindless good-will—not to be believed in. And yet. And yet there was something in people that loved, admired, adored the egg. Doves, now there was an actual fraud, vicious little buggers, persisting in fables. Along with lambs. Coos and bleats. Virgins.

She noticed Mac looking at her from under the hood of his poncho. He turned away. She envied his coloring. In spite of the fact that he had coarse blond hair and fair skin, a pale blue wrinkled vein at his temple and a more diffuse pale blue around his eyes, the whole effect was dark. A blond by Rouault.

She wondered how self-conscious his smoldering was, how many hours of practice, how many reflections cased in shop windows?

She said again, "I think we're semilost." He nodded again.

It began to rain. Anya unbuckled her poncho from her pack and put it on. The group leader announced with a last pathetic attempt at control through good cheer that the best thing to do was to go back to last night's shelter.

A couple of people said, "Well, how far is it?" but the majority said "Shit"—it was the idea of wasting the virtue of the afternoon's hike, as though he'd stolen something, Anya thought. But they were bound to go back to the bus the next day in any case. Perhaps it was revenge for his jolly instruction.

They marched back down the trail, not talking once the first spurt of grumbling was over. Their faces were sealed off on the sides by the hoods of their raingear. It grew dark. One of the girls took out a flashlight. The group leader said it would spoil their night vision. More people said "Shit," but the girl put her flashlight away. They kept on.

One of the girls fell. She sat up and began to cry. The group leader and the girl's boyfriend hovered over her discussing first aid. The girl whimpered. People gathered around her. She seemed to think they thought badly of

16

her, because she said severely, "I'm sorry but it really hurts."

She started to unlace her boot. The group leader said she should leave it on. The boyfriend said they should at least look to see if it was broken. The girl began to cry again, more hysterically. Mac knelt beside her, and she grabbed his forearm. She said to the group leader, "Well, I can't walk, for God's sake."

Mac said, "It's all right. We can carry you. Just rest a bit, it hurts worst at the start, we'll find a pill and when you feel like it we'll carry you back. Just rest a bit while we find a pill."

The girl appeared soothed. Mac said, "I've had the same thing happen, it's worst right away. Rest a bit, there's bound to be a pill in the kit."

The group leader broke out his first-aid kit and rummaged around. Anya noticed that he was shaken; he showed the packet he took out to Mac. Mac said, "Get a cup of water, she can't take it without . . ." The group leader hopped to. Anya decided Mac was a liberal reform, not a revolution. The boyfriend knelt down and took up the bedside chat. It didn't work as well; she obviously knew he didn't know anything.

Mac said to Anya, "Your sleeping bag has a two-way zipper." Anya pulled her sleeping bag out while Mac thrashed about off the trail. He came back with some thick saplings he'd beavered down with his knife. Anya watched the others make room for Mac's new civic virtue. Is that what he'd wanted? Was he redeeming himself? Surely he would have preferred some feat of strength or nerve? But this was woods lore, perhaps that was satisfactory. He certainly didn't want his position in the group to be male nurse . . . Or was he capable of playing it *à rebours*, of emerging more triumphant through humility, more independent through submission, of appearing more rough-hewn while being sweetly tender?

And how had he come to notice that her bag had a two-way zipper? For what reason? What else had he noticed? She watched him and the others watching him as he ran the poles through her bag, stayed the zipper with his blanket pin, notched two crosspieces, and so forth. More deference as he suggested he and the boyfriend leave their packs hanging in a tree, covered the girl on the litter with her

17

sleeping bag and his own poncho, and nodded to the group leader to lead on.

After a short while Mac and the boyfriend were the only two people being friendly to each other. The boyfriend would grunt back, "Watch the rock!" and Mac would grunt and then they'd pass cheerful manly comments the length of the girl's body about how the rain was letting up and how they recognized where they were and its being only a short way now. The injured girl said nothing, whether out of terror or relative comfort Anya couldn't tell.

The three girls (besides Anya) suggested that the rest of them go on ahead of the litter. The group leader said they might get lost. They laughed at him, but they didn't go.

Two hours later they arrived at the cabin. The group leader found the woodpile with his flashlight, but Mac and the boyfriend took over building the fire. Anya felt a poisonous reaction building up in her against public merit. Mac began to whittle shavings on a stick, leaving them dangling. Anya said, "My, that's very pretty."

Mac said, "It's a fuzz stick." He lit a match to it and tucked it under the kindling.

The boyfriend said, "Hey, good idea." Anya laughed.

The group leader came in, penitentially wet. He'd been to get a bucket of water from the pond. Once the fire was going, the three girls approached it with the pots and pans and dehydrated food. They knelt all three abreast in front of the fireplace.

Anya said, "When you girls get the eye of newt in, what say you let a little heat through to the back of the bus."

The moonfaced girl said, "I don't see you doing any work."

Anya sat against the wall and rolled a joint. She knew she wasn't going to resist the temptation; she decided she would take her pleasure, but not by simply being poisonous. No mere poison. That seemed an interesting enough rule.

Mac went over to the girl who had fallen. He took her pulse and felt her forehead. Anya laughed.

She said, "Great moments in medicine."

Mac ignored her.

She said, "Do you think the fever will break by morning, doctor?"

Mac said, "Don't be such a pain in the ass."

"I can't help it. You don't really expect a sprained ankle to give her a fever, do you?"

The moonfaced girl said, "He knows—"

"—he knows," Anya said.

"—he knows what he's doing. After any trauma there's the danger of shock. Cold clammy skin, lower pulse rate." The moonfaced girl turned back to the stew.

Anya said, "Oh, trauma. Shock. Tell me about shock."

The girl said, "Certainly. It's nature's way of numbing you, but—"

Anya said, "—nature's way of numbing you. How delicious, how I envy you that experience—being one of nature's numbed."

Mac said, "You've been in shock."

Anya said, "And missed it? No—when was it?"

"The first time you got laid." Several people laughed happily. "Cold clammy skin, numbness. Postcoital amnesia." More laughter.

Anya smiled. "As a matter of fact you're wrong. Curiously enough I remember everything. I don't think there was any numbness involved. I can't think of any. It was at a music festival, the man was my violin instructor." She stopped. She had their complete attention. "All the girls in the strings were in love with him, and he enjoyed it in a Central European way. It was like the flowers in the fields for him, all those enraptured girls fiddling away with beads of perspiration on their downy upper lips. Even the boys admired him in spite of everything. He was not handsome at all, squat and so forth, but he was a wonderful musician. He was sleeping with one of his girl students who was swollen stiff with pride about it, really obese with pride, obese only spiritually I must say, her figure was actually rather dainty although surprisingly busty. She picked up all his little mannerisms of playing which were grotesque on her, and she also affected a certain sweetness—she went out of her way to say to people, 'You know, Joseph thinks you could be very good.' This was to the less attractive girls and to the boys indiscriminately. One day she said it to me—I was the youngest person there and at that time apparently harmlessly gawky. She recklessly assumed herself to be Joseph's only taste. In any case, I discovered that Joseph went out by himself to pick mushrooms whenever it had just rained—the whole setting strikes me now as—well it doesn't matter—but there he was ambling along in his baggy trousers and brown silk socks and sandals, and I suddenly appeared to him with my skirt full of mushrooms. Actually it appeared to him as though he appeared to me. It was by a stream and at the time I thought the whole thing very Schubert. After some conversation about mushrooms from which he could tell that I didn't know the first thing, I dumped them out and we sat down by the stream and I ended up bathing his face—it was very hot—with the hem of my skirt dipped in the water. His head in my lap and so forth. With complete confidence he unlaced my sneakers. It was perfectly clear from that point what was going to happen, but there was no sudden rush. He stroked my foot and then my leg, but it went on for hours. I *was* drowsy in a way, but certainly not *numb,* aware of every cell. When in good time he reached the ordinarily clumsy stage of taking off my underpants it didn't seem at all—fraught, since we went on, or rather he went on, as before. A sort of stroking so that I barely noticed it when he began to kiss me on the stomach, the lower part, I'm not being coy, nor was he—there was another—oh yes, my sense of time was of course hazy, not out of shock, but I'm sure up to that point it had been a half hour and he had not yet touched me above the waist, or kissed me in any ordinary way and yet I had no sense of his being repetitious. Or rushed. That may have something to do with the shock that you seem to feel is inevitable . . . In any case, I was the one who got impatient, and there was a slight change in tempo but only a foreshadowing. It was when he very slowly put his hand on my—he had very large hands—not so much on as over—even in a way *around* . . . none of your standard bowling ball grip—it was at that point that my stomach muscles began to quiver, jump spasmodically, not really in reaction but coincidentally, at least it seemed that way, and I had a comfortable feeling of pride that I was coming in on cue. In any case there was the change in tempo, but not, as you might think, to a more rollicking movement, but to something slower—a kind of *largo.* His mouth and tongue seemed huge—this was only sense of touch, my eyes were closed though there was still a lot of light coming through my eyelids—but I felt as if I were being painted with gigantic brushstrokes. I admit this part sounds a little hallucina-

tory, but it certainly wasn't shock. And then there was a
sensation of balancing in mid-air. Like lots of stout musical men he wasn't clumsy at all. I came before he did and
for a while I had a strange alertness, I had to keep from
giggling because I'd thought with literary self-consciousness
that it was the sky that had moved not the earth. And
then there was a slow reversal of all the sensations, like a
film being run backward, every feeling that had gone in
was reversed, or rather extracted, but I was left with perfectly clear images of feeling, like blueprints in a way.
So I really can't recall any anesthesia or numbness . . ."

Anya opened her hands to indicate that she had finished
what was to be demonstrated. There was a long silence.

One of the boys giggled, stifled it, and said to deflect the attention that suddenly veered toward him,
"Well, that's a very interesting—story, maybe everyone
should—"

The moonfaced girl said, *"Honestly,* Billy. *Sometimes!"*

Anya said, "Thank you," and smiled at him.

The moonfaced girl said, "This is crazy, she's just doing
it to—" The girl made a gesture which Anya assumed in-
dicated polymorphous disapproval.

Anya spoke, imitating the girl's tight little Midwestern
r and sheet-metal vowels. "I think she's right, girls, I think
we should just not pay any attention to her, just pretend
not to notice her, that's all she wants, is to be noticed."

Anya wasn't enjoying herself so much anymore; she
didn't want to have to deal with the girl any further; she
couldn't think of anything that would be fun. Anya
thought her own story oddly arousing and complexly insulting. Leave it at that. She wondered if Mac thought it
true.

She said to the moonfaced girl, "Oh, let's not ruin a
perfect day by squabbling."

The girl said, "I'm not the one who's—" Billy said,
"She's putting you on." The girl said, "I know."

Mac started stringing a clothesline in front of the fire
near the ceiling, the cooks turned back to their pots, the
boyfriend sat down by the injured girl.

They ate without much talk.

Everyone went to bed. Anya thought the rain sounded
lush and pleasant on the roof even though her sleeping
bag was damp along the edges. She watched Mac by fire-

light as he tried to get comfortable, fussing with pieces of clothing he'd borrowed for bedding, dutifully blowing his cigar smoke into the fireplace so that the updraft pulled it out of the room. She found this bit of conscientiousness touching. Mac finally curled up, threw his cigar butt into the coals, turned over, and said "Oh shit," as something stuck him in the back. He wriggled once and closed his eyes. Anya thought it would be nice to live with someone for a while. It would even be worth having someone who didn't wash the dishes. Just the animal comfort of seeing someone else comfortable. She felt herself waking up to be wary of sentimentality. Who had done the dishes just now? She remembered they'd shoved them out the door into the rain.

CHAPTER

||||||||||||||||||||||||||||||||||||

2

No one spoke to Anya on the hike back to the bus or on the ride back to Chicago.

She spent the time thinking about what she'd dreamed about during the night—the music at Jeannie's wedding reception: the teatime, ship's-cruise, country-club homogenization of jazz, swing, and prewar pop. Suitable for bridesmaids—Tassie, Cissy, Tish, Filly. A few last names were the names of New England towns. The towns were named for their families—other way round from towns and names for European Jewry—Anya's mother's maiden name was Brünner. Someone from Brünn, as it was called in German. In Czech, Brno.

Anya was a bridesmaid too. The only one without a cute first name, the only one not a childhood chum. But the people who didn't know Anya were sophisticated enough to say her last name right. Janek, pronounced *Yahnek,* not *Dj.*

Tassie had once left her a love note addressed to "Anya Janek doodle dandy." It had been that kind of chatter that had made Anya feel silly and intimate and had semibroken her heart.

The wedding that had included Anya had cut her off. She didn't think she'd really done it herself. Maybe she had. But more likely the bridesmaids were already fading, had already heard the high-pitched whistles of their trainers.

Anya suddenly thought that Mac looked like Tassie— odd, since Tassie looked like such a buttercup of a girl.

But her movements were often excited and brutal, some of them the flinging about of a spoiled girl, but some were more powerfully dervish. It was the almost tangible energy that made Mac resemble Tassie.

What she and Tassie had had in common was that they were willing to undergo some trouble and pain to find more than ordinary satisfactions. Tassie perhaps a little different from Anya—Tassie would do anything if it was funny and didn't take too long. Tassie didn't think that about herself, of course. In spite of being self-centered, she wasn't very introspective.

Anya was grateful to Tassie for making her give up being deliberately ugly. Anya had thought efforts to appear pretty were incompatible with vitality, with the chance to burst into flame. She was now startled to remember thinking that. There had been something sweet about her own eagerness.

She was never so unequivocally glad about the physical attraction she felt for Tassie. Tassie had that first year, the first month of college, occupied the role of the crazy innocent of the two of them. Although it was Tassie who was completely at home at Radcliffe, in Cambridge, in Boston, or anywhere within an hour's drive. In any case, whenever Tassie had had enough, she could fall back into the easy social parts laid out for her, without feeling that she'd left Anya at all. Tassie could take up again by saying Anya had been the one who was being boring, who was changing, who was refusing. Useless to argue.

Tassie had a blend of attachment and contempt for the obligatory life she led. "Mother would kill me if I didn't." "Oh, I've known him forever." "You're free to think whatever you want, but what you think just isn't the point." "Of course it's all dead, well almost dead, but that just isn't the point either." The point was Tassie's family's social life in 1959.

Anya loved to hear her say these things. She thought Tassie didn't really believe them as statements, only as incantations that kept Anya swimming to her. Anya didn't know if she'd ever reached her. If she had, there wasn't as much to her as Anya had hoped. No, there was an awful lot, and there was a vanishing point. The hole in Tassie's inner space that it all disappeared through.

Or had Tassie disappeared into the ordinary world? Just

shrunk. Shriveled. How sad to think that maturity, at least in Tassie's species, would be drier, coarser; more husk, less juice. Was there another stage to come?

At that time Anya had wanted—no, she'd known she'd never settle in—she'd wanted even then just to see, to feel what it was like to have all that—all those rooms, all those relatives . . . It was like being caressed or tickled; it was no good if you did it to yourself.

And Tassie was taken with her. Afraid of her. Uneasily charmed. They laughed all the time, bullied each other. Tassie's mother was alarmed. But she kept her distance once she thought the pair of them together had good taste, a girlish snobbish disdain to which Tassie's mother was sympathetic. And perhaps it was that Anya and Tassie seemed childish together, and Tassie's mother was happy to see Tassie's childhood prolonged. Tassie's mother at fifty could have passed for a languorous forty. Except in the sun; Anya remembered her ducking away from being photographed alongside Tassie in the sun.

Had she liked Anya? Tassie said, "Oh, Mummy adores you." Mummy kissed her good night along with her darling daughter when they spent the night at Tassie's house; laughed at Anya's jokes; praised her when she saw a play Anya was in (perhaps she was relieved to see Anya beaming her sharpest energy elsewhere). Liked her for making Tassie read more. Got her invited to some nice dances as Tassie's "out-of-town guest," explained why she really couldn't do more, said, "Anya dear, you'd be bored going to these things all the time—someone as bright as you."

Anya was grateful. She liked the practical arrangements, savored what elegance there was in her slim ration of the slim ration.

Between the people she met at the theater and being Tassie's friend, she didn't have to undergo the dorm mixers. Of course she went once. It was like stepping into an old-fashioned Coca-Cola ad come to life. It seemed all primary colors, but somehow dingy, as though the film print of the event had been run too many times.

It was the last time she saw someone wearing a bow tie with a sports jacket, the last time she saw someone with a crew cut, the last time someone said to her, "Hi there! Wanna dance?"

Anya decided that everything was as unnatural as everything else, so she could take her pick. She knew there was a similarity between the dorm mixer and Tassie's dances—most of the people she talked to were uneasy, claimed they'd just dropped in. Only a few people would admit to really being there. But that was a general problem in those days—no one admitted to really being anywhere. They were caught without a style, in between styles. It wasn't a style to be half-turned away, shoulders hunched.

All that was 1959. What single thing might she have known that would have made it all different? Silly idea—she hadn't *known* anything; if she had, she wouldn't have done any of it, and that would have been worse. The worst thing that year had been being foolish, long enough ago now so that she didn't mind, didn't feel connected in any responsible way. She had been foolish, but had she groveled? Going to Tassie's after-parties without having gone to the dance? Arriving at two A.M. completely sober, trying to imply that she'd had better things to do that she simply wasn't mentioning. She engaged in masquerades. Silly enough at first—by mid-winter they were better.

The odd thing was she remembered now that she then felt as though she'd known Tassie better than anyone in her life.

It was easier to add extra men to the list for the ball at which Tassie made her début, along with two dozen other Boston girls. Anya couldn't remember whether that was her idea. No, that was the kind of thing that Tassie knew, but she must have been the one to—no, they must have dared each other. She rented a dinner jacket. She made a very handsome boy. Five eleven, her dark hair cut short and parted near the middle, long straight nose. Neck a little stalky, mouth perhaps too full, face smooth, but certainly like someone's kid brother.

She was very nervous on her way in to Boston. Wearing men's clothes was a sexual pleasure, while she was driving in it had drawn her out of herself, hypnotized her. But she had been scared walking into the ballroom of the hotel.

She found Tassie. Cut in.

Tassie said, "Now that you're a man, tell me frankly, have I got it?"

Anya laughed. She was still nervous.

Tassie said, "Well, let's try something easier, do your shoes fit?"

She liked her shoes.

Tassie said, "That's enough about you."

Anya said something.

Tassie said, "I like your voice, it's a little bit tough."

Anya said, "I come from a tough part of town."

"Oh, very good."

Anya asked, "Did you tell anyone?"

"No."

Anya began to feel better. She looked around. "It's not as grand as I expected."

Tassie said, "Boston doesn't go in for being grand."

Anya said, *"Jesus."*

They both laughed. Anya was sure Tassie had meant it. Anya pulled Tassie against her. "You know what you need, don't you, you castrating rich bitch."

Tassie said, "Now, that's perfect—God, it really is. Except there're too many adjectives."

Anya said, "—what you need, you bitch, is a good roll in the hay."

Tassie squealed, *"Exactly.* What do I say: Oh—'Stop it, you're *hurting* me. Please *let go!" Let go* is a spondee there. What did you do to your chest? It's hard as a board."

"I'm wrapped up in an Ace bandage."

Tassie pushed with her hand. "God, it's really hard."

Tassie leaned back and said, "You know, what this really represents is that we can't find anyone else who's anywhere near up to us."

They both laughed again, and again Anya was pretty sure Tassie had simply meant what she'd said, hadn't been pretending to be foolish, but happy to laugh if it turned out foolish. Anya liked that at that time, that Tassie just spilled over, kept on spilling. Some of it was her amiable social chat, some of it aimless malice, some of it sexy burbling. Often there was the ironic intonation—"This isn't really me"—but Anya thought that irony in Tassie was just a conversational tic, not a stance she'd reflected on.

Tassie was certainly quick, had very fast verbal reflexes —and she was clever at least as often as she was foolish, but there were lots of times when she just let herself chatter, her feelings wagging her tongue, a blow-by-blow commentary, and out of habit it came out arch. And lavish.

Anya wondered what men were attracted by in Tassie. Her looks, of course—a pound of butter—but then what?

Tassie unconsciously pushed away a lot of the people who approached her by not noticing them. She had a brutal vanity. But Anya had to suppose that the vanity wasn't all that obvious, and that men coming in on a tactile level were taken by surprise. Unpleasantly. They didn't stay to try to figure out that the vanity was part of the remarkable heat, the energy. Or else they groveled; Tassie didn't notice either way. There was always someone around.

But what *ought* to attract whoever came along was the turmoil. Tassie's feelings or wishes or impulses were too big for her habits. She didn't take her brain seriously, she wasn't gong to get caught *that* way—the only things she remembered longer than the day of an exam were the colossal mistakes people had made: the epicycles in the Ptolemaic system, the phlogiston theory, bleeding with leeches, the treaty of Brest-Litovsk, the Scopes trial, "Prosperity is just around the corner." Tassie once saw a costume drama movie in which the peasants revolted against their lord, and the lord went out alone and unarmed to quell them saying, "These are my people, they know their master," and got stuck full of arrows and pitchforks and so forth. Tassie loved it, went around saying "These are my people" until it wasn't funny, another tic. Even Tassie's mother lived more seriously in an intellectual mode. Also in a regulated social mode, which Tassie bobbed along in without considering. As with exams, Tassie had a knack for filling in the right answers without a thought—she had a completely detached habit that managed all that as easily as breathing. But she wouldn't ever change her position because of a thought.

Her life was almost all habit, but her habits were charming, so she seemed to move from one stage of her life to the next gracefully. Her life grew like her hair and fingernails. Or perhaps like her wardrobe.

Anya and Tassie fox-trotted around the dance floor. Tassie said, "I wonder if I could do it sometime."

"They all know you."

"Yes, you have a great advantage." Tassie caught sight of something. She said, "Don't look, there's a girl eying you."

Anya said, "Is she nice?"

"God, no. I've known her forever."

Anya looked at the girl. The girl averted her eyes.

Tassie led Anya over to her and introduced her. The girl's name was Henrietta; Tassie called Anya Tim James. The girl was surprised and wary. She was on the edge of being pretty, but she came off badly next to Tassie. Tassie made Henrietta appear bony, unhealthy and small.

Tassie said, "Timmy insisted on meeting you. I said—"

Anya said, "Actually what happened is this, I said you looked nice and Tassie said you had a heart of stone."

Tassie laughed. "I said nothing of the kind." Her laugh was not reassuring to Henrietta.

Anya said, "Tassie said you stick hatpins in anyone who tries to kiss you."

Tassie said, "That is a terrible lie. That I said it, I mean."

Henrietta was game. She said, "Ho ho ho. Well, a little of that spite is a small price to pay—I mean, if I get to meet some of Tassie's string of followers."

Tassie said, "I assure you—"

Henrietta said to Anya, "You're not from Boston."

Anya said, "Tassie bet me you'd stick me with a hatpin."

Tassie said, "This has gone far enough."

Henrietta said, "How much did she bet?"

"Lots," Anya said. "But—"

Tassie said, "This isn't fair, Timmy, I think they're about to serve something to eat."

Henrietta said to Anya, "You suddenly seem shy, and you were so bravely forward, just a moment ago. You aren't afraid of Tassie, are you?"

Tassie said, "No, of the hatpin."

Henrietta said, "Will you turn back into a frog if I kiss you?"

Henrietta took Anya by the arms and kissed her on the mouth. Henrietta said to Tassie, "He's quite sweet really, but you know—shy."

Tassie said, "I'm going to get something to eat," and walked away.

Henrietta said to Anya, "Run along now."

Anya followed Tassie into a hall. Tassie said, "Just look at yourself, you have lipstick on your mouth." Anya looked in a mirror on the wall. She couldn't see any lipstick. Tassie burst out laughing. She doubled up and then collapsed sideways into a deep stuffed armchair. She lay across it, her legs hooked over one arm, her head thrown back on the other arm, hooting.

Anya watched Tassie melting in her own laughter. Anya still felt giddy. She thought that now Tassie's exterior was loosened, the mesh of her woven surfaces pulled apart, so that the center of her was—visible? tangible? Anya kissed Tassie on the mouth. There was a taste of Tassie's breath, an exhalation as Tassie tried to push herself up, her elbows slipping off the arm of the chair, her hands sinking into the cushion. Anya couldn't tell what was intended, what unintended helplessness. But she could feel Tassie's breath again.

The boy of a couple passing by said, "One foot on the floor. You know the rules." The girl with him laughed.

When Anya looked back at Tassie, Tassie said, "Jesus, you always want to *win*. You and your last-wordism." That was how she treated it. She heaved herself up from the chair, continued talking, asked if Anya was going to go dance with Henrietta. Anya left early.

Looking back, Anya realized that she'd been worried about two things at once—the question of Tassie's worth and the question of her own "invert nature," the delicate phrase from a literary discussion of a book she'd laughed at.

Anya got a big part in a play, a Feydeau farce in which she was a success, surprised herself by how funny she was, slept with the director who confessed—or perhaps boasted of—occasional impotence while he was working on a play. She also spent some time sleeping with a boy in her modern dance class who she'd assumed was at least bisexual; it turned out he just liked modern dance and had gone to a progressive school where it was okay for the boys to dance. He was, however, quite narcissistic, obsessive about his diet (steamed not boiled vegetables, exotic nuts, fruits and herbs which he believed did wonderful things to his joints and organs). He liked to do warm-up exercises, in which he liked her to participate, before making love to her on the straw mat in his austere room in a boardinghouse. The director, on the other hand, was a slob with a great fondness for Italian food and oral sex.

Tassie loved hearing about Anya's life. Anya suspected that Tassie made up some of the stories she offered in trade. They roomed together their sophomore year. They began to bore each other during the winter. Possibly deliberately. Tassie got into complicated rooming negotiations that spring—she finally asked Anya to join Jeannie, Tish, Filly, et al. in one of the off-campus houses for their junior year. Anya was sure Tassie knew that Anya would say no. Tassie acted surprised and sad, but her relief showed through in the happier air she had when she was with her older friends, the childhood chums. Anya at this point was feeling prematurely eccentric, isolated, and arid. Like some kind of artist in a dry spell. Except she hadn't ever had the lush energetic periods to remember and to hope for again. She feared that her condition was a worsening one—that her early impudent daring, which had made her feel breezy and tough and had had some charm for other people, was gone.

She lost her part-time job as an assistant to a producer at the new educational TV station. She'd been sleeping with him. She got bored, answered an ad for Avon saleswomen, took the sample kit, and called on the man's wife. The woman took pity on her and bought some stuff, was obviously lonely and talked a lot. Anya was delighted with her masquerade and told the man.

He said, "Suppose she comes down here and sees you?"

Anya said, "I'll say 'What a coincidence!' And we'll have another chat. We get along wonderfully."

He was scared and angry and fired her. She couldn't remember what she'd expected, what sort of excitement she'd intended. She felt stupid, but because she knew she wasn't stupid, she thought she might be crazy.

She mentioned some of these feelings to Tassie, and Tassie, half listening, said, "Sophomore slump."

Anya, who had started the conversation not only amiably but expecting attention, curiosity, and, finally reassuring praise, said, "I suppose I should have known you and your Windsor friends can't help thinking of life as a series of clichés."

Tassie was alarmed.

Anya said, "One lukewarm bath after another." She knew she was paraphrasing Orwell but was pretty sure Tassie didn't. "Every so often your hairless little bodies get picked up and spooned into the next tub."

Tassie didn't get mad. Her eyes began to puddle up.

Anya said, "Jesus, Tassie."

31

Tassie said, "I was just going to ask you what you really thought of me."

Anya didn't believe her, wouldn't have bought the pathos anyway. Anya said, "It's hard to say, when you're in your débutante-mode."

Tassie ignored that remark. Tassie said, "I'm not like you." Pause. "I need more affection."

"Adoration," Anya said.

Tassie smiled bravely. Laughed. Said, "It's true, I don't mind a little adoration now and then."

Tassie's charm was a little off. It made Anya itchy. A note not hit in the middle, sharped by nerves. Irritating.

At the same time she felt the play, the invitation. She found herself in a prickly fog of feeling, Tassie an obscure beacon.

Anya wished to be moved out of her state of mind without any effort of her own. She was tired of arrangements, of being the one who set the tone. She wanted to be part of someone else's plot. But she didn't trust Tassie's aesthetic sense. Tassie wouldn't know whether she'd left a scene unfinished or not.

Anya compared herself to Merlin in his weary dry period, finally just tired of being cleverer, with watching the slow emergence of men's thoughts, imperfect larvae. Deliberately let himself be imprisoned by Ninianne, enchanted by the spell he'd taught her. She paid him visits. His folly a relief to him, after a numb period of mere knowing, without hope.

Anya took the comparison seriously. Murmured mysteriously, "Ninianne." Tassie cocked her head, looked as if she *thought* she knew what Anya meant but wouldn't mind hearing what Anya meant *exactly*.

The sun-faded institutional green shades stirred in the draft coming through the windows opened a slit at the top. Anya gathered herself, rephrased the story to flatter Tassie. Anya said that Merlin—she touched her own chest—was finally undone by a beautiful nymph who would do anything, who wanted the power that Merlin could give her. Anya improvised. "All for a kiss."

Tassie shrugged and said, "Just for a kiss?"

Anya touched Tassie's neck. She had no idea what Tassie meant, she only hoped Tassie understood.

Anya's own actions had the shock of a dream, her own

voice came to her as though she were on stage—harsh and constricted at first, opening into a clear tone, metallic but open.

Tassie in motion, in fact *acting* too, the little faker, absolving herself by being confused. Alarmed laughter, gusts of response. Miming helplessness, at one point reeling as though drunk so that it seemed it was just another night when Anya had to help her to bed. Anya had the suspicion that she, Anya, was being undercut by another actress.

The heat between them which had been at first drifting and feverish became a solid block. Anya became deaf and blind to the awkwardness, but alert to the progress of their embrace. Tassie still occasionally acted as though it were all a parody, but she didn't interrupt. What probably released them both into the full erotic current was not so much the contact of their bodies as the sounds—their breathing, the crumpling of their clothes, a zipper ticking on the floor, the compression of the pillow as Tassie sat down on it, the grating of metal links, as Anya put her knee on the cot. Tassie pushed Anya's arm away. Anya said, "Oh, for Christ's sake, Tassie, everybody does it *once*."

Anya was cold and suspicious. Tassie was pleased with herself—even delighted. Anya watched Tassie looking at herself in the long mirror on the back of the door. Anya suspected that Tassie had managed to insulate her real feelings—whether from herself, from Anya, or from coming into being wasn't clear. Tassie'd said, "What if I get pregnant?" Anya had laughed, knowing at the time that it was a dreary joke, coarse, mealy. Tassie was going to think of this as another first for her. The first of her Windsor friends to smoke grass, the second to lose her virginity, the first to sleep with a married man, the first to take a nude group sauna. Tassie kept track. She couldn't not keep track.

Tassie was looking at herself in the mirror. A different vanity from Anya's. Tassie loved herself the way she loved her childhood, her family's summer house, her mother's favorite things. A lot of men, Boston lawyers, bankers, doctors, had said to her, "You have your mother's eyes." Older men had said, with sweet randy twinkling, "I remember your grandmother when she was your age." Tassie had pictures of herself from infancy on. Her only bad period had been when she was fourteen or so, a butterball,

33

attractive enough by herself but thick and miserable alongside her mother, an experienced beauty. When Tassie became beautiful, just over a year before coming to Radcliffe, it was about the same time as and very much like her coming into the first part of her trust fund. She became both more independent and more custodial. Blithe with the interest, but "don't touch the principal" didn't even have to be said. She seemed to have received it by genetic transmission.

Tassie left the mirror, waltzed past Anya, touching her waist. Tassie laughed gaily.

Anya thought mournfully that of course that was the point. Tassie could do anything she wanted with interest. She could be daring without touching the principal.

Tassie's family talked about money carelessly. Bought paintings and boats, joked about them—"Mummy's folly" was a rocky little island off Maine. They bought their underwear on sale.

Tassie and her mother talking about Tassie's Uncle Timmy.

"Is he really rich, Mummy?"

"Oh, he has lots of money."

"Much richer than us?"

"My dear, we're comparative paupers . . . but then of course he has to live in New York."

The way Tassie's mother could say the word *money* . . . such blunt good sense. Was that the center?

Tassie's mother to Tassie at breakfast: "Don't go out before you see your father."

"What about?"

"He wants to talk to you about money."

"Oh, God."

"It won't take long, dear." Like the dentist. Turning to Anya. "It won't take a minute. How I envy you two, the way you stay thin eating these big breakfasts."

Anya had felt promoted to Tassie's mother's bosom. She'd also felt her brutally offhand assurance.

Like Tassie's assurance looking at herself in the mirror.

For a short time after that Anya thought that she was in love with Tassie. She compared herself to Swann, Tassie to Odette. "Someone not my style." Tassie moved in with Jeannie, Muffy, Flossie, et al. Anya roomed in a single, but she saw something of them. The ambitious law students who took Anya out, perhaps as an attempt to get a taste of a wild, possibly hostile and artistic girl, perhaps as an attempt to appear mysterious to their friends, were always surprised to take her to parties and discover that she knew the girls. They would turn it into a compliment by speaking of Tassie, Jeannie, and company as silly and social. It was from the crowd of girls that those young men took their wives over the next four years or so. Appropriate and strangely harmonious marriages. Anya once said it was because the girls' vacuity turned with age into comfortable roominess. But there were a lot of other reasons. That group of girls had more training for their lives than any other group of girls.

Of the five law students who were interested in Anya her junior and senior years, three married into the group. The one who proposed to Anya, more distraught and aching than the others, eventually married Jeannie. He was one of the two who didn't sleep with Anya, and the only one who didn't go to Wall Street. He married Jeannie before he finished law school and became less fearful, more determined, and luckier. He worked for the government and took on and coolly defeated, within the warrant of his job, a number of his former schoolmates who hadn't thought he'd amount to much and who—there was some overlap—had fucked Jeannie when her stance toward men had been that of a paralyzed sexual victim.

According to what Anya heard, mostly from Tassie, the husband was unaware of any pattern, and Jeannie was thrilled and terrified. Jeannie and her husband never mentioned it to each other. Tassie took the line that Jeannie had chosen with some calculation to have tasteless (in the delectable not the decorous sense), cold relations with men at their simplest and lousiest. Anya didn't think so. Jeannie's reaction to whatever had just happened to her in her victim period seemed to Anya to indicate that she was both unaware of how fully she radiated helplessness and also unaware of how awfully inviting her helplessness was.

Anya had two experiences that involved Jeannie. One was at a party at which a moderately drunk and sullen boy (who had somehow seemed to Anya vital and puzzling enough to be worth encouraging) had followed her to the bedroom where the coats were heaped up. He closed the door behind him and grabbed her. He was too drunk, or

too much of a meathead, to stop in the face of unwilling-
ness. He lunged again, and Anya sidestepped and whirled
him by his arm into the wall as hard as she could. He hit
flat, without raising his arm to protect himself. Anya heard
his head bounce. He turned and looked at her blearily.
Anya picked up an umbrella. He gathered himself to leave.
He said, "Well, there's always Jeannie."

Anya had been surprised at how horrified she'd been.
She'd asked Tassie and her date to take Jeannie home.

Shortly after that Anya had gone to a ski weekend in
Vermont. She'd gone off with the cross-country group but
had broken a ski. She'd pushed herself back on one ski to
the house, an insulated barn, one vast room on the first
floor and a half loft with cots which served as balcony to
the main room. Anya had gone up to the loft and dozed.
She'd been half asleep when she heard noises in the main
room. She looked over the railing and saw Jeannie being
kissed. She wasn't able to see who was kissing her, but was
struck by how immobile Jeannie was. The boy started to
take off Jeannie's sweater; Jeannie said, "I think someone's
coming." The boy said, "No," as though he knew that was
all they would say to each other. Jeannie allowed herself to
be undressed. Anya thought at first, Like a storewindow
dummy. That was wrong. Then she thought, Like a child,
and felt an uneasy, gristly edge to her aroused feelings.
Jeannie picked up her clothes while the boy undressed. He
left his strewn on the floor. He tipped her down neatly and
handled her briefly. When he knelt between her legs—their
heads were toward the loft—Anya was surprised to see his
face go suddenly dreamy, as though melting off a scaly
hide of determination. It was hard for Anya to read Jeannie's expression upside down, but Anya thought Jeannie
continued to be horribly inert. He prodded in with some
writhing, adjusted his arms, began slowly. Anya thought
that if she were a child watching it would be terrifying,
and a real terror rose behind the thought which mixed with
Anya's pangs of curiosity and arousal. Jeannie's body had
no spring, it didn't just seem inert, but to be absorbing the
impact like flattening dough. Only her head seemed alive,
cocked away from the boy's, which burrowed into a pillow
while his thin ass whipped along—it struck Anya as a
center of stillness in the tumbled space. The boy finished.
Anya turned away, oppressed and stuffy with desire.

She was still for a while, then stealthily set off an alarm clock. There was a scurrying below. Anya went down after making getting-dressed noises. She looked surprised to see them.

Jeannie mysteriously alive again—"Hi, Anya!" with solid notes. The boy faded with uncertainty, pretended to be looking for something, pretended to find it, left. Jeannie made coffee for Anya, began to chat—did Anya think so-and-so was nice, wasn't so-and-so really funny. Jeannie grew cozier and cozier, Anya more and more bewildered. Jeannie suddenly said, "You know, I'd like to be more like you." She let out a short bubble of sound, possibly a laugh. "I don't mean it that way." Anya alarmed now. What sentence had Jeannie just skipped? But Jeannie went on, maddeningly vague, coyly perky, then sweepingly warm. Then, suddenly, "You know, I'm not really unhappy, there are all sorts of things I don't worry about."

Anya, anxious to hear her own voice, said, "That sounds like one of those Zen sayings."

Jeannie burst into laughter. Anya again was taken aback. Jeannie said, "Oh, that's wonderful." *That?* Jeannie said, "Maybe that's what I meant, you can say that everything's like everything else, maybe that's what I mean, you know, when I said I'd like to be more like you."

Anya realized that Jeannie had decided they were going to be friends and was going about it awkwardly. Anya had no interest in Jeannie but couldn't think of a good reason, or a good way, to avoid being friends. After that Jeannie'd made Anya her confidante, but humbly, that is to say, on a monthly basis, not intrusively at all.

Jeannie would occasionally embarrass Anya by quoting her to a group, often some lame thing Anya had said to Jeannie to keep from sinking into silence.

But all during her senior year at college that cumbersome friendship with Jeannie was Anya's only link with Tassie.

Anya stopped acting and took up directing.

The Drama Club voted Anya a main-stage play the fall of her senior year. After opening night it was Jeannie, not Tassie, who came backstage with flowers.

The Drama Club didn't approve Anya's spring production, so she quit the club and spent the winter and spring making a 16-mm. film, a parody of Ingmar Bergman's *The*

Seventh Seal, the Cambridge hit film of the year before. Anya liked Bergman, but thought *Seventh Seal* was finally pretentious. It was Jeannie who helped Anya raise the money and who scurried around doing errands for her.

Anya thought her half-hour film was very funny.

Now two years later, Anya could barely remember the gags. Anya wrote the basic script along with a couple of Harvard *Lampoon* editors. Those two also arranged the showing of the film as a parody of a Hollywood premier. They drove a parade of convertibles through Harvard Square—the last one was pulling an open U-Haul trailer. A man in Ben Hur costume stood in the trailer holding reins attached to the convertible. The sides of the U-Haul chariot were painted S P Q R.

In front of Adams House they had mini-Klieg lights and a block of wet cement they stuck their feet in. It was pleasant nonsense, and they filled the Adams House dining hall three nights at a dollar a head.

One of the Poonies came dressed as a Swedish sailor—supposedly Ingmar Bergman—and was interviewed in front of the audience.

"Mr. Bergman, I understand your father was a Lutheran minister. Has this influenced your work?"

"Yah, dat's right, my work has some metaphysical bias." He pronounced it bee-ess.

"Uh, Mr. Bergman, in English we pronounce it bias."

"No, no, vot I say is metaphysical BS—metaphysical bullshit."

Anya took the film to New York that summer and finally got someone to look at it. Without the college pranks, without a college audience ready to laugh at the parody, or even when they recognized an allusion, the film fell flat. Sitting next to Mr. Danziger in his dingy screening room at Ikon Films, Anya winced. The film seemed to go on for hours.

Mr. Danziger was gentle. "Look, Miss Janek, what can I say?—it's kind of cute. You do the camera work yourself?"

Anya nodded and said, "Me and another guy."

Mr. Danziger said, "You do the script?"

Anya said, "Me and two other guys."

Mr. Danziger asked her which gags were hers, how she raised the money, how much, what the schedule had been.

Anya finally said, "You've been very nice, but I know the film isn't good enough."

Mr. Danziger said, "It's not the film I'm interested in. I might have a job for you. We do a lot of documentary shorts—right now, I've got one on belly dancing in New York, one on poetry reading at the YMHA, and one on a wildlife sanctuary. We also do two or three features a year. One of them is usually a horror show about a girl with big tits. I use the term technically. I am referring to the mood, the third feature at a drive-in. And then one of the features is something I really like. I'm not a gambler.

"I wear a belt and suspenders to keep my pants up.

"My partner runs the distributing company. I run the production company. I have some permanent staff to help in the office, most of the people I work with on production come and go. I'd like a bright kid to be around who didn't pack up at the end of every project. We've been scavenging, but we're going to expand. I'm betting that in five years—certainly by the end of the sixties—more interesting films are going to get made outside of Hollywood. I'd like a little help."

Anya didn't take the job at first. She didn't think Mr. Danziger was sinister, but his company wasn't what she wanted. She looked for a part in a play. She kept going to a dance class until she couldn't afford it. She wrote a twenty-page treatment of a movie about a college love affair. She started to adapt *Twelfth Night*—her idea being to film not only the action but the images that the characters spoke.

She thought of what Tassie and Jeannie and Muffy and Tish were doing. Tassie had gone to Florence to study Italian art. Jeannie was at the Perkins School learning to teach blind children. Muffy was a secretary for the Tanglewood Festival. Tish was taking a postgraduate year of chemistry and biology in order to apply to medical school. Her father told her he would pay her tuition only if her grades put her in the top third of the entering class at Harvard Medical School. If she met that private requirement, her uncle, who was on the faculty, would see that she was not kept out because she was a woman.

Anya thought that was infuriating. It was not favoritism, but it was privilege. An intercession of private law. Of course it was true that it was an intercession to right a wrong, and it was also true that her uncle was a champion of women's admission to medical school and would argue for any woman—that is, any applicant who was above average. What made Anya feel furious, and also forlorn, was the plain coziness of it.

Anya, for all her contempt for Tassie's gang, saw them taking what appeared to her to be an inevitable step toward matronhood. They were all—except Tassie—becoming less foolish, handsomer, and less sexy. They weren't lovely flowers tossing their pretty heads anymore, it wasn't a hothouse anymore, it was the slightly acid soil of New England virtue, but they were still cared for.

Anya rarely allowed herself the weakness of considering how close she'd been to their life. Her mother—Anna Brünner Janek—arriving in Canada by herself and making her way to Boston after Anya was born—had given her up to the couple who'd raised Anya. That would have been fine. But Henry Sewall gave up his job at Harvard and retired to a small farm in New Hampshire—in the Boston tradition, to be sure, of renouncing Boston. The Sewalls hadn't changed her name. And when Anya was still in high school the Sewalls died, eleven months apart.

Anya met Henry's brother Edward only once. Edward had disliked Henry. Anya had disliked Edward. At the age of eighteen her main feeling about her not liking Edward was a sense of freedom, a clean unleashing of an unclean rage that she'd felt for a long time.

But during her last three years of college she'd also rather blithely thought—no, not entirely blithely, she'd been encouraged by various professors, and Tassie's mother, to think it—that she had talent. And she'd decided that her talent was all that she'd wanted. After four months of vainly offering her talent, she went back to Mr. Danziger.

She said, "Is this more than a Girl Friday job?"

He said, "Yes. The hours are longer."

Anya considered this a temporary arrangement, so she was shocked to find when Jeannie asked her to be a bridesmaid the following June—that a whole year had gone by since college. Jeannie apologized that she had to ask Tassie to be the maid of honor, Tassie was her cousin, and their families had always been close. Tassie was due back any day now from Italy. Anya had a reunion with all the endearing diminutives—Muffy, Tish, Filly, Tassie.

The wedding was near Hamilton, about thirty-five miles north of Boston.

Mr. Danziger gave Anya all of Friday off so that she could be in Massachusetts Friday and Saturday. He asked her if she'd mind coming in on Sunday. That marked the passage of a year for her too—she knew she ought to, and she was governed by the obligation without even thinking about it. The company was like the weather.

At the reception Tassie flirted with her Uncle Timmy. Timmy was also Jeannie's uncle, Jeannie's mother's stepbrother.

Tassie said, "Why, Uncle Timmy, you're looking prosperous."

Uncle Timmy laughed, hugged Tassie, and said, "As a matter of fact, I've just counted my money and I am."

Anya remembered Tassie asking her mother if Uncle Timmy was rich—Uncle Timmy, the New York branch.

Jeannie's father, divorced, occasional drunk, showed up at the last minute to give the bride away. Uncle Timmy had come in full fig to do it in case the father didn't show. Uncle Timmy was beautifully dressed, sleek, healthy, and clean. A prize bull groomed for the fair. A suggestion of an Irish tenor at the turn of the century, singing to a parlor full of dovebreasted, swooning women. His starched, absolutely white wing collar squeezed his cleanly scraped throat and neck. He was hot. All his female relatives gloried in him. His wife was not present, summer flu. Prize Black Angus on the green lawn. His morning coat and striped trousers fitted so well they must have been his own. He was the only one who was pleasant to Jeannie's father. He walked off with him occasionally, an arm around the smaller man's shoulders. Politely keeping him off the sauce.

But Uncle Timmy kept coming back to Tassie. Raucous and corny now he'd had enough to drink, but moving elegantly.

"Tassie, why don't you come see me more often now that you're all grown-up?"

He and Tassie inflated each other with their charm.

"You don't think all those teddy bears I gave you weren't an investment . . ."

Rising gaiety. "Oh, Uncle Timmy!"

41

He politely included Anya in the conversation. "You know this fellow Jeannie's married?" He didn't stop for an answer. "Has he got a sense of humor? That's what Jeannie needs. Now, Tassie here"—he put his arm around Tassie's waist, and Tassie leaned back on it prettily—"needs a serious old bear."

Tassie put her head on his shoulder.

He danced with Tassie a lot. It was an old fashioned band that he'd hired. They played jazzy fox trots whenever Timmy came on the floor, songs they apparently knew he knew. Tassie knew them too. While Anya was dancing with the groom, who was being ponderously sentimental— "You're someone who's turned out to be one of the few friends Jeannie and I count on"—Anya heard Tassie singing to Timmy, "I'm getting tired of working all day. I want someone who just wants me to play—"

When she got to the line "a big sweet poppa like you" she looked at the bandleader and pointed to Timmy. The bandleader smiled and nodded without missing a beat. Tassie and Timmy were having a lovely time showing off. A hot summer game. After the bride and groom left, Tassie popped champagne corks, arcing them from the terrace down over the steep back lawn. Timmy ran back and forth catching them on the fly. She opened five bottles. A man passing by said, "I hope you're going to drink all of those." Tassie laughed at him.

Tassie pleaded with Timmy to stay for supper. He had to get back to Boston. Tassie said, "Well, at least you can give Anya a ride to the airport."

Gallantly—"Your good-looking friend? What a treat."

Anya suspected that Tassie knew Uncle Timmy was a game Anya couldn't play as well as Tassie. The car rolled majestically away, Timmy and Anya in the back. Timmy instructed the chauffeur in Spanish.

Timmy was coasting down a slope of well-being, Anya was tongue-tied. Ordinarily she could have made fun of his bottle-green Bentley. She knew the lines, she could hear Tassie's mother saying them. And Tassie would have made fun of the little vases with flowers in them, she and Timmy would have laughed all the way to Boston. Anya felt gritty. She would have liked to be Tassie, gently poached for Uncle Timmy. She had a headache from drinking champagne in the sun. Timmy popped open a bar. Anya was startled. Tassie would have laughed, and Timmy would have patted her knee. Timmy patted Anya's hand, and she was startled again. He asked her what she wanted to drink. He was bored. Anya was sure now this was Tassie's revenge. Tassie would ask Timmy what he thought of Anya. Tassie would list Anya's talents—"but she plays the violin, she's so smart, she was in plays. I can't believe you two didn't say a word." Anya's talents shriveled to boring compensations for being a dull girl.

Anya thought of saying, "You're from Boston originally?" He would say yes and ask her—it wouldn't work, the question was either pretentious or toadying. Well, fuck him.

She thought of "Tassie never told me she had such a charming uncle." Staggeringly simpering.

The car rolled on. Timmy didn't seem affected by her depressed silence. Some people are like that, he probably thought. He seemed to be enjoying the countryside. Tassie had had such a light touch, powdery, she and Timmy fit so well, old smoothies on the dance floor, how pleasant for them, narcissism *à deux*. No, that was just another sour grape. Anya held her mind still long enough to see that she wanted a favor from this man, a judgment. She felt deeply that if he didn't think she was charming she would consider herself a failure. Ridiculous, but she felt it. Was the problem that he'd had such a good time and she'd had a dull time? She refused to settle for the spite of the critic who hadn't had any fun.

The car pulled onto the highway. Timmy suddenly looked at her and began to make conversation. College? What was she doing now? It turned out he knew Mr. Danziger from a group of musical amateurs they'd both been in years before. Timmy told her a long story about her employer's attempts to sing the tenor part of the great male duet from Bizet's *The Pearl Fishers*. Mr. Danziger had, according to Timmy, a lovely tenor, but he was unable to sing against another voice. An elaborate defect—not a tin ear, but a chameleon ear. If there was any note being sung other than the one he should have been singing, he was irresistibly drawn to it. If he struggled to concentrate on his own note, he flatted or sharped it. Timmy did an imitation —first Mr. Danziger's solo intro, *"Au fond du temple*

43

saint . . ." Timmy sang it prettily. Then Timmy sang the main melody:

> *Oui, c'est elle*
> *C'est la déesse plus charmante et plus belle.*
> *Oui, c'est elle*
> *C'est la déesse qui descend parmi nous.*

Halfway through it, Timmy explained, the baritone breaks into harmony. Timmy sang the tenor part again, starting off each line heroically, but wandering off the note at the climax. Timmy had a good enough ear to get it wrong cleverly, plus a talent for mimicking the desperation of a floundering singer. He flicked his eyes from side to side as though trying to find the note through a sense that hadn't betrayed him. Anya laughed.

It was all easy enough once Timmy got started on his musical stories. Most of them involved singing or humming themes. He knew a lot of standard opera and ballet. He was on the board of trustees of a ballet company. Anya had heard some of the stories he claimed to have witnessed. She thought her dance teacher had told her some of them, dating from when she was in ballet twenty years earlier. Anya wondered if they were a hundred years old. It didn't matter, Timmy told them well enough, enjoyed his own performance, held her by her forearm when he laughed. She hurriedly slipped in that she'd danced—so she could very well picture what he was talking about . . . He was off on another story. She asked him why he hadn't had a career in music. Ah.

For a moment he considered giving her a serious answer. Perhaps started to.

"There were so many things I did passably, you see . . ." He laughed. "Let's blame the war. No. I did in fact sing some lieder one evening in front of some musical friends. They were mortally polite." They both laughed. "You know, I remember there was once a very good conductor named Fine who was rehearsing a piece by Stravinsky. In Boston, I think. The piece came to an end, and Stravinsky rose from the back of the auditorium and shouted, 'Fine! Fine! . . . That was terrible!' "

He laughed, Anya laughed with him. He said it again, "Fine! Fine! That was *terrible!*" He said, "You see, if only

I'd been *that* good . . ." He laughed some more. Anya thought, Almost.

She was shocked when she was suddenly on the pavement in front of the airline terminal, slightly hung over.

During the next month her life was not very satisfying. She fell back into the rhythm of working, but it didn't correspond to the movement of her feelings. She stopped being amused by the airs of the cast. She was depressed by the mechanical sentimentality of the movie, for all its quick cuts and jumbled time sequences. Everyone relied on her efficiency, but she didn't take full advantage of it. She was surprisingly good at finding ways to save money, and she didn't mind squabbling. She suggested to the producer that two characters who ran off together for a dreamy love sequence shouldn't go off to an island but just rent a cruising sloop. The director said shooting on water was hell, the light changed all the time. She said shoot at night. He said it was worse. She found a boat free at City Island, and the director fell in love with evening shots of New York from the water. The love scene took place in the cabin. Interior, night. Hooked to the marina power.

She became the good gray lady of the enterprise. She drifted into spinsterish reliability, reflected on it gloomily. She was behaving well on her job because she found it strangely natural to please the people who paid her. Not a happy and not a trivial relationship. She had little energy left over at night. What became trivial were her own pleasures. Her pleasures became sleeping late on Sundays, not having to answer the phone in the office after they hired another girl. And—she was ashamed at how affected she was by it—being included by the producers with the assistant directors when the whole gang went out to lunch at a restaurant.

She had dewy shop-girl reveries in which Timmy appeared and thought she was wonderful. She knew that her reveries of Timmy's charms were precarious, she might find him ridiculous at any minute, and therefore her fantasy had a forced pace, speeding clichés, very like the movie.

She still saw a few people she'd known in college from the theater crowd. They were dislocated. Those that had jobs had even worse jobs than hers. They either inflated them or made fun of them. All of them, employed or not, who had been in New York for a year had lost their fuzz of gaiety. They were still waiting for the lucky break, but silently and grimly. A few sneered at her for being in the production end. More wanted to know when the company's next movie would be cast, could she let them know beforehand, brief them on the director's eccentricities?

She also noted that their boredom and bad luck had a saltpeter effect on their sex lives.

She herself was bored. She'd been bored before, but she'd always thought she could move away from it at will. Now she felt becalmed in a flat sea of boredom. Her soap opera about Timmy now bored her. She decided to see him again. She immediately decided not to. She was timid. She was then scared she'd lost her nerve. Six weeks had passed, he wouldn't remember her, there was no graceful way . . .

She remembered that Timmy had said he knew Mr. Danziger. She asked Mr. Danziger if he knew Timmy. He looked at her a moment and said, "How come you know that son of a bitch?"

She was taken aback. But she said, "Why is he a son of a bitch?"

Mr. Danziger said, "Never mind."

Anya said, "I just met him once at a wedding, he mentioned he knew you. In fact he said you were very talented—"

"Never mind."

Anya wondered what the offense could have been. It increased her interest to imagine Timmy as someone's villain. And Timmy seemed unaware of it. He wouldn't have told the story about the tin ear, not the way he had—or had she missed the real flavor?

She called up Tassie at her family's summer house. The maid said Tassie had gone to New York, she didn't know the number. Not so very strange to call Timmy to ask. Anya looked around the office; it was five o'clock Friday, she poked around to make sure she was alone, looked up Timmy's number, her hands shaking. She decided she had to do it—her feelings were too fresh to waste no matter how trite. She called. Tassie answered, but Anya didn't recognize her voice until she'd said Timmy was out. Anya said, "Tassie? It's Anya."

Tassie said, "Oh my God, where are you?"

"Still here, I haven't—"

Tassie didn't notice. She bustled ahead. "Well look, you've got to come over right away. I want to talk to you before Uncle Timmy gets back. Just for a drink. I want to tell you some things."

Fine. Tassie assumed Anya was looking for her. Tassie's voice struck Anya as both frantic and inert.

When Anya finally got to the apartment Tassie squealed and hugged her and sat her down on a sofa.

Tassie said, "I'm engaged."

Anya knew she couldn't say the right thing, not because of surprise but because of the tedium of the surprise.

Anya said, "No!"

"Oh yes. It's nothing like what I expected, I didn't realize—how can I say it without—I didn't realize I had so much power." Tassie laughed. "Not just over myself, but I've got such confidence. You ought to try it . . . But Mummy and Daddy are horrified."

Anya was surprised at that since the fiancé turned out to be one of the old gang of law students. He now worked for a New York firm, was at the very moment working. Tassie said, "Friday night, for God's sake. We'll have supper together and he'll work some more. So we can have Saturday. When I'm not here he works Saturdays."

Anya asked about Tassie's mother and father.

"Oh, I don't know why they don't like him," Tassie said, "Yes I do. He's not impressed by them. He thinks they baby me. I think Mummy's jealous. Daddy's just worried in general. He asks me in a suspicious way if I'm ready to settle down. I told him I thought that was a dumb way to think about it. As though everything has to come to an end. Of course, he may somehow know about my one little lapse. It won't shock *you*, but after Paul proposed and I said yes and we told Mummy and Daddy and they said, 'Let's wait just a bit before we announce it'—after that I suddenly felt sexy as hell, afterwards I felt awful, not guilty because I was really just absentminded—"

Anya said, "Where was Paul?"

"Well, he was back here and I was up there, doing the regular things, you know, very healthy, but boring at night, and I just wandered over to the house just along the shore which we were all avoiding because it had been rented to someone nobody knew or liked the looks of, so of course

47

he was very touchy about my being on his dock, you know
the one I mean, just inside the breakwater. What was odd
is that I'd always had to be prepared, or at least asked, and
I suddenly thought I could be the one, so I said I was just
a bored divorcée taking a walk, and how would he like to
take me for a midnight boat ride, so we went into the cabin
of his motorboat. We didn't even cast off. He didn't really
want to in a way, but it was too good to be true. He *had*
to do it. And it was the idea that I could have got up and
jumped off and swum away that made it nothing more than
an idea of mine. And when it was over I did just that, put
my bathing suit back on and dove in and swam off across
the channel. I walked back by the new bridge across the
gut and thought about something else, no, I didn't think,
Paul has probably done this once, completely without jealousy. So it was just a part of—getting rid of everything
before."

Anya thought Tassie's interest in herself was now thick.
It had been, once, a feathery caress, so light and silvery in
fact that it often seemed that Tassie was surprised—shyly
pleased—to have someone as nice as herself show such
delicate understanding and sympathy. It had been the most
graceful self-appreciation. Now Tassie's interest in herself
was a dumb headlock.

Anya looked at Tassie closely. Of course you could read
anything into looks once you were thinking it—even so,
there did seem to be . . . Perhaps it was just the obvious-
ness of a summer by the sea—the complete tan. Her eyes
by contrast lighter, more doll-like China blue. Her arms
and legs were tennised and swum out of any hint of baby
fat, only her hands still had chubby palms. Her last reservoir of fleshiness, a beaver's tail of stored babyhood. Anya
looked at her own large long hands.

Tassie's face was thinner. Still a golden girl, a mask of
fine features. She still bit her nails.

Anya thought of her own dull job with pride, a valuable
exercise, a sharpening of her senses.

Anya said, "What does Timmy think? Does he—"

"Uncle Timmy? Oh, he just rattles along. We see him
here a lot, and he makes jokes about being our duenna. He
really is useless. Very charming, very light-touch, but useless. I mean *materially* he'll do anything for me, a place to
stay, theater tickets, but when I want to really talk to him

48

he vagues out. A little babbling stream of pleasant this-and-that. I asked him seriously how he and his wife get along —I mean, I know they have ups and downs and he has his little other interests, but I'm not supposed to know, I guess. He said—as he faded out—'oh, one falls in love with one's wife periodically.' Keep it light, keep it gay."

"Where is he now?"

"He's floating around. There's a performance by some ballet company he has something to do with that he wants us to go to. But Paul has to go back to work. That's another thing, he's very witty about how hard Paul works."

Anya said, "Maybe he's a little jealous. He may have stronger feelings about you than you imagine."

Tassie considered this seriously. She was used to considering people's stronger feelings about her. She finally said, "No. He likes me as a well-made piece of family."

Anya thought that wasn't right but didn't want to go into it. Anya said, "Of course, it's very hard to be anything but cautiously enthusiastic to someone who's engaged. Anything he says can be held against him. What you really want is reassurance that everyone is still going to love you no matter what."

Tassie shrugged. She said, "Well, I don't mind. If his uncle act stops when I start my own life, it's just too bad."

Anya looked around the room, wondering if she could have guessed it wasn't a bachelor's. It was well done. Not their first place. Their own style, she thought, but a style that had been worked out somewhere else first. Almost a habit by now. Perhaps that was a wishful thought.

Did they have separate bedrooms? Was the wife long-suffering?

Anya recognized some of the conventions of decoration from Tassie's and Jeannie's house, but this was sleeker. More New York as the center of the world. An expensive idea to maintain. Not much stuff from Grandma's house here. Anya looked at a piece of sculpture, certainly not from Grandma's house. *Leda and the Swan.* Translucent marble, no, maybe alabaster, veins of opaque darker white. All one piece. Leda was long-limbed, almost awkward, she looked as though she'd just fallen backwards, one hip flattened, her breasts jarred upward, her mouth open. Both arms flung out behind her, the heel of one hand seeming to slide along the earth, the other hand in mid-air. Her face was not as specifically modeled as her arms and legs, particularly the long thigh and bent knee opened by (or perhaps to receive) the rush of the swan. The Swan was amorphous at his base, seemed to be materializing from the earth. He became more detailed and more tranquil from the chest up, his open beak was tucked through Leda's hair under her ear. The neck was not yet fully extended. The touch of his bill on her neck would be gentle by contrast with the force with which he'd sprawled her on the earth.

Anya felt her sexual feelings being tuned. Tensing toward the right note.

Tassie had more to say about Paul and her. Anya wondered if this was the final change for Tassie. Tassie pressed on. Anya thought, Tedious enthusiasm for the inevitable. Tassie probably considered that she was liberating herself from her parents, from her childhood, that she was a princess awakening. Anya thought Tassie was vaulting into a less interesting cliché.

How I met Paul and how I knew.

The thing about Paul is he's not very verbal. (Verbal a pejorative in the new order.)

Paul has a serious vision of the world. Paul is seriously ambitious, not for his own sake but (Tassie floundered a bit) he likes to see things run right (Tassie sensed she was boring).

On to: Paul a whacking great stud. (Tassie looked at Anya to make sure they could still have a giggle about that.) You wouldn't guess it to look at him but my God I've never . . .

Then: But Paul really loves me. I can let myself go completely with him. I don't have to do anything more. Can you imagine the relief?

Anya was struck with horror at that admission. Not having to do anything, not wanting to keep on—it gave Anya a dismal vertigo, a fear of falling out of life.

Then Anya tried to imagine Tassie's feelings. Had things been hard for Tassie? Anya found it difficult to imagine. She'd often been aware of Tassie's symptoms of distress; but she'd always taken them to be dramatized exclamations, on a par with Tassie's squeals, flounces, or clever sayings. She'd never believed Tassie's pain was as real as her own, because Tassie's seemed comparatively formless and variable. Anya had thought it all like complaining about a pimple before a dance.

But now, suddenly, Tassie said, "Can you imagine the relief?"

Anya managed to feel an outline of Tassie's distress: Tassie's distrust of her own mind—a mind good enough to make fun of anything, but not able to hold still long enough to consider or believe anything for her own benefit. Her say-anything wit had been only a part of her charm —like her looks, it was for the benefit of those around her. A brilliant sweetness—like anise—that attracted others but that Tassie herself didn't really crave anymore . . .

After Anya glimpsed that idea (and several other possible anxieties in Tassie's life—e.g. views of Tassie's mother as a shadowy rival rather than cool, long-fingered comforter), she suddenly found herself in touch with Tassie's mood—the urge to gel into substance the bland cream-filling of Tassie's passive life behind the glaze of Tassie's beauty.

Anya recoiled as though from a pregnant woman. She felt a flush through her neck and face.

Tassie noticed this and looked at her intently.

Tassie said, "Well, that's enough about what I'm up to. Except I've thought about you a lot. This doesn't upset you, does it?"

Anya said, "No."

Anya looked again at the *Leda and the Swan*. She began to wish for something that definite and clear to come to her head.

Anya asked, "How does your Uncle Timmy get along with Paul?" She didn't want the conversation to bog down.

Tassie said, "They're not really all that *simpático*. Timmy likes people to entertain him."

Anya thought, That's not right. He just wants things to define themselves. Why *should* he care about things that aren't an improvement on dull matter? She thought, If I were his mistress . . .

The possibility as it occurred to her was connected to the statue. She wanted to remove some harder, clear feelings from the sludge of her life and sculpt them. The *Leda and the Swan* was a better-than-average Edwardian effort, an Edwardian notion of an Italian Renaissance notion of a classical notion. Anya thought that was the line of descent that mattered, that it was possible by an act of will to be ready to take the risk that would put her in touch with the higher molding force. All her earlier yearnings for elegance weren't as important, they were only adolescent preparations. Her dancing, her crush on Tassie, her appearing on stage in farce and comedy, her masquerades. She must either fall out of life like Tassie or move onto a stage that would allow, no, demand that she appear as the best idea of herself.

Anya thought that she was ready for that idea—not an idea of herself that she already had but an idea that was now waiting for her. She felt a thrill of pride at her modest willingness to be transformed into something real and valuable.

But when Timmy finally came Anya sank back into confusion.

Tassie, for all her complaints of the moment before, brightened up, kissed him, laughed. "You remember Anya?"

"Certainly." He shook Anya's hand. "Oh, yes, of course! The dark musical stranger . . . Well, what fun you're both here."

Tassie, gay all over again, plumped him up. Her voice bouncing along.

Anya, tongue-tied and virginal, waiting for a chance to join in.

Timmy made a phone call. Anya figured out it was to his wife in some outlying town. ". . . Yes, there's Tassie and her young man." He looked at Tassie who held up her finger and shook her head no. Timmy looked away. "I don't see how I can manage to talk to the Wheelocks if you're not along. I suppose he and Tassie's young man can talk about law . . . Oh yes, well I'll warn him about that. What shall I say about you? . . . It's *not* serious, is it? . . . Good . . . Yes, that's right, we are having the whole troupe out there on Sunday . . . But that's it, how are you going to say anything if you haven't seen them dance . . . I forgot that. Can you get the channel out there? Another sign of age . . . No, I meant *my* forgetting it . . . All right. I'll come out tomorrow night. In time for supper . . . Yes. Good-by."

Timmy turned to Tassie. Tassie said, "Paul has to work tonight."

Timmy said, "I thought I mentioned this to you last weekend."

Tassie said, "I don't remember."

Timmy said, "Well, *you're* free at least."

Tassie said, "I'm having supper with him—".

"Try not to be late. We'll leave here at half past seven."

Tassie said, "Oh, all right. I'll meet you there. I'll take the ticket with me." Tassie smiled. "Anya loves ballet."

Timmy said, "Of course. I hope you're free. You must think we're inviting you to go to the dentist—"

"I do love ballet, but—"

Tassie broke in. "Don't go back to your place, there isn't time. I've got lots of dresses here, you can keep Timmy company—ease my conscience. Timmy, you've got to insist."

Anya really didn't know—maybe it would be better to leave. After one drink, having said something clever, having caught Timmy's eyes, saying, "I really do love ballet, maybe another time."

Timmy insisted politely. Tassie grabbed her arm, laughing. "You mustn't, you can't, I won't let you, I won't go unless you do. Quick, tie her feet!"

It ended up the way Tassie wanted. The two of them trying on dresses in the guest room, Tassie laughing and babbling. It was hard to tell what was giving her pleasure; perhaps only the disruption. Tassie left. Anya sat alone in the living room wearing a dress of Tassie's. Timmy came in wearing his evening clothes. He was annoyed to find Tassie gone. He said, "She forgot her ticket."

Anya apologized. She wasn't sure how she looked, Tassie had chosen the dress and put her hair up for her. Anya thought her bare neck and bare arms and pale long legs looked too stalky, schoolgirlish. Tassie's shoes were too tight for her.

When the Wheelocks showed up, Timmy introduced her with careful insistence as Tassie's roommate, joked about the chaos. They all chatted. They drank faster than they would have if they'd had anything to say. Anya remembered she and Timmy hadn't eaten anything. At the theater Anya insisted on being the one to wait at the door with

Tassie's ticket. Tassie was fifteen minutes late. The two of them crept into the box and sat behind the three others.

Tassie said, "Anya—"

Anya shushed her. Tassie leaned over, her bare upper arm touching Anya's stickily. She whispered, "Can you smell anything?" She covered her mouth and nose to keep from laughing out loud. "I mean, is it obvious what I've been doing?"

Anya said, "Not unless you announce it."

Tassie thought that was funny.

At intermission Anya talked to Mr. Wheelock about the ballet. He was a clod. He asked why all the men were so short. Anya said it just looked that way when the girls were on point. She swept herself up on the ball of one toe and towered over him. Timmy laughed.

The Wheelocks begged off after the ballet. It occurred to Anya that Mrs. Wheelock didn't like the idea of a group in which Tassie and Anya were the other women. Anya wondered if this was clear to anyone else.

Timmy was hungry. The three of them took a cab to one of the *La Crêpe* restaurants. As they walked in Anya saw the Wheelocks and grabbed Timmy's arm and turned him around. "The Wheelocks!"

All three of them jammed through the door and ran down the street until they were around the corner.

Timmy said, "Good for you."

Tassie's side zipper had popped open. They couldn't fix it. Tassie hailed a cab and got in. Timmy said, "We'll get something to eat at home."

Tassie said, "I've got to meet Paul." She closed the door. The cab drove off.

Anya said, "I'm sorry about all this—"

Timmy said, "The Wheelocks are bores, I'm annoyed at Tassie, but I'm really perfectly delighted with you."

Anya said, "I know a place to eat. Over near where I live. No Wheelocks to be seen."

She was sure she saw Timmy deciding that she knew how to be discreet. She said, "The food is good . . . at least not bad."

When they finally got a cab and got in, she took off her tight shoes. Timmy leaned over and kissed her knee. She kept herself from looking at him but turned her head slightly toward him. She felt herself start to smile, she let herself smile, he couldn't possibly be offended even if he saw it was self-congratulatory.

When they walked from the restaurant to her apartment she put her arm through his. She felt regal. Timmy said, "Makes me stand up straight, walking with a girl as tall as you."

When they went up the steps of her building, however, Timmy began to talk a nervous, slangy chatter. Anya thought, It can't be that he doesn't know? Kissing her knee had been just right. Could Tassie have been wrong about his chasing after nymphs? But who *was* it he'd been interested in? Maybe he had some quirk, only the downstairs maid. He didn't *seem* to be a restricted personality. Her mind snagged on her jargon.

Timmy eyed her long, almost bare single room. He saw her violin case tucked under the round table by the bow window. "What's that? Your submachine gun?" He laughed. She laughed. They kept on laughing. It occurred to her that hilarity was the medium he found necessary. She refused to be disappointed. She still hoped for some lingering, some gilded courtly mannerism. But it became abrupt. She thought of what was instantly pleasant—some strong lotion on his neck and jowl, clovelike breath, his hands pressing anxiously on her flanks—a bright cosmetic daydream becoming heavy breathing.

She turned her back so he could see the hook of the dress that he was having some trouble with. Perhaps she should tell how she'd thought of him, how she'd been stunned with admiration. Too late. Going down the track. She was caught up a little, not enough. It all rattled along like a subway ride, lasted about as long as between stops on an express, settled to a hydraulic stop, the doors sighing open, a noisy subsidence, silence. The sound of a voice returning sharply.

Later on she got up, picked up their clothes. Drifted out to the ice box and stove behind a folding screen. She thought she should offer him a drink. There was nothing to drink. She went into the bathroom, looked at herself in the mirror on the back of the door. Pale long limbs. It occurred to her what she'd thought Timmy's charm was— that he was a great appreciator of women. Susceptible, spoiled—the perfect judge. An oracle. Tell me my fortune, tell me in what mode I'm attractive.

She was glad to be away for a moment. She listened. Nothing. Her daydream lying collapsed on her bed. What was her fortune? She backed away from the mirror to see more of her body. She thought she looked like a Cretan bull dancer, the long developed thighs, the wide flat shoulders. Did Timmy dream of models? Would he think of Crete? He probably only started with Greece, perfect proportions. Did he even *think* about attraction? Or did he just let it rise up in him? What forms? Surely he considered the forms . . . She herself had often thought of the *idea* of women's bodies—the shifting attention of the imagination of each age. Surely more than an exercise in proportion. Refined excitement. Fashion and costumes were an attempt to share alluring daydreams—Marie Antoinette's ladies rigged-out as shepherdesses to make pale innocence attainable as flesh. What was the point of Liberty's naked breast at the barricade? Surely she was the shepherdess stolen from the court—she can be yours, *citoyen,* after the battle. *Empire* breasts, barely veiled, ideally soft, small, round, ribboned off above a waterfall of gauze. Covered more carefully in England during the Regency. The gauze itself the allure? No, there were dainty necks, the tiny slippered feet.

Victorian bathing machines. Wooden harems drawn by horses into the water. All those layers of wet clothes. That daydream must have been heavy and rich.

In public the majestic heads of hair, the majestic singular bosoms. When did the men start passing around those pictures of odalisques, rosy globes of flesh—was that what they dreamed was submerged under the floating soggy clothes? Twirling their moustaches and diving for sunken treasure.

The Gibson girl was an elongation of those notions. Still the monumental head, the pigeon-gorge bosom, the bustle, but now sharper and more androgynous faces. That was closer to her. Curious how the flapper came about. All knees and frantic motion. Girls as boys, that always recurred. And then again majestic anchored ships of women. Softness and stately repose—odalism—seemed to alternate with leanness and motion. The Miss America idea—immobile, the flesh hanging softly on the bones like overboiled chicken. It got worse. From her own childhood and early adolescence, she could remember crinolines and small feet, cute little noses, baby hands. She'd hated them. What a starved adolescent idea—the body a secret white pudding. To be fed on in the dark, under the cashmere sweater, fingers nipped by the elastic band of the bra, creeping around. Boy Scout test: Can you unfasten a bra with one hand? While the other hand plunges up under the pleated skirt across the inert junket of flesh above the stocking. She'd caught the last of that—she couldn't put up with it —the boy alarmed in the back of the car—doubling with his best friend. Feebly nerved to paddle around in her quiet flesh. Alarmed when she'd fingered his prick. Then he'd lain still but rigid. Couldn't believe it. A voice from the front seat, "Hey, did I hear a zipper?" Har, har. The boy biting his hand, then twisting his face into the back of the seat to smother his breathing. Shot up his shirt front. She'd been amazed it worked. She'd been operating on theory alone. She'd half-feared it would make her notorious in the Hillsboro school district, half-hoped it would make her famous. The boy never mentioned it to anyone as far as she knew. She'd had to be her own heroine. Busy with herself in the dark winter valley.

Even the next year at Putney she'd sensed she'd seemed sinister, a gritty problem in spite of all her talents. Such solitary ones. Not a happy girl. Even her few admirers on the faculty never made a heroine of her. Most of them believed in shepherdesses too—the healthy liberal leisure class in blue jeans. She was less bitter about the idea now that she could articulate it; at the time they'd almost convinced her. But she'd certainly been better off in that Nordic preserve of apple orchards and goats and clear long views than in the dark narrow ditchlife she'd been in in her part of New Hampshire. She'd still fiddled and read and skied, she'd had some audience among the students. The heroes and heroines had had authors among the faculty. As doting as Lewis Carroll about Alice. Her violin teacher at music camp hadn't doted. She'd lied a little about that. He'd given her the feeling that he was trying out an American violin. Not bad—for mass production. Maybe we could use it in our grade-school program.

She thought, was it only emptiness in her that wanted an author now? That wanted someone's imagination to make something of her life?

Had she made it all up? Wasn't Timmy a connoisseur? Wouldn't he place her in the proper niche?

All right. She wouldn't insist on an author. A critic would do. To approve her vanity. After all, she'd admired *his* creation of himself. She should have asked him, "Did you have to work to be the way you are, or did it just happen?"

She wanted some acknowledgment, not of her effort but of what she was without effort. Come on, Timmy, a brilliant remark. Her fortune. It really wasn't any fun to tell your own fortune.

She stood up straight and touched her mouth with her fingers. Smoothed back her hair. Looked for the brush. Back in the other room.

She watched Timmy watch her enter. She turned to the mirror over the mantel of the fireplace. She brushed her hair, watched him in the mirror. He came up behind her. A small nervy reedy desire came back.

"You have the most marvelous bottom." A hand on each buttock. He ran his thumbs down her spine, opened her ass. She hoped not.

She was relieved when he reached around the top of her legs, fingers combing apart the damp hair. Her desire now turned bright and giddy. She put her hands on the mantelpiece, went up on the balls of her feet, knees out. Second position *relevé*. She tilted her pelvis up to his hand.

She didn't care what he thought, he could think anything he wanted, dirty little girl, hot little box, so long as he kept at it. She didn't care that he was only being polite, his duty dance with his hostess. If he'd just— She looked at her face in the mirror; her expression didn't change even when he finally got it right. Even while she watched his free hand spidering into view up her chest. She waggled her butt back at him. She could play around, she knew she could come like a shot. She felt her climax winding up somewhere far away—thin, sharp. Her heels lowered to the floor, she pressed her hands on the mantelpiece. It was his hand pulling her along, and yet his hand and her coming were far apart, two wheedling persistences slowly curving together on a plane.

She said, "Oh fuck." She thought she'd missed it, but she came just then, her spine crumpling up sharply, her brow just missing the mantel, her head bending almost to her knees, her hands still holding the mantelpiece.

Timmy was lurched backward as she bent forward. She

heard him knock into a chair. She turned to see him falling, one hand on the chair, the other hand trying to grab a standing lamp that was teetering away from him.

And yet Timmy regained his allure when he was all dressed up again, shirt studs in place, holding both her hands, smiling good-naturedly. He really had a lovely seaside smile.

"What a pleasant turn of events after all."

Anya said, "Do you want to take Tassie's dress back to her?"

Timmy said, "Oh, yes. Well, no. If I walk in with a dress over one arm, it might . . ."

Anya said, "Okay. I've got to come by to pick up my dress anyway."

"That would be lovely. We can all have a late breakfast. Of course, maybe Tassie will rush off with her young man."

Anya said, "Perhaps you'd feel more comfortable if I didn't . . ."

Timmy said, "My dear, I have perfect confidence in your aplomb. Your coming by tomorrow isn't a bit out of the ordinary. I've got to be off right after that, I think we have people coming out. Usually I'm expected in the country Thursday or Friday. Back to the city for the week. Even when I get to stay in and go to the ballet, there are the Wheelocks of this world. I envy you your open road."

Anya wasn't sure what he meant. Was he saying he was all booked up? *Almost* all booked up? She realized she had no idea now bright he was.

She said, "What I really want from you"—Anya saw he looked startled—"is your opinion."

"My opinion? On what?"

"Oh—your opinion on all sorts of things."

"My opinion?"

Anya said, "Yes. Not right away. But some time. At your leisure you can find time to make a few aimless pronouncements on things you're interested in. What you like. One of your charms is that you're a great appreciator. Not just of the physical world but of the spirit of the physical world."

Timmy said, "Well, this is all too metaphysical for me."

Anya was afraid that that was the case.

After he'd gone, however, she found she didn't feel disappointed. She thought the situation might still be interesting.

Anya woke up several times during the early morning, willed herself back to sleep for the sake of how she'd look. She dressed at ten in a white blouse and khaki suit, the skirt crisp, smooth and short, the brass buttons on the jacket shiny and unbuttoned. She looked aloof and para-military, she felt nervous and clever, as though she'd drunk too much coffee. She put Tassie's dress and shoes in a shopping bag.

Walking along the sidewalk up to the door of Timmy's apartment house, she felt tough, she could knock someone down for the pleasure of it. She hoped Tassie would be out, almost certainly she would be. On the way up Anya hummed the song Tassie had sung at Jeannie's wedding— "I want . . . a butter-and-egg man—"

The elevator man waited to make sure someone answered the door. The door opened in. A woman in a gray suit stepped into the small space between the elevator and the door. She closed the door behind her. Anya stepped back. The woman held out a gray cardboard box. She said, "I believe this is yours."

Anya realized she was back against the wall, her hands behind her, her bag dangling against the back of her knees. She thought, I have to do something. The woman handed the box to the elevator man, then looked at Anya again.

Anya struggled to undo the hold on her. She said, "Is Tassie in?" The woman looked at her. Anya looked away. She was emptied of strength, she couldn't lift her eyes, not against the weight of the woman's look. The woman said, "No."

Anya stepped sideways, felt the elevator grille with her hand. She stepped in. She felt relieved. She looked at the woman. She tried to say, "I'll call Tassie later." Her face moved, and she felt how cold her cheeks and lips were. Anything she said would be wrong. She said nothing. The woman nodded to the elevator man, and he closed the door.

As she was lowered down, Anya felt her face grow hot. A spurt of anger. Unfair. How could the woman know? How *did* the woman know? Maybe she didn't know. Maybe it wasn't even Timmy's wife.

But Anya knew it was Timmy's wife and Timmy's wife

had guessed and when she saw Anya she'd known without a doubt and that was that.

When the elevator reached the lobby, Anya realized she still had the shopping bag. With Tassie's dress and shoes. She also remembered that her expression had changed, had taken shape under the woman's eyes—she was afraid that after she got back in the elevator she had looked like a glowering punished child.

She gave the shopping bag to the elevator man. She said, "This belongs—" She corrected herself. "Have this cleaned and sent up." She gave the elevator man a five-dollar bill. The doorman appeared with mysterious smoothness and took the shopping bag and the five dollars away from the elevator man. Anya thought that was funny. The elevator man laughed. Anya thought he was laughing at her. She left.

She thought, This is an adventure. The thought didn't last at all. She felt a shame in her like a snake. It didn't matter what she thought. All her thoughts were food for that hard worm of shame alive in her. She had not thought it possible.

After a few days Anya was able to think of several things about the woman without alarming herself. It seemed a long time ago. Anya thought the woman had done it well. If the woman had shown any interest, been curious, tried to deal with her in any way, the woman would have started a sore in herself. As it was, it was Anya who imagined. She tried to imagine how the woman had guessed. Had she got it all wrong? Finding Anya's dress and jumping to the right conclusion wrongly. The dress had been in Tassie's room, the guest room . . . had Tassie not come home? Did the woman sleep in the guest room? Or had she arrived in the morning? She looked like the kind of woman who would arrive unexpectedly and would immediately begin picking up.

Anya couldn't remember if she'd left any marks on Timmy. She imagined him surprised while changing his clothes, turning quickly to face his wife, who could see the raw marks in the mirror behind him. Served him right.

Anya tried to direct these scenes in her imagination with a Colette touch of sympathy for herself, but she usually had to cut them off before she could make them come out right.

She found it hard to imagine Timmy's state of mind too. The alarmed bourgeois, undone by the morning after? "Oh, how could I?" Or had he sullenly confessed? Anya found her imagination blocked. Except to imagine his retrospective disgust with her, his thinking of her body as coated with habitual stale musk. It hurt her feelings.

She imagined him calling her. Apologizing, sympathizing. Feverish. Herself merely not saying no. Answering the door. Stepping back. Making him— No, she herself was disgusted. The worm in her still alive.

She stayed late at work the next Friday. A beautiful still August end of the day. She sat quietly, suddenly dreamy in the relief of pain ceasing. She watched the crowd spilling off the sidewalk of the gritty cross-town street, the late sun flooding over stone, dirty concrete, faded paint, a spot of glare passing slowly from car to car as the line of traffic crawled. She didn't know why she felt better. She was fastened to what she saw. The crowd moving, shamelessly busy with or busy avoiding the little savageries of city life. The pleasure of observing a landscape she knew.

But even after that afternoon she had to keep herself busy with little tricks. She rejoined a dance class in the evening. That wasn't enough—she did difficult exercises in her room at night. She learned to walk on her hands, taught herself to juggle three oranges. She put herself to sleep reading the film scripts submitted to Ikon.

There was a large party when they finished the movie they'd been working on. Anya felt little satisfaction, although Mr. Danziger told her she'd done good work. Her work had been lots of details, not one thing she could point to or even recognize.

She'd applied to graduate school in English at the University of Chicago. She'd considered getting a graduate degree in drama, but she finally decided if she was going to study, she preferred an academy to a trade school. If she was going to leave the real world for a while, she didn't want to deal with the semireal, the semicommercial, the semiprofessional.

Her mood at the Ikon party reminded her of her mood at the end of music camp. She'd wondered if she would ever play beautifully. The violin instructor, Joseph, gave a recital. Anya was delighted with him. There was a clean necessary cruelty to it. He inflicted a perfect example. He didn't have to say, "If you wish to play the violin, it sounds like this." It was clearly implied, and she moved on, her violin hope amputated so swiftly it was painless.

The situation now was rearranged. The film they'd made was not a perfect example. She'd read thirty scripts that had been submitted and she knew they would not do. The best work she'd done all year had been on a short film contracted for by the chamber of commerce of a town in Rhode Island celebrating the three-hundredth anniversary of its founding. Two weeks there with two cameramen. A week of editing and dealing with the sound-mixing subcontractor.

It was up to her to be clean and ruthless. She wished to withdraw her efforts and spend them some other way.

From time to time she thought that Timmy's wife had inflicted the perfect example that freed her from a hope. She replied to herself that she had never wished to *be* Timmy's wife, only to examine Timmy's situation. Anya felt purged of the worm of shame. But she knew that she was not simply leaving Ikon.

She wished Mr. Danziger well. Mr. Danziger wished her well. Anya was pleased he took her seriously. He didn't kiss her good-by. He asked her to keep in touch. If she wanted to come back, let him know. She'd been a help. Next time would be better.

She thought, not completely ironically, Come back, Dick Whittington, thrice Lord Mayor of London.

* * *

Now, pulling into Chicago on the Outing Club VW bus, she thought she must have been moved to go back to school by some remnant of her New England fostering. Education as cod-liver oil.

She liked the effect on herself of what she learned, but her *life* as a graduate student was as flat and gray as Lake Michigan on a dull day. Her thoughts like shoals of minnows sprinkling up to the surface, then gone again into the dark silt. And herself as still and sharp as a piece of concrete broken off from the sea wall sticking up from the tideless dirty water.

She thought she had the endurance to be an expert. If you were smart enough to begin with, it wasn't so hard as it was long. She was willing to endure, but she was also ready to wish for a change.

Part Two

NORTHERN
LIGHTS

CHAPTER

||||||||||||||||||||||||||||||||||||||||

3

When Mac got back from the rock-climbing trip he was on edge. He thought at first it was because he'd been bad at rock climbing, that he would be uneasy until he redeemed that failure. He thought he might feel better about it after his club hockey team started the season and he had a decent game.

But then, several days after he got back, he noticed that there were a number of girls who traveled up and down his stairwell. They also seemed a source of his disquiet.

He knew that on the third floor above him (which was the top floor) there was only one apartment, occupied by a single man. He knew this because he'd earned some money the spring before by knocking out the walls to make one large apartment out of the two "efficiency apartments." And Mac had seen the man once when the man came in with the landlord while Mac was finishing up the job. The man hadn't spoken to him, although all the questions the man asked the landlord about the work had to be referred to Mac.

Mac hadn't seen the man since he'd moved in that fall. He tried to remember whether there had been the same traffic on the stairs before the rock-climbing trip. He thought so, but he wasn't sure. Now it bothered him. Listening to the sound of the footsteps, he decided there were several different girls. He thought he could recognize the sound of the lightest one. She came up the stairs at a trot, on her toes—*tip-tip-tip-tip*. Slower steps across the landing outside his door. He could hear her heels now—*ta-tick*, *ta-tick, ta-tick.* Up the next flight—*tip-tip-tip-tip.* Fainter now, across the half-landing—*ta-tick, ta-tick.* He couldn't hear her footsteps clearly on the last flight, nor her knock at the door.

He imagined nothing beyond the stairs. And even his imaginings about the girls on the stairs were fragmentary. A hand on the banister rail. The sole of the shoe striking the cross-hatched metal bar on the lip of each step. The movement of the skirt as it was pushed up by the rising thigh.

The year before he'd been more or less comfortable in his isolation—working hard at the School of Business assignments even after he knew he was going to quit, exercising a lot, dreaming and worrying about what his life would be like in several years. And even a month before, when he'd started out at I.I.T., he'd been dully absorbed in his assignments. It took him a while to think it was his encounter with Anya that had alerted him.

The footsteps became like spirits—more beautiful and suggestive than any real flesh. First audible, then swelling in all the shadow senses of his imagination. The girl's breathing came to his imagination, the sensation of her breath, her open mouth, the swell and touch of her lips and wet teeth. The footsteps made their way quicker and quicker each time to the eerie but well-focused magnifications of his imagination.

One evening he was doing pull-ups on the projecting lintel over his front door. The door was open so his legs could swing. He heard the *tip-tip-tip* from the first flight. He thought he should close the door. It was her right of privacy. But he stood still, his arms still raised, his fingertips still on the lintel. He saw the girl's face bob up behind the banisters. When she reached the landing, she stopped and looked at him with surprise. Her head twisted suddenly, and she said, "What?"

Mac shook his head to show he hadn't said anything.

Mac thought it was unfortunate that she was not plain. He hadn't imagined a whole figure or even a whole face. He'd hoped that seeing her whole would put an end to his disquiet, but in a strange way the girl was not whole. She wasn't pretty, but she had a nervous thin beauty that had flashed into her face and then vanished—and not by a changing of her expression. Her expression had remained fixed in alarm the entire time.

He'd made his interest worse. There were new fragments—wispy light-brown hair, complicated light makeup he would never have imagined, a real mole on her cheek. But worse yet was his sensation of her locked trembling. It was still ghostly. The fragile skin of her face and even the prominent loose-jointed thin bones of her body made Mac think less of flesh and bone than of the emptiness they implied. The fine dry edges of flesh defining the ovals of her nostrils made him think of her being only space—without blood, without any liquid, without the necessary strength that fluid gave to matter. Mac thought that when her eyes had widened, her mouth parted, her nostrils flared, the hollows in her cheeks deepened, he had seen nothing, but only felt the shock of her deep, rigid trembling.

Later in the evening Mac was listening to the radio. A knock at the door. Mac opened it. The man smiled and said, "Ah." Mac recognized him. The man upstairs. The man said, "Sorry. Hope I'm not— Curious thing. I live upstairs. One of my guests—"

Mac said, "My name's MacKenzie."

The man said, "Yes." He didn't offer to shake hands. But after a short pause he said, "Henniker. Ah—one of my guests thought—this is the strange thing—she thought she saw a policeman standing in the doorway. This doorway. A policeman in uniform. She said the policeman spoke to her."

Mac stared at the man, at his yellow Indian shirt with white embroidery, at his stomach moving under the thin material. Mac said, "Huh?"

Henniker said, "Hmmm." Smiled to himself. "You don't know what I'm talking about. Of course not. Did you see the girl come up?"

Mac said, "I saw a girl going upstairs."

"You were just coming in?"

"No. I was just finishing—I'd just finished some exercises." Mac touched the top of the doorframe.

"Ah. But you didn't speak to her?"

"No."

"But you *looked* at her?"

"Yeah. I was standing just like this. It'd be hard not to."

"Yes, I'm sure this seems strange to you. It would be hard to explain. You don't mind?"

"No, it's okay, but—"

"Were you wearing a trench coat or a uniform of some sort?"

"No. I was doing a few chin-ups. I was wearing a sweat suit."

"Ah. What color?"

"Dark blue."

"Ah, navy blue." Henniker smiled. "But no brass buttons, what?"

Mac said, "Would you like to see it?" He thought the man was oily, but quick in some way. Working to be supercilious.

What had the girl thought he'd said? She couldn't really have thought she saw a policeman. Was she joking? Mac got the sweat suit.

"No need really," Henniker said. He spoke too late on purpose.

Mac didn't think the girl could be joking. Not the way she'd looked.

Mac displayed the sweat suit.

Henniker said, "Well, it does have stripes down the side."

Mac said, "What did she say the policeman said?"

Henniker said, "Oh, the classic thing."

"What's that? 'Stop in the name of the law'?"

Henniker looked amused. He said, "Close enough, close enough. I'll assure her then that she just saw a graduate student?" He paused and lifted his eyebrows; Mac nodded. "—a graduate student," Henniker continued, "doing his daily dozen."

Mac heard the girl's foot scrape the floor on the landing above.

Mac said, "I can do it myself."

Henniker rolled his eyes upward. "No. More harm than good. Believe me." He was speaking softly. He held out his hand palm down as if to say, "Steady on. I'll take it from here."

Mac said, "You aren't English, are you?"

Henniker smiled with his lips closed. Looked at Mac and said slowly, "No-o."

Mac said, "Okay. Take it easy." He stepped back and put his hand on the doorknob. Henniker went up the stairs. Mac heard him step on the half-landing as Mac swung the door shut.

Mac couldn't remember his face any better than the girl's. Shirt, stomach, dripping voice—slides and sudden edges. Why did he work at it? He thought Mac stupid. Or did he just want to give that impression? Was the girl crazy? Mac remembered she had a mole on her lower cheek. Right cheek. He was sorry he remembered it, it brought her jaw and mouth into focus. The planes of her cheeks and her throat. It was a pale, luminous face. He could see it now.

Mac wondered if Henniker and the girl hadn't made up the whole thing together. What fun.

Two more questions, Mac thought, and call it a day. Why did the whole thing come up exuding so much energy? Was it that his life was barren? So barren that any movement was visible for miles? The girl and Henniker disappeared over the horizon.

Mac saw Anya while he was walking down the stairs. He realized she was one of the upstairs girls from the sound of her footsteps.

He hadn't really believed her story about her violin teacher. He hadn't even really believed the way she'd behaved on the outing. He had believed she had a noble independence, and that it had been their two independences that had held them apart, like two north ends of magnets.

Mac couldn't hide his expression as he saw where she was going. He was sure that Anya could see that.

Anya said cheerfully, "I've been wondering when I'd run into you."

Mac could feel his scowl, could see Anya ignoring it. Or perhaps even being amused by it. He said hello and started to pass by her. She held his coat sleeve. He stopped.

She said, "Do you live there?" She pointed at his door.

Mac nodded. During the moment she delayed him he felt his scowl change to a look of defeated glumness. Anya seemed to bring out an impulse to overact his part. Usually with girls with whom he stood face-to-face he froze into almost immovable heaviness. Only the ritual of a slow rustic courting enabled him to move. Downcast eyes, shifting feet, digging the ground with one toe. The lumberings of the shy boy's part in a slow peasant dance. The girl mincing backwards, her fingers entwined, until tradition authorized her to stop, him to galumph forward, both of them to become hot, swollen, and dazed with dumb sexual certainty.

Anya held his coat sleeve, coolly forcing him to be alert. He should have guessed she would refuse the anesthesia of a set pattern.

He'd had some hopes. Her athletic deftness at climbing, her toughness, her breezy, confident ill-will toward the other hikers had all stirred him. Only afterwards he'd thought of her long, bony handsomeness.

Now he wished to resist.

Anya said, "Do you mind if I ask you a few questions?"

Mac said, "I've got to go out."

Anya smiled. She said, "Well, sometime soon let's have a nice cozy chat over a cup of tea. I've been worried that you thought I wasn't nice."

Mac was annoyed. He said, "You don't talk like this all the time. I'll talk to you sometime when there's no floor show."

Anya tilted her head with surprise and then went upstairs.

Mac was sorry. He thought he should get in touch with Anya and say so. She'd actually been straight enough about herself with him. She was just fooling around, she had no way of knowing how touchy he was.

But the meeting had magnified his sense of her in a way that prevented him from looking her up casually. And he couldn't figure out what he would say that wouldn't strike her as an amusing cliché. She could get a laugh out of his saying "hello."

Shortly after that Mac received a questionnaire in the mail. He skimmed it, was about to throw it away, folded it up and put it in his mackinaw pocket, and took it to the library.

There was a dollar enclosed. A stamped envelope. The pages were badly mimeographed in a purple blur. It was hard to say no. To ensure confidentiality, do not put your name or address on the answer sheet. One of several hundred male graduate students chosen at random in Chicago area. Field of study? On scholarship? Age? Marital status?

"At what age did you begin to fear your own death?" Hmmm. Was there a moment? Yes—but that was the trouble with surveys. The little fear at age seventeen. Cerebral.

Fantastical. The big fear at twenty-four. Physical—clutching the side of the bed. *La grande peur*—serious because it was clear it would return. Okay—*twenty-four*.

"Do you know your life's ambition?" Circle yes, no, perhaps. Easy—no. No? No. *Perhaps*.

"Do you think you should?" *No*. That was the problem —another minute he'd say yes.

"Was the onset of your fear of your own death connected to your consideration of your life's ambition?" Consideration. *Perhaps*.

Did the onset of your fear of your own death follow your first complete sexual experience?

Yes, but. *Yes*.

If yes, do you think there is a connection? No! No, don't know. Don't know. *Perhaps*.

Are you rising in the world: Quaint, that. Yes. Not really. *Yes*.

"Are you romantic about love?" Meaning what? Don't know. *Perhaps*.

"Are you romantic about nature?" *Yes*.

"Are you romantic about politics?" *No*.

"Do you think most people are romantic about love?" *Perhaps*.

"—about nature?" *Yes*.

"—about politics?" *No*.

That was interesting.

"Do you think your studies will help you find the answer to a question that is important to you?" Not bad, that. Will help, yes. But can there be help that doesn't lead to success? How do you know it's help? "Do you *think*—" Okay— *Yes*.

"Are you lonelier in graduate school than in college?" *Yes*.

"Have you ever considered using a computer dating service?" God . . . *No*.

"Do you enjoy filling out questionnaires about yourself?" Having got this far. *Yes*.

"Are you generally secretive?" *Yes*.

"Do you feel the need for uncritical companionship?" I suppose. Yes. Who doesn't? *Yes*.

"Would you settle for critical companionship?" This was getting a little bit like sparring with an invisible partner. *Perhaps*.

73

"Have you you ever offered uncritical companionship?" Hmmm—no. I guess not. It might have *seemed* uncritical, but— *No*.

"Do you think about your childhood a lot?" *Yes*.

"Are you ambitious?" No. Yes. In some ways— *Perhaps*.

"Are you hopeful about yourself?" That's better. *Yes*.

"Do you like tall girls?" What's this? Depends. Perhaps. *Yes*.

"Do you agree to answer part 2 of this survey?" Okay. *Yes*.

By mistake Mac put the dollar in the return envelope along with the questionnaire. Funny. He didn't think about it until he'd licked and sealed the envelope. He was afraid he'd appear foolish. No—it was okay. See if they'd send him two dollars with part 2. He mailed it.

The second part of the questionnaire came. One dollar. It had some questions that were not yes-or-no or multiple choice. They required a word or a phrase to be filled in.

"List several things you think are wonderful."

The command set Mac to daydreaming. He wasn't sure anyone else would understand what he meant if he wrote down northern spring. He wrote "northern spring." He once went north of Lac Gros Caillou with his father's friend, a fishing guide named Albert Meilleur. Half-French, half-Cree. It was too early to fish but they kept going. Half the time on snowshoes, half the time slogging through mush in their waterproof shoepacs. Both of them drunk with the rush of spring. The ice breaking up sounded like huge animals roaring, echoing off the ridges. The constant sound of rushing water, water piling up in green and white haystacks, slicing in deep black cuts between the rocks. Apparently slack pools quivering against a wall of jammed ice. Mac saw a whole uprooted pine drift gently into a pool, bob once and then disappear. Violent and explosive —like a giant fish breaking water to swallow it whole. A minute later the tree emerged downstream beyond the ice jam—twisted, cracked open, held together by a few fibers of raw heartwood.

But it wasn't just the violence he liked. Everything was sterile, but about to burst into life. No fish yet. The force of the water in streams still too powerful. No insects. The wet mud still frost-glazed hard every night. Trickles of water running out from under the mounds of snow hugging the feet of trees. The water filtering through pine needles as clean as fishbones.

Sudden changes. The woods creaking with wind, casts of ice shattering from the branches.

Sudden stillness—water dripping straight as plumb lines. The smells hovering in globes of warm air caught like balloons in the brush. Steaming breaths in a deer yard.

A shift of wind—spring rain—the sky close and gray, the trees black and warm.

A sudden hot sun. Steam.

It was the awkwardness of northern spring that Mac liked. Before life could manage grace.

A moose finding its way to food, plunging knee deep into old coarse snow, new mud. Splashing through pools of new water and muskeg. Basking on a southern slope in singing heat—turning to the sun. Mac sharing the field with it. Suddenly washed by cold air rolling down from the ridge—like a ghost of a snow slide. The yellow grass dried and blowing off, shreds of scrolls. New grass tubed in green; inside, water green and white.

And always the sound—every fold between the tight glacial ridges filled with the roar of its own stream.

It struck Mac as an odd dream to have in the middle of a Chicago January. He tried to remember the rest of it. He'd been hungry for flesh—they were eating only beans and porridge—Albert Meilleur farting into the campfire— saying the lake would be warm enough to fish in three days—the lake filled with floating brush and scraps of trees. Yes, right at the end they pulled out fish on deep streamers. But that wasn't what he dreamed of. He wasn't in the dream himself, not as himself. Just his senses. The feel of the layers of wool and knee-high leather and rubber shoepacs, his feet sweaty but cold. Sometimes his cold face as a sense. Sometimes his dizzy exhaustion from wading through a cold, shining bog, which seemed to tilt toward the lake. Then into deep crusted snow, pulling himself from pine to pine up a dark slope. Growing hot behind the eyes. He could feel his body heat just beneath his cold skin. He felt it as brightness. As the same brightness and painful energy in the sky, earth, water. A heart not yet blooming. They were all in raw noisy motion, but his senses stretched

out to what was still. That was at the core of his wish—
the stillness at the center of the motion.

*   *   *

Two days later he ran into Anya on the street. He stood
up straighter. She said, "You going out to lunch? I'll buy
you lunch."

They went to a hamburger joint. He was as tall as she
was when they were sitting down. They sat, facing each
other in a booth. She seemed giddy and friendly.

She said, "Ask me some questions."

He asked her the questions he remembered from the
questionnaire. She looked as though she thought he was
very bright. He said, "You're giving the same answers I
did."

She laughed. "I'm trying to."

He was impressed. "How can you tell?"

She said, "I've been thinking about you. If I have a few
facts, I can usually guess the rest."

He said, "Is that right?"

She said, "I'll tell you something that happened to you.
A girl was going upstairs in your entryway while you were
doing exercises."

"Oh, yeah. I forgot you know the territory."

She let that go by.

She said, "The girl looked up and saw you. She thought
you were a policeman. She thought you spoke to her."

Mac said, "Do you know her?"

"*About* her."

Mac was unhappy.

Anya went on. "She went upstairs and said what she
thought had happened. Your upstairs neighbor came down
and asked you. You said you hadn't said anything."

"What did the girl say I had said?"

"—'So you're going up there to fuck.'"

Mac was stunned. "God almighty. —And she thought I
was a policeman? That's crazy." He thought of the girl—
pale, a mole on her cheek. He was cured of his desire for
her tuning-fork trembling.

Anya said, "Maybe she read your mind."

He said, "No. Have you seen her?"

Anya said, "Yes. Do you think she's attractive?"

Mac said, "Yes—too fragile. Yes. But he must know she's in trouble. Really drifted loose."

Anya said, "He thought you might really have said something."

Mac didn't say anything.

Anya said, "He's interested in despair—I mean other people's. Attracted to self-loathing. He likes to get a whiff of something from it. But I think he was really scared of her once that happened. Not of her being crazy. Not scared *for* her. Of her."

There was a silence. Mac wanted to seal off the subject. Anya ordered coffee for both of them.

Anya said, "What do *you* do?"

After a while Mac shrugged and said, "Not much."

Anya said, "I'm tired of impersonations. But I never did them to escape. I'm pretty sure about that. I find out things that way—without a costume I can't find out things—not as well. I'm not in despair—I'm not that self-absorbed. I don't know why. No virtue involved. But I am bored sometimes. With how little—" She looked at her fingers and drew them up into a fist. "with, with, with—just seeing things, just trying them out a little."

Mac liked her. Now that she was a little sad, she was likable.

She said, "But I think the worst thing would be to get stuck doing it."

Mac said, "Oh, I don't know. You probably couldn't fool yourself for very long."

Anya said, "Sure you could. Not in one impersonation, but in impersonations. I see people doing that."

Mac said, "What are we talking about? *Who* are we talking about?"

Anya laughed.

Mac kept it in mind—her pleasant side, her easy side— while they talked, put on their coats and hats and gloves. He walked her back to the library. As soon as he was back home at his worktable he dropped straight into a depression. Not a stormy one, just a steady moment of sitting in gloom.

Then he thought Anya might like to go ice skating. He felt like showing off. He recognized it as more of his folkloric notion of courtship. And surely out of place in this case. Downcast glance, transparent nonchalance. A woolly flush on his skin. A stylized animal imitation—pawing the ground. Sudden fever—watch this! Walking a fence top, standing on his hands.

He got up to go to lunch, realized he'd just eaten.

He snorted—laughed at himself—but was left tremulous.

That night he heard steps. They stopped at his door. He opened it. Anya was on the landing, about to knock.

She said, "I'll be right back down."

He said, "What?"

She went on up. Wearing a blue suit and a white blouse he noticed as she climbed out of sight. High-heeled shiny leather shoes. What kind of an outfit was that? And what was she doing? It made him a fool, a spy—a foolish dwarf lurking at his cave mouth.

He thought of the color of the stockings she had on— silvery white. Smooth but powdery, as though they would leave a trace on your fingertips, like new birchbark.

He stood in the doorway. He should close the door. No —go out. Twist *her* off balance.

If she knew what she was doing, she shouldn't do it. If she didn't know, she should know. She should not have been so pleasant at lunch. He was being ridiculous. "Madam, I am much abused." She could laugh at him.

He did not wish to join in the turmoil of her life. She apparently wanted him to. Was he being forced to feel feelings that weren't his? That he did not wish to be his? That he did not wish to recognize as his? Well, *that* wasn't so bad, he shouldn't mind his feelings wrenching loose inside himself. He felt as if he were answering the questionnaire.

He heard her footsteps. She appeared on the half-landing, came down the rest of the stairs. She faced him. His anger rose to his forehead. She clasped her hands together and stepped forward.

She said, "It's awkward, I know, but I had to leave a message. I should have called."

Called who? His anger flew off and disappeared. That puzzled him. He suddenly guessed and said, "You sent that questionnaire."

She blushed, avoided his eyes, laughed a little.

"How did you guess?"

He said, "I just guessed."

"Did you guess right away?"

"Just now."

She said, "I didn't mean it as a *trick.*"

He said, "No. But it was tricky. The mimeograph."

"—I had to find out if you like tall girls."

"What did I say? I said no."

"You said yes." She stepped out of her shoes. She was still taller than he.

She said, "See—" She slipped her feet apart a little, and her eyes came level with his.

He said, "How tall are you?"

"Five ten."

"No, you're more than that, I'm five ten."

"Five ten and a half." She laughed. "I'm stronger than you, too." She struck a pose with both arms flexed.

Mac laughed.

Anya said, "Go on—feel it. Hard as nails."

"I believe you."

"Oh, a wise guy? You think I'm just clowning around, huh? This isn't just beach-boy muscle, buddy."

Mac was charmed.

Anya said, "Wanna arm wrestle for beers?"

She laughed. Her performance left Mac oddly dreamy. Comfortable, entertained, curious, slow. He held out his hand, and she put hers in it.

After a minute, she came inside. He closed the door with his foot. They stood holding hands.

"I honestly didn't mean to pry," Anya said. "I meant it as a friendly gesture. I probably would have told you I sent it. Well, maybe not." She took his other hand.

He saw that she could see his desire flowing up through him, feel it through his hands. Her dark eyes blinked. She let go of his hands. She undid her hair. He felt clumsy and serene. He was surprised at first by the breadth of his feelings. They went to bed slowly. He was surprised when he embraced her at the calm smoothness between their skins. It was all as mild as talcum powder.

Before they went to sleep he said, "You don't have to be anywhere early, do you?"

"No."

He woke up when she got up in the night. She went to the bathroom, but she didn't come back to bed. He got up, went to the bathroom, turned off the light. He could hear

79

her moving in the room. He went toward her, stopped, listened to her breathe. He went around the table. Warily aroused—she might think it was funny. There was no nightglow in the room. But she would hear him. The air was dry and thick. He thought he knew where she was in the darkness. He thought of heat in blackness. Dark heat. He stood by her. He put his hands out very slowly until he felt her without yet touching her. He brought his hands back and stepped closer. She let her breath out. There was a dream like this—turning in sleep toward a desire, hands out, only a step farther. Was that her idea? He moved his hand toward the sound of her breath. He felt her breath on his hand; reached to touch her. He brushed her chin with his fingertips. He stepped closer. He found her neck, her collarbone, her shoulders. She suddenly turned. He put his hand on her shoulder and followed her as she walked back to the bed. He caught at her hips. She fell onto the bed, and he fell after her on his knees, turning her to him. She dark—her cunt was as lush and open as when they'd fin- must have been as aroused as he was in the dark—by the ished before. Their bodies were harder and sharper against each other.

When she came, her left foot shot out and banged against the wall, he could hear it fluttering and sliding on the wallpaper as he finished.

A desire for her—distinct from fucking her, from having just fucked her—spiraled up through his body's nerves. Only a late shadow?

He wished he knew her well enough to speak.

After a while he reached down and pulled the quilt over them. Drowsing off against her back, he pressed his mouth on it, thinking of her cleverness.

Mac woke up when he heard someone banging at the door. It stopped, then started again. It wasn't the door, just someone in the hall. It stopped before he got out of bed.

He was awake for the day. He lay still, setting himself questions. He was giddy. He felt moved to caution—he felt vulnerable, perhaps speared already. His own fault, having led such a crimped life all fall and winter. Another barrenland venture, his project. But still tied to an institution. Whether in Labrador or in his carrel—funny he'd never thought that before—that his isolations were official, devised by a constant center of others, outlying parts. He must ask Anya if her life was like that. A solitary voyager on a string, not a wanderer.

He admired her black hair—long, coarse, a little oily, the strands curling near the end. He lifted the quilt to look at her back, the straight jut of her shoulder. The spine recessed in long muscles. She'd said in her first story she'd been gawky—she was still angular, but athletic now, an edge to her, even lying in sleep.

He thought he liked the jolt of her arrival, she had made him gather himself. He was worried about what next, about being too slow. But he would manage. He was glad he had time now to consider her as a new idea while she was asleep. He'd never imagined her particular appeal, it was different from his imagined admirations. Her skin a very slight separation from her intensity.

She was a good idea he'd never thought of.

He got up, put the kettle on, put yesterday's biscuits in the oven, took the oranges out of the refrigerator, went to the bathroom, pissed, washed his face, brushed his teeth, and got back in beside her. The luxury of company in bed.

When she woke up he was in a rude good mood. She stretched out comfortably on her back. The sides of their knees touched pleasantly.

The kettle began to clatter. He jumped up to pour it in the teapot.

He came back and stood by the bed. Anya cupped her hand behind his knee. He got back in beside her. The length of her fingers, the length of her arm soothed him. He lay quietly with his mouth on her shoulder, his arm across her breasts. His hand slid down her arm from shoulder to wrist. She was entirely relaxed. Her body had seemed wonderfully hard—a dancer's muscled back, like a turtle's shell. Clear furrows between her leg muscles— straight bones—now suddenly it was all liquid, floating under his forearm and hand. His hand caught on the notch of her hipbone, then drifted down the length of her thigh. He slid his hand over her knee, the crest of shin, and took her ankle in his hand. He kissed her foot, the top and the deepest part of the arch, and lay still in a pool of blank contentment, buried head first under the quilt.

*   *   *

As Mac lay still under the quilt, hidden except for his feet, Anya felt her mind start working again. She hadn't guessed that Mac would admire her body so straightforwardly. With such energy.

She had an enormous appetite.

She took a shower while Mac cooked. She ate breakfast in her slip, aware of her shoulders, arms, legs, and feet, comfortable in his admiration and her vanity. Passing behind him on her way to the stove, she touched the side of his neck, was pleased at his rising to her touch.

She gathered up her clothes. She remembered that she'd left her shoes in the hall. With her clothes tucked under one arm she opened the front door, relieved to see they were still there. She bent down and grabbed both heels with the fingers of one hand. The shoes wouldn't move. She looked up, afraid of the open hall. She stepped back. What was this? She dropped her clothes. A little musical panic shimmered up. What? She thought of the girl seeing a policeman. In this doorway.

She looked over at Mac, who slowly raised his face to her. She looked back at her shoes and saw that each one was nailed to the floor. The head of the nail was visible inside the shoe, just where the sole came down from the heel to touch the ground.

Mac arrived and she grabbed his arms. She laughed. She just got it. She said, "That son of a bitch."

Mac looked at her, puzzled.

"That son of a bitch," she said. She felt seen. She felt Henniker's needle of spite.

Mac was looking into the hallway. He bent down and picked up her clothes and reached for the shoes, just as she had. Anya was pleased that Mac was reaching—and then suddenly angry as she imagined Henniker imagining just this tableau—Mac pulling at the shoes, her hands at her temples. I see you.

Mac seemed dully unsurprised; he ran his fingers into a shoe and felt the nailhead. He squatted down and pulled the shoes up one at a time, twisting and pulling gently, working with both hands. He worked the nails out through the inside of the shoes—oversize upholstery nails with large, brass-plated heads and thin, bright shanks. He handed her her shoes.

She stepped back inside and looked at the soles. The holes frayed larger with Mac's pulling. She wondered if it was more than I see you—a nail through her foot. Spite. Clever spite. But only symbolic. No, no *but only*. She'd felt it.

The poisonous cripple.

But imagine the twist in his nervous pride when he saw her shoes. Left out to be shined. Ha. And the nails—he hadn't bought them; they came from his damask-covered love seat.

She stopped. She didn't want to think of him at all. Leave it. She wanted to sail on, leaving her impersonations drowned in her wake.

She looked at Mac. She said, "It shouldn't touch you, or me either, really. He doesn't know me really. It's just scribbling on the wall. Anya fucks MacKenzie. You don't mind, do you?"

Mac was silent, his lips were shut around something sour.

She didn't want him to trust her, she didn't want to be trustworthy, but she did want him to keep on. She could see he saw something loathsome in all this.

She said, "I'm sorry. It spoiled it, I guess. Just the end . . ."

Mac said, "I'd forgot you were mixed up with him."

Anya said, "It's not worth explaining, it's a very small thing."

"Well, everything's small."

"No." She had to go on. That was fair. "Let's go out. Do something. Have lunch. Don't be stubborn. If you think I'm awful, tomorrow morning you can go away then." Anya felt a dizzy gaiety. She said, "I could see you were thinking your way into something back there in bed. Working your way down my leg, wrapped up in a cocoon of intense thought. Meditation on a kneecap."

Mac stared at her. Surprised, then glowering.

Anya said, "But really—there's no reason for you to stop. Oh well, outrage—these white limbs splotched with scarlet harlotry. Priestly rage—'Shall I expound whore to *you?* They're sweetmeats that poison the eater, perfumes that corrupt men's nostrils—' I once played that part, not the priest, the heroine whom the priest, cardinal actually, is slithering at. But—but all that outrage in you would be even more of a cocoon than your meditation on a kneecap. You know much more about my kneecap. I mean we have my kneecap in common."

Anya paused, she'd charmed herself again. Mac was sullen.

"Look," she said, "suppose I began to shriek and wail that you'd seduced me. Just when I'd pulled myself together to seek a better life, you seized me and had your evil way with me. I hope you'd laugh."

Anya stopped talking and put on her blouse, her silklike tights, and her blue wool suit.

"I see I've gone too far," she said. "You're probably the kind of man who doesn't like to talk about his feelings."

*   *   *

When Anya said that he probably didn't like to talk about his feelings, Mac felt the first fusion between Anya and him. It was not a pleasure. At least not a physical pleasure. The sensation was in fact slightly painful. What pleasure there was was intellectual—his recognition that she knew more about him than he knew about her. It was not that her remark was extraordinarily acute but that it was the occasion for him to see that she could comment at will on the way he was. It was also the first occasion for him to see that there was a quality in him that she wished to take pleasure in. He also saw that he didn't know what this quality was.

He knew only that he wished to pursue the matter.

At the same time he had the strange feeling that his desire for her body grew suddenly distinct, as if it took on such a concrete substance and form that she could remove it from him and then examine it as it stood beside him. He hoped it was a good specimen of the desire that she was looking for.

The only analogy he could now remember to this sensation of standing beside a replica of himself dated from the time when he'd been playing hockey three or four hours a day. He'd been able to examine that replica himself—check its learned reflexes, its cardiovascular fitness, its strains and bruises, and, most important, the intensity of its single current of desire. He now thought it odd that there was that

verbal coincidence, as though the word *desire* was an artificial constant, like his bridge of three false teeth (the three
right uppers behind the canine), the only cells in his body
that weren't renewed each time he started something new.

CHAPTER

‖‖‖‖‖‖‖‖‖‖‖‖‖‖‖‖‖‖‖‖‖‖‖‖‖‖‖

4

For a short while, when she was first living with Mac, Anya
thought that he might be malleable, that she might play
Pygmalion to his Galatea.

She then came to realize that this was unlikely. He spent
long periods of each day paying no attention to her what-
soever. Her feelings were slightly hurt until she made two
additional observations. The first was that he spent long
periods of each day paying no attention to himself; that is
to say, he gave his slow attention, in a trance, to things—
his calculations for his work, his ice skates, cooking supper,
sewing patches on his pants—in such a way that she was
sure he was sealed in a sphere of unself-consciousness. The
second observation was that when he did pay attention to
her, it was with the same intensity as to things. It was an
intensity that she described to herself on several days as
ponderous. On several other days she described it, with
more approval, as massive. Later on she thought the right
word for his attention to her was meaty.

She then spent an hour one afternoon comparing him
with Henniker. At first she raised a lot of small differences
—Mac was bluntly careful about money, pinched pennies,
bought few things for himself, and bought those with great
pain. For example, it took him an hour to buy a cast-iron
stew pot. He went to three different stores, asked the hardware-store owners esoteric questions about the composition
of the iron. At first Anya didn't believe Mac was serious,
probably because Henniker would have carried on exactly
the same way, but as an elaborate joke. (Henniker treated

waiters, clerks, policemen elaborately. Elaborate politeness, elaborate rudeness, or elaborate indifference.)

Mac was in fact the stereotype of the Scot. Tight, skeptical, sensible. Happy when he was setting people right. And yet he was a sensual materialist. What he did buy was very good—whether pots, or wool socks, or vegetables. And he knew more details than she cared to hear about iron, or wool, or growing seasons.

Henniker had been careless with money. When he had some, he spent it on restaurants, new clothes, or amusing things. When he didn't have it, he sponged. One of his two or three girl friends of any given moment was bound to be rich, and probably guilty about it.

Henniker had joked about this openly with Anya. His several Persian and Turkish rugs were trophies of his affair with a married woman from the north shore. He had assumed that Anya's attitude toward the very rich was like his—a laugh beyond F. Scott Fitzgerald's. Henniker thought that the function of the very rich that separated them from the mid-bourgeoisie was an elegant patronage of the arts. This elegance could not be achieved by mere civic subscription. Elegant patronage had to be playful and esoteric— the sharpest, riskiest edge of fashion.

One work of art that he regarded as always in the forefront of fashion was his own life.

Anya did not regard this conclusion of his as comically absurd. His life *was* a work of art—it was made up of self-contained systems, illusions, subplots, inventions, and contrivances, all in pursuit of moments of distilled clarity, which, as he brought them into focus for an instant, seemed eternally immune from the ordinary, from laws of weight and decay.

It was theater. A very special masque in which Art (co-extensive in these scripts with Henniker's life and notions) was the central figure.

Since it was closet drama, caviar to the general and so forth, one of the problems was finding suitable supporting players. The ideal player was someone who would also produce and stage manage—that is, maintain the necessary luxury of Henniker's apartment, and the several additional changes of scene, and who also was capable of being subordinate without being inert; who was also knowledge-able enough to maintain the atmosphere of knowingness;

who was also able to emanate waves of delicate psychic energy, fertile but not disruptive.

One of Anya's coplayers had been a good example of the difficulty. A thin beauty whose psychic bruises had attracted Henniker like a bee to fallen fruit. Anya had met her, acknowledged her beauty—the thin perfect skin, the large frightened eyes, the mole on her cheek, the exquisitely thin ankles and narrow feet on which she tottered while her lovely desperate gaze flitted back and forth, saying, "Don't touch me, I don't know what I'll do if you touch me."

She'd made Anya feel too thickly muscled, too coarsely healthy, and too practically intelligent.

Anya had also been attracted to her.

Henniker had enjoyed this girl's tremors. Immediately he'd invited her to take the three of them out to dinner. The girl had been in nervous agony under the interrogation of Henniker's careful silences (a device he'd picked up from psychiatrists). The girl had chatted edgily with Anya (it turned out they both knew Tassie, and Anya had heard of the girl's ex-husband).

Anya had finally said to Henniker, "You're a shit," and had left the restaurant. Henniker had told Anya later that that had been perfect, absolutely the perfect thing to do.

But later still, the girl with the mole had cracked up badly. The concert pitch of her rich-girl voice had become too harsh and off-key, the delicate nervous quivers in her hands and breathing had become tics and spasms. But what had finally ended Henniker's interest in the girl was the girl's hallucinations. He'd been interested in the hallucinations for a while—he'd told Anya about them—but the girl herself, as he'd also told Anya, no longer radiated.

"Whereas she once signaled from her psyche with telegraphic intensity," he had said, "she has now regressed—if I may continue to speak technologically—to semaphore." He'd flicked his hands about in imitation of the girl's gestures. "A girl guide in bloomers wildly waving her flags."

Anya had guessed, however, that the cruelty of the remark had not been entirely spontaneous. In all likelihood it had been a cue intended for Anya in her role as a deliciously wicked conspirator.

The over-all effect on Anya had been to make her fear for her real powers and feelings. If everything became theater, Henniker's theater, then she would gain several new roles, but she might lose her capacity to direct her own theater.

And Anya hadn't been all that crazy about the parts he gave her. She had begun to realize that there was no theater that palled so quickly as one which promised novelty after novelty, *dernier cri* after *dernier cri*.

Anya thought that in a way she'd done Henniker a favor by leaving. She'd given him a chance to nail her shoes to the floor—his sharpest theatrical gesture so far. She noticed, however, that in her memory Henniker's *mots* and *gestes* disconnected themselves from him. It wasn't only that he borrowed heavily from others' works, it was also that so much of what he said and did was for effect, was part of a presentation. The presentations remained; he faded.

But, Anya thought, if being with Henniker meant having to take a part in his theater, being with Mac was like coming on board a ship. She wasn't sure if she'd signed on as crew or as passenger, but even if it was as passenger, it was on a working vessel, certainly not a cruise ship or a yacht.

The vocabulary that occurred to her to fill out her metaphor was not the sailing jargon she'd picked up from Tassie's yachting friends—whisker pole, spinnaker, genoa, committee boat—all of which suggested to her regression to prep-school competition. It was more the vocabulary she'd absorbed from reading Melville or Conrad or Tomlinson— the notions of manly resignation to discomfort, monotony, hierarchy, and formality implied by terms like "eight bells," "storm canvas," "dog watch," "heavy weather," "slow passage," "taut ship."

And yet Mac was not the captain of this vessel. He kept things shipshape in obedience to the ghost of some higher authority.

It was not, as Anya suspected for a while, his father. Anya was fairly sure of that. It was his father who'd persuaded Mac to go to the School of Business, on the theory that his own labor and ingenuity had been taken advantage of by GE, and he didn't want to see Mac get suckered in his turn. Mac stuck out business school for the first year. Anya would have guessed that Mac was the kind of person who compelled himself to finish whatever he started. But after a year Mac hied himself over to the Illinois Institute of Technology and started a program in civil engineering. Anya had no idea whether he was happier with that. He seemed aloof from the program. He didn't seem to calculate what was the shrewdest way to do well in a course, but rather to pursue projects that interested him even though what he learned might never come to his instructor's attention. Anya thought this attitude was admirable, but that it would have served him better in the humanities than at a trade school.

She wasn't sure whether his independence was positive —that he knew what *he* wanted to learn, or negative—that he only knew that he didn't want to be shaped by a program.

She'd asked him, and he'd said he didn't know. What finally struck her was that for someone who hadn't made up his mind, he was awfully decisive.

*   *   *

During another afternoon of reflection, Anya also discovered that she'd got rid of a dissatisfaction. She'd been lonely. Her time spent with Henniker had been lonely. Henniker might have been an inducer of freak-outs for some of his divorcées and waifs; for Anya, his quick changes had induced a sense of isolation while she'd been with him, and a bitter aftertaste of artificiality that made her feel lonely afterwards.

She got rid of her loneliness—and only part of getting rid of it was the week or so of sexual gluttony with Mac, a laughable acting out of old honeymoon jokes that kept turning her wiry sense of sexual parody into slapstick. (Henniker had a self-conscious sense of sexual parody— perhaps he'd imagined himself a sexual prince in disguise among the people. When he'd insisted on screwing in the back seat of his car, or on elaborately double-jointed hand maneuvers at the movies, he would say, "This takes me back to high school. Eating popcorn with cunty fingers." This remark, she later learned, was adapted from someone else's story.)

The other cause of her getting rid of loneliness was the dumb pleasure of sharing daily life—a notion that Henniker had claimed that he held in odium along with "that most bourgeois of all words 'papa.'" Anya discovered this was a line from George Moore's *Confessions of a Young Man.*

But as soon as she got rid of the dissatisfaction of her loneliness, Anya found that there was a deeper dissatisfaction in her. She thought it had to do with her career as a graduate student in English.

As shared daily life lost its novelty for her and became a full pleasure (it didn't seem ever to have struck Mac as a novelty although it was obviously novel to him), Anya found she had a great deal more energy than during the fall. But the effect of her increased energy and interest in her work led to an odd moment. She was sitting in class with the other ten graduate students in her Shakespeare seminar. The professor—a visiting faculty member Anya rather liked and certainly thought intelligent—was commenting on a production of *Twelfth Night* he'd seen. He was trying to reproduce a reading of Duke Orsino's lines in a short scene between the Duke and Viola. He couldn't do it, and he reverted to describing the reading.

Anya, who'd seen the production and had also been in a college production as Viola, interrupted him. She spoke the Duke's lines and Viola's—did the whole scene between the Duke and Viola as in the production the professor had seen. She explained why it was too straight, why it was merely charmingly pathetic rather than pathetic and funny. She said, "The Duke is handsome and noble, even sort of sympathetic, but he's an asshole." She played the scene again, both parts, not as the scene had been in her college production, but as she'd wished it.

She did this not for the reasons for which she usually made a scene, out of malice or for the delight of seeing the effect on surprised clods. It all burst out of her, nine minutes of uncontainable show.

She was embarrassed when she finished. The other students were uneasy. The professor also wasn't sure how to take it. She said, "I'm sorry, I didn't mean to interrupt you . . ."

The professor smiled forgivingly. He said, "No, no, no, no. It's most impressive you know the lines by heart."

A minute later Anya thought, What! Forgivingly! I was fucking terrific.

A minute after that—the professor was saying that there was some evidence that the character of the Duke, Orsino, was based on a visiting court personage of the time, and was *still* warily setting out the problem of the Duke being

91

a figure of fun and at the same time the authority figure—
Anya realized that the professor had said the classically
dumbest thing to say to an actor, what the aunt from
Dubuque would say backstage—"How on earth did you
remember all those words?"

And she had *showed* him how to have the Duke both
ways at once.

She suddenly became calm. She was calmed by an enormous double certainty. The first certainty was that she
shouldn't be taking this seminar, she should be teaching it.
The second certainty was that she didn't want to teach it.

*   *   *

For a few days Anya derived some satisfaction from this
certainty.

One temporary effect was to increase her pleasure in her
sensual life. Not just by a second wave of sexual playfulness, but also by an increased appetite in general for all her
tastes and sensations. Anya went to a master class in
modern dance. She spent two hours a day exercising. She
bought some new underwear and records. She and Mac
prepared several elaborate meals.

She thought this would be a good time to appreciate
Mac *qua* mesomorph, so she went to one of his club hockey
games. She'd been prepared to admire Mac's intensity,
scrappiness, and, even if somewhat archly, the whole boisterous code *duello* of ice hockey. She'd seen several professional games on television while she sat with Mac drinking beer in a local bar on a Sunday afternoon. What took
her by surprise now as she sat just beside the team at the
rink level was the speed. It took her most of the first period
to figure out what was going on. Not just the speed but the
sudden vividness of the sounds—the collisions, the grunts,
the puck off the boards. She thought, How odd, live theater
is usually less physically affecting than a movie.

Finally, she began to watch Mac. All the knotted determination she remembered from his rock-climbing efforts
seemed suddenly to come free on the ice. When he'd been
trying to pull himself up the rock face he'd seemed even
shorter and thicker, more jammed into himself, than he
really was, as though under some evil spell. Now he seemed
elongated, fluid, his center of gravity buoyed up by some

powerful benign spirit. He moved freely at extreme angles. Leaning to one side, careening off the boards, being spun around by someone's elbow, he seemed to end up over one of his skates whether going backwards, forwards, or sideways. The difference, she decided later, less superstitiously, was rhythm.

There was also a quality to his play that she would never have guessed. She grew accustomed to his speed and balance, but she continued to be surprised by his guile. The first time she noticed it was when he was carrying the puck on his stick trying to go around a defenseman to the outside. Mac seemed to stop suddenly and cut inside. Mac and the defenseman both began to shiver to a stop, spraying up ice from their skate blades, but then Mac breezed on. It was as though in stopping Mac had coiled the spring of his forward motion, stored it for a deceitful split second, and then let himself be shot forward. For the defenseman it was a dead stop, for Mac only syncopation in his run.

Anya grew bored during the third period. The game wasn't close and Mac's team began to play defensively to protect their lead. Play was rougher and less well-phrased. The only thing that interested her near the end of the game was Mac giving instructions and/or encouragement to one of his players while they were on the bench. Mac sat beside a dark hulk of a man who had slumped forward from exhaustion. Mac cupped the back of the man's neck in his hand and spoke into the man's ear, emphasizing each phrase by squeezing the man's thick, wet nape.

Anya envied Mac's chance to have someone receive his intense transmission. It was a game, a scheme of things that was ritual but not fixed, that had opened up both Mac and the man. Their intensities—Mac's active and the man's passive—were much more important than what Mac was saying. "Tie up their man in the slot" or whatever. She amused herself by thinking, The medium is the massage.

So, later on, when she reflected about her own intense outburst in class, which the basically kind and intelligent professor should have received with as much passive intensity as Mac's hot, exhausted, open-pored teammate had received Mac, Anya found that this academic cool was part of her new dissatisfaction. It had been masked by her minor dissatisfaction with Henniker and by her minor satisfaction with Mac, but now she was at last in touch with it. The way she was leading her life, for all its academic and sexual variations, was not giving her, was not going to give her, the full risks and satisfactions that she desired. It was not a question of success. It was a question of finding some act that was as large as her energy, that would receive her energy. Some real matter that she could engage fiercely, and in her fierce precision lose herself and her standing in the world.

Provided, she thought after the first rage passed through her, that the world showed up to applaud and take her out to supper after the show.

She ridiculed the idea further. She even compared herself to a housewife filling out matchbook-cover applications to the Famous Writers School ("Do you have a restless urge to write?") or the Famous Artists School ("Let us help you discover your secret talent").

She began to notice names of people she'd known. She read in the *New York Times* that a boy who'd been at law school when she was in college was now an aide to Lindsay. She watched an NBC-TV special and saw that the assistant producer was a girl who'd been in her dorm.

Once she got started she began to see the names everywhere. The old unemployed gang in New York began to show up in magazine reviews of Off-Broadway and Off-Off-Broadway shows. There was a short story in the *Atlantic Monthly* by a girl who'd been a friend of Tassie's.

The San Francisco Mime Troupe had a three-day stand at the University of Chicago, and Anya recognized a girl from her old dance class. Anya studied her closely. The girl had been a fair dancer. She was now a good actress. A confident, funny, and sexy performer. Anya wondered how it had happened—not the good luck of getting the job but the good luck of getting to be good. Anya herself had been better than the girl three years before. Was it simple persistence? Experience? Was the director of the mime troupe a good teacher? Or had the girl simply flowered?

She asked Mac—who had been charmed by the girl—whether he'd ever thought of playing ice hockey professionally. Mac said he had. Anya asked him why he hadn't tried. Mac said, "It was pretty even for a while, for the time I was thinking about it. But after I got out of the Army, I wanted things on my terms again. I guess that was it. If I could have played junior hockey for a year or two and not just turned pro but gone on to play for Montreal I would have. But it's an American business now. They don't just hire you, they buy you. I could have gone on being the right mental age—twenty years old and wired to take the full juice three times a week. It wasn't until I was almost through college that I thought I didn't want to stay twenty forever."

Anya said, "But you think you were good enough?"

Mac said, "I think so. I'll never be as good at anything else."

Anya said, "That must be a demoralizing thought."

Mac said, "No. I was technically very good at a sport. I'll probably be pretty good at something more useful. Nothing wrong with that."

Anya said, "You're the only person I know who'd rather be ruled by virtue than by passion."

CHAPTER

5

Anya and Mac spent their spring vacation in Iowa. Anya
had run into an old college friend, Andrew Bienstock, at
the mime troupe performance. Andrew was struggling to
set up a small theater group near the University of Iowa in
Iowa City. He'd said to Anya, "Dear Anya, I insist—I *desire* that you come see what we're up to. Or should I say
up *against*?"

Anya felt her spirit shrinking as she and Mac droned
along the flat Illinois highway past nothing. Well before
they passed Joliet she decided she was going to be depressed by it all. Mac, at the wheel, was exuberant. He
stopped on the bridge from Rock Island to Davenport to
look at the Mississippi River. He even spat in it for good
luck.

Anya could feel Mac holding back an enthusiastic and
probably detailed commentary on the topography, the soil,
the few green sprouts of crops, the names of towns.

She thought, Let him have his romance now. She doubted
that he was going to be happy with her for the next few
days—not with her or her old home week. Andrew was an
old college friend. Anya wondered if Mac guessed he was
homosexual. The other two members of the troupe Anya
knew were from her New York years—a pair of tough girls
Anya had met in the most grueling dance class she'd ever
been in. There were a half dozen others Andrew had described to her—Anya couldn't imagine Mac getting along
with them.

Mac had bought a topographical map of the Davenport-

Iowa City quadrant of Iowa which he appeared to have memorized. He ignored the directions Anya had written down. He left the Interstate several exits early to take back roads—driving slowly past barns, plowed fields, pigpens. Unable at last to keep quiet, he began to name the small rivers and creeks as they crossed them on cross-planked single-lane bridges.

Mac commented on the fences. Not barbed wire, as he pointed out, but hog wire topped with two or three strands of barbed wire. Mac said, " 'Horse high, ox strong, and pig tight.' "

Anya said, "Only one Boy Scout merit badge at a time. You're working on map reading and navigation."

Mac said amicably, as though she'd finally started a conversation, "I was kicked out of the Boy Scouts."

Anya didn't ask why.

She wasn't mad at Mac, only superficially irritated. The problem she faced with real irritation was her friends Andrew, Alice, and Babette. She wanted the supple pleasures of their company—their small bright vanities, the physical wit of their gestures, the chatty exaggerations of their emotions. But she thought that if they invited her to take up with them she would say no. They'd buried themselves out here. Every mile west of Chicago added a unit of isolation to her forlorn sense of where she was.

Moreover, Andrew, Alice and Babette had been unkind to her in New York when she'd started to work in production for Ikon Films. Now, from her point of view they'd gone into a more barren exile than hers, two hundred miles past Chicago. Anya supposed that from their point of view, their exile was more glorious than hers. But she admitted to herself that she was excited to come warm herself at their small excitement. She was coming to share their thin gruel.

It would take too long to explain to Mac—at least in his present mood. He was like a dog let off the leash in the country.

He craned his neck now to watch a small hawk hovering over a field.

*　　*　　*

Anya's three friends were at first careful to be wry and amusing—My God, here we all are in *Iowa.*

But when everyone began to explain the theory, the inspiration—the Group Theater, Tyrone Guthrie in Minneapolis—they let go, they all believed.

Mac asked how the winter had been.

Andrew fluttered beside him. "Dear boy, you have asked the right person, I hope you have some time." Laughter. "Let me tell you—God, where to begin?—clothes. Just to give you an inkling—a union suit, you know with the trap door. The first week the plumbing wasn't working, so we used the outhouse. Cries for help—stuck to the seat—paralyzed with cold. Snow falling through a hole in the roof. Never ever be the first one in the outhouse on a cold day. By chance I let my sweet young thing barely touch my belt buckle as I was struggling to my feet—like putting your tongue on a door handle—I mean to say it stuck."

Anya saw Andrew thought Mac attractive. Mac was laughing.

"And the terrible shock one day—in the kitchen—the hearth fire and all that—I opened the door to the refrigerator, and it was warmer inside. An intensely surreal experience, I can assure you, warming your hands at the ice tray."

"Well, spring must—"

"Oh God, spring! On my *knees!* Pagan worship—it's not sexual, you know—it's survival. Just to unwrap the layers of scarves and realize that your nose has pulled through. You take off your Dr. Denton's and count your blessings."

Anya had forgotten how pleasant Andrew's all-out conversational entertainments were. And Mac—Mac seemed to be accepting the gift. Why had she assumed he would bristle at Andrew's lavish attention?

Mac's glass was filled again—he made a face at the taste. Andrew said, " 'A naïve domestic wine, I hope you'll be amused at its presumption.' "

"What *is* it?"

Merry Andrew. "Oh dear, you don't like it."

Anya said, "It tastes like bottled farts."

"How terribly crude you've become, Anya, in Chicago."

Mac said, "I'm sure it's good for you."

"It's rhubarb wine. We did a musical soirée once at the Amana colonies, and they gave us twenty gallons of it and a free meal each. They didn't ask us back—their loss."

Anya asked what they did for money. Mac looked surprised (he was on such good behavior—Anya heard Andrew's phrasing in her thought), but he was seriously interested in the answer and the attitude toward money in the answer.

The property belonged to the repertory theater, which was incorporated; the controlling shares were held by two sets of parents. The members of the troupe would get salaries—or possibly shares of stock—when performances began in the spring.

There was of course no rent. For the rest of their living expenses they did odd jobs and pooled the income. Two of them were students at the University of Iowa on scholarship. They put in twenty dollars a month. Two of them applied for county welfare. They received government food —canned beef, a gallon of peanut butter, a bag of oats, a bag of flour, canned butter.

The others filled in at restaurants, late-night shifts at the all-night drugstore in Iowa City, and the all-night gas station at the Interstate interchange.

Mac said, "Why don't you work for a farmer now that spring's here?"

Andrew said, "We're busy here all day."

"They'll be working at night in just a few weeks. They'll be plowing with their headlights on."

"We'll be starting performances in a month." A hint of irritation.

"Are you going to have a garden?"

Andrew took off with shitty brilliance.

"Oh, yes, formal. Paths of white pebbles—fountains shooting out of a sphinx's gigantic marble breasts, a box-wood maze, a fish pond with water lilies, an *orangerie,* tulip beds, a grape arbor, and—and a ruined temple by moonlight." Andrew got up and began to stack dishes. "I really can't live with less." He picked up the pile of plates and walked to the sink.

Mac gathered up the tumblers and mugs.

Mac went to the sink with his load. He said, "Let me get the pots." Andrew nodded. Anya thought, Okay, Mac's being a good scout.

But it turned out to be more than that.

During the next several days Mac had an independent frolic among her friends. Enthusiasms of theirs that she'd never known about conjoined with enthusiasms of Mac's.

Babette Rosen, a small wiry quick-witted girl who'd been
raised as a Jewish princess in Riverdale, turned out (a) to
be a fan of the New York Rangers hockey team, and (b)
to have been a horsewoman of some accomplishment and
actually to be helping a neighboring farmer who kept a few
cutting horses as a hobby. She took Mac off to meet the
farmer and look at the horses.

Alice Adare, Babette's roommate, who put the troupe
through an hour or two of dance and exercises each morning, turned out to be fascinated by Mac's crank theories of
exercise and conditioning.

Ogden Morse—whom Anya saw as an overgrown preppie, and who, possibly for that reason, was the butt of
everyone's jokes except his girl friend's—made eager ad-
vances toward Mac, exactly those of an unathletic weenie
at boarding school who rushes the new boys before they
find out where he stands—except in this case the exclu-
sionary principle was not athletic. Og took Mac jogging.
And it was Og who was the preppie puppy unleashed for
a romp and Mac the obliging dog lover.

Tagh and Bangs, the last two members of the troupe,
were as happy to meet Mac as they were to meet Anya.
Tagh, a short, tense, wiry black Irishman from Pittsburgh
and Bangs, a sweet, slightly maternal woman of indeter-
minate age and modestly theatrical air.

But Andrew was the one who surprised Anya the most.
He took Mac and Anya on a tour of the barn turned theater. Mac didn't say anything while Andrew and Anya discussed the seating, the acoustics, sight lines, possible
rearrangements of the rudimentary stage. Anya began to
gather her thoughts into essays. Andrew took advantage of
this pause in her talk to say, "Have you noticed your boyfriend? He's falling in love with the barn."

*   *   *

When Andrew, Anya, and Mac had approached the barn
from the house, Mac had realized it was larger than he'd
first thought. In the dusk of arriving he hadn't noticed it
was six-sided. The proportions of the hexagonal barn were
so nicely turned it gave Mac the sensation that he could
hold it in the palm of his hand. This was the first pang of a

series—long, rhythmic constrictions of admiration for the building.

Inside it seemed larger still, but Mac realized this was as enlarging an illusion as his first had been diminishing.

The vertical walls of the barn were only twelve feet high, but the sloping roof of six equilateral triangles seemed vast, all the more so because the triangles (trapezoids really, at the last minute) culminated in a bright hexagonal cupola, each side of which was a window frame holding a dozen panes of glass. Mac's vision seemed to him to move simultaneously along all six beams that rose in shadow from the six low corners along the darkest lines of the whole interior until they tapered into the more delicate framework which held up the source of light.

Each beam was square-hewn, $10'' \times 10''$, and was held up by two standing posts of the same thickness—one twelve feet high at the corner and one twice as high halfway to the peak.

The barn loft was a continuous shelf that filled the space between the corner posts and the taller inner ring of the posts. The carpentry was exact, both obvious and ingenious. Each plank in each section of the loft, and each plank in each section of the roof, was mitered to meet each plank of the neighboring sections, and each plank in the vertical walls was beveled to join each corner post, all in perfect 120° angles.

When Mac moved to stand directly under the cupola, he felt a perfect sense of balance, as though all the lines of planking were ripples receding from him, a pebble dropped plumb from the peak. His feeling for an instant was of the hexagon as a circle. But then all the receding movement of the herringboned planks was caught at the corner posts and vaulted back over him along the beams, reaching a new point of balance in the eye of light.

And then his original point of balance seemed to merge with the new balance at the source of light—or perhaps the top point of symmetry descended with the light—until Mac felt the barn balance once and for all in the spatial center at a level with the ring of lofts.

Having discovered his clear sensation of the barn from its middle, he was almost disappointed that he would never have this movement of his sensations reenacted.

Mac clambered around the lofts for a while. He noted

that the corner posts were cut to fit into slots in the beams, perfectly angled in. He poked around the base of the posts, but, since a concrete floor had been poured—he guessed at a later date than the barn was built—he couldn't confirm his guess that both the corner posts and inner posts were sunk deep into the ground.

Most hay barns have tight roofs and loose side walls to air the hay in case a few green bales get packed in. This barn had walls that were tight as a boat. When Mac wanted to ask what Andrew knew about the barn, he discovered that Andrew and Anya were gone.

At supper that night he quizzed Andrew and was pleasantly surprised to find that Andrew had a copy of the plans. The barn had been built by a Dutchman named Van Vlack only three generations before. None of Van Vlack's grandsons wanted to farm. They sold the whole place to a neighbor named Sigurd Olson. Olson later sold the barn and house and five acres to the theater company corporation. He still owned the fields, which joined his. Van Vlack had drawn the plans himself and used local labor—mainly Bohemians from Iowa City—to raise the barn. The wood came from the oak that lined the Iowa River only a mile to the west.

Andrew said to Mac, "So you approve of our barn?"

Anya said to Andrew, "You know it comes close enough to being the Globe." She quoted, " '. . . But pardon, gentles all,/The flat unraised spirits that hath dared/On this unworthy scaffold to bring forth/So great an object. Can this cockpit hold/The vasty fields of France? Or may we cram/Within this wooden *O* the very casques/That did affright the air at Agincourt?' " She added, "Maybe you ought to call the theater 'the wooden *O*.' "

Andrew said, "Maybe. We haven't settled the name yet." He turned to Mac. "What *I* like about our barn is that it has all the pointed aspiration of the Gothic—arrows aimed at heaven—and at the same time it has the comforting quality of a low Byzantine dome. The dome is the sky, which is heaven—you don't have to aspire as hard as the Western Europeans. It's all around you."

Mac at first thought the remark was on the flossy side, but Andrew's speech was flossy in general. It then occurred to Mac that the more interesting and deeper talent that Andrew had was a quick sensing of other people's feelings.

102

Anya had that talent too, intermittently, but behind it in Andrew's case there was a less rapacious curiosity. Mac thought he himself ought to develop the talent as Andrew had.

By the time Mac was through working at this notion, he had arrived at the brink of contracting a loyalty to Andrew. He felt the passage of loyalty and trust. This was the first time he'd observed himself make friends.

Anya said, "Well, what *are* you going to call the theater?"

There was an instant reflex from everyone at the table. As each person in turn stated what was obviously a long-held preference there was an expression of disapproval from everyone else. Each person spoke to Anya and Mac, trying to ignore the rest of the group.

Andrew said, "I prefer The New World Repertory."

Anya said, "I like Wooden O better."

Annabelle said, "I'd like to call it The Middle Earth Theater—you know, like in the *Hobbit*."

Mac said he thought that was nice.

Og said, "I think Black Earth Theater is better."

Mac said he liked that too.

Og said, "Or we could call it Whole Hog."

Andrew said, "Well why not call it Pig Wallow then. Good Lord."

Alice said, "I like West Branch. The West Branch Theater."

Andrew said, "You know what West Branch is? It's the name of the town where Herbert Hoover was born. Why not call it the Herbert Hoover Memorial Theater?"

Mac said, "West Branch is also the name of the creek that runs from the town of West Branch into the Iowa River—it comes right by here."

Anya said, "What other towns are near here?"

Alice said, "Lone Tree."

Mac said, "That's a nice idea."

Anya said, "You're no help if you agree with everything."

Alice said, "Hills, Kalona, Downey, West Liberty."

Anya said, "West Liberty."

Andrew said, "That's where they hold the second state fair. One at Des Moines and the other at West Liberty."

Anya said, "So much the better."

AN AMERICAN ROMANCE

Andrew said, "Certainly—we could have the hog-calling contest as a curtain raiser. And the jelly-judging as the entr'acte."

But Og, Annabelle, Tagh, and Bangs supported West Liberty; Anya said it was best after Wooden O; and Alice and Babette said it was almost as good as West Branch.

Andrew asked Mac if he thought it was all right. Mac said it was okay.

Andrew said, "Well, dear boy, I trust your instinct."

*   *   *

Anya's reaction to Mac's rustic social success was at first uneasy. But on the third afternoon of their visit she suddenly found herself amiable, and him amiable, so she took him upstairs to their bedroom for tea. They carried up their mugs and got under a fat cotton quilt. Anya was pleased to gather him back in. They had a lazy chat as they got rid of the chill. Mac warmed her breast with his teacup, not as a sexual preliminary, more a gesture of polite intimacy, like an Eskimo warming a guest's feet against his own stomach.

From the bed they could see out the window, down a long slope of plowed field, and they could make out a gap where a road must run, and beyond that flat bottom land and then a strip of oak forest that Mac said lined the banks of the Iowa River.

Anya asked Mac if he could guess who were the two members of the troupe whose daddies had kicked in to set up the company. Without much trouble he picked Annabelle.

Anya said, "Because she looks like a rich girl?"

Mac said, "No . . ."

Anya knew it still made Mac uneasy to discuss girls' looks with her. She said, "Annabelle is luscious. All that shiny red hair—"

Mac said, "I'd call it strawberry blond."

Anya said, "So you *have* been paying attention. But she's a good contrast to Alice and Babette. They're both lean meat. It's good to have a piece of pastry for ingenue parts —a sugar glaze and pudding filling."

Mac said, "She certainly isn't tough. But she's not fat."

Anya said, "No. Just bouncy. But you know what's going

104

to be good on stage? Those big wide eyes. You know what those eyes are saying?—'Ooo, what *are* you doing to me?' She's sort of a better-fed version of that crazy girl of Henniker's. You know what makes Annabelle's daze really sexy? It's the three-second lag it takes for a sensation to get from her skin to her strawberry-blond brain. So you're always three seconds ahead of her. Making love to her would be like playing an old organ. You push the key that you want and then from far away and later you hear the note piping out." Anya looked at Mac directly. "Don't you think that's sexy?"

Mac said, "I guess."

Anya said, "I'll bet she gets it from behind a lot and whimpers."

Mac laughed, but was uneasy. Anya could tell she'd transgressed some boundary of his inexperienced gallantry toward woman. It annoyed her. It annoyed her to be his first bitch. Or at least his first bitch he knew was a bitch.

She said, "Who's the other one? Who's the other one whose daddy put up money?"

Mac said, "It's between Babette and Og. I'll pick Ogden."

Anya said, "What? He looks like such a truckdriver."

Mac said, "I think he's a rich kid because of the way he is in that dance-exercise routine that Alice and Babette run. Og's someone who's had lots and lots of lessons. Tagh learned things the way I did. You watch Alice show Tagh how to dance. Tagh will bristle, he won't get it, he'll get more pissed off, and then suddenly he'll get it—*bang*—the whole number all at once. Then Alice will show Og. She coaxes him through it, bit by bit. Og was taught how to learn. I'd guess he learned a lot of sports at a country club with a polite pro at his elbow. So he's a rich kid. The reason I guess it's his daddy is that he's still uneasy—he's not sure if he can relax and get on with putting on a show with the others. Babette's ready to go."

Anya thought Mac's observation of Og and Tagh passably shrewd. She wasn't sure she liked Mac shrewd. She quizzed him about what else he'd observed in the dance sessions.

He'd noticed that Babette was so loose-jointed that when she stretched her leg on the bar, her knee bent backwards under the line of her thigh and shin.

He'd noticed that the oldest member of the troupe—

Bangs—had a beautiful neck, beautiful feet, a beautiful alto voice, and an only slightly sagging figure. He pointed out that when she wasn't in a leotard the soft droop of her lower lip, her bust, and her can looked very appealing.

Anya said, "How old do you think she is?"

Mac said, "I don't know. Around forty. She looks like someone who looks younger than she is."

Anya said, "I didn't know you were such a witty connoisseur of women."

Mac said, "I'm not. A connoisseur is someone who says 'how amusing,' 'quite intriguing,' 'how terribly new.'"

Anya was surprised at how irritated he sounded.

She said, "Bangs was married once, you know."

Mac said, "It's hard to imagine her getting a divorce. Or the guy divorcing her. I mean, having married her . . ."

Anya said, "Oh, easy. Imagine her plain niceness always at your side, a little bit forlorn. Silently demanding attention. It would be like some never-ending chore, to take her quart of kindness every day. A cow silently waiting to be milked."

Mac said, "Cows complain out loud."

Anya said, "Well, there you are. Imagine silent cows."

The sun lowered so that it shone against the window. It was hard to see out through the glare, and the room now filled with dusty light, which brought the details of the interior into focus. Anya felt intimately surrounded by the coarse grain of the walls, the fingerprints on the headboard, the old ashes someone had flicked into the bright inside of a blue coffee can. But it was not the old uncleaned intimacies of the room she found oppressive. She felt as lazy and restless as on a Sunday afternoon in college. Waiting for Tassie. Waiting for her good fortune. What had made her restless was that she couldn't afford to wait. What had made her lazy was her absorbed-from-Tassie superstition that waiting was the proper way to embrace being extraordinary. It was the reverse of the Calvinistic work ethic. Not work, but luxury, the luxury of bored waiting, was a sign of aesthetic and romantic election.

And when the excitement arrived it was proper to vault above it. As Tassie had. Tassie saw everything from above, Anya had thought—her own boredom, her own excitement. Tassie, Anya had thought, was her own Olympus.

How odd that seeing everything from above—at which Henniker was more successful, more articulate certainly— had not been revealed to her as sterile until she saw it in Henniker.

But where was she now, watching the sun sinking through its own glare down the grimy windowpane?

After several minutes of brilliant depression on such a large scale that her questions of what to do were dwarfed, Anya returned her attention to Mac. She felt irritated, as though mildly hung over. After asking him a number of questions about why he didn't feel bad, or adrift, why didn't he worry about not being a genius, she finally irritated him.

She said, "You think you're a nice guy, and that that takes care of it. 'Be good, my child, and let who will be clever.' "

Mac said, "No. I don't know . . . At least I'm not a secret son of a bitch."

Anya said, "And I am?"

Mac apparently didn't really want to fight. He said, "No. You and I have some feeling that we can do something. Your year with that film company—that your boss there wanted you to stay on—that must have helped you—"

Anya said, "Not really. But if you didn't mean me, who is a secret son of a bitch? You must mean Henniker?"

Mac said, "No. That would be too hard to keep secret."

Anya thought they were getting closer to an explosive issue.

Anya said, "You know he was very interested in you. He occasionally got interested in people who weren't rich or clever. For example, there was a student who got a Rhodes scholarship last spring. The boy was a fair-haired enthusiastic outdoor type. A mountain climber. Henniker thought he might like the boy as a pet hero. His real hero is, of course, himself, his dream self. But the boy stopped coming around, and Henniker turned on him. Wrote an essay ridiculing the idea of Rhodes scholars. Henniker used a lot of phrases from D. H. Lawrence's essay on Hawthorne. Stuff like, What's going on in that pretty blond head? Buzz, buzz, buzz. The blind worm of denied lust. The venom in Henniker's piece was amazing. It wasn't just that he'd offered friendship and been denied by this lesser person. It wasn't just envy, though Henniker would have liked to have been a Rhodes scholar. And it wasn't just an attack on the idea of Rhodes scholarships, though the idea is a bit master-racish. I think Henniker was enraged because the boy turned out *not* to be a lesser version of Henniker. The piece was Henniker's attempt to show that the boy was a failed version of being Henniker. Stupidly vicious, instead of cleverly vicious. But deep inside Henniker was hurt by the notion that the boy really was different.

"And so when I came along Henniker was susceptible to someone who seemed like himself. Quick, theatrical. Suspicious of apparent wholesomeness. He was pleased to find I was rootless, a refugee. A child of the Holocaust. He had two superstitions at work: the outsider as free of morals—a sort of Brechtian justification—and also the artist's sensibility as license.

"Henniker's view of people who struggle to behave conventionally is that they're as secretly tacky as people running for Congress. Their wife and kids, and dog and war record, and duty and smiles are fronts. Behind the front they want what he wants, but without the sharpness of taste he has.

"But Henniker has a last doubt that somewhere there is a virtue which has some undeniable aesthetic justification, that perhaps there is some trump that some aristocrat is holding back to play against him. That's why Henniker has done such research on the fine families of England and New England in his literary gadding about. If he can reduce an honorable daughter of an earl to a stupid squeal of pleasure, or see a well-connected girl go crazy in an inglorious way, it helps to calm his fear. If he knows the dirt, if he can do in all the pretensions, then—— But what a long road. That's why I think he was interested in me as an ally."

Mac said, "That's not how I see you."

Anya said, "Well, I *am* rootless, and I *am* interested in seeing into people. And conventional piety *is* shit.

"And I have very little interest in loyalty or gratitude. You know—I don't think I've told you I may have been born in Canada. If I wasn't an ingrate, you'd have a romantic compatriotic claim. Montreal is where the paperwork was done. But I may have been born at sea. My mother must have made it to Boston, because that's where I was adopted. I can imagine how it was all too much for her. A sort of double birth—her squeezing through the cervix of immigration while I was squeezing out of her. But I do know why the Sewalls adopted me. It was a combination of *noblesse oblige* and patriotism. My foster father was named Henry Sewall. He was a Boston drop-out. He'd been teaching at Harvard in the thirties, but it made him so nervous he'd puke every morning. He married and retired to New Hampshire. I was the gesture to the war effort. Or it may have been a gesture toward Western civilization."

Mac said, "Why aren't you named Sewall?"

"It wasn't up to me. I called them Henry and Martha. They believed in my dignity and individuality. And Henry was mad at his family anyway. I never met any of his family until Henry and Martha were dead."

Mac said, "When did they die?"

Anya said, "When I was seventeen and eighteen. I'm coming to that."

Mac said, "You could have been worse off. You're telling this so they sound foolish."

Anya now knew she could get him angry enough to make her angry. She said, "I should have guessed you'd be revering them already. But tell me something seriously. You can name your seventeen first cousins and God-knows-how-many second cousins and your great-great-grandfather and the exact location of the thistlepatch he sprang from. My not having a family must shock you. It must strike you as a psychic disfigurement."

Mac said, "Yes."

Anya said, "Why? Why is that? You don't believe in mongrels versus purebreds or any of that shit." She thought for a second he might say yes.

Mac said, "That's not why. I don't know how much romance I have about either side of my family. The Mac-Kenzie or the Gagnon. But it's your contempt that's the disfigurement. Your mother got you to a safe place."

Anya said, "She got herself to a safe place."

Mac said, "And the Sewalls adopted you."

Anya said, "So? They had no children. Some real craving may have mixed in with the noble gesture. But by the time I got to Boston again, I might as well have been a blank. I had nothing but wishes."

Mac said, "How did you pay?"

Anya said, "I worked a little. And there was some money that Henry left. He died a year after Martha. Here's the neat part. When he died, I was in my senior year at boarding school, and Henry's brother Edward wrote me a letter on his bank's stationery. Dear Miss Janek. He was the executor of the will, and he told me about the money that was going into a trust fund that he would administer. He'd had the school send him my records, and he knew I'd got a scholarship to Smith and a partial scholarship to Radcliffe. He wrote, 'I would strongly advise a young woman in your position to take the full scholarship.' I went to Boston to meet him. He didn't even ask me to lunch. We talked in his office at the bank. I'd half-hoped that he might be a sort of dreary amiable pill like Henry. That he'd take me to lunch and introduce me as his niece. Nothing. But he did let slip that he thought Smith was a pretty good place because his daughter had gone there. I later wrote him that I thought Smith was for dreary minds and that I was going to Radcliffe. It was a juvenile, snotty letter and extremely satisfying.

"It also gave me a snotty little ambition. I knew he would receive my grades every semester, so I worked my ass off my first year. By my second year I'd figured out how to get good grades without working very hard, and I got interested in theater, which was then a sort of outlaw activity. Harvard built a big theater, but there was no theater department. My part-time job was helping a producer do educational television . . ."

Anya suddenly felt tired. There was something in Mac that tired her spite. She said, "Do you think you're better off for knowing all the fairy tales about your family? Does your ancestor worship make you better? Or just smug?"

Mac said, "It's not ancestor worship. It doesn't make me smug. In fact, if you read general history you can always imagine if you'd been there you would have done the right thing, been on the right side. But if you find out someone you're part of in some physical way *was* there and was on the wrong side, you can't be as smug as *you* are about how above it all you are."

Anya snorted. "The wrong side, the right side . . ."

Mac said, "All right. I should have said the side I would have chosen. What I mean is, I'm not free to think of my-

self as above the past. I'm not automatically better just by
being newest. I have to do some work just to keep up—"

Anya said, "—with the Joneses."

Mac said, "To keep up with the best things that have
been started. That are building."

Anya said, "Oh, I see. Now you believe in progress. The
Way West. Manifest Destiny. 'Passage to India, my son.'
Maybe you even believe in the White Man's Burden."

Mac said, "It's not that simple—"

Anya said, "You don't say."

Mac said, "Why don't you tell me what happened to
you?"

Anya said, "Have you seen the future? Does it work?"

Mac said, "Just tell your own story."

Anya said, "It may not link up with the main currents
in American thought."

Mac said, "What happened next?"

Anya thought Mac's patience was in this case a con-
venience. She wondered why he'd told her that an angry
temper was a fault of his. She felt pleasantly exercised.

She said, "Where was I? Names. I once asked Henry
why he hadn't changed my name to his. Henry said, 'When
you buy a good boat, you don't change her name.' That, by
the way, is the wittiest thing he ever said. I did change my
first name, though. It was Anna. Anna Janek. When I was
sixteen I thought Anya was more glamorous. Henry never
used it, but I told all the kids at Putney it was my name. I
went there that year—Henry realized I was miserable at the
public high school and was about to get into trouble."

Mac said, "Were you happy at boarding school?"

Anya said, "I don't know. I guess I was happy from when
I was nine to about twelve. Then I was miserable from
thirteen to sixteen. I guess I was better off at Putney. I was
left alone. I studied a lot. I read a lot. They told me I was
smart, and I suppose the standards of beauty there were
more suited to me. I wasn't pretty, but I didn't think I
was absurd the way I had in New Hampshire. Henry
wanted me to be a doctor. I wanted to do everything. That
was one thing nice about the school—they let you think
you could do everything. Of course, I thought from time
to time if bright people could do anything, what the hell
were the teachers doing at Putney. But more often I went
along with the muddled sense that the kids had that it was

a noble thing to teach us, that we were a joy and a challenge. And then Martha died, and then Henry died. I'd lived in their house for sixteen years, but I hadn't missed them much while I was away, so I didn't take it as hard as if I'd been right there with them. Martha didn't like me much after I was fourteen. Henry did."

Anya noticed that her tone had changed, that she had stated a plain truth, or at least the heading of a plain truth. She moved ahead.

She said, "That summer when Henry was in the hospital, I went to music camp. You asked me if I was happy. I think I decided then that happiness was a passive, and, therefore, vulnerable state, so I started to prefer excitement. Not only daring, but also the minor excitement of projects. Even when I was depressed, I could comfort myself by teaching myself small skills. I taught myself typing and shorthand, photography, stage lighting. You and I are a little alike in that one way. An American foible—not knowledge is power, but know-how is power. Craft, not art. Though I once tried to teach myself Greek. I couldn't do it. I've often wondered why Henry didn't teach me Greek. He knew Greek. But he spent his time trying to teach me the 'natural order of things.' He didn't know what he was talking about. Or at any rate *I* didn't know what he was talking about. I only knew he couldn't even make yoghurt. It's odd—he was raised in a Boston upper-class intellectual tradition, he became what he was supposed to become and then quit. He left Harvard, he left Boston, he left his family. I suppose he wanted me to be a doctor because he himself had a great yearning to be useful and he was useless. Actually, there was one way he was useful that no one ever gave him credit for—his supposedly self-sufficient homestead kept a half dozen local Yankees regularly employed. They chopped his wood, made his syrup, ran his apple orchard, patched the roof, the plumbing. Of course, they thought of themselves as independent."

Mac said, "He raised you."

Anya said, "Yes. I suppose I thought of myself as independent as those sour rural Yankees. I date my real life from the notion that I went to college on my own."

Mac said, "Were you happy in college?"

Anya said, "I don't think anyone is."

Mac said, "You should have spent two years in the army first."

Anya said, "Oh, well—like stopping hitting yourself on the head with a hammer. You weren't really happy, were you?"

Mac said, "If I wasn't, it was my own fault."

Anya said, "I didn't know anyone who was. The reason no one's happy is that . . . you are just smart enough, you've just learned enough to tear up any certainty. You suddenly see that all the people you admire are old farts. At the same time you're close enough to your own pimply attitudes of recent memory to cringe at yourself. So it seems vital to rush on to the next stage. In fact, it would help to rush to the stage after next. I remember starting to admire some teacher, and the instant my admiration was fastening onto him, I could feel it turn into an attack. And I had contempt for the other students. The ones in love— holding hands in the library. The ones announcing how to save the world. There was nothing to do sometimes but sit there being smothered in drivel from all sides."

Mac said, "I don't see you just sitting there . . ."

Anya said, "It was as bad the other way, the ones who thought they could zap people with clean electric shit. Here's a story that finally depressed me. My roommate Tassie went to a big weekend house party out on the north shore. She went with the boy whose parents were giving the party. The boy's mother stuttered terribly. After the weekend, Tassie sent the mother a house present—a little silver cup from Shreve, Crump & Low engraved 'Th-th-th-thanks.' "

Mac laughed.

Anya said, "I would wish I'd done that, and at the same time I'd think No, what a piece of wise-ass shit. I saw everything double. Fitzgerald said the whole point of education is to hold two contradictory ideas simultaneously. Ha! I *yearned* to get one idea off by itself. 'Purity of Heart Is to Will One Thing.' But there was always some notion flickering at the corner of your eye, something tugging on one coat tail. I'm sure there's a fairy tale, some kind of cute fable, in which a man in a forest notices more and more out of the corner of his eye, jerks his head further and further around until he's wound up like a corkscrew. Isn't there a fairy tale like that? Did I just make it up?

Anyway—the only way to avoid that is to let go of your original notions, the ones that hold your feet."

Mac disagreed, but he didn't speak. He thought that for the first time she'd told him a story, even if by accident, as if she were speaking to herself.

Anya said, "Wait. There were a few times when everything seemed to fit together. No—balance. Just for a second everything would balance."

The sun was now behind the trees that lined the river, and they could see out across the field again, though, now that the plowed earth was blacker, the green weeds and grass in the road ditches were gray.

Anya said, "What am I going to do about this place? They want me to come out here. I don't know. Maybe I'd be better off going to New York with the film company. I've been in graduate school so long I don't know if these guys are any good."

CHAPTER

||||||||||||||||||||||||||||||||||||

6

When Anya and Mac got back to Chicago, she hadn't made up her mind.

Other possibilities came up and strayed across her vision—*muscae volantes,* floaters, spots and beams of light, not to be blinked away, but not a part of what she could really see.

Mr. Danziger, her old boss at Ikon Films, sent her a note reminding her that he still wanted her back to work for him.

The English department offered her a fellowship, an underpaid job really, teaching a discussion section of the big undergraduate Shakespeare course. Anya was pleased to be considered a successful graduate student, but the actual papers she was writing became harder to do. She liked her conceptions; it was the formal argument that irked her. She admired wonderful criticism, hers was only good.

Andrew wrote her a letter in which he asked her to join the troupe for the summer at least. They were trying to arrange a tour, since their University of Iowa audience was too small during the summer. Andrew wrote, "I can't think of anyone who is as shrewd as you are whom I also trust."

Anya thought, some compliment.

Andrew's letter ended "Please, please, darling Anya, come conspire with us."

All in all, he charmed her.

She began to think about the troupe's problems more and more often. She liked Andrew's idea that most of the plays they would present during the next school year would be ones that were on the reading list of the huge introductory literature courses at the University of Iowa only five miles away from the barn. She also agreed with him that a troupe like theirs should concentrate on comedy, take advantage of their youth, looks, quickness, and surface charm. No King Lear or Oedipus. Comedy, witty farce, and maybe superb melodrama, like Webster's *White Devil*.

Babette wrote her, too. An echo of Andrew's letter. "We need you, you clever girl." Both Andrew and Babette sent regards to Mac, but they didn't mention how he would fit in. Perhaps they were simply not presuming.

Anya wrote back that she would arrange their summer tour if they would all subscribe to her being a Hobbesian tyrant. They sent a telegram back—Anya guessed Andrew wrote it—saying "Yes. Save us from our horrible state of nature, Anya Tyranna." They all signed.

Anya went back to Iowa for a weekend, and made a 16mm. film of several scenes. She borrowed a projector and took the film—and an earlier film loop Andrew had made—to show to owners of summer theaters and dinner theaters on the north shore of Chicago.

She felt her old good-gray-lady mood return. While she was making a pitch to a manager, she liked it, but when she got back home to Mac, she found she was leaking bitchiness.

Mac was working on his engineering projects, and at the same time devoting an hour each evening to cultural self-improvement—reading the classics. She found his disciplined schedule annoying.

One night she tried to lure him into a discussion. He was lying in bed as still as a felled tree reading *Don Quixote* while she waited for a phone call. She found herself also waiting for him to turn each page. His expression didn't change, his hand didn't move until the last line of each page. When his hour was up, he carefully flattened a cloth bookmark and shut the book. As though it were the Bible.

Anya said, "What do you think? Do you like it?"

Mac said, "Yes."

Anya said, "Is it funny?"

Mac thought.

Anya said, "I didn't see you laugh." She was about to

make him feel bad by summing up what was comic, destructive, and antichivalrous in the book.

Mac said, "It's very consoling."

Anya said, "Consoling? How consoling?"

Mac lay there, the closed book on his belly like a holy hot-water bottle. He said, "I can't say I know *how*."

Anya said, *"What's* consoling? I don't think it's meant to be. It's—"

Mac said, "His affection for me is consoling."

Anya said, "What? Whose affection?"

Mac turned the spine so he could read it, and said, "Cervantes."

Anya said, "You lunk!"

But in a strange way it was settling—his slow belief in the magic of great works. She found out in a later conversation that he actually did get the basic point, and she conceded that there was a charm in Cervantes' virile elegance that could be called affection for the reader. But she was still annoyed at Mac's belief in acquiring virtue by bathing in the rays of the Harvard five-foot shelf.

But consolation? Did he need consolation? What for? Had *she* ever been consoled? Why wasn't she his consolation? Had Mac believed in chivalry and heroism, realized it was absurd, and, therefore, read Cervantes privately, with shared resignation? Was shared resignation consolation?

Mac also told her that he was reading his list of books partly on her account, to catch up on her line of work. This notion made her nervous—as if he thought he was casting some slow possessive spell over her thought. She was, therefore, prompted to make ingenious perverse arguments to him about what he read. He didn't take them seriously—he listened and then shook them off, saying, in effect, that's not the part that interests me.

The great difference between Mac and her, she decided, was that she regarded Cervantes, Fielding, Tolstoy, and Melville (Mac's four month-long spring projects) in retrospect, as builders of steps that led up to her own view of the world from above. But Mac was more like someone *in* these books—Don Quixote, Tom Jones, Pierre, and Ishmael—as they *started out* on their adventures. Mac had an anxious, sentimental freshness that made it easy for her to imagine him wandering blindly into the contrivances of these novels and getting hit on the head with the difficulties the author had in hiding around the bend.

Anya wondered at times how Mac could possibly read about these characters. She thought it must be like a child reading *Tom Sawyer*, *Huck Finn*, or *Penrod*.

There was one argument they had (among the many that they fitted in during that tiring spring) in which she liked the part he took. She couldn't remember how it began, but she remembered that he suddenly burst out at her, "You believe in the hierarchy. You really believe that lawyers and doctors and professors—professors of certain things—are *it*. And the people who have taste. I may have some old-fashioned superstitions, but this is one of yours."

She said airily, "I don't know—I suppose I would say the people on that list *are* smarter."

Mac was waiting for her. "Bullshit. What's smarter? Even I could give them tests they'd flunk. You say someone's smart because they're solving problems that interest you. I say someone's smart when he solves problems that interest *me*. I'll tell you another thing—there're an awful lot of uncertified smart people wandering around thinking up smart things that make dumb people rich. My father was right about his work for GE." Mac said in an ugly way, "General *Electric*. He knows more about electricity than any of the goons running the company. He knows as much as most of their engineers. He makes a living, but no one would think of him as elite. Even he goes around saying 'sir' to the company officers when he's explaining what the hell it is the company is really doing. 'Smarter' isn't what makes you elite. And it's not moral worth. That's not even worth bringing up. And it's not making beautiful things. I could show you a boatbuilder in Labrador—no. Better yet. The man who built that barn in Iowa. You tell me the thing I don't get in *Don Quixote*. I'll tell you what you don't get about that barn."

Anya shrugged and said, "Sure. 'Pushpin's as good as poetry.' There's no way to answer that argument."

Mac was angry, but, she guessed, not really as angry at her as angry in general.

Mac said, "It's laziness. It's inertia. We go on letting people who wear white shirts run the meetings. It's everyone's fault. My father knows how dumb they are, and he puts up with it . . ."

Anya didn't argue. She liked his being a furious democrat, insisting that everyone should be a perfect citizen. She even felt decadent and venal then as she teased this ardor into its other channel, her. She got a hint of what it would have been like to seduce John Brown, or Savonarola. Skimming the cream of innocent righteousness.

So at first it hurt her feelings when he accepted a summer job in Labrador. His old geologist buddy from the mining company wrote him, and Mac answered yes right away.

Anya kept on plugging away at finding work. Andrew landed a weekend in Des Moines. Anya got two weekends at a resort in Wisconsin and a week in a north shore dinner theater. She got an offer from a YWCA camp in Michigan which included running a drama workshop for the campers. She finally accepted it after she got another offer from a summer theater in East Tawas, Michigan. Friday night, Saturday matinée and evening. She promised the manager that Farquhar's *The Recruiting Officer* was bawdy, but not too bawdy.

The troupe would do their *Twelfth Night* in Des Moines, *The Recruiting Officer* in Wisconsin, an evening of French farces in the north shore dinner theater. Anya owed part of this to Annabelle—the owner mailed back all the material Anya had given him except the 8″ × 10″ glossies of Annabelle in a turn-of-the-century camisole, her freckled bust squeezed up into view, her waist cinched in, her hips sweetly exaggerated by the puff. Anya had done her part, too. The manager, like the manager in Michigan, but with a different hope, kept asking if the French farces were bawdy. Anya said, "Yes—but what I'd call them is naughty. Bawdy means someone is looking for action. Naughty suggests that, say, an otherwise proper lady is suddenly struck by an improper urge. More interesting for your kind of audience. More like their own lives, wouldn't you say? It suggests the kind of sophisticated evening you're giving them—tables for two, wine and candlelight . . ."

From then they'd go to the kids at the YWCA camp in Michigan and do *Twelfth Night* again. And then East Tawas.

By then Mac would be on his way back from his summer on ice (as Anya now thought of it). They planned to meet in Stratford, Ontario, and see the three plays being put on

119

AN AMERICAN ROMANCE

there. The idea of the Stratford season put the grundgy parts
of her own summer into relief. The Stratford Company was
putting on *Coriolanus, Henry VIII,* and *Love's Labours
Lost,* in the main theater. There was also *Three Sisters* put
on by the visiting Tyrone Guthrie troupe in the small
theater. It was a shining idea—a repertory company with
two or three actors of great stature visiting for a season, all
in a technically remarkable theater in the middle of nowhere, yet crowded all summer. People drove from all over
—Montreal, Chicago, New York. Anya wasn't envious of
the success—it had been carefully and intelligently earned.
It was the kind of success that was reassuring to Anya as
she spent time wheedling left-over free meals at the dinner
theater and wondering how the troupe would put up with
sleeping in tents at the YWCA camp.

* * *

Anya's first low point of the summer was the party Og
gave at his parents' house in Lake Forest while the troupe
was playing the dinner theater. The only redeeming notion
that came out of it was that she liked Og better—he was
slowly rising above his spoiled childhood friends and neighbors.

The run at the dinner theater itself wasn't bad. The audience was more alive than she'd dared to hope, though the
social and physical types were more or less what she'd
expected. Stocky men in bright plaid jackets, haw-hawing
at the comic turns—the lover hidden under the bed or
behind the chaise longue, the maid's breasts cupped from
behind by the young master's hands. Anya listened to the
wives in the ladies' room after the show. They took pleasure in saying *double-entendre, risqué.* Andrew reported
from the men's room that Annabelle was a hit—one man
sang, " 'She has freckles on her *but* she is nice.' "

But Anya preferred this older self-made crowd to Og's
friends—rich Midwest preppies, heirs to canned meat, steel,
spark plugs, and candy bars. They made a big thing about
getting stoned, although it had the same dreary boisterous
effect on them as getting drunk. It annoyed Anya at first—
she had to fend off one cocksure propositioner. Then it
made her sad. She and Andrew roamed around the house
deducing Og's parents' lives, but neither of them could

120

shake the depressing thought that this party could have been taking place four years earlier at a cast party for a college show they'd been in.

The YWCA camp was, surprisingly, a much happier experience. The large main lodge had a wonderful old-fashioned proscenium, decorated with scenes from fairy tales in a Maxfield Parrish style—androgynous princesses and princes, Rhenish castles, glass mountains, and sexless, but curiously sexy, elves sitting cutely on toadstools. At the bottom left of the proscenium was a picture of a girl in a camp uniform. The conceit was that the entire span of illustration was her dream.

The lodge was originally part of an elaborate hunting camp built by a Michigan lumber baron, an imitation of the Adirondack camps of the New York barons. Anya thought that Mac would have liked the carpentry and the quality of the wood.

The camp director, in a gesture of good will, invited all the people who had summer bungalows nearby to the Saturday evening show. These amiable quiet couples sat in the first row of folding chairs. In front of them the younger campers sat on the floor; half of them slumped off to sleep by the last act. Behind the main body of junior counselors, counselors, and campers, the kitchen staff stood, still in their kitchen whites, their faces and arms still pink from the steam of doing the washing up. Typecast as scullery maids. It struck Anya as medieval in exactly the same sentimental style of medievalness as the Maxfield Parrish illustrations—cloyingly sweet, sweeter than Anya would have thought it possible for her to swallow.

After the show, when all the campers had been mothered back to their cabins and platform tents, the counselors, camp director, and his guests drank toasts in fruit punch to the actors. The camp director, giddy with the success of the evening, raised his glass to Anya and Andrew who were standing together and said, "Well, here's to a really charming couple and the really wonderful time you've given us with your show." Andrew, always a trouper quick to catch a cue, slipped his arm around Anya's waist and gave her a wholesome squeeze and a proper public-matrimonial kiss on the side of her mouth.

Andrew then made a handsome speech back, while Anya hung on his arm. She bit her lip to keep from laughing, not because she feared offending the camp director, but because she didn't want to disturb Andrew's scene.

*　　*　　*

At the East Tawas Theater there was a second letter from Mac.

In his first letter he'd described the long twilights as the sun slid sidewise, disappearing for only an hour and a half. She'd written back, "Goethe said that no intelligent man can really look at a sunset for more than fifteen minutes. What do you do the other 23 hours and 45 minutes?"

Now he wrote back about the northern lights, the beginning of the meteor showers in August. He'd gone off with one geologist on a side trip almost to the northern tip of Labrador, on a parallel with the southern tip of Greenland. He wrote, "The two of us work apart mostly. The silence is wonderful. It's like being asleep with your senses awake.

"I go back to our campsite first and start to cook. He says he can smell the food up to two miles away. I believe him, because once I took a walk after supper and I smelled his pipe smoke from a mile or so off. Most of the time we sit together in a comfortable silence for an hour after supper. Sometimes he'll take me out to a rock face and we'll sit there and look at it, and then he'll talk a bit, and then we'll sit a bit, and he'll add a bit more. It's as though he's writing out loud, or as though I'm reading an outline of geology very slowly. We're both in very good moods, which makes it better than being at the base camp, where some of the men can't wait to go home.

"I don't mean I don't miss you. I do. But it's not painful, partly because everything is in such good order here.

"We go back to base camp (where I'll mail this) and out again together for another side trip depending on what we've come up with on this trip. That may mean I'm up here two or three days longer, but I can use the extra money to fly from Goose Bay to Montreal to Windsor and get to Stratford almost on schedule.

"I hope my senses stay as clear as they are now for when I see you. I don't even try to imagine it."

Anya was annoyed. He really *had* put himself on ice, while she'd been leading a real life. It was as though he'd gone into a monastery, while she'd had to contend with the world—fretful people, money, time. And now he was going to come back late.

After the East Tawas shows the group packed up to go home to Iowa and get ready for the fall. Anya packed her VW to head for Stratford, Ontario. Andrew came to say good-by through the driver's window. He said, "I have a feeling that if we asked you to come to Iowa for the year you'd say yes."

Anya said, "Yes."

Andrew said, "It'll be a lot better. Our own theater. Better audiences."

Anya said, "I said yes."

Andrew said, "What did I say? How has this happened?"

Anya said, "I'll be along as soon as I can. Labor Day."

As she drove into Canada she thought she recognized the part of herself that wanted to run the theater. It was the part of herself she'd admired and relied on long ago, the part that would always take a dare.

But she felt more dislocated than she ever had in college or New York. She supposed she'd been in retreat for the last year.

Mac wasn't at the hotel in Stratford. Anya changed the good seats for *Love's Labours Lost* for worse ones four days later when it came up again. A man in the line at the box office recognized her—he was on the faculty at the University of Chicago. She agreed to have a drink with him. She felt both amused and amusing as she told the story of her summer. She could see the man was considering what next. She was considering it herself, she couldn't tell if she was considering it seriously or simply enjoying considering it, when Henniker appeared beside their table.

Henniker said, "I saw you in your little show up on the north shore. You were really very amusing. I always said you had some talent along those lines—but I had no idea you could perform in public."

Anya was so taken by surprise that she didn't realize for a moment how slyly insulting Henniker meant to be. She thought he only meant to maintain his usual air of comic amusement.

She said, "Oh. Well. I'm glad you liked the show. I didn't think anyone from the university would go all the way out to the north shore to see it."

Henniker said, "Oh, I was staying in Lake Forest. Saying

my farewells. I'm off to New York. I'm on my way there now—to seek my fortune."

Anya said, "Does that mean you have a new job or a new girl friend?"

Henniker turned to the man Anya was sitting with and said, "You see what happens when they spend a summer on the stage. Even if it is quasi-Borsch Belt—I should say off-off-Borsch Belt. She used to be much less vulgar."

The man sitting with Anya apparently thought it was all in fun, and also must have seen Henniker around the University of Chicago. He said to Henniker, "Haven't we met?"

Henniker looked him up and down then said, "No."

Henniker said to Anya, "If you ever get to New York . . ."

He left the sentence trailing and walked away to join a handsome woman who was waiting for him by the cash register. They left.

The man with Anya said, "What a cocksucker."

But Anya was past thinking that. Henniker's appearance had only an odd side effect. It took away any interest she'd had in the man buying her drinks. Nothing against him personally—it was a revulsion against academics and *literati* on vacation, against this acting as though their languid knowingness transported their chat and drinks by some culture magic to the Left Bank or the Via Veneto.

Anya disengaged herself as politely as she could and took a long walk into the countryside. It was dusk when she turned around and completely dark in a few minutes. A cold summer fog drifted in and chilled her knees and fingers. She'd been expecting a long Midwest sunset, but she felt pleased with the fog and at peace with her tiredness. By a happy accident she'd landed in a state of mind and body that loosened the mesh of her spirit as if by a pilgrimage or fast, and made her feel both hungry and satisfied, energetic and passive.

The road she was on entered the town and was now bordered by streetlights, and neon signs, each light contained in a globe of fog. She was prepared to receive the plays she had come to see with a ghostly clarity she had been gathering—not just during the past summer, she realized with surprise, but for a long time, a longer time even than the way she now was. There was a susceptibility

to theater that ran back farther into her past than she could
remember, the only connection still alive, it now seemed to
her, to her first serious wishes.

*   *   *

At six thirty the next morning Anya woke up. The white
hotel room was dim. The fog still held off the sun. The
white enamel paint on the iron bedstead, the dresser mirror,
and the windowpanes were all glazed with condensed fog.
Even the bedclothes were slightly moist. It was like being
by the sea.

There was a knock at the door. She opened it. It was
Mac. His eyes were bright blue, and he was terribly shy.

Anya had the pleasant feeling that neither of them fully
materialized until midday. At first it was as if everything
was the same density—his body, hers, the air, their low
voices, the lead-crystal light. It was all a gentle eddying of
their senses. She could barely distinguish between his touching her hair and her forehead, and making love, passing
into each other like vapor.

Anya and Mac spent five days in Stratford. They went
back to see *Henry VIII* a second time. It wasn't a coherent
play, but there were brilliant scenes. She and Mac had
both been stunned by the interrogation of Catherine of
Aragon. Anya and Mac were high in the balcony and
looked down on Catherine seated in the middle of the stage
while the two ecclesiastical prosecutors revolved around her
in opposite directions, their long trains sweeping behind
them, rustling sideways in wide arcs as the men turned, and
then slithering over each other like silk snakes as the two
men crossed in front of Catherine.

The man playing Cardinal Wolsey, who appeared so
smoothly villainous and flickering with purpose in his
ascendancy, moved Anya even more in his fall. Anya had
from time to time wondered how an actor should deal with
the slight embarrassment of having a hallowed speech to
speak, a speech whose every fifth line had been plucked to
serve as a book title, or to ornament a book review, lecture,
or even a politician's campaign speech.

She had forgotten that Cardinal Wolsey's famous last
soliloquy followed immediately a hotly argued scene in
which he was stripped of his powers. Suffolk and Norfolk

take pleasure in announcing his fall to him. A fast bickering scene. Norfolk exits saying, "So fare you well, my little good Lord Cardinal."

Wolsey, still rankling, still repugnant to the audience, says after him, "So farewell to the little good you bear me." And then in an abrupt silence the actor playing Wolsey let his courtly, snarling posture melt into the empty black floor. His lips, his shoulders, his elbows, his hand holding the upper skirt of his robe, the robe itself, all moved a half-inch down.

The circle of the audience's attention, to which Anya could pay her own attention this second time, had been held away by the flash of the quarrel. Now she felt it tighten around Wolsey. The audience was part puzzled, part alarmed, but eager to feel his well-deserved pain. Before this tightening of attention around his shrunken presence was complete, Wolsey said, "Farewell. A long farewell, to all my greatness."

Then he seemed to feel the swelling up of the huge black silence, but only indistinctly. He turned his head to one side, as though to sense the darkness better. Anya was sure the gesture was a suggestion, a representation that a man in defeat would hope that there might be an audience beyond his contemporary world. So the rest of Wolsey's essay, spoken smally and carefully, seemed to be addressed to his hope of a civilized posterity.

> "I have ventured
> Like little wanton boys that swim on bladders
> This many summers in a sea of glory;
> But far beyond my depth: my high-blown pride
> At length broke under me, and now has left me
> Weary and old with service, to the mercy
> Of a rude stream that must for ever hide me."

There was more speculation than despair in the last thought—perhaps to fail and then to die would be to sink forever out of sight. Perhaps. The darkness gathering about him might be only darkness.

And then his friend Cromwell enters and there is an immediate posterity to address, to teach to survive, perhaps even to save. Wolsey sat on one edge of the apron stage, his pale face clear against its black mat surface. Cromwell stood in shadow at the opposite side so that Wolsey's words were spoken intimately across the whole empty space in which the fiercer action had been played.

At the very end Anya felt it was the insistence on the spoken name "Cromwell," and again "Cromwell," that made them a sudden burst of spoken thought, that saved the famous lines from being sonorous.

> "Had I but served my God with half the zeal
> I serv'd my king, he would not in mine age
> Have left me naked to mine enemies."

The couplet that followed to mark the end of the scene, which was shared between Cromwell and Wolsey, was audible but thrown away.

Anya was so struck by the scene that she forgave the last act, which was mostly propaganda about what a great reign Queen Elizabeth was going to have, amusingly enough orchestrated by the director with processions, fanfares, and enormous and rather beautiful heraldic flags flapped about by extras.

The weather had cleared. Mac and Anya went for a walk and then lay on their backs in a grassy field to watch for meteors. Anya thought she should tell Mac that she'd decided to join the theater in Iowa. She had learned—no, not learned, confirmed her hopes in so many ways. The texts she had read, jiggled about at her own pace, had come back to her whole—released floods that swept up her scattered textual expectations. The play was the gathering of energy into one period of time. Once that time started to move from the lighted stage into the darkness it had to keep moving—punctuated by words, silences, movements, as a music-box cylinder is studded with notes and rests or as sunlight is scattered by the atoms of the earth into colors, but the first and last discipline remained to fit text and invention, each word, each breath and motion, to its proper place against the roll of time.

She had thought she might be confirmed here in this outlandish place in her choice to go to Iowa, another outland, but she hadn't thought it would be a confirmation that stirred such old and primary notions.

But there was the problem of Mac. *Her* romance was with her own hope, and *his* seemed to be with her. She had started with him as a quick infatuation—and yet it still balanced her now. He fitted in so well it surprised her. He'd been as easy as the weather since he arrived. She even looked forward to his plan to go camping for four days by a lake he'd found on his map of Ontario. To rest. To sun herself in his attentions. To be dazed and undisturbed. But she felt for the first time the thorn of a preliminary conscience (as opposed to subsequent shame).

CHAPTER

||||||||||||||||||||||||||||||||||||

7

She told Mac she was moving to Iowa while they were hiking in to the little rockbound lake he'd picked for the end of their vacation. It was a four-mile walk from the road where they'd left the VW, a mile of it down a dry stream bed Mac had spotted on his topographical map.

He didn't seem as surprised as she'd expected. In fact the whole idea seemed to sink into him without a ripple.

She said, "Maybe I can lend you my car and you can come every weekend. It's under four hours."

Mac said, "We can talk about that when we drive back to Chicago."

So for three days she satisfied herself. It was warm enough by day so that she wore nothing but her sneakers. Mac got up at dawn to fish and came back by midmorning to swim with her. She thought their breezing around naked would take the edge off their desire, but their solitude sharpened it in odd ways. Mac fell in with her elaborations —the two of them lying coupled but still at noon on a warm shelf of granite. They were not able to move without some pain from the rough surface. They would lie there glowing with heat, their eyesight darkened by the sun until all they could see was the red-blackness of their eyelids, until all their sensations became as distinct and magnified as their first trickles of sweat.

They would either clamber up and run back to their bedrolls under the tent flap, or else they would try to move spiderwise, still joined, their eight arms and legs inching them toward a moss carpet farther up the bank.

But aside from her contrived pleasure, she was happy to have a holiday—the physical pleasures of a honeymoon. She found herself sleepy at sunset and deeply awake at sunrise. Mac would make tea, warm a fishcake and a piece of bannock for her, and then he'd wander off with his fly rod. Anya loved this little breakfast, which she ate with her legs still in her sleeping bag, watching the mist come off the lake, reading or writing in her notebook until the sun was high. She even took pleasure in looking up from her book to watch Mac fishing. She was surprised at her patient restfulness. She thought it might be that Mac's patience was contagious.

Mac's fishing was not at all as she'd imagined it. She had thought of it as one more variation of hot-blooded slaughter, the brawny hunter sloshing in for the kill with barbed steel. She discovered it was instead a long, blind connivance. It was as though the black water were the mind of the fish into which Mac softly cast an artistic representation, a delicate Miró or Léger idea. The success depended on the insinuation of this illusion into the mood of the fish.

None of Mac's flies, woolly bugs, or streamers would stand close inspection, but, as Mac pointed out, if any predator had to inspect his prey closely, he'd starve. Most of the eaters saw no more of what they ate than an exciting motion or a flash of color in a plausible place.

Anya said, "So much for realism."

She amused herself by thinking of the meals they made of these fish as the result of a perfect match of artist and audience.

During the time they spent by the lake, Anya discovered deeper layers of information about Mac. She thought at first it was his long summer in Labrador, or possibly the fact that he was dazed with pleasure by their daily routine that made the stories that she loosened from him thicker and richer to her taste than any of the things he'd told her before, from the time she'd sent him the questionnaire to the moment he'd left for the summer.

Then she thought it was because the place itself produced a slow upheaval in him, that the rock-bound pond and woods gently cracked open his topmost layers and allowed him to tell, and her to penetrate, what had been preserved in him.

For a short time he forgot that he was wary of her,

forgot her sharp edges—he seemed to think that she was as moved as he was by the place, that she was of the same substance as he so that she could seem to him to be part of himself remembering.

And yet when he told her about his first love affair with his cousin Mireille Gagnon, it was as though he were explaining himself to a spirit of Mireille grown older and more sympathetic. These conversations took place after supper as it slowly grew dark. They sat with their legs stuck in her sleeping bag, their backs propped up against their packs.

Mac started by telling her his feelings about Chicago. Chicago wasn't as strange to Mac as the University. Chicago was a company town. The rich folks' houses stretching out along the lake to the north. The railroads right in the town. The stockyards right in the town. The lakeshore was just the visitors' entrance. Back from the lake a half mile—beyond the visitors' area—flat square miles of dreary company houses slashed with interstates. Daley like a union leader—a squat dinosaur of the labor movement. Mac didn't despise him the way the University did. Daley reminded him of smaller labor leaders speaking to the GE workers, saying—just by their fireplug appearance—more pay in your pocket, remember when there wasn't any meat on the table, we're getting there, we're dealing you men in.

Irish on school boards, Italians on hospital boards, a few squares named after dead Polish sergeants. The way up. The old names were on the letterheads of companies and the art museum. They had to say Mr. Mayor. The union was there to stay. Couldn't lose now so long as the men acted like men. Men worked. Men got paid. Men were on the team. Undefeated, unscored on. The eternal tie. A company town. Mac felt that part of Chicago strongly, as if he were trying to stand in heavy surf. He hated it. It exhausted him. He couldn't talk about it.

He could only wonder how he ever thought that this big city wouldn't be the same as Troy, Rochester, Buffalo, Utica, Schenectady.

When he picked up his scholarship money he felt unemployed. That feeling made him laugh, but only because it would make his father laugh.

All the time Mac was in Chicago he dreamed of Canada as different, but he was afraid it wasn't. Just colder and cleaner. He still dreamed. In his loneliness he dreamed of his father teaching him to skate. Trailing his one-armed father in endless figure eights on the outdoor rink. Behind the goalie's cage, then chopping hard right over left, angling across center ice, into the corner behind the cage (a little bit afraid of the corner boards), behind the cage, and left over right. His father letting him catch up. Resting, looking up at the stars through the dark hole in the middle of the lights over center ice, his breath floating up.

The move to Schenectady—employment took his father off the ice. The company arranged everything. Immigration, the new house. Even the experimental artificial arm. Free.

Mac joined the Boy Scouts in Schenectady and started being in trouble. In a pup tent with two other boys. Scaring each other. "Hey, what was that?" A werewolf. A crazy person. A space monster. A robot. "MacKenzie wouldn't be scared of that. His father's part robot." Why hadn't he hit him then? The two boys giggled over the joke. Until they giggled—a few seconds—he'd thought it was an interesting remark. Then he said, "You little fairies." He should have hit them both. He dragged his bedroll out of the tent.

His bare feet got wet and never got warm. In the morning one of the older boys asked, "Why'd you sleep out, MacKenzie?" It popped into his head, "Cause these two suck each other's cocks." Laughter. Gathering of older boys. "Hey, listen to this." Once more.

The scoutmaster heard. Took him aside. Long preamble —rumbling on solemnly about it being okay to tell some things to a grownup—it wasn't squealing. Mac, for some reason, waited until the man finished. Then he said it was just something he'd made up. The scoutmaster blew his top. Filthy, filthy thing to say. Sent him home. Mac explained the injustice to his father. "They made fun of you. Said you were part robot."

His father was puzzled for a while. Failed to see the insult. The insult had been in the giggle. Mac couldn't explain.

Mac's father: "It would have been better to knock him down. You're getting to be like some New York kid with that filth. Were you scared of him?" Mac was shamed.

Later, his father said he was sorry that he'd said anything about Mac being scared. Okay.

But then there was still so much that Mac couldn't say

—he had just blurted out "suck each other's cocks" as a variation of "cocksucker," the wrong verbal form slipping out of him before he could catch it, his attention distracted by the variation. His father's artificial arm did pain Mac—perhaps disgusted him, not in itself, but because it ,was an intrusion. It was hooked into his father's nervous system, and Mac worried in a way that the arm might control his father rather than his father control the arm. And who *owned* it? If the union went out on strike, could his father walk out too? And the word *experimental* was alarming. It was like an American horror movie.

Things had seemed so natural when they were skating together, his father's sleeve pinned back around his elbow, the cuff flattening in the wind of his father's speed. Mac remembered that when his father hugged his mother then he'd use both arms, his good one and his stump—but now only the good one. That struck Mac as highly indicative, like a vampire not casting a shadow.

Mac said he was only happy, from the time he was twelve till he was eighteen, when he was playing hockey or spending summers in the north woods in Quebec at Lac Gros Caillou. His mother took his family up to the Gagnon family camp there while his father stayed on in Schenectady.

Anya asked if that was when he took up with Mireille Gagnon.

Mac said no, the army came first.

Mac thought he would like the army. His father recalled his own Canadian Army days with fondness. It was during World War II that he'd lost his arm, but he still thought of the men he'd been with as wonderful. Mac took his advice and didn't get a deferment when the U.S. Army drafted him after high school. He would become a citizen after serving. His father thought that would be a good idea.

Mac liked the army at first.

He was bored but happy. There was no thought of war. The favored enlisted men were the athletes, so Mac played linebacker on the regional football team.

He hurt his hand playing football. The coach asked him not to go on sick call with it or they might not let him play.

To open the breech of his M-1 he had to use his thumb. The correct way was to slide the bolt back with the little-finger edge of the hand, the fingers extended and joined.

The sergeant drilling the platoon noticed this. He gave Mac the order, "Inspection Arms." When Mac used his thumb, the sergeant tapped Mac's hand with his swagger stick.

Mac said, "Don't do that, my—"

The sergeant said, "You don't talk to me. I talk to you." He repeated the order. "Inspection Arms."

Mac used his thumb again. The sergeant tapped him on the hand again. Mac opened his mouth. The sergeant raised his swagger stick.

The sergeant said, "Ah! Ah!" as though telling a dog not to move, twitching the stick on each sound.

Mac said, "Look, Sergeant—" and stuck out his hand.

The sergeant hit it with his swagger stick.

Mac dropped his rifle and hit him. He couldn't remember the pain in his hand. He felt it in his shoulder—a little satisfying beam of pain. The sergeant fell down. Mac picked the rifle up. The sergeant crabbed away on all fours, belly up. He got up and kept backing away. Mac went to the orderly room and reported to the first sergeant. The first sergeant called the C.O. and the C.O. called the battalion commander. Mac got locked up.

An X-ray revealed that his little finger was broken. The officer who was to defend him at the court-martial said, "Your *pinkie,* for Chrissake. I'd feel better if it was your arm up to the elbow."

Mac felt like a miniature fool.

But the JAG officer and a friend of his got Mac off. Mac was relieved and grateful, because he realized that he'd been dangerously stupid—not only in hitting the sergeant but in his notion of what he would have said in his own defense. He also realized during his days in the stockade that his bad temper was a worse problem than he'd ever thought before—again, not so much because it flared up so that he hit the sergeant, but because it had isolated him afterwards in a long state of shock. Without his two lawyers, he would have had no good sense at all, would have reveled in having no good sense.

He was tempted by the dazzling white rage that beckoned to him like an arctic desert, a vast interior space that he would have entered with crazy joy. What terrified him later was that the mysterious and alluring white rage was a space in himself that was not himself—if he'd entered it he would have been transformed, he would have lost all sense of direction, his sense of where the paths were that led back to other people.

As it turned out, he explained to Anya, he'd had a solitary time in the army even after he was out of trouble. He'd been kept on in a do-nothing job so he could play sports—he regretted that he never rose above corporal. He spent a lot of time reading in the post library. He read in a daze. Later he realized that the reason he didn't remember much of what he read was because he had no purpose, and therefore he was entirely unreflective. He read as an anesthetic. His attempts to study any subject failed because his concentration was always corroded by boredom. The only things that stuck in his mind were odd bits of military history and a self-study course in map reading, a great deal of which he knew already.

In the spring of his second year—three months before he got out of the army—he was offered a hockey scholarship at Cornell. He got a three-day pass and visited Ithaca, N.Y. He was worried, because his failure to educate himself at the post library had undermined his belief, never very strong in the first place, in his passable high-school grades and aptitude tests. He also feared that he would be treated in college as he had been in the army. A permanent jock corporal. He had to be reassured by the hockey coach (whom he later grew to like) that he wouldn't have to play football, in fact would be discouraged from playing football.

However, Mac was most worried by the thought that two years in the army had grown a mold on his brain. Or, possibly, that by not going crazy in the stockade, he'd made himself dumb.

When he got out of the army he'd said he would go to Cornell, but he was still considering playing junior hockey in Canada if he couldn't read and understand the basic college text in geology before college started. He went up to Lac Gros Caillou for the month of August to take this self-imposed test. Also to go fishing and shed his corruption.

(At last, Anya thought, we're getting to the mystery woman. But at the same time she was touched by the picture of Mac dragging himself away to the deep woods like a wounded bear.)

As soon as he got to the camp he felt wonderful. At the

big dinner in the lodge with the various Gagnon relatives, he noticed immediately how pretty Mireille Gagnon had become, but he thought little of it. She'd been fourteen when he'd seen her last, now she was seventeen, almost eighteen.

He'd planned to go immediately to the far end of the lake and camp in the lean-to there. But he lingered a few days. He liked the swarm of small children, the rituals of family life, especially after the routines of the army.

He felt as if he'd waked up from a long dull dream.

The sun was still up at nine at night. The children went swimming. Mac went along. They played king-of-the-mountain on the raft moored twenty yards out from the little canoe dock. Mireille swam neatly around the raft, encouraging the children to throw Mac off. She dove under the raft and reached up with her fingers to pinch Mac's foot through a gap in the planking. She finally climbed up on the raft and rested, dangling her bathing cap, still encouraging the children to pull Mac off. She filled her bathing cap with water and doused Mac. When he moved to push her off, she said she couldn't get her hair wet. When he turned away, she jumped on his back. He felt the stretched elastic of her bathing suit, and then the heat of her cunt against his spine.

He was toppled into the water and into a new fierce dream.

The next morning before breakfast he loaded a canoe and fled to the other end of the lake.

The new feverish dream did not obliterate Mac's delight in where he was. He caught small lake trout, read his book, climbed the low surrounding hills at night to watch for the northern lights—they came, not in their full colors, but in their pale green version, like the green flickering of a chain pickerel seen in the bright water between dark rocks.

The weather was bright, all his senses were clear, all the life in the woods and the lake seemed to him as quick and musical as the dance of light on water. Most of the time he was as happy as he'd ever been. But three or four times a day he felt the pull of his new trouble. It jerked his attention sharply, making his body twist.

There was a rough trail around the lake, and once a day he jogged it. It joined the dirt road that linked the camp to the nearest town, ran along that road for a quarter-mile on the far side of the lodge and cabins, then left the road and re-entered the woods, and followed the lake shore back to his lean-to. When he reached the dirt-road section he slowed down and hoped to catch a glimpse of Mireille in the clearing where the main lodge was. He couldn't see the cabins, the laundry house, or the canoe rack.

He decided to fish the section of the lake where the main camp was. The lake was shaped like an askew hourglass. He couldn't see the camp from his canoe until he got to the narrows joining the two sections.

When he got to the narrows, he saw Mireille waterskiing behind the one old motorboat his uncles owned. That meant fishing was out, so he paddled purposefully along the bank as though he were on his way back to the main camp. Mireille swung by him several times. When he got near the dock she let go of the tow rope, glided abreast of him, and slowly sank, smiling at him. He was charmed.

She took the skis off and asked if he would be at his lean-to after supper. He nodded dumbly.

All during the long sunset he thought of her face bobbing beside the canoe. A dark ivory oval. Her hair and eyebrows dark, shining, shedding water like the pelt of a mink. He thought of her in alternating pulses: as a sleek, compact water animal, and then as an embodiment of the first French women in Canada, shiploads of strange pious women, their thin pale limbs weighed down by stiff wool habits, surviving on cod, daily sacrament, and eels. The combination of high-strung piety and coarse, even savage, common sense had always put Mac in awe. It was not just the combination—which could be said to occur among the Scots (though their piety was played on lower notes, with less melting sweetness)—it was the speed of the shift between the two.

When Mac saw Mireille's white blouse at the narrows, and, straining, heard the faint brush of her paddle strokes across the flat water, he felt as though each draw of her paddle washed him with a scalding liquid.

As she drew near he really believed that he would be a brute if he allowed her to land.

Mireille stopped paddling and let her canoe glide toward the bank where his canoe was pulled up. Mac waded into the water up to his waist and caught the prow of Mireille's canoe on his chest.

(Anya was touched by this detail too. The picture she formed of Mac's embracing the prow of the canoe summed up for her what was raw and dark in Mac, turned against himself, she imagined, by what she least understood about him, his stony Scottish Catholicism. And yet, like his father, he was drawn to the softer, hotter company of one of the Gagnon girls, as though hypnotized by the flame and sweet smell of a thick beeswax candle in the stone vault of his will to be good.)

Mac said, "This isn't a good idea. *Il vaut mieux que tu rentres.*"

Mireille laughed at him at first, thought he was teasing, and so teased him back, said he was like a bear. But when he persisted in turning her away she got mad, said that he imagined himself to have an irresistible splendor that now struck her as ridiculous. . . . All this in a rattle of French that Mac had to concentrate to follow.

She drifted away and Mac climbed back onto shore. Mireille listened a moment to the water running out of his clothes. She said, *"Et maintenant t'as l'air d'une vache qui pisse."*

The next day it clouded up and began to blow. He thought he would paddle back to the main camp and take a hot bath in the laundry room, the only place where there was a water heater except for the kitchen.

It began to rain and the water ran up his arms as he paddled, mingling with his sweat as he worked to keep the canoe on course against the wind. He began to think of Mireille swimming under water, himself reaching out and feeling her moving through his hands.

When he got to camp he didn't stop. He walked out the dirt road to the nearest town and thumbed a ride on the hard-top to the next town. He waited until the druggist was alone and asked him for *"une prophylactique."* The man gave him a toothbrush. Mac finally had to use the slang word, *une capote.* The druggist sold him a dozen of the most expensive.

Mac was struck by how often he got in trouble in French, for all his good will. He remembered the time he'd

gone to confession at a church where the priest insisted on
speaking only French. None of the easy euphemisms in
English were available. Such as: "Bless me Father for I
have sinned. I accuse myself of impure thoughts, and—
uh—impure deeds."

"The impure deeds were by yourself?"

"Yes, Father."

"How many times?" As easy as that.

In French Mac hadn't known any phrase but *"Je me suis
tapé la queue, mon père."*—I beat off, Father.

"Tu peux te confesser en anglais, mon fils."—You may
confess in English, my son.

Both incidents slid together and reminded him that what
he knew was not French, but the half-forgotten small-town
French-Canadian of an eleven-year-old boy. All he could
really understand was the radio broadcast of a hockey
match. He spoke American, not English; he could understand the Mass, not real Latin. He thought it was no wonder he found it hard to keep his feelings from breaking
loose. All he had was a wordless sense of how they worked.

Mac got a ride back to the dirt road and started walking.

He remembered his thirteen-year-old sense of taboo
about the woods. On a fishing trip with his father, a friend
of his father's, and the guide, Albert Meilleur. Albert
started the fire with a cup of gasoline. Mac was shocked.
Sitting by the fire at night, the men passed around a bottle
of whiskey. Albert got up, stooped, ass to the fire, and
farted. A faint puff of blue flame. They all laughed. The
fire died down and they watched the northern lights. His
father's friend from Schenectady said to his father, "Jesus,
Walt. They can't do that at GE." More shock at the breaking of taboo.

Mac thought he would now have a worse moment than
Albert farting into the fire: Mireille watching the northern
lights while he tore open the tinfoil envelope of his pre-
lube Lam-skin.

(Anya thought, Inside every muscle-bound jock there is
a thin poet wildly signaling to be let out. She didn't say
anything.)

Mac moved the envelopes from his back pants pocket to
his front shirt pocket so he couldn't feel them. He was still
more aware of them than of the wind and the huge clear-

ing sky. Later he couldn't think of the road, the woods, the camp, the lake, or Mireille without thinking of that walk —his senses swollen and clumsy, his urgency seeming to him a foolish change in himself, too large and unbalanced to stop. A part of his feelings—his timidity, his good sense, his desire for peace and order—tried to ally itself with the wind blowing in his face and the hard light from the clearing sky, but there was another part of his feelings that rolled him dizzily forward, stopping his thoughts, exhilarating his senses until what they received seemed unreal, seemed to unweight him, gave him a giddy feeling of removal from his past life, from consequences, from everything except his present movement through the woods in a ball of light and wind.

Of course the funny thing was that Mireille really had given up on him, meant to avoid him, had felt confused, insulted and, for all her adroit airs, frightened. He learned all this somewhat later. What he saw when he got back near the camp was Mireille and her sister crossing the dirt road with empty pails. Mireille had a pimple on her right cheek. She turned her head to hide it. Mac slowed down, Mireille slowed down, they half-turned to face each other but kept walking—Mireille following her sister toward the big raspberry patch, Mac stepping out briskly toward the camp.

A blank in his memory. How had he got to the bathhouse? He must have rested for a while. He went to the kitchen to get bacon and eggs to take to the lean-to. Packed his canoe. He thought he should shave. His feet were sore, he went barefoot to the bathhouse.

The bathhouse had an enormous bathtub with claw feet —hauled in on a sledge one winter, along with the kerosene water heater. The concrete double sink for washing clothes had been poured on the spot. There was also an enamel wash basin because the women said the rough concrete snagged everything but blue jeans and work shirts. There was also a kerosene space heater which threw flickering rosettes of light on the ceiling. By fiddling with the wick the rosettes could be brought into focus. There were no windows, only a vent. There was a kerosene lamp on the wall in front of a shiny tin-can top which served as a reflector.

Mac had helped build the house three years before. It

still smelled of pinesap once it got warm and steamy. When the water heater, the space heater, and the lamp were all burning, the inside planking grew gummy and sweated. A heavy, yellow, still heat.

Mac lit everything and went back for his razor. The second walk to the bathhouse was completely clear to him. He suddenly became very alert even before he saw the laundry basket outside the door.

He brought in the basket. Mireille was running hot water into the concrete sink.

She was startled when he put the basket down. Put on an air of exasperation. *"O, c'est encore toi qui m'embête."*

He said, "That's my hot water."

She rattled along, *"O dis donc, je dois faire la lessive, c'est plus important quand même que ton bain. . . ."* It was clear though that she was enjoying arguing. He stamped around. "Oh for God's sake I've waited a week." She was enjoying his bad temper. He said, "And who heated up the water anyway?"

He turned on the faucet in the bathtub. She pulled the plug. He put it back in. She went back to the sink and elaborately busied herself, hummed for a minute, pretended not to notice him. He laid out his shaving kit in front of the mirror. She tried to sneak back to pull the plug while his back was turned. He caught her by the arm. She laughed.

"Vas-y—prends ton bain. Ça me fait rien."

But she began to hit him with one of the pillowcases stuffed with laundry. Mac half resisted, taking it as a ritual beating after which Mireille could resume flirting.

(Anya thought, Wrong again. She could easily imagine Mireille's nerves as Mireille pummeled Mac, waiting impatiently for Mac to lead them out of childishness. But Anya also sympathized with Mac's dazed stupor, his blood rising to his skin.)

Mac couldn't remember how the next few minutes went. They began kissing. Mac was happy enough holding her by her stocky hips, feeling the thick wool of her long skirt on his palms, dreaming of what might happen. Mireille suddenly went to the door, stepped outside, looked around, came back inside, and hooked the door shut.

Her practicality was what allowed Mac's daze to unlock. He fell to his knees in gratitude, wrapped his arms around her legs while she turned off the bathwater. He touched the calluses just under her kneecap—calluses from the hours of kneeling on a wooden *prie-dieu* at the Catholic school she'd gone to before starting her nurse's training.

It was that detail of touch that caused the second part of the eruption of Mac's feelings.

Mireille became a saintly vessel of irresistible sin. At the time Mac didn't think of that idea as confused.

After several minutes of his feverish reverence, during which he continued to kiss her arms, her knees, and feet—and Mireille unbuttoned her clothes—Mac's notion of what was going on changed once more. He began to think of himself as a quick mink as he hovered over her (she'd gathered the spilled laundry into a heap and sat down on it), his length springing through his shoulders and neck without his moving his planted forepaws as he darted his open mouth.

He hesitated for a moment—he'd heard the usual unpleasant talk in the army about eating pussy, he'd heard the New York-Canadian border jokes (How do those Canuck girls hold their likker?—By the ears)—but his sense of himself as an animal burned it off. It was like finding the cheek of a trout—the most delicate bite, the hard piece of cheek muscle to be pried off with the tongue and lips from the hollow of the trout's jawbone.

His own part was short. After he fumbled on the rubber and entered her, there was a brief astonished writhing and then his spine seemed to curl up like a hooked worm.

They met at night in the woods. Mac spent the days at his lean-to as he had before. After dark he would paddle to the narrows, pull his canoe up and walk along the trail to the main camp. Somewhere along the path he would meet Mireille. She wore her nightgown and bathrobe and sneakers, as though she'd just stepped out of her family's cabin to go to the outhouse. Mac brought his bedroll. They would find a pocket of warm air, usually in a hollow up the slope from the trail. It was like standing in a humid breath.

When they saw each other at the main camp, she behaved the way she had before, paying attention to him only occasionally in a childish, teasing way.

One night she told Mac that her mother had told her not to be so rude to Mac.

He finished the geology book, thought vaguely that he might as well go to college. He was still busy during the day—fishing at dawn, cooking, reading, working out. Visiting the main camp after lunch to help work on a shed being built by the wharf.

It was as though Mireille came to him under a spell which set limits on what she could feel. Later on, in his last two years in college, he came to recognize this arrangement as it was practiced by a few more sophisticated but less mysterious girls there, and he understood that he was a safe experiment. There was his surprise at a girl's interest in him, his dazed eagerness—the girl's certainty that he lived in such a way (only partly because he was a jock and had to be off jocking it up) that he would not be her slave, or her master, or even try to play a trick on her.

But at the time of Mireille it was entirely mysterious to him that she came to him, that she seemed to release herself in such a concentrated way.

Even later when he figured out that the limiting spell she seemed to be under was her own plan, he still continued to *feel* that the spell had been cast by the place itself, that their connection had been narrow in order to be intense, in order to give him a deep core-sample of the place—the circle of northern forest reflected in the water, birch, pine, aspen, and knobs of granite breaking through the pine needles, moss, and thin soil around the steep edges of the lake.

The first week in September Mac's father came up, and he and Mac and Albert Meilleur went farther north for three days. When they got back it was the day before the last big family meal. Mac helped board the cabins up. Then everyone went out to pick the last berries. There were bear tracks near the bushes, so they all stayed close together.

Mac watched Mireille. She was minding the small children. She didn't look at him, but he could tell she wasn't mad at him—in fact, pleasantly conscious of him. She was wearing a long gray skirt and a dark red shirt. Her hair was loose. She looked older. She played tag with the children, moving slowly in the middle of their scurrying.

When everyone took a rest from berry picking, she brought him a beer and sat down beside him. She told him she'd had a dream. In the dream she'd been playing on the float with the kids, pushing them off. The children started pointing at her. She looked down and saw that her legs were covered with sheets of blood. It didn't bother her—it didn't seem to be real blood. She said something to the children. They jumped in the water together and swam quickly to shore. She lay down on the float and whispered through the planks to Mac who was under it.

And then?

No, that was the end.

Mireille laughed. Mac leaned forward and hooked his elbows around his knees.

Mireille said, *"Tu as du chagrin, Mac?"* She pulled up a handful of orchard grass and dropped it on his hands. She said, *"Moi, j'ai pas de chagrin. Je suis contente."*

What made her so comfortable? The sun? The meandering family strung out around the raspberry bushes? The wind blowing far above the top of the hill, moving the clouds but not even the top branches of the trees? He felt her last feeling for him with a shock.

She looked around to see if anyone was watching—his eyes followed hers—she leaned toward him and kissed his forehead.

For an instant, he felt like her—imagined he had kissed her on the forehead and was feeling her surprise and pleasure. His hand began to shake.

He didn't feel sad, but he felt shocked by certainty—the certainty that she would drift away. But now they hovered in that place for an instant not themselves. Unfleshed and out of time.

It had been at the far end of the lake, years before, that he'd first been seized by that kind of disembodied joy—watching sunlight pour through the shallow water and be soaked up by the water-rounded stones settled across the bottom in layers of brown, gray, and white. A completely satisfying order—by no hand, for no purpose, but pulling his deepest wish out of him.

And here now with Mireille, he felt that her dark head, the jut of her shoulder, the ripe blur of color of the seed-tufted orchard grass, the stillness of the air, the slow turning and passing clouds in the pale windy sky—all were arranged for an instant so that his deepest wish was again exposed to him—tasteless, touchless, motionless—his senses not pushed away but, for a moment, gathered together at rest like the smooth stones in the pool of water and light.

It turned out he wasn't faithful to that end. The next spring at the end of the college hockey season he went to Montreal to see Mireille.

She wasn't glad to see him. Her mother was—and introduced him to all the neighbors with an air of displaying a suitor. Mireille had long work hours at the hospital. She went out with him only once, to the ballet. They sat far back in the auditorium, but were affected by the distant flashes of athletic, sexual movement. Mac thought it must have been that. They walked to his hotel in a spring snowfall, and Mireille motioned him up to his room with a move of her head. They made love. She now had a diaphragm.

They dozed and then woke up when someone in the next room turned on the television. Mac took Mireille home in a taxi and then walked back to his hotel. The snow was still falling, large wet flakes falling out of the opaque city sky into the area of the street lights, signs, and windows. The wet snow reminded Mac of his exhaustion. He was too tired to feel acutely unhappy. He kept stopping to rest against lampposts and walls.

He did not feel remorse, but he was convinced that he was being punished in two ways—by loss of strength and by being cut off from ordinary life.

Later, he saw the foolishness of this feeling of heroic punishment, but he didn't see it as funny. It was just another way he'd been wrong.

He recognized, however, that his feeling of having to regain his strength and serve out his exile had rendered him an incidental service. He had become dogged. He could exercise only three or four hours a day—after that he wasn't getting anywhere, so out of boredom he tried to penetrate the mysteries of the courses he was taking. He was too contrary to have his reading be an intellectual awakening visible to his instructors. He distrusted the way in which they and his intelligent classmates were able to digest theories provisionally and skeptically. But Mac acquired a crude sense of what was necessary academically.

He found that history and geology yielded most successfully to doggedness.

For the next three summers he didn't go to Quebec, he went instead to Labrador on a geological survey team.

The third summer he feared he was doing something harmful to himself. The vastness and emptiness no longer induced expansion in him. It seemed instead to move against his senses on all sides, like deep water, until it squeezed them into a ball. Sometimes doing tedious work in college he'd wished he could take a pill to know a subject; in Labrador he thought, I am the pill, compressed essence of Labrador.

The final weeks the mosquitoes were so bad they all wore head nets and gloves and elastic bands around their pants cuffs even sleeping inside the tents, which had their own netting. They put on layer after layer of bug dope.

The job over, he decided to go to Boston for a vacation. It was the first time in his life he'd wanted crowds.

He spent a couple of days wandering around town, paying too much money for a hotel room. As he walked in the late-summer city heat, even his fresh sweat still smelled of bug dope. He ended up in Cambridge where he wandered into a party that moved from the riverbank into a large apartment on Western Avenue where a dozen people flopped down for the night. Mac suddenly found his threshold of suspicion lowered. One of the guys who appeared to live in the apartment invited him to go sky diving. Mac said sure. The guy was a drummer in a rock band that had just lost a job. They all drove out to the town of Orange in their van. It turned out they were college students too, blowing their summer money. Rich kids with fancy hobbies and things—guitars, cameras, scuba gear. But their equipment and voluntary rags didn't put Mac off. He was glad to be caught up in their swirl.

Mac sweated out the last of the bug dope going up in the plane with them. He jumped off the static line—the air shot up his nostrils—one whiff of clear, cold fear, and then he floated down into the warmer air.

As easily as they'd swirled him up, they swirled away.

Mac tired of doing nothing. He took a job stripping old wallpaper. He worked all day along with two others. Two dollars an hour. The owner showed up and asked if one of them would spend the night. Sure. The next day it was just the owner and Mac working.

The owner turned out to be an associate professor just hired by Harvard. He was moving from California. He asked Mac to call him Stan. He asked Mac if he'd stay in the house and keep working while he flew to California and drove back with his family and furniture. And would Mac stay on and help them unload? Sure.

For Mac it was like watching birds. First one flock would swirl in, and swirl away, then another. Now Stan.

The weather was hot but pleasant. Mac worked happily. The house grew brighter as Mac painted. He washed the windows and pried open the paint-stuck sashes.

It pleased him to think that he was painting the scenery for years of a family's life.

Mac ate lunch by twelve thirty—the same food as breakfast at six thirty: canned fruit and a piece of cheese and a bottle of Poland Spring water. Then he knocked off during the heat of the day.

After the water, gas, electric, and phone companies showed up, he kept milk and beer and a box of cigars in the refrigerator, and made tea and scrambled eggs for breakfast. It was still too hot to cook lunch.

From one to three he sat on the front porch, read *Moby Dick* slowly, and watched people passing by.

Inside the house he was struck by the network of light—shafts of angled sunlight and reflections from the windows of other houses, and patches moving across the walls and ceiling cast by the windshields of passing cars.

(Anya recognized this mood. It was like her last days in the Ikon Films office, as she lazed alone looking out the window.)

Mac liked the feeling of time passing—a shallow fast sunlit stream over a clear sandy bottom.

Stan called up from California one afternoon to see if everything was hooked up. Stan said, "Annie wants to say a word." Stan's wife got on the phone—"Hi, Mac? This is terrific! How on earth did Stan ever *find* you? Well look, don't go away before we come, okay?"

She asked him what the colors were like, and what the street looked like, whether there were trees. Had he met the neighbors?

Mac finally told her he had to get off the phone to go close the windows—it was about to rain.

Annie thought that was terrific too—no rain all summer in California. "Well, we'll be along. You'll be there to let us in in a week?" Mac promised.

Two days later, when Mac was taking his midday break on the front porch, a girl riding by on a bicycle stopped. She recognized him from the Western Avenue apartment where she'd spent several nights.

She parked her bicycle and sat on the stoop.

The girl, whose name was Sara, seemed to him to be an example of the free-floating fertility. She chatted on— she'd been making a few bucks a day as a guinea pig in an experiment in hypnosis—"What a trip! The final bit was a free dream period. The best vacation I've ever had. I dreamed I lived in the sea, just swishing around."

When Mac started painting again, she asked if she could help. Another bird swooping in.

She spent the night. She laughed at the nest he'd made for himself—his bedroll on top of a pile of old curtains that were to be thrown out. She laughed at everything— Mac's earnest schedule, his being a good burgher sitting on the porch with his cigar.

She was short and stocky with sturdy legs, small ankles, and plump feet. Her skin was thick and loose. Mac could move her scalp two inches with his fingertips. When she lay on her side her cleavage started at her throat. She wasn't fat, just loose-skinned. Under her skin she was hard rubber.

She was monochrome—she had dirty blond hair and an even dirty-blond tan and light brown eyes.

She stayed for four days.

She found it amusing to disrupt the morning painting session by seducing him—it didn't take much, if he was up on the ladder she only had to brush her hair against his leg.

Or she'd bring him a glass of juice, take a swallow herself, and then squirt it into his mouth from hers.

It all seemed to be a joke for her—a pleasant joke—but it kept her strange to him, even shocking. The shock was in part at himself, how physically free he was, letting himself go on the front or back of her wide elastic body without any fear of hurting her, spurting out a string of seed into her damp flesh, each string a week of pale Labrador nights. It worked out that way—he'd spent seven weeks in Labrador. He noticed it because when she left she made a joke about being paid. At two dollars an hour for her painting it came to seventy dollars. She giggled over ten bucks a shot.

Mac was surprised both that he missed her cheerful company and also that he was glad to be alone. The house became his campsite again after he cleaned up the kitchen, hid Stan's money again in a can under the sink, hung his bedroll in the sun, finished painting the front hall.

The California family arrived tired but boisterous. The wife was exuberant and kind. "It's wonderful!" She hugged her husband. She flew upstairs and called to the teen-age daughter, "Honey, come look at *your* room."

They had a huge stationwagon—an International Harvester Travel-All—towing the biggest U-Haul Mac had ever seen, as big as a van. All the furniture—two beds, a table, various chairs and couches—was made of light-colored wood. The disassembled parts and bags of nuts and bolts were tagged. Navajo rugs. Two oil paintings by the wife— one of the foamy spread of a wave on a beach, the other a huge design of circles. There was also a red, yellow, and purple straw bird with a hardwood beak.

Mac was alarmed for their brightness. Amazed and curious. The husband and Mac went to pick up fourteen cartons of books that had been mailed fourth class and were being held at the post office. The husband approached the postal clerk holding up his right hand as though greeting Indians, his face and teeth shining.

Mac closed his eyes. Chatting, smiling, shining—the whole family would be done in by the sour people who worked at lousy jobs and could see that Stan didn't. Now that the carnival of Harvard summer school was over, and before the real students arrived, the mood on the streets was tougher.

And yet the husband—Stan ("Hey, c'm*on,* call me Stan")—must have had some strength and clarity of mind. He had a rank in civilization. Mac thought that he himself was a barbarian.

The wife ("Annie, for heaven's sake") asked him at lunch if he ever came to Boston. "You're our first Boston friend." Mac was by then used to her effusiveness. He'd never seen it before in a grown woman.

Mac said, yes, he came down to play hockey. He thought, It's like being a gladiator. And their house was a Scandinavian/Californian temple, one of the important calm cults toward the end of the empire.

Mac said, "I'm a barbarian."

Stan smiled, Annie leaned forward in her chair and put her elbows on the table, both showing they were interested in this kind of discourse.

What he meant was that if there hadn't been some early tic of feeling—between Stan and him? Annie on the phone? —he would have been part of the horde of dreary passers-by who resented this fragile, bright household. But having been looked at trustingly, warmed at the hearth, he felt like their tamed Goth.

There was a silence. Stan said, "It's interesting, it's a word you don't hear much anymore. I guess Englishmen use it."

"Not about themselves," Annie said.

"Oh, some angry young man from the north," Stan said, "with a kind of self-hating pride. Emphasizing a Yorkshire accent, taking the word out of the mouths of sleek Londoners."

Annie said, "But what did *you* mean?" Mac realized Annie was sweetly drunk on three glasses of white wine.

The daughter said, "You don't always have to mean things." A little bit of daughterly sourness.

Stan said, "Of course not."

Annie said, looking at Mac, "But I think he does." Her eyes large. "I think you mean—" She shrugged slowly and then smiled as though she knew something. She looked slightly foolish but handsome.

The daughter said, "It comes from the way the northern tribes sounded to the Greeks. The Greeks thought they were saying bar-bar-bar."

Mac said, "Is that right?"

Stan said, "Yes."

Mac said, "What I mean is that my mind seems to me to be just one more *thing* in the world. I think civilized people think of their mind as something that can contain the world. I'd like to be able to do that, to think calmly about the world. But the only time I'm calm is when I'm doing something."

Stan said, "But I could tell right off I could trust you. That you like to make things. That you worry about what's fair, what's decent . . ."

Mac said, "That's all superstition. Once I started working in this house I felt good. I had used up all the credits from having worked in Labrador. I had to find a safe place to earn some more credits. I don't mean money."

(Anya thought that here again there was a faint resemblance between Mac and her. He'd been a good gray lady too.)

Stan, Annie, and Mac ended up talking all afternoon. What struck Mac finally was that this was the first time he'd ever tried to talk about himself. The safe credit that he'd earned by working in the house he spent lavishly in talk—more lavishly than in fucking Sara.

Mac had the sensation that he could be completely abandoned in what he said—that Stan's sympathy and, more important, authority and learning all made a vast net into which he could let himself fall again and again.

Now—talking to Anya under the tent fly—Mac couldn't remember exactly what it was that he'd said to Stan about himself. He remembered only how he'd felt, the sensation of being unburdened, of being weightless at the end.

Anya asked him, "Are you sure that's the only time you told anyone about yourself? Wasn't going to confession like that?"

Mac said, "No. Confession wasn't like that. And probably it shouldn't be. The priest isn't someone you want to have consider you personally. At least I never did. I just wanted to scrape my sins off into a common pile. That afternoon was the only time, until now. And what I'm telling you is different. I'm letting you in. Then I was really throwing myself head first. Stan was the first teacher who had the kind of knowledge I was supposed to be getting in college whom I didn't dislike. I'd spent most of my time in lectures really pissed off. The whole idea of someone presuming to sum up people's experiences—my life being a fraction of all that—made me mad. But with Stan, I was glad he had all this secondhand knowledge. I remember saying to him, 'I don't want anyone to try to explain why things are the way they are. I just want someone to show me *how* to do things right.' And Stan said, 'That's interesting. Hemingway said something like that.' And I felt a great relief. Ordinarily I would have thought I was being put in my place. Oh, the Hemingway syndrome, or complex, or fallacy. But then I thought it was pleasant that Stan was able to keep track. That he had a big collection of all those specimens."

Anya thought that her old desire to be appreciated as a classic form, particularly by Tassie's Uncle Timmy, had been like that.

She said, "Are you sure you didn't have a crush on the wife?"

Mac said, "No. In fact it made me uneasy—she was a little corny the way she liked to break into the conversation physically. She'd say, 'Oh, I know!' and squeeze whatever part of you was at hand."

Anya said, "Feeling uneasy at being squeezed isn't inconsistent with having a crush."

Mac said, "I feel ungrateful even saying that . . . I'll tell you what I felt for the first time with them—that there is a single geography to everyone's experience. I don't just mean a topography, something you can follow with a flat map. But a globe. I had a feeling Stan was saying it's all round—that no matter how angry you got or how uneasy, you don't shoot off in a straight line into nothing. If you just keep on, you come back."

Anya said, "Well yes, we all die." She was sorry she said it, but it didn't seem to matter.

Mac said, "Another feeling I got was that what people announce as knowledge is about as accurate as sixteenth-century maps."

Anya saw a certain pathos in Mac's metaphor, in his effort to reduce the problem of what he didn't know to the difficulties of navigation, to a semi-intellectual skill he was good at.

She also felt sympathetic relief that for that moment in his life Mac had been encouraged by another person. She had been as solitary, but she'd known how to nourish herself on other people to keep from being lonely.

She had used to think that she was a lot smarter than

Mac. Now she thought she was just smarter, and she wasn't sure what advantage this gave her. However, she was, on the whole, reassured by his story. Not just because she now knew his sensuality ran deeper into his imagination than she'd thought—deeper than her own (in fact in her it was the other way around; imagination nurtured sensuality)—but also because she now knew he would be able to understand what she planned to do in Iowa. This was important because she guessed he would follow her there.

* * *

Their last night it began to rain. In the morning it was still pouring. Mac irritated her by accepting it with satisfaction, as if he liked the idea of paying for his pleasure.

Mac got into one of his let's-do-it-right fits. He asked her if she had the car key. He told her to be sure to wear wool socks for the walk out. She knew he was going to add, "Wool keeps you warm even when it's wet."

He also said, "I hope the car starts."

She said, "Why shouldn't it?"

He said, "The points may get wet."

Anya thought that a needlessly irritating notion.

Mac waterproofed her boots, pointing out that the dry stream bed they'd come in on was not going to be dry on the trip back.

She tried to annoy him by lingering in the tent to smoke a joint after breakfast. But he sat with her patiently. Anya thought that he seemed to be able to store up pleasure, he had a whole camel's hump of it, whereas she was herself again, a shrew who needed three times her own weight in pleasure every day.

She said, "Let's stay in a motel tonight. Eat a lot of greasy cheeseburgers and take a hot shower. Put quarters in the bed and vibrate."

Mac nodded. He didn't want to talk about it until they'd left the lake.

Anya thought she wasn't sure what it was that attracted her to him—whether she liked his carefulness, patience, stubbornness, as a counterweight, or whether she liked the possibility of transforming him, of teasing him into different displays of energy, even making him yield in some way.

153

She thought that perhaps what she liked was the elastic tugging between her two notions.

There was one comfortable thought. She wasn't afraid to ask him to do anything—he wouldn't ever think of blaming her for anything she asked for. He imagined that he decided everything in his life.

* * *

Mac hadn't intended to consider the problem of Anya's move to Iowa while he was hiking out from the lake. But as they climbed the stream bed, crossing and recrossing the flow of water, he felt himself delivered of several statements. He didn't argue with them in the intervals between them. He simply let them occur one after the other. Occasionally he had trouble getting every word. The words were pronounced all together as though the sound were a photographic print being developed. But he saw nothing, he only had the impression of hearing. Then a blank quiet until the next.

If you go to Iowa, you may get your ass handed to you.

If you're scared, put a uniform back on.

Don't worry about any uniforms.

You have been thinking of (up?) pale ghosts.

You've been camping out for a long time, even in Chicago.

You could go on staying away from your life and preparing yourself for it forever.

These pronouncements came through again. This struck him as a decent arrangement, because he could tell when it was all over. He felt relieved that that was all. He'd thought that he might have been more worried about himself. All in all, he now had the impression that he'd been told not to worry very much.

He didn't speak about his thoughts to Anya, because he wasn't sure how to explain that she wasn't mentioned.

He crossed the stream again. The rocks and earth were slippery from the rain, and it was hard to walk fast. His pack seemed more cumbersome even though there was less food in it. The tent had probably soaked up some water.

He let Anya go in front of him, and he was immediately struck by an attraction to the backs of her wet brown legs below the hem of her poncho. He caught up and touched the back of her knee as she paused after taking a long step up onto a flat rock.

She said, "How far is it now?"

He said, "I love the backs of your knees."

She said, "It's pouring rain."

He laughed—he'd just figured out what a creature of daily habit he was. It was time for their midday lay in the sun. Mac thought how easy it would be for someone to tame him. He'd never thought that of himself. He'd always thought he was too wild. But now he seemed to see himself from far away, tramping behind Anya—a creature of habit. He'd always thought his loyalty was his one unchallengeable virtue. But perhaps that loyalty was part of the same reflex as habit. If any piece of time or matter gave him pleasure, he lurched into a loyal reverence to it. He realized that this loyalty tipped him off balance as often as Anya's curiosity tipped her.

But, of course, she wasn't off balance. He sensed her motion and her pleasure in her move to Iowa, and it gave him more confidence in her than her curiosity did. Her curiosity had given rise to their screwing in the sun, making the hot noon sun a third party. She was a connoisseur of her own taste, a traveler in her own sensations. Mac thought that when he first met her she had probably been dangerously vague, but now, even though she hadn't given up her interest in sensation or her attention to the echoes of sensation in herself, she was more solidly happy than she'd been, and on that account he trusted her. He wondered if this was a blind reverence on his part for anyone making an effort.

He also wondered what she would say when he said he wanted to go to Iowa. He prepared his presentation of the practical advantages, an outline of the ways he could be useful.

*   *   *

Walking back to the car in the rain, Anya thought she deduced from Mac's story what had made him so close-grained and condensed. It seemed to her that Mac had always been secretly resisting what was happening to him.

He didn't like it when his father left Canada to work for GE in Schenectady. He tried to like it since it was good for the family. But he'd sensed he was in trouble from age fourteen to eighteen.

He didn't like it when he was drafted at the age of eighteen, but he tried to make himself perform correctly. He'd felt himself an alien, and got in even worse trouble.

When he'd gone back to Canada for the summer after he got out of the army and fallen in love with Mireille, he'd felt even more helplessly in trouble.

He'd gone to Cornell on his ice-hockey scholarship. The trouble there was that he sensed he wasn't a real college student. He felt segregated as a jock, but he was also slightly at odds with the other jocks because he was older and couldn't hide the feeling that they were not doing their job as seriously as he was, that they were accepting their scholarship money carelessly. He was a perfectionist, trying to give value for every penny, but a sullen perfectionist, because he felt by the time he was twenty-two, midway through college, that ice hockey was not a cause that moved him closer toward membership in the community of civilized people.

What she deduced from his stories moved her again almost to pity. But the ferocity of his energy as he had again and again tried to make himself perform his duty kept her from pity. She was more struck by the danger to herself she sensed in being attached to such fierceness now that he'd mixed her into his cloudy purposes. It was on the whole an exhilarating sensation, more exhilarating than masquerades with her old slyer lovers.

Even Tassie had been better than Mac at getting what she wanted. Henniker had been perhaps the best at achieving his small wishes. But Mac seemed almost never to have got what he wanted, and was all the more fiercely energetic for it.

Anya didn't think that it was just the novelty of this that appealed to her. It was not just the exhilaration of the risk either, she was pretty sure. It was Mac's unconscious vehemence.

Anya thought again that there were several pleasures available to her from Mac. The pleasure of making him more or less conscious, or more or less vehement, or even simply the pleasure of feeling his energy even if she failed to make him clearer to himself or to her.

It was not a question of her molding him. She knew she

understood his story better than he did himself, could sum it up better than he could, and in fact had pried him open to get at it in the first place; nevertheless her seeing into him had not given her an advantage. It had concentrated *him*.

She should have guessed he could not stay inert. Now she could feel him pressing toward her. Shyly—even after eight months, even after their recent middays of hot, naked lounging—but urgently.

Her dealings with her college boyfriends, with Tassie, Timmy, and Henniker had been exchanges of exploring and trading parties, perhaps even a few raids. Mac seemed to be a migration—a migration of some upheaved tribe that had a keen sense only of its integrity, and very little sense of its effect or even of its graces.

Part Three

WEST LIBERTY

CHAPTER

8

Mac met Raftery in the woods by the Iowa River. Mac was carrying his fly rod. Raftery was wearing a white lab coat over his pants and shirt. Strolling. His beard flowering from his face under his bright rimless glasses. They saw each other. Raftery examined him. Raftery said, "Good evening, sir." Mac was surprised. Raftery came up to him and said, "Buenas tardes, señor," in an American accent. Mac laughed. For an instant he'd thought Raftery was a madman.

Mac said hello, and Raftery asked him how he came to be there. Mac said, "I thought there must be a river, and I looked at my map and there it was."

Raftery said, "The map."

Mac said, "The river."

They came out of the woods into an open space dotted with hummocks of broken reeds all bent downstream. The reeds were speckled with dry silt. Mac asked when the last flood had been. Raftery said last spring. The river was low now, ten feet below the lip of its dense mud banks. Mac climbed down and waded in. Raftery sat dangling his legs over the bank. He said " 'A minnow! A minnow! I've got him by the nose. But what a nasty surprise. It wasn't a minnow at all but Jack Sharp the stickleback all covered with spines.' "

Mac laughed again though he didn't know what Raftery was talking about.

"What's that?"

"Jeremy Fisher. Monsieur Pêche-à-la-ligne. 'He didn't mind getting his feet wet and he never caught cold.'"

Mac put his rod together and worked the line through the guides.

Raftery said he wished he'd brought his son.

"How old is your son?"

"One and a half."

Mac understood it was a children's book.

Raftery lay his head back against a pillow of vines.

Mac thought there might be some largemouth bass in the river. He tried a streamer fly upstream. He waded out carefully after a few casts to see if there was a sudden drop-off. There was. He cast upstream and out and brought the streamer back several times, darting deep under water. He thought he'd got the bottom. No, the line tugged sideways. Raftery jumped up and slid down the bank yelling, "'A minnow! A minnow! I've got him by the nose!'"

Mac carded the line in around his left hand. The fish didn't feel big after the first tugs. He shifted the rod to his left hand and netted the fish. A largemouth bass, under a pound, but longer than he'd guessed. Big enough to eat. Raftery waded right in to look at it, laughing at his own excitement.

Raftery seemed fascinated by the insides—Mac turned the stomach inside out. There were digested bugs; Mac couldn't tell what they were. He stuck with his streamer for a while, caught another, same size. Ten retrieves, and then he switched to a buglike fly, a fat little ball of hair.

"Do you mind if I join you?"

"No." Mac looked at him. Mac was surprised he, Mac, didn't mind. He caught something he liked about this man —his agile foolishness. Mac felt vaguely protective, although Raftery reminded him of something tough and nimble. There was something about his apparently deliberate whimsy that Mac would ordinarily have thought was affectation. It was okay.

Mac wanted five or six fish for the group. Eight or nine pounds. Raftery offered to carry the gunny sack Mac used as a keeper net.

They waded up toward a tree that had fallen down the bank. Mac put his bug upstream of the branches that stuck out into the water. He saw the movement just under the water and twitched the bug too soon.

He said, "Damn."

But the fish hadn't seen or felt the hook. He snuck the line back out and hit the same spot, just above where the branch disappeared under water. The bug ticked the branch as it floated over. The fish sucked it in. Mac didn't have to set the hook. He couldn't tell where the fish was going at first. Then it was clear he'd gone deep into the middle. Mac let him have the line from his hand, played him on the reel. He waded back downstream, bumping into Raftery. He wanted the fish clear of the tree. He slowly lifted the rod high. He felt the steady deep runs of the fish. Some size here. Strength. He let him run against the flex of the rod until he felt the fish weaken. He brought the rod butt down to his chest, taking in line. Surprised the small hook was holding. He took in more line, eased the rod up to see if he could bring him to the surface, control his head. He saw the fish, dark and thick in the dusty water. The fish saw him, too. Dove hard. Mac took the run in his arm, lowering the rod, afraid the thin hook would unbend or slice loose.

But he didn't have to give any line. That run was it. Raised him back up, the fish throbbing rather than tugging. Mac took in line, led him into the net. This time Raftery was disappointed. "I thought he'd be as long as your arm."

Mac said, "He weighs five times as much as the others— four pounds, I'll bet."

"There was ten times as much drama."

No insult in the tone, but Mac decided not to explain. He unhooked the fish over the gunny sack Raftery held open. The bass had taken the fly halfway to his stomach. Mac pinched with his left hand and delved down the gullet with his right. The hook was okay.

He waded up twenty-five yards farther and after twenty minutes caught another one-pounder. He asked Raftery if he wanted one. Raftery said he didn't eat meat. For some reason that made Mac laugh. Raftery's turn not to be in-sulted. He took his turn.

Mac said, "What are you doing helping, then? An ac-complice."

Raftery said, "There aren't any rules." He laughed.

Mac stepped back and caught the throat of the sack as Raftery deliberately let it go.

Raftery said, "Consistencies are what keep people from moving around."

Mac looked at Raftery. He was glad an impulsive premonition had made him grab the sack.

This stringy little guy would do anything. Was he showing off?

Mac climbed up the bank, took his sneakers off, dumped the water out. The sun was behind the trees and the air was still soft. Raftery climbed up and sat beside him. Mac wondered how Raftery knew he was safe with him. Does Raftery calculate? Or had he made one good guess and then let himself go? Raftery lay down on his side and propped his head up with his hand. Mac felt suddenly like a large dog who is puzzled by his master. Knows he is loved but doesn't know what he's being told to do.

Raftery said, "Señor, come to my house."

Mac asked where it was, Raftery told him, Mac didn't get it straight, said he had to take the fish back first anyway. Raftery said no, he should take him, Raftery, home first. Mac said he didn't have a car, he was walking, too. They both laughed. They got up and walked as far as the small creek that ran through the woods, crossed the old tree trunk that lay across it.

Raftery said, "You must be an oldest son."

Mac said, "Yes, why?"

Raftery said, "Oh, you have the disposition. Oldest sons go around feeling like Jesus or Adam. Sitting on the right hand of God the Father Almighty. You're Adam enjoying the well-run world made just for you."

Mac thought awhile. He said he couldn't imagine what Jesus or Adam felt like. And even if he could he wasn't sure about oldest sons in general.

"But you were first in the Eden of your family childhood. There was Adam, watching everything grow. Probably making some sense of it. Yum, sense, yum, yum. Measuring, tasting. After all the trouble begins, Adam can always remember what it was like when there was just him and his dominion."

Mac wanted to know the details of Raftery's life. He worried that Anya wouldn't like him. He still wasn't sure why he liked him. He did like Raftery's uneasy impulse to talk—perpetual motion, Raftery's thoughts starting out evenly on top of one another, then toppling weightlessly upwards.

They walked across a flat pasture to the dirt road. On the

other side of the road was a slow round hill of corn, the rows in long, concentric arcs except where a sharp V of a wash cut into the hill. The wash was filled with knee-high meadow grass, the spears all fully open, the filaments purple in the shadow of the tall corn.

Raftery explained to Mac again where he lived. He drew a map on the dirt shoulder.

"But what you're saying is you're just down this road we're on."

Mac looked up and pointed at a white frame house visible between the trunks of tall oak trees. Mac said, "You mean right there?"

Raftery stuck his finger in his mud map. He said, "Right there, reader of maps."

Mac heard and then looked up and saw a flock of starlings fly up against the sun. The light streamed between them and through their stretched-out feathers—a dark hand against a light bulb. The flock rose and wheeled together, a single liquid drop floating up, squeezing flat and then whirling into a comma that disappeared point first back into the corn.

As immigrant to this continent as his great-grandfather. More immigrants. Came from England in 1890. The starling and the house sparrow and the common pigeon, all from Europe. All over North America now.

Raftery invited him to come to his house that evening. Mac said yes.

Mac hefted his sack of fish, still wet. His pants cuffs were dry. The mud on his ankles, stuck full of wild seed, slowly gathered a layer of dust as he walked toward the theater. He felt at home now for the first time.

He'd thought deeply about Iowa—what else was there for him to think about? He'd collected and stored facts until at last his imagination slowly drew his map and the place together.

The slow decency of the farmers. Businessmen really. Means of production were mechanical—each farm lot full of equipment. $500,000? Maybe $100,000. The bankers probably covered one-half, two-thirds of that. Local bankers, cousins of the farmers. The deals were local, the money from farther away. New, low-slung brick ranch houses; old, tall, wood farmhouses. New metal sheds and squat wire corn cribs like fat rockets. The old tall wood barns. It was a silly way to run things—each farm a duplicate: tractors, trucks, wagons, corn picker, auger. The same tinker-toy set every half mile or so. But the soil was so rich it yielded to any system. You could still be a yeoman—completely independent—so long as you were willing to work twelve hours a day.

And here was this band of nimble actors fallen into a seam between two farms—living and working in the husk of a farmhouse and barn, the land long since gobbled up on both sides by the two neighboring—and prospering—farmers.

Most farms in Iowa had started out as quarter sections—four farmers to a square mile. Now there were usually two. "You're in the wrong business, boy." Sometimes only one. Six hundred and forty acres of black earth. One hundred bushels of corn per acre, without even pushing. A dollar a bushel. Of course, you couldn't plant the whole section every year. There was some grazing land, some fields of oats that went to seed and moldered back to richness.

Almost no touches of superstition, whimsy, or aesthetics. No flower gardens. No ornaments. Everything square, slow, and powerful. The trees were cleared right up to the banks of the creeks that sliced through the sections. This part of the state had been half forest once. Mac thought he felt his own superstition about the forest more strongly here than he did in the north woods. The strip of woods left along the rivers—the Iowa, the Cedar, the Skunk—were ancient. A quarter mile on either side laced deep with roots that held the earth. The flood waters couldn't be controlled the way the land could, couldn't be owned, parceled out in north-south, east-west squares.

It balanced here. Iowa—the mean state in size, in population, hovering between the swarms and hives of the East and the vacancies of the West. On the west bank of the navigable Mississippi, up whose valley wet warm southwinds blew from the Gulf—but, when the wind was northerly in the winter, crushed by arctic cold—no barrier over a thousand feet between Iowa and the North Pole.

Mac thought again he thought too much in maps.

Anya had laughed at that—she'd asked one night during a dumb, comfortable conversation in bed, "Do you think more in words or pictures?" and he'd said, "Maps." She'd been amused.

166

One of the many little things that kept him away from the group—not just thinking in maps but an interest in the place, a lack of surprise. All of them laughed a lot about Iowa. " 'Ioway! Ioway! That's where the tall corn grows.' " Or, "Wow—here we are in Iowa." After almost a whole year.

That, more than their shop talk, was turning him into the house mute.

It was with some sullenness that he went in the kitchen door.

*   *   *

Being a dog's body for the theater didn't bother Mac. What bothered him was the swirl of emotions—no, not of emotions, of temperaments. He felt the disadvantage of being the only person in the group who had no claim to artistic temperament. He also found it hard to sort out what was transient, even just preening and display, from what was seriously felt.

When he came into the kitchen Alice and Babette were bullying Annabelle about being late now that it was her turn to get dinner ready.

Alice and Babette were built along the same lines— loose-jointed, leggy, hard-backed, tight-rumped dancers, except that Babette at five feet two was a miniature of Alice at five seven. They dressed alike, shared a room, and— Anya had told him—occasionally slept together. Mac's guess was that they were both interested in men, too; just not any of the men in the group. They liked (or at least thought okay) Anya, Andrew, Mac, and Bangs. They were short-tempered with Og, Annabelle, and Tagh, who were the youngest in the troupe (both in years and in general).

At the moment Alice and Babette were a little shrill because there was only one good female part in the play the theater was about to put on—*Wozzeck*, by Georg Büchner. Annabelle was playing Maria, Wozzeck's faithless girl friend.

Mac told Annabelle he'd fix the fish for supper. She squealed and then rushed over to hug him, saying "Mmm— *mmm!*" as she squeezed.

Og loomed behind her, a twitch of jealousy pressing through his face.

That's how it is, Mac thought, someone always gets pissed off.

Mac said to Og, "You interested in fishing? I can rig another rod."

Og—immediately soothed—"Hey, yeah, man, let me see those fish. Hey, all right."

Andrew came in and inspected the fish, too. He began to talk about a deep-fried spiced flounder he'd once had at a Fukinese restaurant in New York. "You could eat the whole thing—even the fins and bones. They were the texture of crisp french fries, and the whole thing was engulfed in ginger."

Mac said he'd filet these and make a white sauce. Andrew said, "Oh God, Mac, stop." Obviously politely exaggerating.

Mac was pleased to try to accommodate Andrew's fancy —Andrew paid attention to what he ate. He was also the only one who owned a cookbook.

Andrew was the easiest person for Mac to get along with. He'd liked him right off. Andrew managed to convey a feeling of intimate friendship from a formal distance. Mac had realized this after three weeks. From time to time everyone else in the troupe—including the heterosexual Og and Tagh—prickled Mac with some sexual tension: flirtation, jealousy, rivalry, flaunting one thing or another. Annabelle, for example, let her role splash over into their life—whirling about in a sexy, giddy flutter that was bothersome because she didn't seem to understand its full effect. Og sulked.

Andrew kept his love life entirely separate from the theater. Mac had met Andrew's lover only once, in the barn-theater lobby—a rather ordinary-looking man who was an assistant professor in the English department at the University of Iowa.

Mac and Anya were going through a neutral period, which alarmed Mac. He knew in an abstract way that it was only a period, but he'd never gone through it with anyone. He'd been blissfully neutral most of the time in Labrador, happy that his sexual feelings were in repose. It was clear now that the cause of their neutrality was simply long hours of work, and perhaps the fact that, when they were together during the day, Anya told Mac what to do.

Mac noticed that the man playing the captain—Ray, a

teacher from the Iowa drama department, prematurely bald from forehead to crown—was staying for dinner.

Anya had told Mac in one of their brief conversations in bed before they both slumped dispiritedly into sleep that Ray was more trouble than he was worth. The troupe needed another man, especially for older parts, and Ray was smooth and professional. But—and here Mac was surprised at the line Anya took—he was responding to Bangs's overtures. Anya was contemptuous of them both. "It's so corny," she'd said. "If she just wanted to fuck him—she hasn't, by the way—well then, that'd be fine. But she's being his second wife. His second, nicer wife. And he brought his two kids out for the day. Wants to keep his sex life all part of the family, I suppose. And there's Bangs oozing sex appeal through being a good den mother."

Mac had said, "I still don't see the problem." He'd been upset at Anya's cold tirade. He'd taken it to be against sex.

But Anya had said, "If he leaves his wife, it's going to upset how we get along with the University drama department. The old farts there are very stodgy. And that's where we borrow our extra light trees. And coolie labor. Those grips we get are freshman drama students, they get credit for coming out here."

Mac said, "What goes on with Ray and Bangs is between Ray and Bangs."

Anya said, "Not when she comes on with his kids. She *mothers* them, for God's sake. And Ray loves it. And when they have a crisis, the two of them are going to expect us all to make way for it—see, they're not just kids fucking like the rest of us—'it's heavy,' 'think about the kids,' and so on. And *really* they'll both love the serious agony of it. That's why they're being so blind now, so they can suddenly find themselves in a mess and say 'I don't know how it happened.' Shit . . . And they'll talk about it to anyone. But the old farts will think we're' *all* just kids fucking around."

Mac didn't say anything. He thought she might be right, but he was alarmed both at her harshness and at the tyrannous range of her worry. He didn't want to have anything to do with either one. But that's what she usually talked about before he fell asleep.

He was glad he was going to visit Raftery later on in the evening.

He cleaned the fish, fileted them, made their sauce, cooked them, and served them around the large table in the main room.

Anya was talking to Andrew and Ray about the set. Mac sat at the other end and listened to Og talk about a plan for making cider to sell at intermission. It only served to remind Mac of all of Og's half-assed schemes. Og had bought a potbelly stove—fine—but Mac had to rig the stovepipes and collars, make another trip to town for a damper and pipe hanger.

Og had bought a gasoline motor with an attachable pump, lawnmower, and cultivator. It was a wonderful idea, but the engine had a leaky gasket. By the time Max fixed it, it would be time to store it for the winter.

Mac imagined the hardware-store owner brightening up every time Og came by, thinking, "Here comes a live one."

Now it turned out Og had actually ordered a cider press. Mac foresaw it cluttering up his workbench backstage, disassembled and missing one part which Og wouldn't be able to remember the name of so he wouldn't be able to write away for it.

Annabelle brought in a bowl of fruit for dessert and began clowning around.

Mac realized he'd been taking the same view of Og that Anya had of Ray. Why should he be so sour? Here was a chance to build a new and perfect city in the middle of this rich place.

Annabelle did an imitation of Mae West saying, "Beulah, peel me a grape."

Mac thought back to the rehearsals, the dance exercises, the improvisations. They were after something. He should be generous enough to like that. He could see and hear them from backstage while he worked—the sharpness they were after in a gesture, or a sound, or a pause. From time to time he could feel the words of the script suddenly accept their efforts, become almost real words.

Was it because he knew that he could never do that that he failed to have the proper feelings that a member of the group should have? He realized that he did wish to become a citizen, to stop being a stranger, to tame himself to these people as well as this place. What was hard for him was to make himself easier. His taste had always been for effort and patience and ordered accumulation. He wished all benefits to be earned, preferably by a slow grinding of enormous forces. He recognized his fault—to accept the labor theory of value as an aesthetic. This struck as a corollary of his other northern barbaric fault: to be over-impressed by simple monoliths—by the sea, the sky, the mountains, or the wall keeping out the barbarians. Out of England, out of China, out of the Mediterranean. Out of the lemon groves.

Annabelle caught his eye again as she hootched up and down the room. He felt grumpy at being interrupted in his thoughts. He watched her coldly, recognizing that she was being gay and vulnerable, swirling and belly dancing around, but he wasn't able to stop his irritation.

He'd heard that in communal living there was supposed to be a slow diminishing of attraction, but he found himself surprised by what he noticed. It had happened already with Babette. He'd thought her too small at first, but when she danced she suddenly filled the space she danced in. But there'd been more than her growing larger and more ex-tended—as she danced, all of her became strange, part by part. Mac, watching from backstage, had been amazed to see the neat jut of her ass disappear as she demonstrated a contraction. One line, one arc, ran unbroken from the back of her knees to the crown of her head. When her body re-appeared at rest he saw her trim body with alarm—she was a magician who'd pulled herself out of thin air with a back-ward twitch of her pelvis and buttocks.

At that time Annabelle, attempting the same move, had appeared clumsy. Now it all tumbled the other way, and he saw Annabelle sashaying toward him, her short pudgy toes gripping the floor, the tassels of her braided belt swing-ing across the thrust of her pelvis (which made the mound under her tight blue-jean fly seem as sweetly pudgy as her feet). Her bare stomach, pouting above her hip huggers and below the sleeveless jersey ending at her bottom rib, was as moist and smooth as yoghurt.

Annabelle was carrying a bunch of grapes. She danced up to Og and popped one in his mouth. She held another grape between her teeth and fed it to Og. Mac shoved his chair back to give her more room to get at Og, and she smiled at Mac. She looked at Mac's eyes. Mac thought there must be a graceful way to deflect her, an easy, comic way, but he couldn't imagine it. Even as he felt stupid that this silly milkmaid of a girl could embarrass him, could affect him, could read his mind as simply as if he were a bald-headed businessman at a nightclub, he felt himself tighten and stare, slack-lipped and serious, into her eyes.

*   *   *

Anya looked down the table at Annabelle and Mac.

Anya had had a long conference with Annabelle about flirtation and enticement that afternoon. The problem was that Annabelle in her portrayal of Wozzeck's girl friend played sexiness as hard and sophisticated, a clever vamp. What Anya wanted from her was something sweeter and dumber, a kind of child's attraction to her infidelity, the great big drum major with shiny boots and buttons. And then, when he starts to take off his boots and buttons, a belated alarm.

Anya had thought that would be a natural for Annabelle; surely something like that must have happened to Annabelle when she was seventeen or eighteen. But Annabelle, who was in many ways a harder-working and better actress than Anya had expected, suddenly switched tracks when it came to being seduced. She acted the seductress.

Anya watched Annabelle sidle up with her bunch of grapes, still twitching in her amateur belly dance. Annabelle couldn't dance very well, but she could mimic dancing.

Anya thought that perhaps Annabelle had the same mimetic relation to sex. She could act sexy without having a very strong sexual feeling.

Annabelle's body reminded Anya of Tassie's—the same butterball softness over bouncy summer muscle produced by approximately the same kind of American wealth and schooling.

The coloring was different of course. Annabelle's skin was white with an undertone of blue-green, perhaps negatively induced for Anya's eye by Annabelle's dark red hair.

Annabelle stood still for an instant. She held her hair with one hand, swinging it beside her ear. With her other hand she dangled the grapes. Anya tried to see, to feel what Mac saw—she thought she was receiving his impression of Annabelle's milky skin above the braided belt, the hovering of Annabelle's slow, soft body, the side of one thigh now indented by the edge of the table.

Anya looked at Mac's face and was surprised. He was tied in a knot of attention and embarrassment. Anya thought, *That's* what Annabelle should have as Maria, she should receive the advance of the drum major with embarrassment, paralyzed attention, a little numb timidity at first so we can *see* the inert flesh that the drum major is working on—at first clumsily and stupidly, and then hurriedly, as he dimly realizes his dumb luck. The girl should be dazed and immobile for a moment so that her flesh is a clear backdrop for the drum major's crude and finally comic groping. And then she can join in once it's too late —the line Wozzeck overhears—"Don't stop!"

Anya saw Mac staring up at Annabelle's face. She was only mildly jealous of his attention to Annabelle; she was much more struck by what she knew was a feeling that was strange to her. He was such a believer in absolutes—no, in keeping everything whole. Here he was at a loss because of a small tweak of lustful gazing. She blotted out Annabelle and felt a fresh curiosity towards Mac. What was it like to feel what he was feeling?

When Mac abruptly got up and left, Anya had a rush of feeling—pity and alarm that she had for several weeks let him drift out of her attention. She was aware that her fresh interest in him had an element of play and sexual desire, but as she followed him outside she held her first feeling steady, unidentifiable but caught between currents of curiosity and sympathy.

The farther they walked down the road the more interested Anya became. Mac walked slowly but steadily, clearly going somewhere. But it wasn't where he was going that held Anya; she caught hints of his present pleasure in the way he glanced across the field or up at the moon. The night was still, there was only a dry froth of noise from the leaves on the standing corn. The straight gravel road looked whiter than by sunlight, the dry wheel tracks seemed covered with talc. Toward the river there was the mass of trees, a piece of black that ran parallel to the road and seemed as unending.

She was afraid Mac's pleasure was relief to be away from the group; she hoped it might be for the night fields.

Anya caught up to Mac as he turned in at the first farm-house south of the crossroads. They stood for a moment looking at the house. Anya by now was on edge with desire. She considered asking Mac to step into the barn across the yard from the house. She decided he'd worry too much.

The side door of the house opened. Mac spoke to the man, took Anya in, and introduced her to Raftery. Raftery in turn introduced them to his wife, Dulcie. Anya's buzz of desire was temporarily buried by her social attention.

Anya liked Raftery right off. He was precise in his whimsy. This precision gave him an odd cricket charm. Raftery told a story about how he got fired from his most recent job as a lab technician, and he slowly wended his way back through his history of short-lived occupations to his arrival in Iowa City as a graduate student. In spite of his unhurried and ornamental narrative style, Raftery seemed to be working with an intention. Anya couldn't make up her mind whether he was being a teller of tales in the bazaar hoping for praise (and alms) for his mere extra-vagance, or if he was a Chinese merchant beginning a long and delicate negotiation in the proper way.

His wife seemed to be his blushing shadow.

Anya saw that Raftery was as watchful as she was—she sensed the glitter of his attention behind the stories, which were well told, polished but not enameled, allowing Mac and her to exclaim and intervene.

What she also liked about Raftery was that he was ob-viously taken with Mac.

They drank cheap jug red wine, heated and then smoothed with honey. Raftery passed around a small corn-cob pipe of marijuana. It was home-grown, slightly harsh in taste but a very mild hit. Dulcie made the mugs, it turned out, and sewed their clothes, and grew their vege-tables. But the house didn't exude the serious organic sweet-ness that Anya usually associated with whole grain, cover-alls, and other objects in the neohomespun mode.

Anya guessed it was the carelessness that both Raftery and Dulcie had that saved them—if they were ideologues for their way of life, if they thought there was sacramental grace in their rituals it was not a recent belief. Rattling on, Raftery was certainly as cozily unevangelical as a witty old Jesuit to his dinner partner.

Then Anya began to think of how different Mac's pleasure was.

What probably had alarmed Mac—as the neohomespun had alarmed her—*was* Raftery's carelessness, his impudence toward the lore and craft of his jobs. What probably charmed Mac she was less certain of—Raftery mocked a number of categorical skills, but he was obviously observant in a most skillful way, in a way that Mac would admire. And Raftery obviously had bursts of sensual enthusiasm that Mac would like.

Anya watched Raftery laughing at a story Mac was telling about Og, and she recognized that Raftery called out Mac's talkative side, even a kind of wit.

Mac asked about the river—Was there a dam between where they were on the Iowa and its mouth on the Mississippi? Raftery asked why Mac wanted to know.

Mac said, "I like the feeling of being on water that goes someplace. I like to think that if I was paddling a canoe around here I'd just let go and end up in New Orleans."

Raftery said, "You have a canoe?"

Mac said no, but he might build a little duckboat.

Raftery said, "Would you like to go down the Mississippi?"

Dulcie said to Raftery, "Not this year."

Raftery explained to Mac, "Two years ago I walked to New York."

Mac was amazed and delighted, asked Raftery a string of questions, not stopping for the answers. "What did you carry? What did you eat? Was it all on roads? How long did it take?"

Anya said, "Why did you do it?"

Raftery said, "It seemed the right moment."

Dulcie said, "I was pregnant with Hugh, and I had a job at a library."

Raftery said to Mac, "I carried thirty-seven cents, a notebook half full of poems, and two pairs of wool socks that I got in Cincinnati. All in a bag with a shoulder strap."

Mac said, "Where did you sleep?"

Raftery said, "Oh—all sorts of places. When I got to a town I'd go see the editor of the newspaper and tell him what I was doing. Sometimes I'd sell them a poem for a meal and a bed. One editor bought me a new pair of shoes. If the newspapers didn't work, I'd look the jail over. There were two nice ones. Or I'd sleep in a barn. When I got to the Appalachian Trail—that was near Harpers Ferry—I slept in lean-tos or cabins. I only slept out three nights out of forty."

"What did you do when it rained?"

"I had an umbrella that I found on a golf course near Louisville. It was stuck in the ground point first. Only a future king could pull it out. I also used it as a sunshade— it was light-blue and white. And I used it to frighten away attacking dogs. If they wouldn't stop when I spoke to them, I'd open the umbrella at them. I only had to stick one with the point. I also carried some newspaper clippings. The Louisville and Cincinnati papers came out with the story the next day, while I was still in their range."

Mac said, "How did you pay?—oh yeah, your thirty-seven cents."

Raftery said, "No, I just clipped the story. I started with thirty-seven cents and I ended with thirty-seven cents."

Mac said, "How did you eat?"

Raftery said, "Very well. I gained weight. I ate three meals a day, which I usually don't do. I'd stop at houses or churches. Sometimes I had to work, sometimes I gave them a poem. Eating was a pleasure, but the chief pleasure was sunrise—and thinking and talking. And after I got to Ohio I had a sense that I had great physical power. It was my askesis, my priestly training for fatherhood."

Anya said, "When did you get back?"

Raftery said, "Just before Hugh was born."

Dulcie said, "Yes, we were both waiting for you."

Anya couldn't tell whether Dulcie's tone was dry or whether her voice was always flat and metallic. Kansas? Missouri? Anya looked at Dulcie's face. It would be pretty if it were softer. It was a face set to resist—not resist anything in particular, just resist. Mac would like that, would say Dulcie's face was set to endure.

But when the baby cried upstairs and Dulcie brought it down in her arms and did look softer, Anya noticed that softness on Dulcie's face looked like pain.

Raftery disappeared upstairs, and Mac tried to amuse the baby, who stood on the bench beside Dulcie, holding on to her. The baby turned its face into Dulcie's hair.

Dulcie tried to persuade it that Mac was a nice man. She smiled apologetically at Mac and at last looked pretty.

Raftery re-entered, and Anya said, "I think it's time we went back to—"

Raftery said, "Yes, it's bedtime. I've made up our guest room for you, madam."

Anya laughed.

Raftery said, "Don't go. We must conspire further in the morning."

Anya said, "Okay." She liked the idea of going to bed with Mac in a strange room.

But what struck her as peculiar was that the room didn't seem strange to Mac. There was no electric wiring to the second floor, they each carried a candle lantern made from a cut-out number-ten can.

The bed was a low platform of thin planks covered with a thin mattress and a pile of quilts. Near the windows, through which she could see the moonlit road and the corn, there was a single-plank table. Each end of the plank rested on the level spoke of a wooden wagon wheel, grayed with age. The wheels were hung from the ceiling by old harness leathers. She was sure the device was Raftery's— there was a sense of theater in Raftery's house, intimations of wizardry, that she thought had the right amount of open pretense and ingenuity.

But Mac seemed to find it as familiar as he did the dirt road and moon. He lay on the bed, sunken into the layers of quilts, his head propped on his hand, watching her examine the room. His face was mild, not on guard, like the third son in the fairy tale whose simple heart is not surprised when the raven speaks to him, who believes the crone by the road who tells him the way to fetch the water from the well at the world's end.

The skin of his face looked fragile by candlelight—she came and touched it, moved her fingers slowly, hoping that he would catch the rhythm, the tang of touching so slowly that she wouldn't lose her sense of place, so that she could half pay attention to their skin, half pay attention to the mustiness of the dry bare wood of the room, the cool air, the small heat of the candle, the clumsy bulk of the quilts.

She lay awake afterwards, strangely alert. Mac lay asleep, it seemed to her more securely and childishly asleep than she'd ever seen him. Was it an effect of candlelight?

Or was it contentment in the kind of place he'd lived in in Canada in his version of a happy childhood?

But what kept her most alert was her puzzlement that they both found pleasure here. She wasn't sure that she liked the idea of their different pleasures so neatly counter-weighted.

But, completely separate from this bud of perversity, she felt a great tenderness. She smoothed Mac's hair with her hand, surprised at herself, at the pleasure she took in admiring her hand in this sentimental gesture.

CHAPTER

|||||||||||||||||||||||||||||||||||||

9

During the next month they spent several more nights at the Rafterys. It was a hair less than a half-mile cutting through the field. Mac worked hard during the day back at the theater house, as though against a deadline. He hauled tree limbs from farmers' brushpiles and filled the woodshed with logs, helped the plumber get the flush toilets in, fit the stovepipe into the chimney, had the big Jeep station wagon fitted with an electric engine heater and buried an extension cable from the house to the garage.

Og wanted to build a sauna. Anya asked Mac to help him, since Og was still sullen about not playing Wozzeck, although he'd resigned himself to Annabelle's not loving only him. Mac said that just talking about the sauna and walking around looking at places to build it would satisfy Og. That seemed to be right.

Mac put two bushels of apples in the cellar and made another four gallons of applesauce in quart Mason jars.

There was a fire at a lunch counter in Iowa City, and the firemen used so much water to put it out that they washed the labels off ten cases of six-ounce soupcans. Mac was in town at the hardware store. He overheard the lunch-counter owner tell the story to the manager of the hardware store. He offered to buy all the cans for three cents apiece. Sold.

When he got them back to the theater, everyone complained. The cardboard cases had decomposed before the labels washed off and Mac had gathered the cans up pell-mell—there was no way to tell without opening it whether a can was chicken soup with rice, mushroom, pea, navy bean, or vegetarian vegetable.

Mac took all the cans down to the Rafterys.

Anya guessed he wanted to move in with them.

She talked to Andrew about Mac and her moving. He was dismayed.

"Anya, you and Mac are the only two I can talk to!"

She was touched.

Andrew said, "Who are these people to you?"

She said, "No, it's not that." She thought of Dulcie. She said, "The wife is going to sew costumes and the husband—" She couldn't think of anything Raftery could do. "—is going to help Mac. It's not us leaving, it's more of an expansion."

Andrew mimicked, "I'm not losing a daughter, I'm gaining a son-in-law."

Anya said, "I thought you'd like our room for yourself."

Andrew said, "Well, I hope everyone realizes it's yours to bestow."

She gave up. "Don't be so fucking cute."

Andrew liked to fence, had in fact got the better of her, but he disliked having to hear a real rip of anger. She'd snarled at him, hoped he would pale. He didn't. He said, "It's all right with me, do what you want. Just don't try to con me."

She was annoyed at having appeared a simple wheedler. And hurt—she realized she'd had an easy understanding with Andrew and now . . .

That night in their bedroom she told Mac about the conversation. He said it was true he'd been thinking of moving in with Raftery and Dulcie, but he was surprised she wanted to as much as he did. He was surprised, too, that she'd been so clumsy with Andrew. He said he thought Andrew should go with them, he could have the single room off the kitchen. It was always warm. Besides, he spent two or three nights a week in town anyway. What more could you ask from a housemate?

After a moment Mac added, "I thought you knew how Andrew felt. He's the one who's the most for you. They're all pretty well satisfied with what you're doing, but he's the one who really knows that what he wants is tied up with you."

Anya was suddenly uncomfortable. She wasn't sure she wanted Mac to know enough to be helpful.

Mac said, "If something came along for Babette or Alice or Og, some real job in Chicago or New York, they'd take it. I don't think Andrew would. As long as you're here."

She thought that was true. She was now angry with Mac.

She said, "Annabelle would like to fuck you."

Mac grunted.

She said, "Go ahead and smirk."

Mac said, "I'm not." He laughed.

She said, "You've already fucked her."

Mac said, "When could I? Where?"

She said, "Your giggling is disgusting."

"Oh, for Christ's sake."

She said, "You'd like to fuck her, wouldn't you? Just fuck something pale and soft and dumb."

Mac didn't say anything. Anya was through. She'd really been angry at him, but it was a thin sizzle of anger. What disturbed her was that she hadn't meant to get angry at Andrew or Mac, and she hadn't been relieved by her anger. In fact her anger seemed puny and useless. It seemed that the more capable she became talking to people in the theater, the more ungainly and ineffective she became outside the theater. She thought, Cliché of the executive life—I need a vacation.

*　　*　　*

What finally precipitated their move to Raftery's house was Raftery's landlord. Mac met the landlord, Sigurd Olson (former owner of the theater barn), when Mac and Raftery were collecting firewood from Sigurd's brushpiles. Sigurd told Mac and Raftery that he needed a farmhand more than he needed rent money, and the only way he could hire help was to fix up Raftery's house and offer it as a fringe benefit. Mac told Sigurd that he and Raftery could work for him.

Sigurd considered the idea.

Mac said, "That way you won't have to fix up the house."

Sigurd looked Mac over.

Mac said, "And you won't have to be paying steady wages when you don't need us."

Sigurd nodded, and he and Mac discussed possible schedules.

When they got back to Raftery's house, Raftery had misgivings.

Anya and Dulcie were waiting for them to discuss sharing the house. Anya had misgivings too; she wasn't sure she wanted to share Mac's work-energy with anyone else.

Raftery said to Mac, "Will this work make me wiser?"

Mac said, "One day a week isn't going to kill you. He says he can get by with twenty man-hours a week most of the time. Less during the winter, a little more during the spring."

Anya said, "I suppose you think it's real work." Mac looked puzzled. Anya said, "As opposed to building make-believe sets."

Mac said, "We need to keep the house. That's the point."

Raftery said, "Will this work increase our exaltation in life?"

Mac laughed.

Raftery said, " 'Distrust any enterprise that requires new clothes.' "

Mac said, "If it's too hard we can always quit." He turned to Anya. "Look at it this way—for my working there, you'll get Raftery working for you part-time, Dulcie sewing for you, and a place to live that's not already full. *You* and me better off. *I'm* the one that'll be getting up in the morning, and I'm willing."

Anya considered the idea.

Mac said, "I'll give up fishing."

Anya looked at Mac. Mac realized he'd let himself in for two bosses.

Anya said, "Okay."

Raftery said, "This is how Sigurd is going to make serfs of us. Next we'll be tugging our forelocks, sending him our daughters. Then he'll abolish our druid rites."

Mac and Anya moved in. Andrew got the single bedroom off the kitchen. Dulcie put in the harvest from her garden, which was partly in cans and partly in the root cellar. Anya bought Dulcie a sewing machine.

There was still a spare bedroom next to Mac and Anya's room, across the hall from Hugh's. Anya decided not to mention it to the rest of the troupe.

But the new arrangement didn't help Anya with Mac.

She saw his loyalties go leapfrogging down the road from the theater—a half-mile to Raftery's, then another half-mile to Sigurd's. She knew she was being unfair—after all, she'd moved to Raftery's too—but her feelings were hurt. She said to herself that if Mac wanted to exhaust himself that was his business, but she couldn't help considering his exhausting hours as a drug that removed him from her. When he'd just been working at the theater, at least they'd been getting drugged together.

Mac seemed happier, however. He and Raftery got along wonderfully. Mac seemed less wary than back at the theater house. Anya realized that by moving she'd removed one unfairness of hers—she hadn't liked it when the members of the troupe treated Mac as the hired help, but she hadn't liked it either when they began to ask his opinion about their performance. At least now she thought she would have his spare time to herself.

But after the first week she realized he had a new preoccupation. It wasn't Dulcie—Mac treated her with a formal kindness that Anya found pleasant, for reasons she couldn't explain. Mac was really more intimate with Raftery, and that too Anya found pleasant. It was Mac's preoccupation with the child that Anya found unsettling. Not irritating. It simply made her nervous. Mac played with Hugh with a passionate intensity that Anya at first couldn't believe was real. She thought for a while that it was one of Mac's odd politenesses to the Rafterys.

Then she saw Mac alone with Hugh. Mac lay on his back on the kitchen floor, and Hugh climbed over him. Hugh put his face an inch away from Mac's and babbled at him. Mac was enchanted. There were two details that struck Anya as odd. One was that Mac seemed to understand what Hugh was saying. The other was that Mac answered Hugh matter-of-factly—Anya had expected baby talk. But Anya's main vision was that Mac was concentrating his attention, his sensual attention, in a way that shocked her. Mac didn't even notice her come into the kitchen. Anya knew that Dulcie caressed Hugh with as much tenderness, and she hadn't paid much attention to Dulcie. But now, watching Mac hold Hugh by the hips and kiss his shoulder as Hugh flung himself forward, she found the caress distasteful.

Hugh suddenly sprawled motionless on Mac's chest and

lay there, his face glowing, his eyes open but unfocused. Anya guessed that Hugh thought that Mac couldn't move. It struck Anya that Hugh's expression represented satisfied physical possession of a kind that she herself couldn't remember or imagine.

Hugh grew restless after ten seconds and began to pull Mac's hair. Mac noticed Anya and said to Hugh, "Who's that? Who's that? It's Anya."

Hugh looked at her, and said "Ah-ha," and immediately turned back to Mac's hair.

Since the two best cooks (Dulcie and Mac) were at Raftery's, Anya thought it only fair to invite two or three of the group for supper in those midweek days when Mac didn't have too much to do.

It was good for them to get a change of company. Raftery charmed them. Dulcie was mildly jealous when Raftery recited Elizabethan lyrics to Annabelle, but otherwise it was all very cheerful. Dulcie, it turned out, played the guitar and sang rather sweetly.

Anya herself felt that she sat several rows back.

The worst part of her day now was when she wasn't working. The only time people talked to her, it seemed, was when she started the conversation. She wasn't prickly anymore, but there was an eerie distance between her voice and the other voices. Whenever she spoke there was a moment of attentive silence on the part of the troupe. As though everything she said might be a bulletin. As soon as it was clear she was just talking, or that the bulletin didn't concern them, they turned back to their own talk.

Anya began to wish Mac would surprise her—astonish her with an advance toward her, not a sexual advance but an astute penetration of her mood.

CHAPTER

||||||||||||||||||||||||||||||||||

10

The only disadvantages to Raftery as a housemate were that he left unexpectedly and reappeared unexpectedly. The annoying thing about his disappearance was that he sometimes took Anya's car. He was very cheerful when she asked him not to; he made no excuses, made no attempt to justify the practice with communal ideology. Anya was almost sorry she'd said anything. The next day he took it again. He left a list of seventeen places she might find him.

The annoying thing about his reappearing was that he often brought someone with him—especially at mealtimes when there wasn't quite enough to go around.

When Anya got back from the theater that day the car was back, and Raftery and a strange young girl were eating heartily, while Dulcie and Mac served up the meal.

Raftery was unabashed when Anya came in. He asked Dulcie to fix Anya a plate. He turned back to Anya and filled her in on the conversation. That was to say, his monologue. He said, "I am considering the question of why people fail to do what is necessary to be happy."

Anya withheld her irritation. She was beyond irritation. Raftery was beyond monologue. He was preaching. It was his improve-each-shining-hour line.

Anya looked carefully at the girl. She was sitting hunched over so that the oversize sweatshirt she wore hung loose, hiding the shape of her upper body. She had stringy blond hair, hacked away in something like an old-fashioned bowl cut, so that it hung to her eyebrows in front but revealed the back of her neck.

Raftery said, "Why shouldn't every minute of life be ecstatic? Why shouldn't every minute be like hearing the 'Ode to Joy'? Or seeing the Sistine Chapel?"

Dulcie said, "You only saw it on television."

Raftery said, "I'm speaking figuratively—or like first looking into Chapman's Homer."

He passed his pipe to the girl. Anya saw she had strong, beautiful fingers with chewed nails.

Anya said to Raftery, "Sure. 'Spend all you have for beauty's sake and never count the cost.'"

Anya turned to the girl and said, "Are you staying long?"

The girl was not as hang-dog as she'd seemed at first. She met Anya's eyes and held them. She said, "Who are you?"

Anya said, "Anya Janek. And you?"

Raftery said, "Peewee."

The girl said, "I'm called Peewee. My name is Lucinda Nadl."

The girl seemed to have suddenly gathered her energy. Anya thought the girl might be alarmed that Anya would send her away. But Anya felt an interest in the girl's face. Even when her mouth was closed the upper lip appeared to be rolled back. On the lip itself, which was quite full, there was a thin shiny scar that ran diagonally. It was only visible at certain angles to the light. Anya guessed the girl was seventeen or eighteen. She had an Iowa accent.

Raftery went on about the question of happiness— "Everybody is happy at one time or another. Why don't they just keep on doing what they were doing that made them happy?"

The girl lowered her head again. Anya saw that the hair on the crown was cleaner and softer than the ends.

Raftery said to the girl, "When were you happy?"

The girl said, "I don't know. I don't think about it much."

Raftery said, "But what else is there to think about?"

The girl said, "Well, I remember once I was at a picnic on my uncle's farm. I was happy then."

Raftery said, "There. When was that?"

The girl said, "That was back near Rock River when I was twelve. We used to go over to my uncle's every Sunday

because I wouldn't be in his movies anymore . . . and all his guys were looking for me. And the University. You know what *they* did? When the dean heard that I'd tried to kill myself—*that* shit—she wrote me a letter saying I was on probation. And if I did it again I'd be expelled. Jesus."

Anya laughed. Peewee watched her a second and then laughed too. Anya realized she had control of the girl for the moment. But she also realized there was something uncontrollable about her, a brutal numbness. Anya didn't know whether this brutal numbness was a defensive ring around the girl's core or whether it *was* her core.

Anya said, "How do I remind you of your Spanish teacher?"

Peewee looked at Anya's eyes. Anya resisted an impulse to look away. Peewee's lips rolled back. It took Anya a second to see it was a smile. Peewee had large, very white teeth that weren't quite even. The canines were pressed forward.

Peewee said, "I guess it was just that you came in looking—tight. But you don't talk like her." Peewee cocked her head. "I mean, if you wanted to make it, you'd just come out and say it. Right?"

Anya thought Peewee was testing her. Anya looked at Peewee without saying anything, but Peewee didn't lower her eyes. Anya then wondered if Peewee's remark was unplanned.

Anya said, "Tell me something—how did you decide to come to Iowa City?"

Peewee said, "I didn't want to stay on the farm. My father wanted me to stay on a year and help him, and then he'd let me go. But it got worse and worse. My uncle's a pretty good farmer, but my father isn't. He got so nervous one time he couldn't drive the tractor. If you can't take a full day of driving a tractor you can't farm. He came in to the yard one day with his hands shaking and asked me to finish the field. I went on out to the tractor, but he'd let it run out of fuel so it had an airlock in the fuel line."

Anya looked puzzled.

Peewee said, "It was a diesel. If you let a diesel run dry, you have to blow out the fuel line. It's not like a gasoline engine.

"Anyway my father was still shaking so bad he couldn't

189

fit the wrench to the fuel line coupling. My cousin started calling him Uncle Shakey. So already in the summer things were a mess. I left last fall. I wasn't sure when I started out which way to go. I hitched a ride to the Interstate and that's when I thought about where it was I could go. The only place I could think of where any of the kids from around Rock River had gone was to the University of Iowa. Iowa City."

Anya said, "You don't like farm life?"

Peewee said, "No. I like the city."

"You mean Iowa City?"

"Yeah."

"But here you are on a farm again."

Peewee laughed. "This isn't a farm."

Anya said, "What do you think you can do around here?"

Peewee said, "I can do chores. I spent a couple of months in a house where I did the chores."

Anya said, "Maybe you could learn to help Dulcie sew costumes."

Peewee said, "Sure."

It occurred to Anya that Peewee's parents might come looking for her. Anya said, "How old are you?"

Peewee said, "I'm eighteen now."

"Are your parents worried about you?"

Peewee snorted. "They're less worried than my uncle." She laughed. "When I signed up for school and I had to pay tuition, I called my uncle up and said I'd left because I got knocked up by Dwayne. I got him to send a thousand dollars for an abortion."

"Didn't he ask Dwayne?"

"Dwayne wouldn't know. He used rubbers. You can't tell for sure with them. I got an IUD now. Mercks got me to. That way you can't get stoned and forget. I'm not used to taking any kind of pill. And a diaphragm—if you have a whole scene, what are you going to do? Run home each time and squeeze some more jelly in?"

Anya wondered if Peewee's year in Iowa City was representative of any section of undergraduate life there. She doubted if Peewee could tell her. She wondered if Peewee even had any idea that her story had an edge to it. Anya wished to find out—to examine Peewee's mind, or, perhaps more to the point, her nervous system. Was Peewee's story

a stance she adopted that was at odds with her real feelings? Or a stance that showed that Peewee thought, in some way, that she had sharper desires than the rest of the clods around her? Anya thought that direct interrogation—like Raftery's—would bring out more shreds of experience, but not the main impulse of Peewee's life. Or perhaps there was no main impulse, only an enormous vacuum at her center.

Anya sent Peewee up to the theater to find Dulcie and start to work.

Anya thought it wasn't Peewee's tough talk that interested her. Behind it there seemed to be an awkward yearning—awkward because Peewee probably couldn't think in any other way than the way she talked—but the yearning itself (it must have been a quick energy that made her want to latch on to Raftery, to Anya) seemed to Anya both alarming and oddly familiar.

CHAPTER

‖‖‖‖‖‖‖‖‖‖‖‖‖‖‖‖‖‖‖‖‖‖‖‖‖‖‖‖‖‖‖‖

11

There was a flurry of activity at Sigurd's. Mac spent three afternoons in a row there. The corn was being picked by a contractor with an eight-row picker. Sigurd needed Mac to run the auger to load the picked and shelled corn into bins.

The second afternoon Sigurd decided to dehorn his thirty young steers. Mac asked why they had to be dehorned. Sigurd explained that he was going to fatten these steers up in a feed lot on corn. When they bellied up to the feed trough they were likely to gore each other.

Sigurd rolled out a portable stanchion into his barnyard. It was like a regular dairy stanchion to hold cows being milked, except that the part that held the steer's neck was hung from a heavy metal frame that was on little rubber wheels. The whole thing weighed around four hundred pounds. Sigurd asked Mac to stand on the base of the stanchion and hold one horn while he hacksawed off the other horn. Mac had to grit his teeth as the saw bit through the horn. But it was the sight of what was under the horn that left Mac weak at the knees. After Sigurd cut the horn off he took a pair of pliers and ripped out a rubbery white ganglion from the socket.

The steers all stood still for it.

After they'd done a dozen steers, Sigurd's wife called Sigurd to the phone. Sigurd handed Mac the saw and told him to keep going.

Mac stood on the base of the stanchion, held one horn with his left hand, and started the saw across the base of

the other. The steer rolled his eyes at the first stroke. At the third or fourth stroke the steer braced his forefeet and lifted the stanchion off the ground. It came down unevenly and bounced on its little wheels. Mac dropped the saw and held on to the frame with one hand and reached for a horn with his other. The stanchion rocked back and forth as the steer shook his head. Mac tried to calm the steer as he'd heard Sigurd do it.

He said, "Go easy, go easy, go easy, boy." Then he yelled for Sigurd.

Sigurd appeared as the steer bucked and lashed out with his hind legs. Then the steer again lifted the stanchion and Mac. Mac's feet flew into the air. He held onto the horn and the frame, and tried to keep his feet clear as the stanchion bounced on the ground.

Sigurd said sharply, "Hey you, cut it out!" He came nearer, and the steer saw him. Sigurd said more softly, "Hey, you better just cut it out."

Through his hand gripping the horn, Mac could feel the steer's strength ebb, pulse up again in a slow roll that lifted the stanchion gently, like a wave lifting a boat, and then settle, as though the steer's force suddenly drained down its forelegs into the ground.

Sigurd said to the steer, "What do you think you're doing there, you better just stand still."

Sigurd took his glove off and put his bare hand on the steer's muzzle. Then he ran his hand over its neck and shoulders and down its chest. He said to Mac, "He didn't hurt himself, did he?" Mac didn't know. Sigurd said to the steer, "I better learn you some manners."

Sigurd picked up the saw. He said to Mac, "How about you? You didn't get hurt, did you?" Mac shook his head.

The steer stood perfectly still while Sigurd cut off his horns and plucked out the ganglions. Sigurd opened the stanchion, and backed the steer out. Mac edged around to the far side as Sigurd walked the steer down into the feed lot. Sigurd called back, "You can climb down, Mac, he ain't mad at you."

Mac bent down and picked up the horn he'd held onto. For an instant he imagined he felt some glow of energy. Then he pulled his thumbnail across it—just like his thumbnail, old horn. It was scummy around the rim and inside.

Sigurd said, "You can fix them horns up. I saw some for

AN AMERICAN ROMANCE

sale in an antique souvenir store once. You boil the scum
out and then sandpaper them and shine them. Genuine
antiques."

Mac listened, although he wasn't interested in the idea.
Mac's mind was still on the enormity of the steer's strength,
but he listened because he recognized that Sigurd had a
calming effect on him. He felt as calmed as the steer, as if
by the same magic that drained the steer's frenzy. He thought
that it was ridiculous of him but he still thought it was
magic, even though Sigurd himself didn't prize this relationship to his cattle as much as he prized his talent as a
go-getter businessman, all-around engineer and mechanic.
But still Mac felt it—Sigurd's vitality, emanating from his
hands and voice, Sigurd's coarse good will measured out in
the serene open portions that could come only from a man
who lived in tides of abundance, who knew that all his efforts would surely flow back to increase him.

*   *   *

Mac had come back from Sigurd's in a daze. Anya had
been able to tell he was thinking by his blank look. He'd
eaten a bite of supper at five and gone up to the theater to
bang away in the workshop. Into bed like a felled tree at
nine thirty. He wore his sweat suit as pajamas now that it
was cold.

Anya had spent the afternoon at the University watching
a film class. All very earnest. Everyone at the theater was
being earnest, too. Anya had gone through a numb earnest
period herself, pleased at everyone's earnest work. Now she
was irritated. It was a sensual irritation—everything she
touched or saw or heard prickled her. But she saw clearly
that she couldn't afford to become any more of a bitch
than she now was.

It was odd, she thought, no idea or mood ever left her—
they all orbited around until some chance brought one of
them plunging back into the central density of her brain.

She'd thought for a week or two that she was reconciled
to her busyness, Mac's stolid helpfulness, their clear vigorous sex on their hard bed. The slow advance of projects
through the group. Now suddenly she was struck by impatience—a jumpy allergy to all the efforts she'd been care-

fully promoting. An old asteroid of rebellion crashed through her atmosphere.

She tried to blame her mood on the thunderstorm that had been building all afternoon. She didn't trust that idea. She was sick of her good-gray-lady common sense, of the pattern of thinking.

She blew the kerosene lamp out and listened to the rain on the roof.

Through the crack under the door to Peewee's room she could see the glow of Peewee's candle. Peewee, it had turned out, was afraid of the dark. She always lit a fresh candle before she went to sleep.

The light now annoyed Anya, and she got up to stuff a pair of pants along the crack. She heard Peewee stir.

It was chilly now in the room. Anya pulled an extra quilt up on her side of the bed. She lay still for an instant and she guessed, she knew almost certainly, that Peewee was going to come in. Anya held the idea until it became clearer, until she had a languorous control over the scene.

The rain was distinct on the metal roofing over the front porch just below the bedroom window. Anya leaned over and felt Mac's pulse in the artery in his neck. Slow and deep. He rolled toward her hand. He was used to being surprised by her in his sleep.

Anya thought of Peewee, imagined a path to her feelings through the darkness. Peewee not thinking, only stirring. Not restless, more like a reptile slowly feeling the need for heat.

Anya thought, Peewee will be the only one for whom it's not strange. She herself would make Mac slide, float with her, neither of them able to touch the sides of what would happen.

It would all happen under her, under her gaze. She thought she felt Mac's pulse go faster. She wished she could will it. The trick was to hold both the girl and Mac in her mind, to prolong the thought, deliciously. It was like the dark sun by the lake in Ontario.

But Anya was taken by surprise when Peewee came in. Anya didn't hear the door. She saw Peewee's thin legs back-lighted by the candlelight. The girl was in the middle of the room. Anya got up. Peewee said, "I can't sleep in that cold in there."

Anya said, "Get in here."

The girl stood still until Anya pulled her by the waist. They sat down on the bed with a thump. Anya laughed. She sensed her edge as a familiar taste. It was the girl herself—her nerves, not her flesh—that gave the new taste, like the sharp cold ozone after a discharge of electricity into the air.

Anya lay still, listening to the shallow breathing of the other two. She imagined the girl floating between Mac and her. Anya thought Mac and the girl were in her spell. She guessed that Mac was waking up. Every minute that went by the nervous film covering all three of them grew more finely conductive.

Anya waited a long time. She had no idea of how many seconds or minutes, but she sensed the tension diminish, go smooth, flare up again. Several times. She pulled the quilt sideways. She imagined she could feel the others through it.

She touched the girl's foot with hers lightly. The girl moved her foot, pretended she was asleep. Anya pressed a little harder, heard the girl's breath hiss.

Anya heard and felt the girl's other leg move. Anya imagined the net of feeling, the lightness. She guessed that Mac would move toward her. She tried to feel him transmitted through the girl.

She enjoyed drifting, wavering between what she knew and what she had to guess. But suddenly she again felt her prickly irritation.

When she put her hand on the small of the girl's back, she felt the girl become suddenly heavy, dense, as though the girl's body had just become half marble through the hips, weighing down heavily into the hard bed.

Again a hiss of breath.

Anya reached her arms around the girl to touch Mac. She pulled one of his arms over the girl, pressed the girl against him. The girl turned on her back toward Anya. Anya kissed her mouth, returned her toward Mac. Anya put her mouth on the girl's ear, breathed into it, stuck her tongue in. A small bitter taste of wax on the tip of her tongue. Anya said, "Go on, go on." Anya grabbed the back of the girl's neck, felt how thin it was, reached around and felt the girl's mouth; the girl took Anya's fingers into her mouth, gobbling at them.

Anya touched Mac's hand, was surprised at its size—of

course, she thought, compared to the girl's small bones. She didn't want his hand to touch her, not if he knew it was her. She thought he was still more asleep than awake.

Anya pressed forward until she and the girl were both piled across Mac. Anya's forearm was still around the girl's neck, her hand on the girl's cheek. The girl began to kiss Mac's face, still with that old thirsty gobbling motion with her lips, like a fat-mouthed, toothless fish. Anya could hear it, could feel the girl's cheek with her hand. The girl moved down to lower Mac's sweat pants. Anya smoothed his hair.

Anya thought, This is at last beyond me. At last something to submit to. She had meant to reduce this girl to a quiver between her and Mac, a flow of sensation between them. But through her left hand following the girl's cheek, her right hand barely touching Mac's forehead, she realized she herself was in the middle.

She lost track of the design of their bodies on the bed, she began to move only by touch, by her desire to be touched, to keep going on and on. She was only able to measure that first period by the fact that from time to time she reached with her hand for the girl's strange mouth, the full peeled-back upper lip.

Later she lost the girl's mouth, she found her hands in Mac's hair, her own mouth imitating the girl's, gobbling at Mac's skin.

Later she felt Mac begin to move. She and the girl were already naked, entwined, as they both touched Mac's bare legs, touched his stomach and chest under his loose sweat shirt. Anya felt a tang of fear and satisfaction that they were all giving in, all intent on their blind trembling hands. They all touched each other.

She held her own cunt while the girl rode up on Mac, each whinny of the girl reaching her through her breastbone. She was for a moment the little girl, she lay down against him, against them, wriggling and begging with little whimpers. She knew she was not like that, and it was for an instant deliciously strange that she could feel so strongly that she was.

She thought coolly at the same time that Mac could keep going only if they stopped him short, kept him engorged but restless. She touched the girl, and she stopped. Anya was deliberate again. She felt the girl's mouth more care-

197

fully, just with her fingertips. The girl's throat, the girl's thin arms, sharp elbows. Small tight breasts.

Anya said, "Are you always this thin?" She moved onto Mac.

The girl said, "No. Just lately," as she moved off.

Mac held Anya's hips, and Anya felt how much thicker and stronger she was than the girl, a pleasant feeling—as though she were admiring herself with her own hands, held by Mac's hands, floating apart from her body.

He and she were both rigid, their slow motion making themselves heavy with their tense muscles. Anya leaned forward to kiss him—even his tongue seemed hard as a spoon.

The girl put her hand on Anya's mouth. Anya opened her mouth, sucked the edge of the girl's hand, held on with her teeth. The girl's other hand began to tickle Anya's breast—it was annoying.

Anya rolled to one side and got Mac on top of her. She wanted to become soft, to feel soft, but the effect of their bodies was still harsh and gymnastic. She was tired of her idea.

But she relaxed, felt comfortably absent-minded, came sharply and locally. Mac came with a sharp release of his breath.

After a moment Anya and the girl moved him back to his side of the bed and massaged him as he lay on his stomach. He seemed to be trying to rouse himself against the weight of their hands, but he finally collapsed back into sleep.

Anya got up and stood by the window, listening to the rain, feeling the push of the cold air through the window.

Peewee came and curved her body against Anya's. Peewee's body seemed hot and delicate. Anya felt a delicious pity for Peewee's small smooth skin, for the wiry nervousness that seemed to require a softer embrace than Peewee's rough experience or imagination allowed. Anya found herself thinking softly that she was in Uncle Timmy's position. She wondered if Uncle Timmy had felt this same detached pity for her body as he had handled her after his first rush of eagerness had passed. Anya listened to the rain until she heard Peewee mew and press against her hand.

Peewee settled down to sleep, and Anya was left awake. She was more amused than worried about this flurry. She knew that Mac might take it seriously, but she let that thought slide away. She held on a little longer to the thought that this sortie had ended up a defeat of the imagination, but, she thought finally, not of the main force of her imagination. She felt an odd neutral contentment as she thought of what she meant to do at the theater the next day.

* * *

When Mac woke up both Anya and Peewee were downstairs. He remembered, he felt a panic: Anya can change everything.

He felt disemboweled, dispossessed of the power to claim anything, to be angry, to instruct.

An odd splinter of erotic feeling—he remembered the girl, her smallness, her ferocity; he had done it with pleasure, with a thin heat. Odd then that he should have moved with such timidity, as though approaching a clearing with difficult stealth, pushing aside springy branches.

That pleasure now stabbed him with fear and helplessness.

He forced himself to dress and go downstairs. He was surprised to see them both. Relieved. He could make amends. They were sitting together. They were laughing. He thought for a second they were laughing at him because they'd made him dream it. This was such good news that he decided he would not be angry with them.

A second later he knew again—though it was hard to believe, it was also impossible to disbelieve. Everything was sharp as the edge of the table.

He made himself speak. He said, "I've got to go work for Sigurd today."

Anya said, "What?"

He mumbled again that he had to work for Sigurd.

Anya said, "Well, we'll get you breakfast."

His speech had exhausted him. He sat down. He felt he'd been shouting across a valley.

Anya said, "Peewee, the milk can is outside in the pumphouse."

Mac sat at the table while the two of them began to mix some batter. When he heard Raftery and Dulcie getting up he drank a glass of milk and left.

It was a windy, brilliant fall day.

Sigurd offered him a cup of coffee, joked that getting up early and having to work had got Mac down.

Mac worked furiously and silently all morning forking out manure from the sheep barn. The wind slipped through the long slits between the standing planks and lifted bits of straw through the bars of cold sunlight. Mac felt hollow and endlessly enduring.

At lunch he started to eat a lot but couldn't finish what was on his plate. Mrs. Olson's feelings were hurt. She joked about it awkwardly. He thought what a pleasure it would have been—he liked the Olsons' loud cheerful voices, the plain order of their lives, Sigurd's delight at having a new audience to whom he could explain his machines and systems.

"This manure spreader here is a little bit different, I improved it over the way it was . . ."

Mac thought, *Domine, no sum dignus ut intres sub tectum meum . . .*

As he thought that, he felt the influence of the off-and-on year with Anya come into focus. He wasn't overwhelmed with how ridiculous he sounded—he *was* unworthy—but he was alerted to a possible mimicry—as though the rolling soundwaves of his remorse were baffled by his idea of her, and then were echoed back to him more thinly and with a slightly different phrasing, so that he heard, not parody, but a tinny clarity that was vulnerable to parody.

He maneuvered away from his sense of being observed. After a while he felt tired and steady.

When he left the barn to drive a tractor and wagon down to Sigurd in one of the lower fields next to the woods, he noticed that the wind had dropped, the light was slanting and full, the sweat, dust, and bits of straw on him dried into an ammoniac plaster (like a pig's mud in the sun). The air was sweet in his mouth. He felt cradled between the rising fields east of the road and the woods growing along the river. The air, the earth, himself, all softening into each other. The center of the world.

At the end of the afternoon he asked Sigurd why he didn't plant corn in the fields next to the river.

Sigurd said, "They don't drain right. It if rains more than usual in the spring, and it usually does"—Sigurd laughed at his joke—"then the seeds rot. It'll sometimes flood right up to the dike. Then the only thing living down here is mushrats. You probably say muskrats."

Mac said, "Why don't you plant rice?"

Sigurd laughed. "Supposing you could find a rice that would grow here, and supposing you got all the machines —see, you couldn't pay a work crew even if you could find them—supposing that, and that you found a buyer, then I guarantee that year it wouldn't rain at all. Or maybe you could get them Mexicans to bring it in, like the tomato farmers hire over by Muscatine to pick tomatoes. I wouldn't do it. I wouldn't want to treat anyone the way they treat them. Of course I don't blame them farmers. A whole gang of strangers you can't even talk to. No, I'll tell you, corn and soybeans. You can't beat it around here." He pointed across the road. "And pigs. If the market's right, maybe cattle. The way the cattlemen think they're better than pig farmers. You wouldn't think so, but pigs is the way to grow meat. They breed faster. You can get twenty times as many pigs as cows in a year. And then cattle can't clean up a field the way pigs can. You watch the way pigs eat corn, and you tell me what you see. The trouble with most farmers is they won't look at what their animals really do all day. Now, I'm at a stage in life where I look at what I'm doing. I'm looking for some pleasure. I have them sheep just to see. They're dumber than pigs, more likely to get sick. But we'll see. You got to keep yourself interested or there's no sense in being here." Sigurd smiled a square-toothed smile. "Of course I made quite a bit in real estate so I can afford to stand around and talk awhile."

Mac found himself attuned to Sigurd. The man's health and boisterous optimism were not false—they were flung up from the man's land as thick as the corn and soybeans. He'd planted himself and cared for himself and was well pleased with himself.

And yet Mac felt at the same time that the affection could only go from him to Sigurd. Sigurd couldn't know him, and that made it all false. They were attached to each other only by a thin cord of language. Otherwise Mac was sure he would drift away from Sigurd and Sigurd wouldn't notice.

Mrs. Olson invited him to stay for supper. Mac said he should get back to the others. She gave him one of the pies

201

she'd baked. They discussed the crust—she asked with some surprise if he did the cooking over there. Mac said they all shared it, but Dulcie and he did most of it. Mrs. Olson said, "Now, I don't mean to ask you questions. That's your home and you keep it whatever way you see fit."

Mac didn't get it for a second. He couldn't tell if she was embarrassed that she'd raised the subject of who lived in the house, and therefore who lived with whom, or if she was simply embarrassed that he might think she'd disapproved of his doing woman's work.

Sigurd offered him a ride, but he said he'd rather walk. Halfway home he realized he was exhausted. He'd never felt so tired and wobbly. It wasn't just his muscles, though he knew he would soon stiffen up—five hours out of ten in the sheep barn—it was his emotions that seemed to have a pitch and surge of their own. They were almost colorless, unfocused, but their motion was tireless, sloshing without meaning over his numb mind—their motion and his own dull reeling both only echoes of some earlier collision of energies.

He deliberately tried to think of a detail of the night before that would arouse him into a response (a stirring in his gut or prick, then a constriction of shame). He couldn't do it. He thought of Anya—no feeling, only her as his observer.

He was no longer appalled by his defeat—he could barely remember how it was a defeat. He had once thought that his careful goodness was a restraint against her deliberate wildness. That notion was certainly gone now—that wheedling golden rule: "If I don't do anything wrong, nobody else ought to either."

But that wasn't it—there was also something he was sorry to see go. Did he fear that she'd maneuvered him? Or that they'd lost their importance to each other? That something slowly acquired had been quickly shattered? He was too exhausted to settle his thoughts, to see if anything he was thinking was right. At that moment he had a desire to lie beside her as numb as he was and, in lying next to her, measure her physical presence against all the notions of her that were winding and unwinding in him. It could be, he thought, that she still matched one of his better ideas after all. That would be a great relief.

By the time he reached the house it was dark. He

smelled the smoke from the chimney and saw the moonlight reflected in the back window of the green Volkswagen. By then he was happy to reach the kitchen and sit still in the warmth.

Anya was in the bathroom—she'd lit the kerosene water heater and was pouring another bucket into the tank.

Mac drew another pail of water and went in. Anya said, "You must be exhausted." She thought it was funny.

Mac undressed and got in the empty tub and sponged the dirt and straw off his ankles, wrists, and neck.

She said, "What are you doing?"

He said, "I don't want to sit in my own crud."

He pushed the mess down the drain with his foot and poured the rest of the pail after it. He dried himself, and stuck his hand in the open tank. It was lukewarm. He lay down on the pile of laundry behind the door. Anya lay down beside him.

She said, "I had a terrible day at the theater."

Mac didn't say anything.

Anya said, "Bangs has done it—she got Ray to spend the night. I think he told his wife he had to spend the night in Des Moines. But I'm sure it's going to crack open—they're being—"

Mac shook his head and said, "Oh. That."

She said, "Well, it's going to be a problem. We've done pretty well with *Wozzeck,* though. It's pretty well booked for this last week."

Mac closed his eyes. Anya put her arms around his head and stroked his forehead with her fingers.

The cool sweetness astonished him. He felt himself letting go.

Anya laughed. "We must look like the *Pietà.*"

It didn't bother him.

Just her cold fingertips. It was just right.

He thought of her as somewhere else. He remembered her. Not at any specific place. He was being forced to admit that she rose up in him—not just that he was drawn to her through his eyes, the flare of interest in her looks, her long arms, the shape of her face. That could happen with Annabelle's belly, Bangs's droopy soft mouth, with any girl, with any flicker of light on almost any surface of skin —the side of the knee, the cheek, the soft blue white be-

203

tween the breasts—any rustling single step hollowing the ankle. He was a barbarian, without any art, so what else could he do but want to touch? The desire to devour by seeing, touching, the ravenous touching running back into his deepest nerves. A barbaric urge to get what he saw, to spoil his own sight.

But he felt Anya's resurgence within him. Was that cleaving to her? Beyond his senses—an appetite for her presence. An appetite that no movement of his senses toward her could satisfy—only the movement of her presence in time.

Anya got up, checked the water, let it run into the tub.

He realized he was enormously hungry. Anya left to go help with supper. He thought that one of the things that had been bothering him was that he was afraid this life was letting him become dumb again. He was pleased to consider this worry, turn it this way and that in his mind, not really bothered by it; there was lots of time, there were plenty of ways to take care of it.

Later he was lying in bed, Anya lying beside him, watching him and listening to him. He was trying to explain what had made him so tired walking back from Sigurd's. He was struggling to say it had been like walking on shore after being in a boat, still having to struggle with the pitching—the phantom movement more tiring than the real. She was laughing because he wasn't making what he was saying clear. He was too tired. He was absorbed in the pleasure of being tired.

She said, "You really are a work junkie."

He tried to explain.

He heard her say, "It's like trying to understand you when you talk in your sleep."

He gave up. She said, "You do, you know—you even try to answer questions."

He said, "This feels good. I can feel myself falling asleep, it's up to me." He felt his face go slack.

CHAPTER

The next several days were bright and cold, filled with surface irritations and worries. On Saturday there was an all-day pecking of gunfire in the distance—the first day of pheasant season. Raftery stopped two hunters cutting across the yard and recited his poem against hunting to them. They left bemused. Dulcie was cooking a bean casserole to take over to the theater. They were entertaining some newspaper people for supper—from the University paper, the *Daily Iowan;* the Iowa City paper, the *Press Citizen;* and the *Cedar Rapids Gazette.* And a reporter from the women's page of the *Des Moines Register.*

Peewee minded the baby.

Mac went for a walk. Saw a lot of squirrels and rabbits, a few ducks resting under the far riverbank. On the way back he saw a cock pheasant pop through a square of woven wire fence and disappear into the knee-high wind-twisted grass. He tried to scare him out. Couldn't find him.

Mac thought quite a few birds might come down to hide near the woods. Sigurd's land was posted on the river side of the road, but he gave permission to friends to shoot in the picked corn up across the road. Chains of five or six men had been beating through the last bit of standing corn all morning.

Mac walked down to Sigurd's and asked if Sigurd would mind if he shot along the bottom land. Sigurd ended up selling him an old side-by-side sixteen gauge for an extra half-day's work. He threw in two boxes of shells, no. 7½ and no. 5, light loads. The gun had been for his daughter

—that was why the loads were light, and why there was a cheek pad on the stock.

Mac realized it was a favor.

On the way back to the house Mac stopped into the ditch to piss. His fingers were cold on his prick. He glanced up and down the road—no cars—started, and gasped with pain. He tried to stop pissing, that made it worse. His eyes filled with tears and the tears made cold streaks down his cheekbones. His piss was burning. It felt as though it was scraping out his urethra. His head lolled to one side. He said, "Oh Jesus!" and ground his teeth, first one side then the other while he finished pissing.

A white plume of dust appeared down the road. He tucked his prick in. The pain was over. He guessed it was gonorrhea—he tried to remember the army training film—surely it wasn't syphilis, no sores. Clap then; it wasn't that bad, but was it contagious? or infectious? That was it. That meant Peewee had it. And Anya. There was only one way to get it, that was true, wasn't it?

But after his initial calm he began to worry again. His nervous shame, which he'd thought he'd put in its place and which the cheerful indifferent way Anya and Peewee behaved had lulled, re-emerged in him.

After supper at the theater house he walked home alone. Anya was having a good time talking to the newspaper people. She'd probably stay for the performance.

Dulcie was sitting by the stove playing her guitar.

* * *

When Anya stepped onto the porch she stopped for a moment outside the door to listen to Mac and Dulcie talking. She was surprised once again at how awkward they were with each other. Or did they just *sound* awkward? Did they even sound awkward to each other?

Anya thought of the love scene between Wozzeck and Maria—that should have that same pathetic, mute quality, as if Wozzeck were an animal who'd learned to speak. But of course Dulcie and Mac were not mute, only unbearably slow with each other as though the words they spoke—to each other—had to be without resonance, certain and pure, as though they were explaining things to a child and were fearful that the child might be shocked by a word carrying any of their real feelings. Their language to each other was not so much censored as puréed.

Anya laughed through her nose. Dulcie heard Hugh cry. Anya went in.

She had to take Mac back to fix the equipment for the last scene—Wozzeck drowning himself. If it wasn't just right, people giggled. Wozzeck jumped off the stage upstage—blackout—sound effects of water—black light on—Wozzeck in an invisible harness appearing to be swimming and struggling—only his treated hands and feet and face showed up in the black light. The visible effect was that he was writhing in a current. The noise of the harness was supposed to be covered by sound effect. He was swung into long underwater weeds, which were also treated and lit by black light. Weeds entangled Wozzeck's feet—sound effects up—Wozzeck undulating with weeds as though floating submerged.

The problem was working the ropes that ran from the harness through a pulley, which in turn was on a short metal track, without making a racket. The effect of Wozzeck's face and hands and feet whirling in desperate slow motion across thirty feet, the long luminous strands of water wrack winding around his legs, his tangled suspension in what appeared to be mid-water followed by a sound effect of the bubbling emptying of his lungs (a recording of a large jug glugging under water in a tub) was wonderful and horrifying, and, Anya admitted, mostly Mac's idea. After the first performance one of the people in the drama department of the University had told her it looked like a nightmare of drowning. Right. But at the third performance the illusion didn't take—Anya couldn't tell whether it was the creaking of the block and tackle or the rollers on the I-beam's rims, or a crackling in the sound-effects tape; or if a backstage light had been left on and showed a stagehand working the strands of weed. She had Andrew make a new tape and had Mac check out the mechanics—grease the wheels, oil the pulley. She made sure Mac was the one who worked the rope—it seemed to give Tagh more confidence to swim and twist around. Tagh was terrified of falling.

She was now suddenly angry with Mac. She hated to have to order him to do something. The only decent way to run things was if everyone did everything without having to be told. She realized she was angry—unfairly angry—

exactly because Mac was usually good at guessing what needed to be done.

And here he was wallowing in Dulcie's mother love.

She restrained herself. She explained—overelaborately—why she wanted him to run the drowning scene.

In the car he told her he thought he had the clap. She said, "Well, it's not serious, is it? You don't feel bad, do you?" She knew she was being a prick, but she was running the whole thing. She recognized the harried-executive cliché and was annoyed at herself.

Mac said, "I'm not complaining. I'm telling you because if I've got it, it must be that you and Peewee have it, too."

Anya said, "I see." She wondered if their theater-group Blue Cross covered gonorrhea.

She said, "We'll go in Monday to the doctor."

Mac said, "Let's try to find someone tomorrow, okay? This gunk is pouring out of me. I had to put a sock over my prick so it wouldn't run down my leg."

Anya stopped the car in the theater barnyard.

Mac said, "I am worried about— Do you know for sure that the only way you can catch it is fucking? I'd hate to have Hugh get infected."

Anya said, "I'm pretty sure." She laughed. "Darling— our first social disease."

Walking outside the theater barn she was excited again by the eerie silence of a still audience listening. *She*'d caught them in that cage. At the same time she was filled with pleasure at all her feelings—alive in the shadow of the barn. She hugged Mac from behind, leaned against his hard back. He hadn't laughed at her joke, but he was somehow charmed by her again, she was sure. He hooked her elbows with his and they half-struggled, half-embraced, and finally stood still.

Then they went in through the door behind the stage. The space was half lit by the blue nightlight at the steps and the glow from the hooded gooseneck lamp on the prop table.

She thought, Just as well he's got clap, it's the perfect penance.

She then thought, Is he another audience I've lured into a theater? Do I need a private audience as well as a public one? Is that what he is? And I have my backstage to myself. Is that what I do?

*   *   *

Mac decided he liked the life at the theater and at Raftery's because the people could behave in more ways than would ordinarily be possible. For example, both Anya and Raftery would have been considered crazy show-offs by the people he'd gone to high school with, by his parents and sisters, by his father's friends, by his mother's family in Canada. He didn't count the army; he himself had been considered a misfit there. But all the other circumstances he had been in, had enjoyed being in—including his circumstances at college—had been straitened, had allowed very little impersonation.

Mac recognized that this was an obvious observation, but it had not occurred to him so bluntly and deeply as when he withdrew for a period after Anya, Peewee, and he went to the doctor.

The treatment was routine—the doctor was bored but pleasant, perhaps amused at the three of them trooping in to the hospital on a slow Sunday. He was sympathetic to Mac's fears, told him that gonorrhea was common as a cold around the University. Ran a swab up Mac's urethra to get a culture. Mac closed his eyes and clenched his fists. The doctor ran another swab up Mac's ass. Mac said, "Wait a minute—"

The doctor said, "This is the way we do it."

Mac said, "Why don't you come out and ask me if I've been buggered?"

The doctor said, "Look, the whole area is susceptible to infection, it's a question of proximity. This is the way we do it."

Mac asked him if the amount of his discharge was normal. The doctor said that, yes, sometimes it really pours out.

Mac said, "That first piss hurt, but it's not so bad anymore. Is that the way it goes?"

The doctor said, "Usually. If it does hurt as severely as at first or you feel like your urethra is constricted, let us know."

Mac said, "One other thing—"

The doctor said, "Stay out of action for a while."

Mac said, "I was going to ask about contagion."

"It's not contagious. You get it through direct contact."

"So the child of some friends of ours couldn't get it."

"Not from you. But in general, dormitories and student houses and so forth are unhygienic, very fertile media for disease, so if this inspired your group to clean up—nothing wrong with that."

Mac thought their house was clean but said nothing.

Monday he worked for Sigurd storing corn in the drying silos.

Tuesday he worked on the new set.

Whenever he was at the theater or around the house he kept busy—without forcing himself, just letting himself drift into work. He sawed wood, replaced a wick in a kerosene lamp, put up the storm windows and chinked them.

At meals he just listened.

Peewee said one night at supper, "Where do you get your grass? It's not Mexican."

Raftery said, "I don't know his name. I don't know where it's from. The stuff we're down to now is local. I didn't know you were so discriminating."

Mac thought Raftery might be pissed off because all the grass was his except two ounces Anya had. Peewee smoked after supper without seeming to enjoy it very much. Mac had stopped even his few tokes.

Peewee said, "Do you know Mercks? I went on a buying trip with Mercks last summer. He never smoked while he was dealing, so he got me to smoke a little before he bought any. You know, just to see it hit. It got so I hated it. Just while I was down there."

"Down where?"

"Mexico. We went to three places before he finally bought some. Way up in some mountains. I had to tell him if it was better or worse than the last place. He'd take one toke, just for taste, and then he'd watch while I smoked. You see, he'd seen me smoke a lot of different stuff that he'd smoked too, so he could tell . . . The last time was really bad, we drove with this old guy all one night. I was scared to begin with and we got to this field and there were all these Mexicans with guns. So they said, 'Have you got the money?' I understood that much and Mercks just said yes, and waited. And then they argued and shouted at him. It was like a movie. A big adventure scene, the moon over the mountains, and there we were"——Peewee laughed——"the hero and heroine. Except I knew we couldn't think of anything. So finally Mercks rolled me a joint and I smoked it. I was just about fainting but I knew he was using me. It was a turn-on in a way, there we were about to die—that's what I thought—here he was about to die and still being the same old shit to me. Cool. He said, 'How's it hit, Peewee?' So I began to laugh, and they all laughed. Mercks smiled. What a bastard! It was good grass. Good taste; good deep, clean hit—not sneaky. Didn't make your stomach feel bad, in fact it seemed to me to kind of be calming. This was somewhere near Oaxaca. So we drove with the old man and two of the others with the grass, and we went to a house and these women there packed it into cones of newspaper. You know, with the top folded over and tucked in. It took all night. And then we had to stay in Mexico another three weeks, I don't know why, doing nothing except drinking beer and smoking different stuff. That's how I know the names of all the places and what the stuff's like. If he'd let me alone I would have been really stoned all the time or else quit or maybe tried something else, but we'd only smoke a little at night. I was out of my head—I got to hate grass, and him, and being there."

Raftery said, "Why did you stay?"

Peewee said, "Well—it's funny . . . Because he only gave me just a little grass, and just a little piece of him . . . I really didn't mind hating it. From just smoking that little and from just *being* with him—we didn't talk much and he wouldn't ball, I blew him, and he watched me beat off—from that little bit of grass and him, I made a picture. No, not even a picture, a kind of—paste."

Peewee looked at Raftery. She said, "Do you see what I mean?" She held her hands up as though she were squeezing a ball. "Everything mashed together. Everything. Feeling sick or feeling good all mixed in so that while we were still there I couldn't feel any difference. You see? I couldn't feel the difference between scratching an itch or having the squirts or giving him head or drinking a beer or driving the car. On purpose."

She shook her head. She said, "You don't see what I mean, do you?"

Raftery said he did.

Mac thought that he himself didn't—he understood Peewee's telling the story and ending up saying she did something on purpose, but he wasn't interested in thinking about what it made her feel. He could think of a lot of questions he could ask her that would make the whole thing clearer, but he had no interest in asking them. He was horrified that Anya began to question her after Raftery.

He went in to the bathroom and lit the water heater and then cleaned his shotgun with a pull-through while he waited for the water to get hot.

When he was lying in the bath, Anya came in. He made a great effort and said, "Don't worry. It won't last long."

He realized she thought he meant the clap. He couldn't find the strength to say what he meant. His depression settled back over him.

*   *   *

Anya couldn't help thinking that Mac was being self-indulgent. He didn't say anything, but he emanated a silent dirge.

She would have been happy to take the blame and call the whole thing finished. She resented that he thought he was being good by not blaming her. She didn't think he was being so good—it was his crazy wooden vanity that made him pretend that everything that happened in his life was up to him.

As far as she could tell he wasn't giving any thought to what she was thinking *now*. And she had a great many other things to think about.

Peewee seemed happier and happier. She was very comfortable with Dulcie—Anya noticed their voices sounded alike, Dulcie's tone was richer, her Kansas accent more extreme in its crushed-glass *r*'s than Peewee's Iowa version, but they had the same rhythms, said "Anya" the same way, a narrow *a* as in *ani*mal. Peewee filled a gap in Hugh's life, since Mac didn't play with him the whole week after Mac went to the doctor.

Peewee took the green Volkswagen to town one afternoon and came back with a four-pound steak. She flopped it down on the kitchen table proudly. Raftery guessed at once that she'd stolen it, and he was delighted. Dulcie was alarmed. Dulcie didn't eat any, and silently disapproved of Raftery's eating meat. Mac didn't eat any of Dulcie's pie either. Anya and Raftery were cheerful and gluttonous enough to make Peewee feel pleased.

Anya had this to say for Mac—while he was brooding he didn't scowl at their pleasure, and he didn't increase the intensity of his brooding in order to get noticed. He really did try to be unnoticeable. She would have noticed any acting tricks.

She followed him one late afternoon when he went hunting.

He seemed dreamy, moved slowly. He sat down for a while. He roused himself with a great effort. He walked up to the fence and shook it. A bird got up. He swung the gun after it but didn't fire.

The short day grew darker. She yelled at him and waved. He appeared so startled that for an instant she was afraid of him.

He came over and said, "What is it?"

She said, "Nothing, I thought I'd walk along. How come you didn't shoot that bird? It looked like a pheasant to me."

"It was a hen pheasant."

"What's wrong with a hen?"

"Only cocks are legal here."

Anya laughed. She said, "I wish you wouldn't keep on being depressed."

He said, "I know. I'm stuck with it."

"It's not just your dose of clap, is it?"

"No. Even before that—the day after . . . the rainstorm—"

"What a pretty euphemism."

"Okay, the day after we fucked Peewee. I suddenly got tired. It doesn't just have to do with fucking Peewee. It's being up in the air in general. I thought I was okay again that night. More than okay—restored. And simple-minded, as though I wanted nothing else except to stick to your bones."

Anya knew a but was coming. She said, "But . . ."

Mac said, "It's like being lost in a fog but moving in a fast current. I haven't ever felt—No. I felt this way once before in the army, the time I was in the stockade. I thought I might go crazy. I thought I might go crazy if I ever let myself get as angry as I felt like getting. I had a glimpse then—I need the physical world to be the center of my attention. I think that's what my going crazy means —that I let something besides the physical world be the center of my attention. No. It's when the physical world has less influence on what I'm thinking than what I'm imagining has. That's not it either. It has to do with balance. I'll get it back. A good month of work ought to do it."

Anya felt desperate. She saw him from a great distance, walking through a flat meadow by himself, his prick still dribbling pus, the day darkening, herself no comfort—not even there (she thought her picture was accurate in that regard; she wasn't there except as a dramatic convention, to be able to hear what he said), speaking calmly and hollowly of what he saw was a flaw in himself, a flaw he thought was opening even though he couldn't really see it, only feel it—no, guess that he felt it. She could imagine what it was like for him—a constant fearful dream underlying everything.

She'd always thought if she ever cared about anyone she would be marvelously potent toward whoever it was, work wonders. In fact, now she didn't even have anything to say.

She also knew, however, that her understanding, for all its feeling of suddenness, did not depend on what he'd just said, that her view of him was not one that she'd worked for. She was struck by how their lives had merged, in an ordinary, lumpish way, from a sharp physical attraction— but no sharper than a lot of others, surely—to this weight of knowing him.

That was the surprise, and that was what made her flutter with revulsion, that his feelings could settle in her, and that she had less control over them than she did over her own feelings, and yet they were mixed with her feelings, and by some dark impulse (of his? or hers?) were supposed to *be* her feelings.

She thought, In all fairness . . . then she thought, Fairness has nothing to do with it.

One thing that had pricked her was that he seemed to be saying that he did not expect her to be any help. He hadn't made a complaint, there was no tone of complaint.

She resented that he thought he was an independent atom, that he was so blind and wrong. And she admired his effort.

Had he begun to speak to her about his depression in a way calculated to drag her into it? No. After all she'd *asked* him. And his tone had been only expository. But she'd never believed in anyone's simplicity.

And yet she believed they were in that one way alike— she wouldn't like to ask him to lament for her. They both had drawn rules of self-sufficiency. Of course it was his self-sufficiency, his trust in his own good balance and density that was the very thing he feared for.

She couldn't bear to be in phase with his slow processes. Let him mend and then join her again.

She thought perhaps she could arrange her sympathy from a distance. She was interested, she could take a knowledgeable interest. It was not necessary that she choose— that she either had to be swirled down into him or cut herself off.

And she had a curious faith in him—that he might surprise her after all by bulling his way through, healing himself with a brutal will.

Easier now, she felt an urge to touch him, to see if perhaps he'd eased up too. A friendly examination.

But when she touched his arm he dropped the gun and seized her—shaking her hard. He wasn't angry, she realized after a second, he was shaking her because his arms were trembling, his chest and shoulders in spasms.

She let him calm himself against her, but she had to keep herself from pushing him off, from saying something angry and cruel.

She thought he might have guessed because after a moment he let go, picked up his shotgun, and walked back toward the house without looking around.

She thought it was what he'd wanted, how deep what he wanted was, that had alarmed her. Revolted her. It was not his fear rattling at the gates, it was the weight of his longing to reach her center. Her defenses had never flung up so instantly and reflexively.

* * *

When Mac got to the edge of the house yard he saw that the green Volkswagen was back, that whoever had been using it had left the lights on. There was another car in back of it. Peewee came out of the kitchen door and stood

215

on the porch. Two guys got out of the car in back. Mac stopped and watched.

One of the guys said, "C'mon, Peewee. Mercks wants to see you again."

The other one said, "Yeah. He's not mad at you."

Mac couldn't hear what Peewee mumbled back. She wasn't wearing a coat, she tucked her hands under her arms and shifted her feet. She suddenly walked down the stairs and got in the front seat of the boys' car. The two boys got in on either side of her. The driver started the car and the three of them sat for a moment while the car idled.

Mac looked around to see where Anya was. He couldn't see her.

The car backed up, wheeled around the yard in a circle, and shot out the gateway onto the road. He thought he could see the boy on the right pull Peewee toward him as the car accelerated out of its turn. He wasn't sure. It struck him as odd that the car turned right, away from town.

He turned the Volkswagen lights off. He considered following the car. He could see its lights still, almost to Sigurd's now. He walked to the fence and looked after the car. It had stopped. It turned around, taking several backward and forward rolls to come around on the narrow road. Mac was sure now he should stop them but he couldn't make himself move fast. He got into the Volkswagen, lay his gun on the back seat, and put his hand on the key. But the boys' car stopped at the gate. Its lights went out, and it rolled into the yard past the Volkswagen, past the house, all the way to the back of the yard beside the small hay barn. It wheeled around to face the road and stopped with a jerk. The two boys got out and stood by the open doors. Peewee got out on the driver's side, and the driver seemed to embrace her.

Mac still found it hard to move. He watched through the windshield. It was hard to see what Peewee was doing, whether she was being held or whether she was moving freely against the boy.

The other boy came around the front of the car and stood by the couple, cutting off Mac's vision. Mac closed his eyes. He couldn't think—Sigurd's barn, Peewee's hands tucked under her arms—she hadn't wanted to go, she'd got in the car, they were all in the yard.

The three of them were walking to the barn door. They rolled it open. Mac picked up the shotgun, ill at ease and cramped. He took the flashlight from the glove compartment and walked over to the barn. He stood beside the open door. He listened. They weren't speaking. He knew he couldn't stay and listen, but he couldn't leave. He walked in slowly. He could hear them, ahead and to his right in the dark. He said, "Peewee?" There was no sound.

One of the boys said, "Hey, what do you want?"

Mac heard the other boy moving to his left. He shone the flashlight at him. The batteries were old. The light was yellow and unfocused. The boy stopped for a second and then kept moving toward him. The boy said, "Hey man—"

Mac said, "Stop."

The boy said, "Hey, just a second, man, you don't want to come in here."

Mac shot in front of the boy's feet. Mac had to stop himself from firing again—his finger was already on the rear trigger, the butt was tucked under his armpit, the muzzle floating into the space between him and the boy. There was a fluttering of wings as several pigeons flew out the doorway.

Firing the shot had released Mac, he breathed deeply, as though the shot had given off cold ozone like an electric arc. He was terrified of firing again, but he felt exhilarated. He knew he shouldn't say anything, it would be foolish to say anything. He backed to his left, still shining the flashlight to find the other one. The boy was fully dressed but his pants were open and his belt buckle dangled loose —a pair of saddle-girth rings.

The rings jingled as he stood up. The noise embarrassed him—he held the rings with his hand—but he was unwilling to take the time to fasten his belt.

Mac shone his light back to the boy in the middle of the barn. He motioned with his flashlight beam toward the one with the jingling belt. They moved together.

Mac felt a satisfaction that they all knew the rules, the steps of the dance, but he sensed already that he was going to feel overblown, ridiculous.

He broke open the shotgun with his right thumb on the lever and the empty shell popped out. He slowly reached in his pocket with his left hand, holding the flashlight in his left armpit, the gun in his right hand. He could feel the chill of the two of them. Mac inserted the shell and pulled the flashlight from his armpit with his left hand. The weak light wavered around the pair. As Mac slowly closed the gun the flashlight clinked on the bottom of the barrels.

Mac waved the two out the barn door with the light. They stopped in the doorway. The one with the unbuckled belt said, "Hey, Peewee, tell him it's okay, it's not—"

Mac said, "I'm not going to shoot you."

The pair went outside. They both turned around. The unbuckled one started talking with quick amiability. "You got the wrong idea—Peewee's an old friend, she's an old girl friend of this friend of ours, we all used to hang around together, it's not like we just came along, so it's not like something you need to get your gun out for."

Mac thought, or meant to say, It's not your place, you shouldn't push Peewee around. I don't want my yard a place for cheap shits with jingling belt buckles. He said, "It's not your barn."

The two looked surprised, looked at each other, started to get in their car, looked back at Mac to check on him. Mac lowered the shotgun. They got in and drove away.

Mac went inside, filled the water heater in the bathroom, lit it, and cleaned the shotgun with a pull-through while he waited for the water to heat up.

Anya came back into the yard in time to see Mac come out of the barn holding the light on two men. She'd heard a shot but it took her an instant to see Mac was pointing his shotgun at them.

They drove away, Mac went into the house, and Peewee came out of the barn.

Anya said, "What's going on?"

Peewee shrugged. Then she said, "Ask Mac, he's the one acting like a crazy old farmer."

Anya went into the bathroom. Mac didn't look up from cleaning the detached double barrel. Anya thought Peewee was right, he was choosing to act like a crazy old farmer. She thought it was hokey, and it alarmed her. She didn't think he knew as well as she did what he was doing. She was also, to a lesser degree, irritated that he probably wouldn't admit how deliberately he chose a role, that he was choosing to regard his difficulty as some uncontrollable piece of nature.

Raftery and Dulcie served up supper. Raftery finally asked what had happened. Anya suddenly felt sorry for Mac, knew he wanted to say he'd stopped two men from raping Peewee—no, he wanted someone else to say it.

Anya said to Peewee, "You didn't want to go off with those two?"

Peewee said, "They wanted me to go to Mercks' in town. I didn't want to do that, so I came back here."

Anya waited for Mac to ask. He didn't. So Anya said, "But you didn't want to go out to the barn?"

Peewee said, "No, it was too cold, but then I didn't want them in here."

Anya said, "Well, you're not much good as a prosecutrix."

Raftery said, "In Madagascar there's no such thing as rape." He beamed. "Everybody consents!"

Dulcie disapproved. She said, "Mac, you shouldn't shoot at people no matter what they're doing. If you just tell them . . ."

Raftery said, "Or stun their minds. The best martial arts are mental."

Dulcie said, "Can't you be serious?"

Raftery smiled at her.

Anya said to Mac, "There were a lot of other things you could do." She knew they were ganging up on Mac. There was some pleasure in seeing Mac in the wrong, she couldn't help it. "You could have driven over and got Og and Tagh. It doesn't take a minute in the car. There were only two of them."

Peewee mumbled, "What are you getting so excited about? I used to ball them, I just don't want to anymore. They can figure it out themselves. You know, if it's no good, they'll leave."

Anya thought of Jeannie in the ski lodge. It was different. Peewee was denser, stringier. And deader—deader at will in her flesh. Jeannie had oozed a sweet, ambiguous, genteel distress, had possibly savored her infected connections to propriety.

Anya said, "Besides they would have got the clap."
She saw that Mac gave up completely at that.

*   *   *

It got very cold the next day. They all disappeared from
each other under double layers of clothes. Peewee cut a
hole in a blanket and made a poncho out of it.

Anya offered to drive Mac to the theater after breakfast.
He said he'd walk up later. The night before he'd slept in
the bedroom off the kitchen. By Anya's reckoning it was
time for them to see the doctor to make sure they were
cured and could start screwing again. She'd thought they'd
cured the shock he'd felt: she remembered pressing against
his back outside the theater, his rolling forward and lifting
her a little. She missed that kind of fooling around—mock
combat, mock sex—the comedy of her as the aggressor,
subduing him into impossible coupling. How evenly they
were matched, balanced, how pleasantly she could forget
herself, how she could let her thought of herself lapse
entirely, go blank, trusting his feeling for her to take its
place. Not imagining herself as he *saw* her, but feeling herself formed in the dark by his complete attention. His attention, when she wished for it, commanded it, was a slow
mute heat which, as it focused on her and pictured her for
them both, rendered him to her.

She had tampered with that. She hadn't imagined he was
so unadjustable, might be baffled, do himself harm. Was
that what had happened?

He was angry, but without an object. In fact, barely
seemed to know he was angry, but turned away angrily
when she tried to probe him.

There would be some time for them. The theater was
closing over Thanksgiving weekend. If she had time
enough, he wouldn't be able to hold out.

The sky was gray and close, it felt like snow. She thought
that might cheer him up.

Mac turned to Raftery for comfort. The morning of the
next day Raftery came into Andrew's bedroom off the
kitchen where Mac was sleeping. Andrew was spending
several nights in town. Raftery brought Mac a cup of tea

220

and a cup of bean soup. Raftery sat on the foot of the bed
—a squat, ugly platform Raftery had built out from the
wall as bed or table or shelf. Mac remembered that during
the night he'd heard the squeaking of Raftery's bedsprings,
so old and loose they were almost a metal hammock,
muffled by the eiderdown and bolsters—Raftery and Dulcie
maintained an old-fashioned bed—and he'd heard Dulcie's
soprano crying out short fluted high notes, though without
any breathiness or tremor, or even urgency. Delicate and
regular.

Mac hadn't felt any twist of sexual feeling—no, he had
a little when he'd heard the bedsprings, but then Dulcie's
music had dispelled it. He'd been surprised, having feared
that his feelings would quicken and begin to grind, but
he'd been calmed. Not hushed and calmed, but brightened
and calmed. Then he'd gone to sleep, been wakened by
some other noise, and lain awake. Finally got up and
padded around the downstairs rooms, cold and anxious,
waiting for some thought.

Now in the morning, with Raftery on the foot of his bed,
he still felt anxious and expectant—he felt he wanted to
declare himself, to trust himself, to give himself to
Raftery.

Mac said, "This is good soup."

Raftery said, "The real way to have soup for breakfast
is to put it in a thick porcelain bottle at night and take it
to bed to warm your bed and then you end up keeping it
warm and then you have it for breakfast. Like drinking
your own blood's warmth."

"Have you ever tried it?"

Raftery laughed. "I only read about things."

Mac said, "You have Dulcie keeping you warm."

Raftery said, "Yes. When she was still nursing Hugh
—it was like that—the two of us keeping her porcelain
jugs of milk warm . . ." Raftery was pleased with the idea,
his hands flying up.

Raftery said, "You and Dulcie are a lot alike—your
serious blond instincts."

Mac said, "I think she's wonderful."

"I know, it works out—she has a sense of household
decorum that you satisfy. What's good, too, is your mute
gallantry. Not just to her, to women. It's amazing to me
how I admire qualities in you I find boring in most people.

Your respectful attitude toward a day's work, too. Were you ever involved with anyone like Dulcie?"

"No."

"Do you ever imagine what it would be like to be her?"

"No. No, I don't think I could. Do you?"

"Yes. But then I try to imagine lots of people. I'm promiscuous in that way. I bet you think it's an intimacy. An improper advance. Anya imagines what it's like to be other people. Have you heard her describe what it would be like to be Annabelle?—the slight retard between being touched and feeling you've been touched. It's very funny, but Anya imagines it as very erotic. For Annabelle and for the toucher, too—like playing an organ in a huge cathedral where the pipes are far away from the keyboard so you only hear the notes long after you've touched the keys.

"Have you ever imagined what it would be like to be fucked? Imagine your innards aroused instead of being the dull untouched meat they are now. Of course the whole thing could be still better—suppose you could have every other molecule of yours make room for every other molecule of someone else. Maybe that's why feeding is a pleasure —what it's like to be a large cat, you know, a bobcat or a mountain lion—leaping on your prey. Wouldn't that have everything?—all your nerves, flesh, and appetite flying, no weight—"

Mac said, "You must be a terror in Andrew's improvisation sessions."

Raftery said, "Well, that's applied science, mine is pure." He laughed.

Mac looked at Raftery's tight black hair, his eyes blinking through his glasses. Mac felt very tender about Raftery's spasmodically rapturous state of mind. He *could* imagine what it would be like to be Raftery, to be so light and volatile and be swept or sucked this way and that by unpredictably igniting wishes. Every idea Raftery had immediately set out on its own for the edge of the universe.

CHAPTER

||||||||||||||||||||||||||||||||||||||||||

13

Anya stopped worrying about theater expenses versus income, audiences, the fact that Ray (the professor from the drama department) left his family and moved in with Bangs, the protein content of the diet of the troupe, the publicly sulky fights between Og and Annabelle or their publicly smarmy reconciliations, the insurance agent's warning about the theater company's liability for passengers on the hired buses from the University dorms, the grant applications to foundations, the suspected pilfering from the cashbox at their ticket office in the Student Union, the wise-ass reviews in the University newspaper, Andrew's distress that his one pleasant friend and lover might not get tenure in the English department and might therefore leave before his contract was up, the flagging invention of Alice and Babette in the dance workout in the morning—

—and in the Raftery house she gave up worrying about Raftery's mad project for an American pageant in verse, she gave up worrying about saying exactly the right thing about the pages of scenario or declamation he showed to her, she gave up, as much as she could, worrying about when Mac would come back to her bed.

She couldn't help but notice, though, the affection he showed toward Hugh and Dulcie. It occurred to her, in the serial argument she carried on internally with Mac, that the way he and Dulcie played with Hugh between them was not unlike—not unlike, she carefully thought again—the incident of Mac, Peewee, and herself.

She rephrased her delineation of the parallel several

times even though she knew that if she ever spoke of it, Mac would be more offended than penetrated by the argument.

He would understand her other notion—that her feelings were hurt by the infidelity of affection. She didn't like the idea of asking—it would be begging—for his return.

She thought that when he came to her bed, even if his wanting her was constricted by his pride or sullenness, he would stay.

She thought that she wanted to talk to him again, but that she didn't need to.

What she concentrated on as much as she could was what parts of her success with the theater she wanted again, and what satisfactions had so far eluded her.

She thought that her position gave her less pleasure than she would have expected. Seeing her name and title— Anya Janek, director—made her think more of problems and imperfections than of achievement. The notices in the Iowa newspapers seemed to her a necessity more than a pleasure. She also realized she thought of them as foreign in some way, as though she'd written a story and it had been published only in Swedish in a small handsome magazine in Stockholm. A pebble in a deep well.

She knew she was happier than if she'd been studying for her Ph.D. orals or still working at Ikon Films. But to reflect that way struck her as weakness.

The thought that her work disappeared forever when each show closed saddened her. She tried to think that in each audience there must have been at least one person who was seized in just the right way, in whose brain the image and sound of her notion of the play (and her enticement of the actors to that notion) would recur again and again until that brain was dead.

It didn't work. It made her feel better, it reminded her of the seven fan letters she'd got—of which three seemed pleasant and intelligent—but it didn't answer her dissatisfaction.

One night Raftery, standing beside her behind the last row, had said, "Anya, this is excellent." She believed him, believed that he could tell.

Mac once said he'd understood what she'd wanted to do. He admired her deduction of the strengths of *Wozzeck*, her shortening of the weaknesses, her perseverance.

She wondered—she thought perhaps he couldn't separate his admiration of her from his admiration of the whole process of transformation, of incarnation of the play. She took some satisfaction in his education. Of course he'd always liked ballet, he'd spoken to her several times about that. She'd been pleased with the unlikeliness of it—his gnarled jock body hunched in a seat, dutifully receiving the plot in the program notes, glowering around him until the curtain went up, then stunned into himself. He said he'd felt a pleasant tickling envy, he could feel the control, the elongation as though he remembered having done it, though of course he knew he couldn't—he said at first he felt a restless sympathy for the dance in his spine, in his pelvis, joints, and thighs, but soon he completely forgot his body, he felt held in perfect immobility.

Anya had been surprised and touched. She thought that that was the point of dance—to produce a sensation of perfect immobility, a moment of balance of all the wishes of the dancers' bodies. Symmetry, order were dead unless they were precarious. It was balance; he was right.

But why was he being such a shit? So inert with her, so deliberately exhausted . . .

She slowly wheeled around to her real worry—that there was something wrong with her taste. It was exasperating that it came back to that—now that her control, her brain-to-stage coordination, was there. For years she'd admired others' competence but thought, If only they had taste. If only they had some real bite. If only they dared . . . Now here she was. Not wrong, but befuddled, slowed. Was she worried about everyone in the audience getting it? Was it condescension making her bland?

Or was it just the opposite, that she guarded so warily against sentimentality, always making sure there was an exposed irony at every crucial moment?

She couldn't experiment—there was no time now. Her evenings were spent standing behind the back row fretting that an act, a scene, a speech, a line was dragging. She spent half her day working out tactful praise for the actors in which to wrap her sharper wishes. The other half day was worrying about little problems. Mainly money in small bills. She felt a sympathy for her old boss at Ikon, Mr. Danziger. She'd always thought he was funnier than he thought when he'd said. "I'm Gulliver tied down by

Lilliputians." Or, once she knew his code, "Keep these god-damn Lilliputians out of my office."

Now she was sitting by herself—at last—in the long front room of Raftery's house by the sheet-metal wood stove, wearing two sweaters. She watched the wisps of heat splotching the inside windowpanes, reviving a fly to buzz in the dry dead ones piled on the sill between the double windows.

The troupe had almost all gone off for the Thanksgiving weekend. Except Bangs and Ray. The two of them drooped around with obviously enjoyable self-reproach and yearning for his children, who were off to grandmother's with the wronged mother/wife.

Anya would be off herself on Monday. To Des Moines with all the women in the troupe to tape *The House of Bernarda Alba* at the TV studio. It would fulfill a local programming requirement. Thank you, FCC.

Dulcie came in with the suit she was fixing for Anya for her after-the-show interview. Dulcie was filled with good cheer. Anya stripped to her thermal net long johns. Dulcie rubbed the brown velvet against her cheek. "It's really wonderful. Hugh can't keep his hands off it."

Anya's original estimate of the opportunity to put a play on Des Moines TV had been cool. Too little money. What kind of jerks would they have to deal with? But she'd finally decided the exposure couldn't hurt. Des Moines TV reached Cedar Rapids, maybe some people would drive the thirty miles to the theater to see more plays.

Dulcie gave a running commentary as Anya tried on the short skirt and jacket. The spot that Hugh made, you couldn't really see it. Was the skirt too short? What did it look like when she sat down? The jacket looked nice, nipped in all along her waist. Be sure to keep it buttoned, or there's no neatness to the line.

Dulcie felt the small of Anya's back. "It fits so well in the back, it's a shame about that spot. You can see the shape of your back, the material's right against the skin."

Anya went up to Dulcie's room where the big mirror was. She was surprised by how white her legs were—like roots grown in a water jar—and by how the hair on her thighs seemed to have grown longer by being covered with layers of long johns, pants, and her knee-length sweater. She rummaged through her things until she found a pair of powdery white tights to wear. She suddenly had stage fright.

Sunday night they had a depressed rehearsal—what did she expect? Their vacation had upset them. She should have foreseen it. Only Bangs was glad to get back to work.

All the girls in the Jeep Wagoneer the next morning. A bitter-cold bright day. Anya couldn't figure out why their nervous tittering was making her so mad. By the time she drove to the Interstate she guessed it was because they seemed to regard television as a step up from theater.

But she herself was carried with them into their mood. They drove into Des Moines, following the directions to the studio, being stared at from the downtown sidewalks— a giant station wagon full of *wimmin!*—What were they? A basketball team? Bridesmaids? Now—look there—it says some kind of theater. They're actresses!

Anya felt her jangling nerves making her eager and tough. She began to think maybe this would be it. Des Moines, Chicago, New York. She enjoyed the sudden glamour of her ambition, she enjoyed being released from the details of the house and barn—sawing wood, mystery soups, the slow water heater, Dulcie's sewing machine, drunk fraternity boys in the audience, Mac fixing this, fixing that. It all resolved itself suddenly into anecdotes about how they'd struggled.

She met the television director, introduced the cast, felt the effect they had as they trooped through the lobby. They did look good, her girls. Not so much pretty (though, of course Annabelle was pretty) as sensual. They knew how to move. Hours in front of the dance mirror made them expert show-offs.

Dressing rooms, green room, a stage area. The set was okay, a sparser reproduction of the one they'd built in the barn. She'd sent ahead a picture of their set and Andrew's sketch of the bare minimum. Anya told the hands where to put the trunks of costumes. She heard her professional but gushy tone with the TV director. "Oh, you're terrific. It'll all drop into place. Shall we just do a run-through for you, or shall you and I have a little talk first?"

It went on like that for her—the rest of the morning, lunch with the director, afternoon, right through the shooting. She was speeded up, zipping around, talking too much

—she knew it, liked the part of her that was so high, was pleased with herself, congratulated herself for getting on so well with everyone. She was sure everyone could tell she was doing it for the good of the show.

The show was taped at two thirty. They were ready to do her interview at four thirty.

The on-camera host showed up. Anya said to the TV director, "Who is this asshole? He hasn't even seen the show."

The TV director said, "He's the host, honey. Wait'll you hear his beautiful voice."

It was going too fast. Anya was surprised when the TV director told her she had a few minutes to do her hair and face. She felt she was falling past them all. She went to a dressing room. She looked at herself in the mirror—the whole day showed up in her face. Tight, nervous, sliding around—a slithery mask of panic and foolishness seemed to be hiding the handsome intelligent arrangement of features she had in mind.

She changed into her brown velvet skirt and jacket. She thought, We don't need an interview.

When she got back, the stage hands had already struck the set and laid out the chairs and backdrop for the interview. When she stepped into the area she felt as though she were stepping onto a wrestling mat.

The TV director called, "Over here."

He said, "Let's try a couple of one-minute conversations, sort of program notes. Let's just run through it. Anya, if you could come up with that thing you said to me—you remember?—about the costumes—'Because these women's bodies are buttoned up to the neck, their passions are that much clearer in their voices.' Dah, dah, dah—'It is a play of passionate voices,' that's a good closing line, maybe let Bob have that, a kind of summary of your point."

Even in her lightheadedness, Anya was embarrassed at that—she couldn't believe she'd said anything so corny, she thought the TV director must have simplified, made it sound stupider than it was. Maybe it was his voice that made it sound so embarrassing.

The series host had not looked at her. He was immobile, immaculate. His tie and shirt front seemed to have grown right there, never to have moved. They began a run-through. The host beamed at her.

His voice was as wavy as his hair. "Well, you're certainly the best-looking director we've had on this series."

Anya said, "Wait'll you see my girls. I'm just the madam."

The TV director cut in, "Okay, wait a second, that may be a problem, honey. This isn't a late-night talk show."

When they started taping, however, Anya couldn't help showing off—resisting the host's elocutionary manner. Through all six takes he didn't stir a hair, and, except for dropping his opening remark, didn't change a word. Anya said different things each time, but the repeated takes had an effect on her—she did regain her concentration, say a pretty speech about how the women's pale limbs, shrouded as they were in black costumes, were not visible but audible. She said the play was Spanish, that is, both Moorish and Catholic, and it was ambivalent: Was the house of Bernarda Alba a harem or a convent or both?

She knew it was bullshit, but she could feel it going over with the audience she imagined. Glass beads for the natives.

The television people took them to rooms in a downtown motel across the street, took them out for dinner, and on to a cocktail party in a penthouse that belonged to the head of the major sponsor, Ryan's Trucking Company.

Anya was surprised at the paintings there. The TV director said they were all by Mexicans. She thought they were wonderful—one especially; she finally saw what it was after she'd admired its shapes and colors as design. It was a dead bull in the sand seen from above, flattened by the perspective and—she thought with amusement—by being dead. The blood on the massive shoulder was a film, thin and delicate like a wave slowly spreading a sheen of water across hard sand. There was, in fact, blood *in* the sand of the painting—a visible connection between the bull and the sand—but there was another connection suggested, that the bull was becoming part of the sand not by decay but simply because in death that which separated its form from the sand was fading.

Anya suddenly felt the dead weight of the body pressing against the sand, a curious sensation because she felt herself seem to rise in order to accommodate the perspective— the bull beneath her eyes, pressing down, away from her.

And then she felt the impression of weight fade, the perspective flatten and change—she saw the bulk not from directly above, only from a superior angle. Strange—no longer weight but still a massive deadness supported by the sand, a portion of the earth's surface after all; as though the earth itself were firm only because of an inflating breath.

She felt uneasy now about her day of exhilarated babbling, her little taped piece of chat.

Had this painter been clever or was the effect a product of long dumb contemplation? It didn't matter, the painting was careful, his good luck earned by his care.

She didn't look at the other paintings as closely or as long. She wondered how it came about that this Des Moines businessman took such an interest in Mexico, in Mexican painters. The taste in furniture was not so good, but not terrible—chunky, bright, modern. A little more late forties movie musical than Danish.

She wanted to leave but she did not want to be alone. She sat on the corner of a yellow-and-white obliquely striped sofa. She thought that what she wanted was going to take longer than she'd thought—it was not going to be an arrival, a triumph.

Here she was. She had her lucky break—made it. Here she was in middle show biz. A fly in honey. In Des Moines. Going home to an outdoor crapper, someone else's baby, and a crazy boyfriend.

That wasn't the problem. The problem was that she'd been getting by on cleverness, nimbleness, a little bit of daring. But she'd got stuck somehow—too much footwork? —dancing away from large enthusiasms. Of course, the risk in "thinking big" was to end up like Raftery—babbling away with lines from Whitman, Blake, Isaiah. Romantic ambition.

Or Mac—another kind of romance. He was as mad as Raftery.

But surely both of them were more admirable than this TV director, slick pep in his double knits. Both of them more admirable as characters.

She needed a rest, to pull away from all of them, to enlarge herself, to gather her energy. Let Andrew direct the next show—have his way with Ben Jonson. The madmen in her life were distracting her. Making her guard against failure because she could see how they failed. She knew why Henniker, for all his supple verbal talent, was a failure. She knew why Raftery was a failure. More noble but still . . . That was a knowledge that could make her desperately careful unless she could ignore it. Those people were worse for her than this TV director with his zippered boots and flowered shirt.

She needed for just a short while to get away from her feeling of having become inert at a midpoint, stopped by the thickening of small successes.

Henniker—writhing with envy, trying to ease his self-disgust with a career of contempt for everyone else, lost in his mad reductions. Only I know art.

Raftery lost in his mad inflations. Incantation—"If a fool persist in his folly he will become wise." Wishing to be a naked giant. Not knowing the meaning of envy—charmed by himself, by his sensations, by other people. Whirling rapturously, childishly.

And this bell-bottom-trousered TV director with square white teeth, mindlessly content to be a technician—arranging minutes on his notepad with a flair-tip pen. "Wow! Dynamite!" Unwittingly resigned. Smooth—rolling along on the ball bearings of a job.

This absent Mexican was the only success she'd felt in a long time. How did she imagine him?—some squat Indian chewing coca leaves, suddenly getting lucky, feeling himself getting lucky, without a word. For years not knowing how bad he was, ignoring his teachers, his failures, their failures, and then brutally doing it right with his short, thick hand.

She walked back by herself across four empty blocks of downtown Des Moines to her motel room. She watched the late movie on television. She gave in to groggy insomnia, lying in her velvet suit, listening to the whir of the machine pumping air into this sealed room. She thrilled to an ad for the world's one hundred greatest melodies. Ten seconds of "Song of India," "Ave Maria," "William Tell," the Waltz from *Eugene Onegin*. Don Ameche asking her if she could name this beloved tune. She could name them all. It shocked her how much junk she knew.

There was a knocking at her door. She opened it. The TV director spoke over the chain lock. "Is there anything else I can do for you?"

Anya said, "Yes, there is."

He wanted to say another line but she closed the door to undo the chain lock. He came in, she redid the chain lock. His smile wavered brightly.

Anya said, "I'm watching TV but I'd love a leg massage." She searched under her skirt and pulled her tights down. "I hope you're a leg man." She was comfortable with her cheap lines. They itched her. This was a bargain at the price.

She sat on the foot of the bed watching *Captain from Castille* with Tyrone Power. The TV director knelt, took her bare foot in his hands, and kneaded it.

He said, "Is this the idea?"

Anya said, "Yes, it's up to you, do what you think feels good."

Eventually, after he caressed her feet and calves, he grew restless. She said, "That's great, it feels wonderful."

He moved between her knees and slid his hands up her thighs; the skirt was stuck under her, she lifted herself up. He licked the inside of her leg. She watched the screen, following the movie with her eyes and a narrowing part of her attention. She liked the sensation of mental resistance as he began lapping and pressing his tongue into her. She thought of another line. She said, "I hope you don't mind missing the show."

A moment later she was sure she could feel his pleasure and triumph as she let go and fell flat and began lifting and squirming. As though it had been a real struggle between her coolness and his energy.

She was surprised at how intense he was after she came. He leapt up and quickly threw his clothes in a pile.

She said, "Shall I skip the foot part?" He didn't speak. He knelt on the bed, reached for her shoulders. She touched the bubble at the tip of his prick and spread it around with her finger. He leaned sideways to make it easier for her to reach his prick with her mouth, but as she took it slowly in her rolled-in lips, he lurched toward her. She had to grimace to keep from biting him. He grabbed her head as though he was about to leapfrog over her face. He began to hunch.

Anya thought, He's fucking my mouth.

She knew she could stop him by closing her teeth, she didn't know why she didn't, it was uncomfortable, not awful though; it was right that his will should flare up this way, she felt her own will—that part of her will that was engaged here, that had said the things she'd said—give way to his irritated flurry. But he suddenly began to move more gently and more rapidly. She curled her tongue back—the bottom of the tip slid along his prick, springing against it but sliding with it. He groaned through his teeth and wriggled. She had to breathe in gasps through her nose, her head jerking as much from her breathing as from his now strangely fluttery hunching.

He suddenly stopped, shot into her mouth, and then across her upper lip and cheek as she wrenched her head away.

Her right arm was asleep from being caught under his knee.

She understood perfectly his neat pleasure. She wasn't sure what he would like now—for her to try to be cocky again, in vain? for her to curl up and whimper? for her to say "you son of a bitch" while he laughed and got dressed?

Nothing. She wiped her cheek and mouth on the bedspread. She decided she should shut up.

She watched him put on his underpants, which looked like track shorts, notched up the thigh, hemmed with red piping.

She stood up on the other side of the bed and smoothed her skirt and jacket.

She felt the repulsion of their two bodies across the room. Not unpleasantly. She realized, however, that this man, a more spindly, paper-thin figure than anyone else she'd encountered, had initiated her in a way, released a shadowy presence in her, at a depth far below her irritation, below her sneering at him, below her laughing at herself, below any of her ironic amusements. The presence in her was not so much this specific humiliation as a doubt about what had prompted her to give up. She'd always thought she would *never* just give up. Give way for tactical reasons, give in for some trade-off of pleasures—but she could see now that she hadn't had any other thought in her head—taken by surprise—knocked down by his flurry, his concentrated vehemence. Like Leda by the swan, but without divinity or fertility. His part in it was sterile. Except for that doubting presence now released in her. Even Timmy's wife—who had shamed her—had not made her give up.

He came around the bed and took her hand. He said, "Look—now we know we're both cool, okay. So we—" He stopped. She could tell he was looking for an exit line. She hoped he would think of one. He turned back at the door and gestured toward the television set. But he decided against speaking. His mouth closed and he left.

She hoped that would satisfy him, she didn't want to think about it anymore.

* * *

The next morning it was snowing, not sticking to the Interstate but clinging to the weeds along the embankment and lining the furrows in the corn fields. Everyone seemed anxious to get home. Anya drove slowly, however. Justified, of course, by the slick road. She hoped she wasn't going to be uncontrollably unpleasant.

All the men except Mac and Ray were watching the television set Og had brought back from his Thanksgiving visit to his parents in Lake Forest. Anya called a rehearsal for a reading of *The Alchemist* that afternoon. She knew the *Bernarda Alba* was going to be terrible that night. Tired. And a small house—the snow would keep people home. Mac hadn't seen a performance yet. She thought she'd get him to come—Annabelle and Bangs would perk up if they knew he was coming to see them. But she also wanted him to share her distress. She wondered how much of this mess was let-down, the sag of a midmorning return.

Bangs came back in the car with Ray. She reported that Mac was out hunting with Sigurd. Anya thought, Good. Then she felt a sudden rush of feeling through her defense (a reserve position that *he* was the one who'd pulled away). She feared that she was bitter, that the taste of her skin would be bitter, and she wished that she could make herself as dumb, sweet, and slowly flowing as Annabelle. Or Dulcie, or even Bangs. Screw them. But it wasn't Mac's fault they liked him—she clicked her teeth—were sweet on him. She thought of Tassie—Tassie had been sweet in just that way she envied. Had lost it . . .

But if she'd given Mac what he wanted— No, Mac and Raftery were madmen, they thought that you could arrange everything internally. Grow it all in your soul. Build yourself. Before *she* started trying to be whole, shut herself up in the closet convent of her mind, she wanted to *do*. To be stretched large by events. There was a difference between big and little, for God's sake, and she could see it. This whole fucking mess was little. Last night was little.

She recognized that she was a little desperate. But she still thought that she would feel better when she reached an event. Not with this two-bit vanity of arranging your feelings as though they were pieces of the real world.

She went back to work. She thought the cast, the whole company in fact, could use a dance session. They had time for an hour before lunch. During lunch she would look at Alice's sketches for the *Alchemist* costumes with Andrew— that would be the time to see how strong Andrew was now, how filled with good, coarse energy.

* * *

When Mac came back from his long Monday at Sigurd's, he found Raftery, Dulcie and Hugh, and Andrew sitting around the kitchen table. Raftery had heated the bath water and made him a cup of tea. Mac left the bathroom door ajar so he could hear their voices and smell the kitchen. He held his cup of tea and settled in the water. He was shocked at how pleased he was with this kitchen gathering —it gave him a physical pleasure, as though he'd just passed through a gateway into a perfectly proportioned square of a small walled city.

He drank his tea and drowsed in the bath, hearing the voices but no words. The oven door creaked open, and a moment later the smell of banana bread reached him.

He thought dimly that it was just as well for this sense of pleasure that Anya was away. That was where his shock had come from, he thought—it was shocking that he could enjoy her absence, that without her he suddenly felt the proportions of the affection he had for the people in the next room, that Anya had been a distraction between him and them.

It was as though he'd been dozing on a bus or a train and suddenly came awake, lifted his head from against the vibrating window, suddenly heard the voices around him, the hum of voices breaking suddenly into words. Normally a disquieting sensation, but this was all strangely reassuring, the words seeming to contain a message that he didn't have to understand to be comforted by.

He thought that perhaps his problem during the past weeks had just been sadness.

He then felt a current of desire pass through him, and

he was reminded of how deep a nervous response he still had for Anya: It ran through him underneath his tiredness, underneath the pulled-apart and swollen fibers of his muscles. It was a response that drew him on—not like the harmony of the kitchen square, which stilled him. Anya drew him on the way a wild place did—a path into a birch wood, or a curve of running river, or a stretch of windswept black ice. Most like a running river, he thought, always tangible, visible, or just there and always disappearing further, inviting him to move into its movement, to risk its movement, which it would be foolish to think existed for his ends, or could be influenced by his virtues, or could do anything but draw him on.

If what was making him feel bad was just sadness, then he thought he should bear it better.

He went upstairs in his towel and rummaged in his drawer in the dark hall for a clean pair of long johns. He heard Hugh climb the stairs. It interested him that Hugh, having grown up in half-lit houses, was not afraid of the dark. Mac picked him up at the top, and Hugh clapped his hands on Mac's cheeks.

Mac said, "Tough guy, huh. Want to get rough." He pushed Hugh's stomach, poking out between his diaper and his short shirt. Hugh wriggled and Mac felt the warm satin finish of Hugh's belly move against his fingers. The whole round belly fit like a bowl into his hand.

Mac carried Hugh down the hall while he looked for a clean shirt. He was amazed how Hugh threw himself around, confident through no other sense but touch that he would be held in mid-air in the dark.

Mac said, "Where's your belly button, Hugh? Where is it?" and he felt Hugh roll back against his arm and pull up his shirt front. Mac put his mouth on Hugh's stomach and blew. Hugh laughed and wriggled. Mac turned his cheek, and Hugh held onto Mac's hair, his stomach hot against Mac's cheek and nose.

Mac said, "You're an old sweetheart, Hugh."

Hugh said, "Go downstairs to Dussy."

Mac said, "Wait'll I get my clothes on."

"What?"

"Wait."

Hugh said, "Okay." Mac put him down and felt him slide easily from standing to sitting, a small hot Buddha. Mac

236

felt faint with love for Hugh. A short rush that gave a dark pause to his breathing and seeing. He opened his mouth and held the bridge of his nose.

It occurred to him that his feelings of joy and his feelings of depression had very like physical effects.

He dressed, then scooped Hugh up and settled him on one hip. He said, "Okay, now we'll go downstairs."

He was determined to break out of his isolation, to let the love he had for Hugh break out to all the people in the kitchen. But by the time he'd finished eating, Raftery and Andrew were reading out loud from *The Alchemist,* stopping only to comment on how the scene they'd just read should be staged. Dulcie was taking notes of what Andrew said.

. The barncat came and yowled on the porch. Dulcie took out a saucer of milk and grease. Mac thought, That's what they do to me. He immediately blocked the thought, gritting his teeth with shame at his self-indulgence.

Andrew asked him a question about a piece of the set. Andrew explained, "Anya made a drawing, but she draws so badly I can't tell—did she say anything to you?"

Mac shook his head.

Andrew began to talk about a set in a production of *Bartholomew Fair* he'd seen. For a moment Mac didn't realize it was another Ben Jonson play; he thought it was a Dr. Seuss story about Bartholomew and the thousand hats.

Andrew said, "We should try to get the same lewdness in. There's that wonderful line about screwing the pig woman. Someone says it's like falling into a whole shire of butter."

Raftery said, "Ursula the pig woman! That's right. 'All fire and fat!' That's right—the whole idea of *rendering* people into their humors—*The Alchemist* is doing the same thing. The bubbling cauldron. We need an alchemical apparatus, a lot of beakers and pipes that gurgle."

Andrew said, "Of course it's a *fraud* . . ."

Raftery said, "Of course. An extravagant, superb fraud. It works backwards. It turns metal into nothing."

Andrew said to Mac, "Can you build something like that? I know we're still a little vague—"

Raftery said, "I can get glass tubes from my old lab."

Mac said, "When you get a sketch ready—I can't say for sure."

Andrew and Raftery went back to their reading out loud. They both read well—the words came off the page for them in runs of live speech.

Mac took a gas lantern and his tools and went upstairs to finish his improvement to Anya's bed. He could still hear the voices through the whistling of the gas lantern, but once he started concentrating on screwing the wood pieces he'd made into place, he lost them.

What he needed to do to be able to sit with them, he thought, was to join the pieces of his life into one purpose.

Raftery, for all his whirl, had a single gypsy sense of adventure that bound him to his life.

Andrew was no longer dependent on Anya; he'd always had good ideas, and now he'd found his voice again.

The whole troupe, for all their bickering, were united in their dreaming of success, both next year's and next week's.

But Mac also knew that the barrier between him and their life was one he'd put up. He had no idea why. He only knew that there was a grim endurance in him that he could not yet control. It sometimes isolated him, but it eased him too—to build their sets, to get their food, to walk down to Sigurd's to maintain them.

He wondered if Dulcie felt the same way about her position.

He finished off the screw holes with bungs he'd cut from dowels. He'd be finished in time to get to bed so he could get up at dawn to go deer hunting with Sigurd. Anya would find the new bed when she got back from Des Moines.

That was the thought he decided to stop on while he fitted the horse blanket that was to be the canopy. Hewer of wood, hauler of water. Building a bower.

* * *

Anya drove down to Raftery's to get a clean leotard from her drawer in the upstairs hall. She went into her bedroom to change and saw that Mac had finished his work on the room while she'd been away. He'd put up the inside shutters he'd made for the two windows, and turned the bed into a four-poster with a canopy. He'd replaced the stubby legs with six-foot-high posts. The canopy was an old horse blanket he'd got from Sigurd—white with a red and black design. The hole for the horse's neck was over the pillows. A string ran up to the ceiling to give it a peak. Around the bed there were curtains made from old blankets. Each blanket was battened, and at either end of every batten there was a screw eye through which a cord ran from bottom to top. The blankets were raised and furled by pulling the cord ends and cleating them to small metal cleats screwed to the bedposts.

At the same time that she thought how much warmer it would be, she thought how clearly it was one of Mac's ideas—that whole side of his taste—ingenuously grotesque, practical, ideologically homemade. The labor unconcealed.

The blanket curtain on her side of the bed was up. She poked her head under the canopy and looked at the design of the horse blanket—it was impressive: tiny stitches along the thick overlapped seams, the overlap covered with black and red strips. The collar fringed in red. She realized the collar was now arranged to be a vent for their kerosene lamp and candle. Sensible.

The whole thing was touching and slightly, annoyingly, pathetic. Mac's maternal side. She wondered how consciously he displayed it—his primitive tenderness. The side of him she was most uneasy with. Maybe it did just rise up. But he certainly knew what she was making fun of when she made fun of it.

She changed into her tights and leotard and tied her hair back.

Mac walked by the open door in his long underwear, the sleeves rolled up. He came in.

She noticed he'd just washed his hands but there were flecks of dried blood above his wrist.

Mac said, "How did it go?"

She said, "Oh—I'll tell you later. Not much for all the excitement. I want you to see the show tonight. What's the blood from?"

Mac said, "I cleaned a deer. It's hanging at Sigurd's, we're going halves. It's a lot of meat, but—I'll tell you later."

Anya laughed. "I guess that just leaves us and our new

bed." She didn't want to be sentimental and make up. She knew he admired her in her dance clothes.

They embraced. She unbuttoned the front of his wool underwear and slipped it down. He stepped out of it. They embraced again. She thought how it must feel to rub his skin against the tight silkiness of her leotard.

They lay in bed awhile before she undressed, bone against bone. His head seemed enormous in her hands. His back seemed hot and large. Her body pressed into him all on its own, rose up like a wave under him.

She didn't recognize herself at all—clinging to him, whining against his cheek.

When she got up to take off her leotard and tights, she was still trembling and dazed.

He understood she didn't want to start right away—just be raised up against him. Her teeth were chattering, she wasn't able to stop trembling even pressed hard against him. He scarcely moved even after his prick came in. She didn't move except to pull herself closer. Their bodies were locked with all their weight and muscle, but her sensations were only clear and small. Strangely distributed through every part of her. Her longing was larger—disembodied but hovering over her body. Her sensations clicked through her skeleton below her cloud of feeling, like tiny Zuñi dancers trying to get the cloud to burst into rain.

*   *   *

Lying in bed afterward, Mac thought that periods of time once lived through became spheres set in motion—altering each other's orbits, charged with negative and positive memory, discharging at different rates, obscuring each other, some dull and large masses of a somber influence, some bright and small, apparently emitting the new order of energy. Mac wasn't sure if he was thinking of planetary systems or molecules; what affected him was the thought of the inchoate gas of future time spinning into spheres, his mind a space undefined by outer boundaries, only by the center of the accumulated system.

What started him on this thought was the terrible shooting and butchering of the buck suddenly completed and whirled away to a great distance by Anya's return.

The day's dawn was now a remote globe—sitting on a

plank between two branches of an oak on a folded sheep-skin taken from Sigurd's tractor seat, his neck, hands, and armpits, and boots anointed by some concocted musk of Sigurd's to mask his smell. The snow piling up on his wool cap, on the branches, on his legs, each stretched out along a branch. On the dead leaves below.

Through the falling snow the bare branches of trees settled into his vision, the design weaving deeper and deeper the longer he stayed motionless. His eyes took in layer after layer of pattern, triangles and trapezoids, every fork of a tree or branch cut by another tree or branch. He could finally see about sixty yards into this network.

He sat with the fingers of his left hand across the bridge of his nose, the other around the grip of the shotgun, his fingers curled just inside the shooting slit of his right mitten.

The falling snow became static lines. He could no longer distinguish its motion from the implied motion of the lines of the trees.

Every so often he half-closed his eyes. After a time he knew the design before him—all of the areas of it so delicately balanced and divided in his eyes that it became a spiderweb—so that when the buck moved into it he was obvious, an obtuse, warm-blooded animal straying into an abstraction. The buck walked calmly along, slanting closer and closer. Mac observed all of the many colors in the buck's coat. There was an undisturbed dusting of snow on its back. Mac slowly crept his hands down into position and sank his body down to the gun, pointed the gun at the same time, and then shot the buck where Sigurd had told him the heart was.

Mac yelled after the gun went off, before the sound of the shot was completely formed. He had scarcely begun to know what he was doing or anything about the buck, it was all done by instructions, so when he shot he instantly knew he had done something he should not have.

The killing shot curled up all the morning of seeing the network of branches. The luminous falling snow.

Sigurd thought Mac had whooped for joy. Sigurd strung the buck up to bleed, and then they went to bring the tractor and a wagon to the nearest field. They dragged the buck out to the wagon, sweat running on their foreheads in the falling snow. At Sigurd's they worked with knives for an hour, left the carcass hanging in Sigurd's side porch.

The butchery rolled into a ball, whirled back away. When? On the walk back? Lighting the water heater? It was when he was examining his hands. They were burned hairless from reaching into the wood stoves. His skin smelled of woodsmoke all the time now, and there was a faint smell of onions under his nails, no matter how often he soaped them or how hard his hands sweated in his work gloves. Sliced onions in every stew, whether bean or meat. Bean here, meat at the theater. Common onions. A peculiar sweet smell—he hadn't recognized it at first, the sharp sting of the juice turned into balmy vegetable decay under his nails. Perhaps the smell was cured into the quick skin by the little licks of flame and heat. The other day he'd smelled Dulcie's hand and fingertips—woodsmoke, onions and apples, and skin. She had turned her hand in his, and they saw the same burned scar on the back of her hand as he had on his.

Surprising, it never hurt to stick a chunk of wood in, even when the flames seemed to lick around the flesh for a second, but if the fire threw up sparks his hand jumped and often caught the hot iron edge of the opening across the back. Hence the scar.

He was back from the deer hunt when he stood in the kitchen and smelled his hand. The smell of the deer came off with water, but not his home smell.

And then upstairs there was Anya, back from Des Moines. Taut in her leotard. At first she seemed the same —the impact of her strong body, the hard prow of her breastbone, her grin, the sinking of her pelvis as she bent her knees outside his. He put his left arm around her, his right hand floated on the stretched mesh of her tights over her thigh and knee. The cool hard river of her body again.

But then she shrank. Not a withering, not a condensation—it was an inner reduction as though her spine suddenly sucked the heat and size away from every bone. Her mouth too seemed smaller and colder on his cheek. His own heat vanished into her. All their bones, their whole touching seemed held in a small space.

She got up and came back naked. Why was it all so small? As though they were the embroidery, the tiny double stitching on the quilt. When they moved it seemed minute and precise. Lying still later, Mac thought their breathing, their heartbeats and pulses were as large as their bodies.

He tried to imagine what made him content in this sensation. He thought it was that Anya was for a moment fragile—but not helpless. She had, it seemed to him, deliberately presented what was usually secret in her life. It was the deliberation that struck him as wonderful. She had not let herself burst, as he had, for example, that evening in the field. But Mac didn't worry that he'd done it wrong, now that Anya had done it right.

After she went back to the theater, he felt buoyant in all the plans of communal life. *The Alchemist* set, what they would have for Christmas dinner (even the deer now seemed justified), the odd jobs at Sigurd's (easier now that the fall work was over). Everyone in the group again seemed to him worthy and full of good will now that he had the feeling that there was a balm in his living with Anya in their own bed.

He looked out the window. Four inches had gathered on the metal roof. He sacrificed a small portion of his mood to the natural order—he probably owed some of his well-being to his yearly pleasure in the first snowfall.

CHAPTER

▪▮▮▮▮▮▮▮▮▮▮▮▮▮▮▮▮▮▪

14

Winter came in hard.

It snowed two days a week the first three weeks in December.

They all gathered one night at the theater house to watch an NBC-TV hour-long special on communes. Annabelle started giggling when the camera showed a woman from a nude commune in Boston sitting with her back to the camera and facing the interviewer.

Annabelle said, "I can see her heinie crack."

Andrew laughed.

Og said, "Look at the interviewer's eyeballs, you can see her tits."

Alice said, "Oh, Og, you are so locker room."

Og was good-humored. He said, "You aren't taking this seriously. Are you?"

Raftery started saying "Amen" after each sentence the commentator spoke. They all joined in. Then they chanted amen. Og started singing "Bullshit" and they all did that for a while.

The color slipped and the commentator had a green face and a pink ghost. Annabelle said, "Oh, I see his aura." Everyone laughed.

They kept the TV on to watch *Gunga Din* on the late show. The living room was very warm from all their bodies huddled together on the floor on blankets, coats, and pillows. Mac fell asleep, and they all picked him up without waking him and put him on the dining table. They were all giggling and hushing each other. Annabelle said, "Let's all get under the table."

Og said, "Let's put his hand in warm water and see if he pisses."

Alice said, "Og, you are so boarding school."

They all hid under the table. The table got pulled apart where the extra leaf fit in and they began to pinch Mac's ass through the crack. Mac rolled over and woke up. He got up on his knees and looked down through the crack. They shrieked with laughter.

The snow melted a little and then froze again, making a coarse brilliant crust.

The question arose—about *The Alchemist*—was Alice pretty enough, sexy enough to play Doll Common? Annabelle was pretty enough and sexy enough, but could she appear cunning and tough enough? Anya thought she herself could do the part best, but since Andrew was necessary to play the Alchemist, she would have to direct.

They settled on Alice for Doll Common.

Dame Pliant—a dumb, soft, and buxom widow—was between Annabelle and Bangs.

Anya asked Mac what he thought. Mac said that since they needed to cast a girl as one of the men, the logical part for a girl was Kastril, the angry boy who wanted to learn to have duels. Cast Babette as Kastril with a red fright wig and clothes that were slightly too long—the comedy of the feisty runt. And then it became clear that Dame Pliant, who was Kastril's sister, would have to be Annabelle, for her red hair which matched Kastril's fright wig and for her bosom—she should be almost laughably desirable. She should resemble her brother but on a larger scale—as though she'd been pumped up with cream.

Bangs had the juicy female part in *Mandragola*—that would keep her happy.

The surprise was Raftery. He sat in on the readings and took over as Sir Epicure Mammon. That was fine since that left Andrew for the Alchemist and Ray, Tagh, and Og for Face, Tribulation, and Surly.

Babette was delighted to play Annabelle's quarrelsome younger brother—to push Annabelle around, to pick a fight with Og. She worked out a comic bit with a foil from the costume room. Her arm was too short to draw it from the scabbard at her waist; she had to work it out hand over hand—which ended with the handle being offered to the person she was accosting, the bell of the foil waving like a flower on a metal stem.

The wind stayed in the north for several days. The stream to the river froze over thick. Mac skated up it a half mile, pushing a coal shovel to scrape the snow off. There were fallen tree trunks and branches frozen into the ice, and low branches sticking out over it. He came out of the woods, and there was a hundred yards of the stream leading up to a bulldozed impoundment with a culvert through it. The dammed-up pond was about the size of a hockey rink. It occurred to Mac they could all have a pleasant time skating on it together, but he decided that the next day he'd go downstream, see if he could reach the river on good ice. What disaffected him from the artificial pond was the ugliness of the corrugated pipe sticking out from the dike and then through the snow with a frozen, muddy dribble hanging from the lip.

*   *   *

The play they put on for the first two weeks of December was Machiavelli's *Mandragola*.

Bangs was the apparently virtuous but strictly sequestered wife whose husband (Ray) is induced to force her to sleep with an apparent stranger (Tagh) on the advice of a doctor (Andrew) who actually is in league with the seducer. The doctor warns the husband that the first man to sleep with the wife after her peculiar illness will die a horrible death.

The show was clever and stylish and Anya couldn't figure out why the house was so small. The roads were plowed and sanded, and their buses were running. She and Dulcie drove to town to shop, and Dulcie pointed out that the art movie house was playing *Mandragola*, an Italian film of the play.

Dulcie tried to hold Anya back, actually held onto her sleeve, but Anya barged into the manager's office.

The manager didn't know what she was talking about at first. She explained.

Anya ended up saying, "Don't you read the newspaper? Don't you pay attention to anything? We posted our schedule in September, for Christ's sake."

The manager said he hadn't noticed—but it was the owner who set up the schedule anyway, which was also available at the Student Union. The same place the theater's schedule was distributed. Perhaps Anya had overlooked it.

Anya bit her upper lip.

The manager said, "I'm sorry it turned out like this— just bad luck. Would you like to see the show? First afternoon show starts in a half hour. Ends at five fifteen. It's a good movie, even with subtitles."

Anya said, "How has it been doing?"

The manager said, "Not so hot. These kids come to foreign language films only if it's got Belmondo or Mastroianni, *ec cetera*. Or if the director's got a name. This one's slow."

Anya noticed *ec cetera*. She said, "I'm sorry I yelled at you."

The manager said, "Well, you did take me a little bit by surprise."

"Who owns this theater?"

"Bill Ryan, up in Des Moines."

Anya said, "The same one who sells trucks and farm equipment?"

"That's him."

"Do you have his phone number in Des Moines?"

"Yeah, I'll give it to you, but he's most likely down in Mexico." After a pause. "You know him?"

Anya said, with some airiness, "Not very well—he's the sponsor of a television show we did."

The manager said, "That's him, all right—a finger in every pie."

She said, "What are these pies?"

"Well, there's the business his dad started. The International Harvester franchises. There's a few of them—Waterloo, Cedar Falls. That's still going. Then his dad did some hauling and that's still going. Then there's Bill's ideas—a couple of movie houses that just about break even. He backed a night club in Des Moines that closed. Then there was a hunting camp out in Colorado—that never made money—most of these old hunters go out in their own campers, but Bill sold the land for a lot more than he paid.

He's not dumb, he's just restless. I could make him some money here, but he's friends with a foreign-film distributor from the East and that's that. Like I say, he's not dumb, but he's not a regular go-getter."

Anya remembered him. She'd been introduced—he'd said something polite—better than average but she couldn't remember. He owned the painting of the dead bull. What else did she remember? Fleshy, a soft, well-oiled tan—not the windburn of a farmer. The Iowa version of Uncle Timmy, it now occurred to her. She couldn't remember him very well. Wasn't there going to be any other significant figure in her life?

How had she ended up way out here where there were no hierarchical sanctums? No guarded mysteries. Her instinct was right—Bill Ryan wasn't a figure, he wasn't even a figure to this employee of his. Here was that Midwestern openness that Mac liked—anyone driving by could see your land, measure it, count your hogs or cattle.

Dulcie said she'd like to see the show. She and Anya went and had a beer at the bar across the street. Dulcie was full of gaiety—having a beer, away from her kid, getting in free to a show.

Anya said, "Is there anything else you want?—in the way you're living, I mean."

Dulcie said, "No—not these days. Raftery's having a fine time. I don't think he's restless. You and Mac keep him interested."

Some foam caught in the blond hair on Dulcie's upper lip. She had a lovely high forehead. There must be more she wanted.

Anya said, "What about another baby?"

Dulcie smiled. "Oh yes. Sure."

"How is it, being pregnant?"

"Well, I don't see what the fuss is about. But then I wasn't sick at all. I got tired of lugging around so much belly, but I didn't ever feel ugly. Raftery was away a lot, but a girl friend came over and spent nights." Dulcie laughed. "I just sat in my rocker and rocked and rocked. I rocked on the porch when it was nice out, rocked inside when it wasn't. It was very dreamy. I rocked grooves in the porch floor. It was really calm. I had the best garden ever—I think because I did everything so slow. I had a part-time job in the local library but I hardly noticed it. I can scarcely remember it. I guess I just drifted in and drifted out. I wasn't even worried about Raftery getting back on time from his trip. I generally worry a lot when he's gone, not just jealousy but that people might beat him up or put him in jail—you know how he can be sometimes—he attracts attention somehow, but when I was pregnant I wasn't worried at all. All I remember is those hot, dusty days and being calm. Most of the time I need someone around—someone besides Raftery—to get me calm. But then I didn't. Sometimes I'd read poems—usually I worry about whether I understand a poem or not or about what Raftery thinks, or else I get stirred up by it . . . But then it didn't matter if I even finished it or not."

"But it hurt to have the baby?"

"Oh, it hurt some, but I felt strong—I was completely rested up for it. It didn't take more than four hours. Now if it were to take a long time I can imagine it being painful—being tired and getting scared and then the whole thing seeming too much. The doctor kept telling me what was going on and I would say, 'I know.' When the waters broke the nurse called him in, and he rushed to explain . . . I don't mean to be unappreciative, but the people involved never really worked out as much of a help.

"Now, when the contractions came faster toward the end it was powerful—like being too close to the tracks when a train comes through. That's not quite it." Dulcie laughed. "Maybe being *on* the tracks. It's inside and it seems discordant—almost wrong. Once—during one of the contractions—it seemed as though everything was pushing the wrong way but then it straightened itself out. Then the doctor said, 'Here we are,' and I looked at the mirror and I saw the head come out. Then the doctor pulled him and turned him and one arm came out on my leg—it was just like the books say except when the hand flopped on my leg I was afraid it was dead. Then the hand moved by itself on my skin. After that I was just watching—I don't remember pushing the rest of him out, or the placenta. Or being sewed up. I was just one of the heads around the table."

Anya believed Dulcie, but was sure she'd either left out something or added something.

"What about the postpartum depression?"

"Oh, Raftery had that." Dulcie laughed.

Anya laughed, too. It always surprised her when Dulcie was sharp.

Dulcie said, "Of course I was fairly numb the next day, and the breast feeding didn't start up right off. . . ."

Anya thought it wasn't a story she could be a character in. It wasn't that she disliked Dulcie, that they disliked each other.

She wondered what Dulcie's girl friend had been like. She wondered what Mac would think of it. She knew what she thought, transcendental bovinism. And yet she felt a stab—in her mind she was fleeing from being a way she hadn't yet explored, or even imagined.

And surely it wasn't Dulcie she fled from—only Dulcie's passive goodness, the watery, scrubbed sanctity.

Anya wondered if she was irritated by the near miss. If Dulcie was more lively—just a little more bite in her and she'd be wonderful. Dulcie had moments. And had more than ordinary good looks—her gray eyes set wide, slanting down a little, clearly pointed at the outsides, like Moorish arches. Her mouth wide, with thin lips. The broadest part of her face was her cheekbones. But for all the breadth across the eyes, the cheekbones, her face was thin. A sharp, narrow chin. The line of her jaw was too defined. And the nose—starting high between the eyebrows—a narrow, long ridge. Almost witchlike in profile.

All of her strong and bony and fine—the bones and tendons visible under the skin. Her collarbone—her forearm and hand. Her fingers around her glass.

Here she was telling a story to Anya about her body—how her bones had spread. In her Kansas accent that sounded as though the inside of her throat and mouth were hard. Anya felt the insistent openness of the story—Dulcie appealing to her, admitting her. Of course Dulcie was inclined to—it was Dulcie's wish to have clean, direct good will in her house.

Anya knew she herself was being a shit, but she couldn't stop her retreat from this handsome woman who wanted to be friends. Anya thought, If she wants me enough to try again, maybe then. But Anya had to admit there was something more than her own taste or toughness or pride keeping her at a distance from Dulcie. Dulcie's bright gray eyes made her think of a plain, still life. Anya shrank from the idea.

Dulcie said, "I guess there's no way to really tell it. Raftery was up at Sigurd's one time watching one of the ewes lamb, and he said it was just the same as watching me have Hugh. Sigurd was really shocked. He just can't talk about people and animals in the same breath. When I was still nursing, Sigurd told Raftery to give me beer—he gives beer to his sows to help their milk—but he talked around and around about how it wasn't the same. But what's good about it, about having a baby, is that it *is* the same. You go right back inside into the dark. It doesn't matter what you're thinking."

Anya said, "But making love can be that way, too."

Dulcie said, "Oh, no. Well, maybe just at the end. Is that what you mean?"

Anya said, "You're the one who's done both."

Dulcie said, "Yes. Then I'd say it matters a lot what you're thinking about. You can always float up and think and it can all change. But having a baby is just going on and on. It's like the sun coming up. Right through you."

Anya said, "Well, don't tell Mac. He'll want to get in on it."

They went to the movie. On the ride home Dulcie said, "I think ours is better."

Anya said, "But don't you think it's a malicious play? Everyone is made a fool of. Including the wife—the idea that she's been waiting for a secret prick—that whole idea of secret lust under rich brocade gowns of pious wifeliness. I mean, she's not a heroine at all. The movie is very Italian about it—she turns out to have been a sly hot pussy all along. And our version isn't better—it's better theater— when the pale wife comes out the morning after pink and radiant. Surprised and transformed by her night with a good cocksman. It's comic, but it's a terrible cliché: 'All she needs is a good lay.' And she gets it and now she's alive. Of course Bangs does that entrance very well. The suddenly fulfilled woman. Whose idea was the bells hanging from her belt?"

Dulcie said, "Raftery's. He wants to put bells in the lover's codpiece, too."

Anya said, "That's too much—that makes it corny. Like 'she rings my bell.' It's a sly play, not corny."

Dulcie said, "That's what I told him."

Anya found herself about to change around and be for codpiece bells. She bit her lip.

CHAPTER

||||||||||||||||||||||||||||||||||||

15

There was a van parked in the yard. Dulcie and Anya went in. Anya guessed right off that the stranger in the kitchen was Mercks. He was much better looking than Anya had imagined—thin, graceful, with sparkling clean hair drawn back in a pony tail. He still had his sheepskin jacket on. He wore pale yellow leather pants and a pair of handsome half-Wellingtons. Under his open jacket he was wearing a royal blue Mexican shirt of coarse linen.

He said, "Right, you're Anya. I'm Jimmy Mercks." He smiled and made an open-handed gesture, palms up. It reminded Anya of a trader making friends with natives who lived by a lagoon rich with pearls.

Mercks said, "Heard lots about you and your theater. Thought I'd head on out."

There was a formal tension—everyone standing—Peewee holding Hugh, Raftery curling his beard with his fingers, Mac drawn back.

Anya said, "How do you do. You planning to stay for the show tonight?"

Mercks said, "Oh, yeah. I hear it's good. I heard the one in Des Moines went over real well, too."

Anya said, "How did you hear that?"

Mercks said, "I talked to Bill Ryan. He saw the tape."

"You know Bill Ryan?"

"Oh, yeah. We have some negotiations."

Anya said, "You sell him your Mexican grass?"

Mercks said, "I'm out of that now, that's all in the past." Anya thought this was only a *pro forma* denial. "I sold him some paintings I got in Mexico. Safer work, right?" Mercks smiled and opened his hands again. A milk-and-corn-fed, big-boned and blond Levantine trader in a sook. Caressing you with his smile across the rug in question.

Anya said, "The painting, the one with the bull, do you know the one—?"

Mercks said, "Yeah, the dead bull on the sand. Yeah, I got him that." He obviously sensed her interest. "It's by a guy I know." Anya doubted it. Mercks said, "You liked that one? I go for that one, too—it's the best of the new stuff. Most of the people don't get it. But Ryan has a real eye. And enough bread. Now it's all going out on loan to the museum in Des Moines—the Ryan collection Modern Mexican. Olé, right? And I go down and get another truckload for all the other businessmen. They don't like Ryan much, but he's the only style in town. And there's all that wall space in those office buildings, right?"

Anya couldn't help smiling. A go-getter, a freak go-getter. But then he'd found the painting she'd liked. She tried to remember the other paintings.

Mercks said, "I don't mean to, you know, make them sound too dumb. They all have *some*thing, some idea of what's really good. I couldn't just con them. And I couldn't do it without Ryan."

Mac lifted the lid of a pot to check the stew. Anya invited Mercks for supper. Mercks changed the subject to the business end of the theater. He kept saying, "Hey, you really did it," in a smarmy way, but there was sense in his questions.

Anya asked him, "Did Ryan ask you to look the theater over?"

Mercks grinned, meaning yes.

Anya wasn't sure whether to believe him.

Anya then felt a trickle of panic start in her—which was the way up? Was she here for the rest of her life? Was this the peak? A scrap book of reviews from the Iowa *Press Citizen*, the *Cedar Rapids Gazette*, the *Des Moines Register*?

Or would she herself begin to hopscotch—move on alone to San Francisco, or Minneapolis, or Pittsburgh, someday back to New York?

She looked at Andrew, her affection clouding her picture of him. Smooth and charming on her stage, but what scale was that?

Was she improving them? Had they all reached their full growth here?

Or was it the audience that limited what they were doing? She felt the great danger in her contempt even as her contempt became visible to her imagination—a half-dozen stocky fraternity boys in identical windbreakers, punching each other's arms, yukking it up as though they were at a Big Ten basketball game—"Hey Duker, wanna go backstage and get her autograph?" The pair of assistant professors of poli sci in good suits, a little uneasy to be in a crowd not in their classroom, worried about their wives saying something dumb, hoping their wives would count this as a big night out, reading the program notes over and over, a little reassured by the good schools in the company's past (Anya made a note to cut those out, they all had enough working credits now), hoping for and fearing lewdness. The busload of freshman girls—plaid jumpers and knee socks—their voices pitched sharp, bleats of laughter, shushing each other—better than staying in the dorm and reading the play, but this was a tiny bit scary . . .

All of them wonderfully intimidated by theater—they all knew there was something more excitingly sinister about theater than about the movies. Part of it was sympathetic nerves—what if an actor forgot his lines?—terrifying embarrassment. Or came down off the stage, like the man in the gorilla suit at the circus? They all knew about that. They knew that they were going to be in the dark in just a minute—in the hands of these actors and actresses who were going to come out to do things right there. They might do something crazy—this was their building—everyone was right there together, there wasn't the safety that other audiences had been through what was going to happen right here.

Anya loved that brief atmosphere of alarm. She knew that the more sophisticated part of the audience loved it, too—the people who dressed up with casual dandyism, made overhearable remarks about other productions they'd seen, getting themselves on edge to laugh first. The graduate students in English and comp. lit. and art history, and the aspiring musicians, writers, painters, sculptors, and other actors at the University of Iowa workshops—all a little jealous that here was a group out of the cocoon. Really doing it.

In the erotic broth of waiting, Anya loved the spice of their envy. Her contempt was not as severe as she'd thought —honeyed disdain.

And here was Jim Mercks checking up on her theater for Bill Ryan. She felt wary.

Mercks said, "Hey, this stew is primo." He looked at Dulcie.

Dulcie nodded toward Mac and said, "Mac made it."

Mercks laughed. "Well, I knew it wasn't Peewee's."

Anya saw Mac tighten even more. Why did Mac act like such a male dog? Was it just Mercks' sweet white smile, clean beautiful hair?

Anya got it a moment later. Mac wanted to come out and loathe this kid—there was a spermy air of the pimp about Mercks—Anya remembered Peewee's stories—she imagined Mac was thinking of them, too—and Anya could feel that Mac had started to condemn Mercks and had been as suddenly stopped. After all, Mac had screwed Peewee too. Anya knew Mac would not make any excuses, any nice distinctions. On the contrary he might very well imagine that the dose of clap that had been his penance had originally—or rather by the way—come from Mercks.

So Mac sat there brutal as grinding rock.

Mercks was physically safe. Anya knew that Mac in a reflective mood—or what passed for his reflective mood when he was taken up with someone's wrongdoing— thought only total obliteration was worth administering.

She suddenly realized something about him—she hadn't understood his wish for a simple unity of his mind and feelings before. All his talk about how pieces of nature worked, how *things* worked. He wanted everything to come out single after all, all processes to be reduced. He didn't really want his core of thought and feeling to be complicated or various—he was thirsty at his very center to make things an intimate part of his life or to have nothing to do with them.

He didn't in fact allow this to break out, but it was there —the tendency to want one final answer for a person. I adore or I abhor. Any progress he allowed his feelings to take was toward a volcanic decision.

That was why he feared any flaw in himself—himself

being the cauldron in which he would render the whole world.

Anya considered herself and thought how different she was, how easily she lived with her flaws, her good parts, her skills and pleasures—the whole variety of her life —everything was made up of pieces. She had no desire to tidy it up according to some final answer. She did desire the luxury of temporary intimacy with anything or anyone.

But Mac . . . Anya, without looking at him, could feel his dense body compressing even more. She felt a cool pity for the fury that was squeezing him. She even felt pity for his adoration of Dulcie. And, Anya thought, the adoration he wished to feel for herself. She couldn't allow it. She had wondered what it was that kept her always at an angle to his direct approach. It was his terrible ravenous pride—that what he finally took into himself would be finally rendered either good or evil.

Anya felt herself relax. She hadn't known she was tense until she relaxed.

Raftery and Andrew were talking to Mercks about what was worth seeing in the Southwest.

Anya cooled into a pleasant state of mind. Had she just learned something about Catholicism? About ex-Catholicism? Had she just discovered a cultural type of insanity?

She found it hard to keep believing Mac lived in such a dark furnace. What was his relief? It occurred to her it was his satisfaction in the physical world—tamping in a cedar fence post—"There, that'll stay for a few years." Fire. Sunlight. Rain. Snow and ice. Trees growing, anything growing. Beans and corn. Hugh.

Her thought tripped on Cervantes—Mac said Cervantes gave him relief. How was that?

And herself—did she give him relief?

She laughed—she thought it was time to send him another questionnaire.

There was no question but that she had never felt anything toward him like his urgency toward her.

Dulcie took a loaf from the oven, tapped it to see if it was done. Mac took it outside—Raftery said to Mercks, "He always walks the bread before he cuts it up." Mercks laughed, but it was clear he didn't know why he laughed. Dulcie said, "It has to cool a little before it'll slice nicely."

Raftery said, "No, he just likes to walk the bread."

Dulcie brought the pail of honey to the table.

Mercks said, "Hey—where'd you get that?" He peered into the depth of honey.

Dulcie said, "Kalona. Ten pounds for five dollars. You should see the cheese."

Raftery said, "A whole wheel. Mac keeps it in a cage in the larder. No walks for the cheese—he's very strict with it."

Mac came back in and sliced the loaf.

Mercks went through the larder door and down the steps. He called back in, "Hey—it is in a cage."

Mac said, "Close the door, will you? Stay in or come out but close the door."

Mercks came back in. "Yes, boss, I don't want to be alone with that cheese."

Raftery laughed.

Mercks said, "What else you got out there?" He spoke to Mac pleasantly so that Mac couldn't avoid answering.

Mac said, "Cheese, apples, turnips, onions, potatoes."

"What was that hanging from the ceiling?"

"A piece of deer."

"How come everything's in wood boxes?"

"So mice and rats don't get at it. Something tried to gnaw through the outside door. A raccoon, probably. That's why the piece of deer is wrapped up. Keep the smell in."

Anya thought, The right way to keep a larder. Knots; knife sharpening; waxing and oiling floors, boots, hinges. Working order. Anya remembered how his explanations used to exasperate her. Now they touched her. Walking the bread—Raftery was right. Raftery loved him and made fun of him. Mac had to weave this intricate net of satisfying chores. To contain himself.

Hugh slid out of Peewee's lap and stomped over to Mac. He grabbed Mac's leg. Mac said, "Well, what's it called, Hugh? If you want some, you have to know what it's called."

Hugh said, "I want some."

Mac gave him a piece of bread. Hugh complained and thumped Mac's leg with his hand.

Mac picked him up. Hugh pointed to the honey pail. Mac said, "Honey. Honey." Hugh laughed and said something, a chattering of sounds. Mac sat down with Hugh on his lap and covered Hugh's bread with honey. Hugh took a bite and then shoved the slice into Mac's lips.

Mac laughed and took a bite. Hugh then tore the bread into pieces on the table and began to stuff them into his mouth seriously. Anya watched Mac watch him. She wasn't sure what *her* feelings were—there was no question but that Mac was inflamed with love.

Raftery combed the bread crumbs out of his beard with his fingers and beamed at them.

Anya wasn't jealous, her feelings weren't hurt. It was less than that and yet more than that—she felt some fear for herself, some loss of balance toward Mac and Hugh, Raftery and Dulcie.

Mac didn't know—he was talking to Hugh again, one hand cupped lightly around Hugh's stomach, the other under Hugh's bottom. For all the blond hair and fair skin of the pair of them, it was a dark, hot picture, Hugh finishing off his bread, listening to Mac with pleasure but not looking at him, only rolling his eyes sideways, the heat of Mac's looking at Hugh almost visible as dark blue sheets of northern lights.

Mac said, "What are you doing, Hugh? You aren't even chewing. Use your teeth, Hugh. No point in getting all those teeth and not using them."

Hugh opened his mouth at the word teeth and pointed in, smiling at Dulcie and at Peewee. Even Peewee, Anya thought. All that meant was that the kid went for anyone who went for him. Well, why not.

Mercks said the obvious thing about a child commanding the attention of a roomful of grown men and women. Anya was the only one who noticed what he was saying. Mercks said he wondered what difference that made to a kid; he himself had grown up the other way, a roomful of kids and one grownup.

Anya said, "Oh, you're from a large family."

Mercks said, "No, a small orphanage."

Anya laughed. Anya was relieved to see Mercks making his way back to center stage. There was a pleasant childish impulse in Mercks—he really couldn't sustain the sinister role Mac cast him in—pimpish doper and seducer of Iowa girlhood, autopornographer.

Anya knew she could attach herself to Mercks' perma-

nent sentimentality. She said, "I'm an orphan, too." She saw
Mercks' mouth open wide.

He said, "Is that right? You're telling the truth—"

Anya explained.

Mercks said, "Hey—I didn't guess you were that old.
Hey look, we ought to compare notes here. What did Peewee tell you?"

"She never mentioned you were an orphan. Wait. She
said you were raised by a woman over in Bettendorf. I
supposed it was your mother."

"No—it wasn't my mother. I was adopted out of the
Davenport orphanage by a couple and then he split when I
was four or five.

"And then she and her kid sister lived together, the kid
sister was divorced, too. I called them both aunts."

"Mercks is their name?"

"Yeah. It was Aunt Jo's married name. And then I
split when I was sixteen—the kid sister moved to California
and I started out with her and then came back, but I never
got on with Jo after that. I went to work in a drugstore and
then the guy who owned the drugstore said I should go to
college. He wanted me to take another year of high school
but I couldn't face that so I came up here and took the
A.C.T.'s and got in here. I was going into pharmacology
but then one thing led to another. I wasn't ever convicted,
but it looked pretty sure I couldn't ever get a license so I
quit. I went back to school after I met Ryan. I went back
for a year as an art major, he loaned me a thousand dollars.
But then there was just too much else to do. I started
making bread in various ways. But I don't know. Maybe
I'll work it out, now I'm back in town for a while. What
do you think?"

Anya said, "I don't know. It's up to you. Why not learn
something?"

Mercks said, "Hey—I'm always learning." He smiled his
charming smile—I'm-cocky-but-don't-take-it-the-wrong-way.

Anya said, "You could always do toothpaste ads."

Mercks laughed agreeably.

Anya thought, I could be a significant figure in his life.
A pretty, hippy punk. But touching—his now-version of
Dale Carnegie—his nerve, his vacuum.

Mercks said in a low voice, "The kid's father there—I
get a lot of hostility off him."

It took Anya a second to see Mercks' mistake.

She said, "You mean Mac. He's not the father. He lives with me."

Might as well get that straight. She thought Mercks' coming on sexually would be mechanically nimble but boring.

Anya invited Mercks to watch the show at the theater.

When Anya and Mac went to bed that night, Mac said, "There's no room for him."

Anya said, "I don't think he wants to move in." She wanted to avoid talking about Mercks. Or even talking about the perfect city that Mac had in mind for them all.

*   *   *

Several days later it all seemed to turn out according to Mac's forebodings.

Mercks dropped by in the late afternoon to bring Raftery a small chunk of hash, and Raftery fired it up in his pipe. Everyone but the Rafterys was over at the theater.

Almost immediately after Mercks and Raftery started smoking a deputy from the Johnson County sheriff's office came in and arrested both Mercks and Raftery.

Mac found out these details the next morning when he drove in to pick up Raftery. Mercks' lawyer sprung them both (questionable search under the Fourth Amendment). The lawyering was Mercks' treat.

Before they left the county office building, they had a talk with Mercks' lawyer. The lawyer told Mercks that he (the lawyer) had objected to harassment of his client. (Mac gathered from the conversation that the sheriff's office followed Mercks when they had nothing better to do.) But—the lawyer continued—Mercks should lay off for a while because the sheriff's office did have pretty good reason to be on his ass.

The lawyer turned to Raftery and said, "The problem you may have is this—if they catch people who're parents smoking dope the county has been known to move to have the parents declared unfit guardians. There's less of an evidentiary problem at the board hearing. Now, they've never actually taken anyone's kid away, but they use the threat as a way of getting these rural communes to pack up and move on."

Mac began to speak, but the lawyer stopped him and

said quickly, "Yes, it's outrageous, an abuse of power, a way of enforcing extrajudicial criminal sanctions, possibly unconstitutional in one way or another, etc. etc. If you have a lot of time and money, or if you have a friend in the ACLU, fight the good fight. If you don't, you shouldn't stick your finger in the sheriff's eye. He's usually willing to let well enough alone. He doesn't bother homosexuals, or kids living together, or general hell-raising. But Mercks here stuck his finger in the sheriff's eye a year or so ago. If Iowa City gets generally known as drug city, the voters get on him. The State House gets on the University and the University gets on him. Then he needs to get a reputation as a hard man. When every citizen who gets a traffic ticket has just seen some stoned kid wandering around, the sheriff has just lost a vote. And the way things are now, the sheriff thinks Mercks—and his friends—are responsible. So a word to the wise."

Mac drove Raftery back home. Raftery was unfazed by it all. He said he liked Mercks, that Mercks was potentially an interesting spirit.

Mac closed down.

He recognized that there was something beyond his distaste for Mercks that upset him. It was the idea of being in trouble. He'd grown used to the feeling that by his outside work he held the group in harmony with what surrounded it. He was annoyed that he'd been caught relying on sympathetic magic again.

Raftery chattered on about his night in a cell with Mercks. He said, "Part of him is a snake-oil salesman, but part of him is pure butter."

Mac said, "Aren't you worried about what the lawyer said about taking Hugh away?"

Raftery said gaily, "We'll have you declared guardian. You'll walk into the hearing with your broad bright face and your gum boots covered with pig shit and you can recite the 4-H Club motto, the Grange Creed, and William Jennings Bryan's cross-of-gold speech."

Mac felt the grayness of the day as an ache—the lack of perspective down the road, across the fields. He thought he'd come close to satisfying some urge of his here—knowing the distances, the order of whole, solid shapes. But now, not just through Raftery's mocking, everything was again unattached, unformed, at no fixed distance in the grayness.

Mac reported the conversation with the lawyer to Anya that night. They talked upstairs in their bedroom.

Anya said, "What do you think?"

Mac said, "I think we've sprung a leak."

"What does that mean?"

"It means we shouldn't go on messing around with Mercks."

Anya said, "But he's not dealing anymore. That'll blow over. Especially if we get rid of all the dope." She looked at him and said, "You might as well say get rid of Peewee for her shoplifting. Or Raftery and Dulcie. For smoking dope. For having been on welfare. For bouncing a check. For having a kid."

Mac said, "It's their house."

Anya said, "It's our house. But I'm not suggesting it, I'm just saying it to show we shouldn't cut people out. We can *not do* certain things, but I don't want to be pushed around about who we have in the house."

She could see Mac shy away from disagreeing with that principle. But winning that point was too easy. She felt like a fight.

She said, "I may have a use for Mercks. And even if we lost this whole house, we could still run the theater—you and Andrew and I could just move back up the road."

Mac said, "And Dulcie and Raftery and Hugh?"

"We'd have to see about them."

Mac said, "Now you're being a shit." It was half-hearted and gloomy.

Anya said, "I would prefer to have people around who make a real contribution. Motherhood and banana bread don't do much for me. I imagine it's pretty nice for Dulcie, though. She gets to be Raftery's wife and your Virgin."

She'd pricked him.

She said, "You probably think Hugh came out of an egg. The Immaculate Conception."

Mac said, "You don't understand the Immaculate Conception. It's not the same thing as Virgin Birth. It's—"

Anya said, "Well, don't explain it."

Mac shrugged annoyingly.

Anya said, "Just tell me the Latin for Dulcie's pearly little cunt."

Mac got up.

Anya said, "You leaving? Did I say the magic word? Did I—"

Mac turned smoothly and quickly, scaring her for a second.

Anya picked it up again, her phrasing edged with a little teasing snag at the end. "Should I wash out my mouth? Gargle with holy water?"

He still wouldn't say anything.

Anya said, "You want to know the difference between us?—when I'm a shit I know I'm a shit, but when you're a shit you think you're right. You think you're a force for good because you feel so bad." She stopped for a second, pleased with herself. "You think you're the scourge of the wicked. That you're the only honest man for miles around. That stomping around in your gum boots in the great outdoors has filled you up with goodness. You think anyone who goes for a ten-mile hike on snowshoes gets a shotgun full of virtue to shoot the bad guys."

She regretted saying that since she'd bought him a pair of snowshoes for Christmas. She'd had them mailed to the theater where the unopened package hidden in the costume room gave her pleasure. But, she thought, there was the limit on how long he could be mad at her, the two days until Christmas.

She still wanted to make him shrivel.

She said, "What are you going to do? Sulk for a month? We've had that."

Mac said, "No."

Anya snorted.

Mac said, "I'm used to your shittiness."

"Ohh—right. The cross you have to bear. Your hair shirt."

Mac appeared to think about that. He said, "No."

Anya thought he wasn't standing up to the fight the way he usually did.

Mac said, "If I stay here, it's because I want to."

Anya was alarmed. For an instant she thought she was betrayed. She thought, The son of a bitch got me all the way out here—up to my neck.

She thought, He wouldn't leave Dulcie and Raftery. He

wouldn't leave his work at Sigurd's. He wouldn't leave the theater.

She thought, He's so badly suited to my life.

She really didn't admit she was in Iowa. Iowa was the park near her theater. There were other theaters in San Francisco, Minneapolis, Pittsburgh, Boston, New York. But Mac was really in Iowa.

She uncleated the curtain pull and lowered the curtain. She lay down on the enclosed bed. She heard Mac approach the curtain. She put her hand against it and pushed a little.

She said, "Mac?"

He didn't answer but she could see his fingers poking into the curtain.

She thought, He has more sensual heat than I do. His hands and feet are always warm, his forehead and cheeks. I take advantage of his skin. No, if I didn't draw off his heat, he'd burn up inside.

Their hands moved, pressing through the curtain but not touching yet.

She had ignored him for a long time during the fall, while taking his heat, not just while sleeping with him, fucking him, taking his work. More than that.

She could feel an echo of his heat in her now.

He craved her with as much heat as a year before. She was as compelling as a landscape to him—it was laughable to her and terrible. She was nimble with him.

She admitted, analytically, that his physical heat fired her own heat. She certainly feared his taking it away. All right, yes—what else did she have to admit?

His hot, blind idea of his goodness. Or his idea of *her* goodness. That was a problem.

But he approached her openly—showed her what he feared in himself, what he knew he didn't understand in himself. He allowed her to consider him. Was that his arrogance, or his submission? Or just the flow of his heat toward her?

Her hand grazed his. She let her hand trail across the curtain, circle back, graze his hand again. She stopped wondering—the way a glutton suddenly stops wondering whether he should or shouldn't, forgets the plan, lets the instant desire call itself a need.

It was his pleasure, his heat she felt, rising faster now.

Her pleasure was her carelessness, letting the prospect of physical pleasure inflate her brain with nothing—nothing, surrounded by a prickling rim of awareness from her outer nerves, her mouth, her tongue, her fingers, all her skin now rushing back out to itself through her brain.

*　　*　　*

But the incident of Raftery's arrest, Mac's feeling of disharmony, and perhaps his quarrel with Anya had a longer-lasting effect on Mac than on anyone else.

Mac refocused his feelings within the smaller perimeter of the household. He felt himself shrink into the domestic shell, even that a loose fit.

He thought about Anya less frequently, but when he did it was with a sudden urgent pain—as though an ember cracked out of a fire onto his skin, blown hotter by its trajectory onto him.

The sudden remembered sight of her wide shoulders and flushed throat and upper chest—her breasts flattened and covered by the dark quilt, held tight by her long, white arms—made his spine jerk. He breathed in with a hiss.

She seemed to him deliberate with him.

They took a sauna late at night—he had just broken a sweat when from the tier above him Anya slid her feet over his shoulders. The crust of the pads of her feet brushed down his chest. He knew he wasn't meant to move. He couldn't. The first light scraping held him rigid. He did not interrupt her program. Each unfolded panel stuck in his mind. Her fingers trickling over his face, then her fingernails pricking his forehead. Then slowly tracing the rim of his ear. The weight of her heels on his stomach. Her loose calf muscles just touching his chest.

Each time she approached him with such care, it was as though she peeled him to his nerves. But he didn't ever resist or break away, even though the tone of her touching him was elaborate and mocking, and even though he knew that by the time he turned and moved into her, the whole stretch of his body would be humming with numbness, his joints would feel weak and misty. The whole physical occasion far away. His rib cage, his skull, the length of his prick from root to head drawn in fine outline, but his whole core light and spongy.

He was struck by the thought of these arranged occasions, and also of the strangely sharp vision that came by chance two or three times a day (Anya under the quilt, Anya's long legs gleaming with sweat in the sauna, Anya's hand untucking her hair from her jacket collar). He didn't understand why he should be troubled, even fearful, as though she was far away or on the other side of some event when she was in fact right there almost all day and apparently contented.

Everyone was in a better mood. Not having performances over the Christmas break was a great relief. The weather was fair and windless. The snow was a foot deep and crusted across the fields. In the oak woods it was still powdery where it had never thawed.

They all ate together, mostly at Raftery's, occasionally at the theater house. They made a toboggan run on the slope across from Sigurd's.

CHAPTER

||||||||||||||||||||||||||||||||

16

The Christmas feast was a great success. In the morning when he started up the wood range, Mac felt in the mood to cook. He roasted three pheasants with apple and sausage stuffing. The haunch of venison was in the oven of the gas stove. Dulcie made red cabbage and chestnuts, potato puffs, braised celery, and acorn squash filled with melted butter, honey, and crushed almonds. At the theater house Andrew made a cake out of layers of meringue, the layers glued together by, and then the whole smeared with, thick, granular, harshly rich chocolate sauce. Alice presented the group with a barrel of Baskin-Robbins vanilla ice cream she'd bought the day before and left in a snowdrift overnight. Og had been saving six bottles of champagne he'd picked up at home in Lake Forest over Thanksgiving.

Raftery brought out the last of the grass he'd stashed in the barn and carefully rolled a Christmas joint for each person's place.

They ate in the front room on a trestle table brought over from the theater, covered with all the house plants from both houses. The room was lit by the fire from the stove, lanterns, and candles. When they sat down they could still see through the front windows the light from the sky squeezed into a violet line above the crest of the slope across the road.

Alice offered Hugh a sip of champagne. Hugh bit the glass in his excitement. The piece came off cleanly. There was a flurry of alarm during which Alice cried and Dulcie pried open Hugh's mouth and groped. Raftery found the piece of glass on the floor. It fit perfectly into the V of the glass, not a crumb missing.

Mac hardly stirred to the alarm. He was in a daze of melancholy—dull, without words.

He watched the last light refracted in the beveled rim of the oval front-door window.

He hoped it was a short sag after the day of good luck while he was cooking.

He roused himself to go get the birds. He lifted the lid and admired them, nesting side by side in the roasting pan. The leg meat was almost falling off the bone. Two had hung for a week, one for ten days.

He honed the carving knife on the whetstone and took the slivery curl off the edge against the leg of his jeans.

He looked in on the leg of deer. Stuck into it with the knife. Another half hour wouldn't do it any harm—they wouldn't want it bloody. He basted it and left the cover off. Tasted the pot of red cabbage and chestnuts on the back of the stove. Just warm. Wet enough to stand some more heat.

Dulcie and Annabelle came out to get the squash. Annabelle said, "Oh, Mac! Don't cut them up out here." She wiggled the leg of one of the birds. "We should put the feathers back on and march around the table."

She and Dulcie put on two of Raftery's lab coats as aprons. Mac noticed that Annabelle left the top button open and carefully spread the lapels to show the upper quarters of her freckled bosom.

He thought, If I were solid as a rock I'd be free to dabble in there—that's all—just dabble my greasy fingers. Just bounce in with all ten fingers—two bouncing spiders with fat legs.

He was annoyed his only exuberance was thick.

He returned to a calm. Annabelle and Dulcie were having a good time sneaking bites and giggling. He let them carry in the birds on the carving board. He thought that perhaps he'd start having a good time in a minute. He felt the beginning of an appetite—he hadn't eaten all day except to lick his fingers.

Mac got a jolt from Raftery when he went in. Raftery was brimming with cheerfulness at the end of the trestle table—lordly and comic. Mac felt withered by contrast, the skull on the banquet table, even though he was filled with love for Raftery, rejoiced for him—his glasses lit by the candlelight, sparkling the length of the room over the jungle of potted ferns, parsley, and ivy, over the pale-blue Mason jars of pickled apples and pears, various mugs and glasses, loaves of dark, sticky fruit bread, the odds and ends of plates, and past all the faces turned toward Raftery, who was preaching out of his black, silky beard, chanting with pleasure about pleasure, his head tilted back so that the dark tube of his lips and gullet aimed his words down the length of the table.

Applause. Laughter. Raftery blessed the birds and the stuffing.

He kissed Dulcie on the lips. He began to narrate a fashion show about Dulcie and Annabelle's lab coats. *"Blanc sur blanc"*—he pronounced it *blahnk*—"for a quiet evening in the arboretum. Gathered at the waist"—he put his hand through Dulcie's legs from the back—"and at the crotch . . ."

Dulcie held the carving board to her chest to keep the birds from falling off. She squirmed and laughed.

Raftery turned to Annabelle, who backed away. "And here we have a décolleté outfit for a leisurely afternoon of freckle counting."

Andrew said, "Yes, there's—let's give a prize for the person who guesses how many freckles."

Annabelle said, "Don't be mean."

Andrew said, "They're beautiful, you know we all think they're beautiful."

Og said, "I'll count them."

Tagh said, "No fair, we'll all count them."

Annabelle said, "You mean how many show or how many—"

Tagh said, "All over! He means all over!"

Alice said, "Don't get excited, sonny."

Dulcie brought the birds back to Mac's end. Mac cut off the legs and started slicing the breasts. Og said, "Hey, where's the white meat?"

Annabelle laughed.

Og said, "I know, for God's sake."

Annabelle said, "I know you know, sweetie, I was laughing at your joke."

Andrew said, "You mean it's all dark meat?"

Alice said, "The dark meat is better for you."

Og said to Raftery, "I thought you were a vegetarian."

Raftery said, "I am, but there's no point in being a pharisee."

There was no conversation for a while once food was in front of everyone.

Mac was pleased with the birds—they were small enough to be tender—had got just high enough—hadn't dried out in the slow oven. The apple and sausage stuffing had absorbed a lot of pheasant juice.

Og and Raftery and Anya each took a carcass to pick clean.

Annabelle lit her joint and passed it around.

Mac checked the deer. Another quarter of an hour wouldn't hurt.

Tagh asked Raftery if he'd ever been an altar boy.

Raftery said yes.

Tagh asked when he'd left the church.

Raftery said, "When my brother was ordained."

Dulcie said, "Oh, I thought it was later."

Raftery said, "The last time was later. One time another brother, Francis—he works for Hallmark Cards—he once offered me a job writing for them—Francis came to see me to complain about Tom, the one who'd become a priest. Francis had gone to Tom and asked him exactly how many souls had been damned and exactly how many had been saved. Francis had heard from a friend of his in the Holy Name Society that when you got to be a Jesuit, they told you all that. Francis said to me, 'So I asked Tom just what the story was, what percent of the people born since Christ died had gone to hell, what percent to heaven. You know what he said? My own brother. He said he didn't know!' "

Tagh laughed.

Raftery said, " 'My own brother! He said he didn't know!' "

Tagh said, "I have a sister who's a nun."

Raftery said, "My sister Kate's a nun, too. She was Dulcie's best friend. What about you, Mac?"

Mac said, "No. My sisters have my father's attitude. I have a cousin on the French side who might."

Anya said, "Not Mireille—"

Mac said, "No. She's a nurse."

Annabelle said, "Who's Mireille?"

Raftery said, "I'd be for my brothers and sisters becoming priests and nuns if they were happy about it, but they're locked in the closet."

Dulcie said, "Kate's not locked in the closet."

Raftery said, "But she's not in ecstasy. She gave up. She became a nun to stay numb."

Mac said, "How do you know?"

"Because I know her. My God, it was grim. Her novitiate was one long prayer to go numb. Ask Dulcie."

Dulcie said, "She was unhappy at first but last time I saw her, she seemed—"

"Numb," Raftery said.

Dulcie said, "—she seemed pleased."

Raftery said, "Why were you crying then?"

Dulcie said, "Because I thought she might be wrong. I was just pregnant then."

Raftery said, "What about Tom then?"

Dulcie said, "*He* seems numb. But he would have been numb if he'd been anything else. Besides, people might be happy inside their numbness."

Raftery said, "No. If there's no intercourse, no flow— then they'll become more and more numb."

Tagh said, "Suppose they think they have intercourse with God?"

Raftery said, "Well, don't you think they'd let us know? Pretty chintzy to keep it a secret." He said again, "I think they're numb."

Anya said to Dulcie, "You were happy when you were pregnant. Did you tell everyone?"

Raftery said, "But it showed. She was radiant—sparrows came to fight over a strand of her hair as it fell from her comb."

Anya laughed.

Mac said, "Why were you walking to New York then?"

Raftery said, "I was jealous. But at least I was looking for something like ecstasy."

Og sang, "Ecstasy—I was looking for ecstasy."

Anya said, "How's it coming?"

Raftery said, "Not bad. There's more room at least. Out with the bad air, in with the good."

Anya said, "You mean it's just breath control?"

Raftery laughed. "Lungs, heart, liver, palate."

Anya said, "You mean it could start with any cell of your body?"

Raftery said, "Now it's in my beard." He pulled Anya's hand to his chin and rubbed his beard in her palm.

Og said, "It can come in any open wound."

Annabelle gave a shriek of laughter. Alice said, *"Jesus, Og—"* but she laughed too.

Ray said with careful seriousness, "Ecstasy is really a very selfish idea. You can't just disappear into your own head. Love is an interpersonal equation. . . ."

He was holding Bangs' hand.

There was an embarrassed silence.

Og sang, to the tune of "Love Is a Many Splendored Thing"—"Love is an interpersonal equa-a-tion. . . ."

Ray smiled a compassionate smile.

Babette said, "Og—" with drawled exasperation.

Ray said, "It's okay, Og."

Og said, "Hey Ray, I'm just fooling around."

Ray said, "I understand, Og."

Alice said, "It'd be okay if you were funny, Og. I meant aside from the way you look." But she said it lightly, even tenderly, and linked her arm through Og's. She turned and scratched the front of his shoulder with her other hand and said, "You are such a moose."

Mac went to the kitchen and brought in the deer and red cabbage and chestnuts. Dulcie got the potato puff balls. She and Raftery filled all their plates with potatoes and cabbage and chestnuts. Everyone loaded up on the deer as fast as Mac could slice it.

At first Mac thought the red cabbage was too sharply sour. Then he thought it was good—the deer was sweeter than most meat, he'd forgot that, the soft purple sweetness. Like the sweetness of the chestnuts. The potato puff balls came mildly between the vinegarish cabbage and the chestnuts and deer. A shame they didn't have a good red wine, even a rough one.

Mac began to eat in earnest. It seemed to him he hadn't eaten in months; he couldn't remember his last big meal.

He crunched a potato puff ball between the roof of his mouth and his tongue. Stuffed in a piece of meat hanging with strands of red cabbage. He looked at the colors of the food on his plate. A beige-and-cream-ribbed chestnut. He smelled the cabbage first, rising from his mouth and throat to the back of his nose. Then the sweet, dark deer. At each slow movement of his jaw the colors, smell, taste, and texture—he could feel separately the shreds of potato crust dissolve—all rose together as an intact thought to his brain. Washed up from an obscure grunt in his brain stem to a light shimmer in his frontal lobe.

Mac nodded without looking up. He carefully prepared another bite, filled with affection for his food and all the appetites around the table.

Mac let himself stay lumped in his chair, drugged with pleasure. Someone brought him a cup of coffee. Og gave him a large Jamaican cigar as a Christmas present. Og gave Raftery a new corncob pipe. Og gave Annabelle a silver napkin ring with an A on it. At first she thought it was a bracelet, but Og explained.

The others began to traipse out to the kitchen and back, cleaning dishes, bringing presents. Hugh came and sat in Mac's lap. Mac saw himself as his father, felt himself as his father. He put his fingers into his hair and pulled his scalp back. He let his hand rest entwined, a gesture of his father's when about to speak to the gathered families in his fluent, badly pronounced French, his face smooth, a blossom of patriarchal contentment.

Hugh grabbed Mac's unlit cigar and tried to bite it. It broke in two. Mac said, "Goddamn it, Hugh!" and slid him to the floor.

Hugh cried. Mac picked him up again and said, "It's okay."

Hugh said, "Sorry! Sorry!" still crying.

Mac said, "It's okay, Hugh. I only wanted half." Mac put the broken cigar on the table.

Dulcie came over and petted Hugh. She was laughing. Hugh clung to Mac's neck.

Dulcie said, "It's all right, Hugh. Mac loves you."

Mac kissed him, and Hugh climbed up to Mac's thigh and launched himself into Dulcie's arms.

Babette, who had just got a vest from Alice covered with embroidery and thirty or forty dime-sized mirrors, said, "Ecstasy is getting presents like this."

That started Raftery off again.

Mac took out his penknife and cut off the broken cigar end and minced the leaves so that Raftery could smoke them in his corncob. He lit the large stub of cigar.

Raftery went on about the Irish monks in the eighth and ninth centuries. "The only men of learning around. Bishops.

They'd get up one morning and feel an urge, hear a voice. And they'd climb into their currach, a dozen of them, and sail to Egypt or Scotland, or Iceland, or America. Cowhide boats that they waterproofed with butter. Singing all the way."

Og said, "Bells on bobtail ring."

Mac said, "Oh, there's no proof they got to America."

Raftery said, "They went everywhere else. They were all over the Near East and Germany and the Balkans. Hairy, smelly, ecstatic."

Mac said, "Well, it didn't take, and it didn't last."

Raftery yelled, "Nothing lasts! Nothing lasts, you smug historian."

Anya and Dulcie laughed. Hugh began to yell along with Raftery, who was waving his arms shouting, "They paddled all over the world! Filled with ecstasy!"

Mac laughed too, but he kept arguing. "Lots of people went all over the world. The Arabs once they got going—whenever the Hegira was—in fifty years they were in Spain—"

Raftery said, "Spain. They could *swim* to Spain."

"—and Indonesia and Central Asia. And the Mongols took over Russia and China and all of Eastern Europe. The Vikings, for God's sake! They were up and down Russia, and the Mediterranean, and Iceland and Greenland. And they really got to America."

Raftery said, "The Vikings couldn't sing. They couldn't carry a tune in a bucket."

Mac said, "And the Portuguese, the Dutch, the French —they went all over Canada and probably right here where we are and out to the Rockies, down to the Caribbean. And even the English."

Anya sang, " 'From Greenland's icy mountains to India's coral strand—' "

Mac said, "Greenland is Danish."

Raftery said, "I don't count people doing it for commercial reasons. I only count people who go all over the world because they're high. Let me have men about me who are high."

Alice said, "The Jews are all over the world."

Raftery said, "But that's been on gloom. The high period was earlier. Like the Chinese."

Anya said, "What do you know about China?"

Raftery said, "Just the cream. I've skimmed the cream."

Mac said, "Are the Chinese great fish eaters?"

Anya said, "Please, Mac, no, not that."

Raftery said, "What?"

Anya said, "His fish theory of genius. The Scotch, the Jews, the Yankees—"

Mac said, "There you go, the Yankees were all over the world, too."

Raftery snorted. "You mean like Captain Ahab."

Alice said, "How do you account for the Italian Renaissance?"

Anya said, "Fish. It was partly caused by the invention of double-entry bookkeeping, but more by the invention of the treble fishhook."

Alice said, "I like Raftery's *joie de vivre* theory. *Joie de vivre* over technology."

Anya said, "We can have both. First you eat fish, then you start singing."

Mac said, "Look at how smart animals are who eat fish— otters, seals, porpoises."

Tagh said, "Sharks are the dumbest things going."

Anya said, "They don't breathe air and they don't sing."

Peewee said, "Are any of you serious?"

Anya said, "Mac is."

Raftery said, "I'm serious about being high. What else is the point?"

Og said, "It's the only way to travel."

Mac said, "I don't know. No high without a low. Isn't that part of Newton's third law? Besides- -"

Raftery said, "No! No! You really believe that what goes up must come down? You really believe in little balls, rolling down inclined planes, and x and y and graph paper?—that the whole world is a high-school physics lab? You're worse than a smug historian—you're a Newtonian physicist!"

Anya laughed.

Raftery said, "The worst kind of fanatic!" Raftery stood up and began to jump up and down. He shouted, "You're a bulldog! You won't let go of anything! You keep on being the way you are—because you think it's part of the rules! You want to join the army of unalterable law!"

He ran around the table and knelt beside Mac's chair. He said in a sweet stage whisper, "Look, Mac, I want to

help. You can tell me. What would you like to be? We'll
fix it up. When no one's looking. One dark night when
they're all asleep—Newton, Pavlov, all those guys. We don't
even need to leave the universe. We'll just go to the half
they don't know about."

Mac was charmed. He thought that Raftery, besides
capering around to please the crowd, was showering him
with friendliness. But still Mac continued to think of arguments, even after Raftery got up from his knees and kissed
him on the top of the head.

When Anya gave him his snowshoes, Mac was delighted.
He was flushed from the wine, too much chocolate (he
thought he was like a dog, his system couldn't handle
sugar), and from Raftery and Anya's attention. He went
outside and buckled on his snowshoes to go wish Sigurd
Merry Christmas. He climbed the fence and started out
over the crusted field. He wondered if his system couldn't
handle pleasure any better than it handled sugar. He grew
flushed and had to burn it off.

Selma must have seen him coming. She came out into
the yard. She shook hands, wished him Merry Christmas,
and asked him what on earth were those things on his feet.
She said she'd meant to bring over two pies she'd baked,
but Sigurd took sick and she hadn't had time to come over.
She turned and went back inside and brought out a pie
basket. Mac said he didn't think Sigurd ever got sick.
Selma said that was right, he hadn't had so much as a cold
in ten years. She asked how they all were over there. Mac
said they were all fine.

Selma said, "Well, he must have picked it up in town
then. Those college people have all kinds of germs. I try to
stay out of town. When I go to town I notice they're always touching each other."

Mac was befuddled. Was she being insulting? He said
he'd be back in the morning. Selma said she was sure
Sigurd would be up by then.

A hundred yards across the field, Mac looked back. The
farmhouse was dark except for the light from the television
set, watery gray light coming out through the double panes.

He thought it was sad—inviting them over wouldn't have
helped.

It was a shame the Olsons' daughter hadn't come home

for Christmas. Sigurd was proud of her in St. Paul, but Selma spoke of her with cold puzzlement and resentment—maybe because she wasn't married.

Mac forgave Selma her rudeness, he thought he suddenly understood her prim farm-wifery straight as a table edge, as closely focused as the rule book for jelly judging at the West Liberty fair. Watery eyes behind thick, clean spectacles, two inches from a spoonful of jelly. Squinting at how clean the spoonful broke from the mass. Points for the quiver, the translucence, the fineness of the edge.

Letter-perfect skills—copied from the square sections, the straight roads, the railroad lines, furrows, rows of corn, the plain barns set square to the road, the roads square to the poles of the earth.

Why not copy the rise and fall of the land? The easy curves of the creeks and rivers? The disc of the sun or the moon? Or the radiation of branches—the drooping wings of a fir, the candle-flame cedar, the squat thrust of an apple tree, the capitol dome of an oak sprouting to the whole arc of the sky?

Of course it might not be up to Selma what shapes she chose. No more up to her than up to the trees or the rivers. The rectilinear life was all there was for her.

Mac stopped, looked back. He could barely see the TV light in the window now. The three-quarter moon was bright. He could see his snowshoe tracks—fish silhouettes nuzzling each other across the field.

He changed the pie basket from one hand to the other.

The feast was gone now. He felt hollow, hypnotized out of his body by the bright, cold night. He remembered with one small fragment of his senses while the sky was alive over him: family, carols, cousins, midnight Mass, *terrines* and *tourtières* crammed and layered with seasoned pork and rabbit, hot maple syrup poured over pans of fresh, packed snow. You could write your name in syrup and peel it off in sugar. Mireille having to recite " 'Le ciel est noir, la terre est blanche.' " He had wished to reconstruct that kind of feast. He had prepared the physical equivalent. And then he himself had failed. Sagged away from the affection, wandered away . . . as soon as a kind of carelessness began.

He had taken a preserved feast out of a Mason jar and

laid it out. He wasn't so different from Selma, canning and bottling, putting things up according to the rules.

Raftery wished him yeast for his life. Mac now thought he'd wished himself a preserved rightness.

Even Sigurd had yeast—the bounty, the healthy greed, that periodically soiled up the order of his farm.

Mac looked toward Raftery's house. The two windows of the front room visible on Mac's side shone dull yellow, barely visible through the white moonlight falling and reflecting from the shining field.

He wondered what it was that had made him pull away. He thought the answer might be that both Anya and Raftery were capable of opening him.

But surely he'd known that for a long time now.

And surely they both valued him.

What was the matter then?

This night, this moon, snow, and frozen air had as much power. Or the oak forest and the river. Or longer ago the lake, the hills around it, the northern forest—all had power over him. Once, he'd noticed a layer of stones lying in the clear shallow water of a cove at the end of the lake. Their dull weight was abruptly and terrifyingly drawn away by shafts of dark sunlight and water-luminous shadow. Each color, each shape, each distance became perfect—what he saw was as alive as his eye.

It had made him wish for time to stop. The wish had burst through him: Now. No more, only now.

There had seemed then to be a chance to leap over time, over his own life.

What could make him shy after that?

But he thought Anya and Raftery did.

He didn't know why. It occurred to him that perhaps it was because they were not fixed by any rules he knew— they weren't family, or sergeants, or teachers, or players in a game. Or wild or tame . . .

They were not held off by anything he did. He thought again, They could open him.

When Mac came back in the house, they'd pulled the table to one side and started dancing. Anya and Dulcie had got out their violin and guitar and were playing a jig. Raftery was keeping time by blowing on a jug. The rest of them were cavorting around—step dancing, double-bopping, doing quick turns and slow erotic poses. Mac thought it looked better than what he remembered seeing at college parties—there was more wit in their dancing. Even Og, the lummox of the morning dance class, was pretty good. They'd all worked up a sweat—the room was warm for the first time in a month. They'd removed their outer layers (everyone was used to wearing three or four), so there were piles of sweaters, sweat shirts, wool ponchos, down vests and shawls in the corners.

Raftery put his jug down and started stamping one foot and clapping his hands. He sawed his elbows forward and backward with sharp jerks that pulled him in a circle around his planted foot.

Og said, "What's the matter—your foot nailed to the floor?"

They were all show-offs, but from time to time noticed each other, parodied each other's footwork. Someone said, "Oh I remember *that*—that's from that show . . ." Tagh did a little tap number and then jumped onto a chair, balanced one foot on the back, the other on the seat, and slowly tipped it over. Og tried to do a cossack dance, managed three or four kicks, and then lurched onto his ass. Babette did it neatly, flicking her feet out with her toes pointed. Og took off his overalls, tried it again in his long underwear, and managed to do five or six.

Annabelle took off her next to last layer, steadying herself by holding on to Mac's elbow. She shook off her jeans, smoothed her tights, and tied the tails of her shirt across her stomach. She said, "Don't you dance?" and looked at his face. She didn't seem to be able to focus her eyes. She said, "Watch me"—and spun away and shimmied. Her shirt tails came untied. She stopped to retie them while her hips continued to twitch, as if she'd forgot they were still in gear.

Ray and Bangs were swinging each other with great heartiness by their elbows, both of them drenched with sweat.

Anya and Dulcie stopped playing, and someone put on a record.

The effect was one of steamy nakedness. Although Mac had sat around in the sauna at one time or another with most of them, this seemed more fleshly. Annabelle bouncing around in her silk blouse, Og in his BVD pants and a

280

purple mesh tank top through which his thick back and chest hair sprouted. Bangs dancing hard in her thigh-length sweater with the sleeves rolled up. Tagh stripped to his old wrestler's singlet which he wore as underwear, but he kept his leather shoes and socks on—an effect that made his bare legs look as knobby as a businessman's in a department-store changing room.

Peewee roused herself from a catnap under the table and joined in, dancing closer and closer to Tagh—not looking at him but jerking up to him with tight little convulsions. She finally led him out through the kitchen and up the stairs. Everyone else kept on swirling and thumping around. Their vision seemed blurred by the sensation of dance, as though each person's concentration were a simple string of a musical instrument twanging different, privately audible notes.

Anya and Raftery were the only ones still clowning around, mimicking the others, chattering to each other; imitating folkloric effects. The others were ecstatic.

Mac looked away. The inner windowpanes were beaded with drops of water that held the light in the room. Whenever someone thumped the floor near Mac, some of the drops of water ran down the pane, leaving clear streaks in which the outside blackness was visible.

Mac slowly began to move his feet, still facing the window—a slow clog dance in his low boots, hopping on his toe and stamping his heel. He could feel the sweat begin to run down his chest and face while he watched the tremors of his dance loosen the beads of water on the window. He moved from window to window, with a simpleminded satisfaction at making each one run. There was an underlying half-imagined notion—that between his face and chest and the glistening window was the balancing point between the quiet darkness outside and the whirl of pale clever bodies inside the house.

CHAPTER

▮▮▮▮▮▮▮▮▮▮▮▮▮▮▮▮▮▮▮▮▮▮▮▮

17

It turned out that Sigurd had stomach cancer.

After he was sick in bed for three days, he went in to the University hospital. At first they thought it might be an ulcer, or hepatitis, or acute gastroenteritis, or appendicitis (the white cell count was high), or cancer, though they didn't even mention cancer until after the biopsy, which they took without explaining. When they found the cancer they told him.

Mac went in to see Sigurd at the hospital. Mac was shaken to see how afraid Sigurd was. Sigurd's dark face had lost its trace of red. He had a tight grip on himself. He tried to sound the same, but his voice didn't rise the same way.

It took Mac a moment to think of anything to say. Mac finally started giving a report on the work he was doing.

Sigurd cut him off. He said, "If you got a problem, you get Ergenbright to come over. He don't know a thing about money, but he knows how to do things."

There was another silence.

Sigurd said, "They don't know if they're going to cut me up or not. I said, 'Go ahead,' but they got to make up their own mind."

Mac had never seen Sigurd so motionless—he kept his arms on the bed on either side of him. His fingers twitched as he spoke.

Mac sensed it wasn't pain that kept Sigurd still, but fear that if he moved he would stir up the cancer.

Mac felt constrained to be still.

Sigurd said loudly, "Hell, I seen all kinds of *growths* on things." His mouth twisted up with irritation. He controlled himself. "But I guess they know as much as I do." He laughed at his joke.

Mac felt himself enter Sigurd's fear and be penetrated by it.

Mac said, "Are you in pain?"

Sigurd said, "No. The pain isn't enough to talk about."

Mac moved closer to the foot of the bed. He hoped to feel Sigurd's strength stir inside the fear. Nothing moved.

Mac made himself speak. "Well, I won't do anything complicated before you get back. I guess that won't be too long—whichever way they decide to treat it."

Mac folded up the list of chores he'd meant to check over with Sigurd.

Sigurd said, "What's that?"

Mac said, "A list of things for you to approve."

Sigurd said, "You just check with Ergenbright. I'd just as soon not talk about it."

Sigurd looked past Mac and said, "I think this thing is changing me."

Mac was caught by the alarm. Mac didn't know what Sigurd meant but he knew it was terrible.

Sigurd said, "There's a prayer meeting Selma's at this evening. A whole roomful of people and they don't know. The pastor came in here earlier. He said it was his experience—and he looks about your age—he said it was his experience that sometimes people think sickness is sin. He didn't want me to think that. He was that far wrong.

"And the doctors here took out some pieces of me—nothing big, just samples—and they're looking at them, and they've sent a piece on an airplane up to Minneapolis and *they're* looking at it up there. They may find out something. But not what came before the cancer. That's the thing that's changing me. The cancer may make me sick." Sigurd opened one hand. "Might as well say it out, it may kill me. But this other thing . . . the thing that's changing me. That's what's the matter."

Mac said, "The flaw in you."

Sigurd looked at Mac. Sigurd said, "Jesus, yes."

Mac hadn't meant to say that.

Sigurd held up his head, his blue eyes to Mac's, for a long time. Mac couldn't even raise his hand to signify that he hadn't meant to say it, that he wasn't even sure what it meant. But he felt his feeling for Sigurd open up, a bare nerve to receive what now passed through Sigurd's eyes.

Sigurd said, "You know the last time I was in a hospital? It was when Sigrid was born. They showed me the soft spot on top of her head. But you're right. All your work— all your good plans and strength and all your getting it done—it all has a soft spot, no matter what. I figured I'd made it all one piece. I'll tell you how wrong I was. After I was in here a little while I got mad at the farm. I thought this was just one more thing had gone wrong on the farm. And you fix it by being hard-headed."

Mac knew if he tried to say anything, to explain anything, he would make it worse. It wasn't just Sigurd seizing on the phrase that he'd blurted out. That had swept on by. He was more affected by how right Sigurd was and at the same time how far from any help or any truth.

When Mac got outside and felt the day again—the push of the sharp still cold—he was relieved. He realized that what caused his relief was a semiconscious listing of all the differences between Sigurd and him—a hasty fence to make a physical boundary. For all their differences, Mac had felt paralyzed with sympathy for that part of Sigurd that trusted in the magic of order and endurance.

* * *

The temperature dropped to twenty below zero. It stayed that cold for the first week in January. The days were bright but no warmer than the nights, because of the wind. Cold gusts blew into Raftery's house, the theater house, even into the theater, and stayed there. Sculpted pieces of cold hanging in the air. Anya called off the dance classes and finally the on-stage rehearsals. They all sat around the wood stove in the kitchen and did flat run-throughs. Voices speaking out of quilts, scarves, parka hoods. It drove Anya nuts to watch Andrew wiggle his finger out of a hole in his mitten, lick it, turn the page and tuck it back in.

Raftery received four checks in the mail—a total of fifty-eight dollars—for poems that he'd sent out during the summer that were just published in *Prairie Schooner, The Carleton Miscellany, Bellerophon,* and *The Red Clay*

Reader. He hitched into town to cash the checks and disappeared for three days. Anya was furious.

It took two hours of foresight to start any of the cars using the electric dip stick or plugging in the engine warmer on the Wagoneer.

Between working at Sigurd's farm and building the new set, Mac was too busy to do any cooking. They all ate at Raftery's—minus Raftery—and finished off the last of the mystery soup.

Anya was grateful for a warm bed. Mac got in first and flapped his arms and legs as though making a snow angel to take the chill out. Anya lowered the curtain behind her.

Peewee went in and slept in Dulcie's bed, Hugh radiating baby heat between the two of them. Anya tried to imagine what it would be like to be Hugh. The thought drifted for a moment, then snagged. She decided she couldn't imagine herself helpless and unintelligent.

Andrew spent the nights of the cold spell in town. His friend picked him up at the end of the day and delivered him each morning. It was only one morning when Andrew was late, delivered by a woman in a different kind of car, that Anya guessed that Andrew's lover was married.

She raised the subject with him.

Andrew said, "It really is *not* that it's none of your business, Anya, it really is that it would just be far too difficult to explain. If you are *worried* about me, and I assume you are more worried than simply *curious*"—Anya nodded, and Andrew continued, "—then I'll say that my life is not as difficult as you might imagine. That is what you wanted to know?"

Anya said, "Yes, of course. You know how fond I am of you."

Andrew said, "And I of you."

Anya said, "There is one small thing."

Andrew listened.

"I wish you wouldn't lick your finger so ritually when you're turning the pages."

Andrew said, "Oh. Well. No need to bring it up. I'm word perfect as of last night."

After three days of cold and thin eating, Anya got Mac and Dulcie to cook a good big meal, and, as if drawn by the smell, Raftery came back. He'd walked the five miles from town—only two cars passed him, neither one even slowed down. He had on a naval officer's double-breasted coat. It reached his ankles. He'd run into an old college teacher of his who now taught at the University of Iowa who'd asked him for supper. He'd stayed on for three days because of the cold. The man gave him the coat—in desperation, Anya imagined.

She decided not to spoil the meal—she could talk to him after he got warm.

Andrew bridged the silence of the various resentments against Raftery.

Andrew said, "Mac, you and Dulcie are one of the bases of civilization. You make our necessities better than necessary." Andrew raised his glass of beer. They all were obliged to join in.

Andrew said, "If we only lived in a warm climate, we'd be entirely civilized."

Mac laughed. He said, "The January thaw ought to do it. Any day now."

Andrew said, "I wonder why it is that American civilization isn't based in New Orleans rather than New York. It's a terrible mistake."

Babette said, "I don't remember any January thaw last year."

Mac said, "Every year."

Anya laughed. "How do you know? Did the groundhog see his shadow?"

Mac said, "There's a VHF radio station that does the weather. There's a radio at Sigurd's that gets it." He turned to Babette. "You ask Ergenbright about the January thaw."

Andrew said, "It's not enough to build a civilization on."

Mac said to Babette, "Ergenbright tells me you're good with his horses. He hopes you'll come around again in the spring to take their winter coats off and exercise them."

It occurred to Anya that Mac's good-neighbor policy, if left unchecked, would have them all working for farmers at three dollars an hour. Babette had been a horse-crazy girl from ten to fifteen at summer camps—a curious if not odd combination, Anya thought, of a Jewish princess from Riverdale and a WASP hobby. She'd even shown horses in Madison Square Garden. Fortunately, Anya thought, dance had won out at fifteen, and then at twenty, drama over dance. What Anya admired about Babette was that Babette's own story of her life was a history of her acquiring skills rather than of things happening to her. Anya wondered if shortness in a girl produced the same effect as shortness in a boy—peppery competitiveness, contempt for softness in large people.

Andrew said, "But besides cooking, what does the civilized life require?"

Alice said, "I don't know, I miss New York. There was a real grit to it. All those people working on the main chance. You got goosed by it. Here we're like girls in a dorm, all on the same menstrual cycle."

Annabelle said, "I miss sidewalks. I miss people on sidewalks. I miss seeing models carrying their portfolios—their faces still made up so they aren't moving them. And then some beautiful boy with frizzy hair comes up and smiles at one of them, trying to get her to smile." Annabelle paused. "Of course, I miss Chevy Chase, too. There were a lot of flowers on the trees. Dogwood, plum, magnolia, cherry. And all those bushes—forsythia and lilac, and camellia. The lawns under the trees covered with petals. I always wanted to fill a bathtub with lilac petals and roll in them."

Andrew said, "Annabelle, you take my breath away. —But I want more than flowers. I want court life. Alice wants the electricity of intrigues. Annabelle wants the elegant appearance of courtiers—models and beautiful boys." He turned to Raftery. "I'm sure there's a place for you—a sort of benevolent Rasputin."

Raftery said, "But where is the court? Surely you don't think it was that notion of the White House as Camelot? Or Lynda Bird's wedding? And surely not some assemblage of pinched Republican businessmen? And certainly it's not secretly on Wall Street. There is no *court* connected with politics or money. Just lobbies. You're just as well off hanging around universities if you want some remnant of court life, some miniature faded reproduction of it. Some little arid anthill of stored mental order. Cozy small pretensions—hooded and gowned once a year. Intrigues in hallways. Pawning Isabella's jewels to get a grant to study the Van Allen belt. Some dean in a gray suit supporting the arts. Our own Lorenzo Medici. I'd rather be an Irish monk."

"Oh, no."

Raftery ignored the groans, took a breath, pulled an end of moustache out of his mouth. "There is this to be said for the Midwest, you don't have to dream East Coast dreams about courts to get high. And you don't have California dreams about revolution, whether it's grapes and lettuce or the latest guru word." Raftery's voice rose up. "*Here* is where the next great rebuke will come from. *Here* is where independent ecstasy will come from. New York and California are prosthetic devices!" He paused neatly on that hard note, like an ice skater stopping short in a spray of ice on the edge of one blade. He fell to eating.

There was no answer. Anya was struck by the effect of oratory—the timbre, the flow, the cadence. She thought, a perfect Sir Epicure Mammon, if only he'd rehearse. But she was more interested than that—Raftery's gift was not only that he was unembarrassed by his own intensity, or by its occasionalness, but also that his playfulness shaded into seriousness—or rather mixed in—without dimming.

He had, she also realized, a beautiful voice—rich, Midwestern, Missouri (none of the pinched Wisconsin or the parched Kansas). And control—he could shade with a word from one thin note to a big, thick sound, not smooth but crackling with overtones. A projectable field of crickets.

She said to him, "Do you mind if I shape your beard? Just bring it to a point?" She remembered she'd been mad at him. She added, "And don't miss another rehearsal."

It occurred to Anya that she disagreed with him—about New York; she didn't know about California. But it didn't matter much what he said when he was on.

She said, "In fact, let's you and me do a line-through in the other room. When you're through eating."

She was surprised. He had his part cold.

*　　*　　*

The talk about court life, culture, civilization came back at the next three suppers, like a leftover stew.

It seemed to be all of them, but Anya finally figured out it was mostly Raftery working on Mac. Raftery didn't seem to care what the others thought—although he was occasionally stirred by Annabelle or Alice yearning for this or that sentimental or sensual effect—but Mac's remarks seemed to strike him deeper. Anya was surprised. It was as though Raftery had just discovered Mac's particular loyalties, and had to tug at each one, test its deep-rootedness, see how it fit in to Mac's system.

Raftery asked question after question, sometimes with a clever grin ("But if you really think that, how can you . . ."), sometimes outraged ("No! No! No!"), but always swarming and bouncing around. Anya was annoyed —sometimes because she thought she could answer better from Mac's point of view, sometimes because he told Raftery things about himself she didn't know. And because Raftery and Mac were oblivious to her.

She said, "You two really aren't getting anywhere."

They both looked at her, acknowledged by looking that she spoke, were glazed and silent for an instant, and went right back at it.

No one else seemed to mind as much as Anya did.

The second evening she was annoyed because she noticed they didn't care what they sounded like. She said to them, "You sound like a freshman seminar on great ideas." Again they looked at her, puzzled and uninsulted, and, after a moment of eating in silence, they each thought of something to say to the other.

What she'd said wasn't true. They *sometimes* sounded like freshmen in a dorm, and then suddenly they would sound like strange old men. Mac, curiously enough, had as wide a range of voices as Raftery, though he stumbled into them. Raftery seemed to choose his voices consciously, quoting Plato, Epictetus, Buckminster Fuller, the Old Testament, his own poems. Mac would strain to understand, looking straight at Raftery. Then he would begin to answer as though against his will, shaken by Raftery's rhythm, but speaking in a voice and diction that Anya recognized as one of his styles of intimate thought and feeling. It struck her as odd, and then offended her, to hear him speak in these styles in public.

She tried to ignore her feelings, joked to herself, "What'll he have left for marriage?" which led her to think that she would rather have Mac and Raftery be casual lovers, be known as casual lovers, than be at each other this way.

She tried to draw Andrew back into the discussion—

after all, he'd started the whole thing—but he wouldn't cut back in.

The third night they went at it again. Their voices were flatter and strangely alike. Raftery pushed harder, obviously wanted the conversation to be difficult and risky. He half-discovered something about Mac that Anya thought she herself had not—that Mac considered himself dangerous. Mac had at times said to her he thought he was a barbarian, told her about conversations he'd had long ago in which he'd wondered what a barbarian was. But Raftery was drawing out something stronger.

Raftery said, "But about the boy whose head you banged on the rail—you say you wouldn't have done it if you hadn't been in a strange country?"

Mac nodded.

"But you aren't in a strange country anymore?"

Mac said, "No, it's not. Not here."

Raftery said, "Not here in Iowa." He flickered toward that point.

Mac didn't. Mac said, "Not here. Not around here. In Schenectady I was a barbarian in a strange country. Or maybe I didn't think I was really there. When the other boy started the fight, when he started whatever it was he wanted, a fight with rules I guess, I suddenly felt that by destroying him I could get somewhere. I could get bigger, get power to become someone who could be somewhere. That's what was frightening and primitive. That's why the other kids didn't stop me for such a long time. They felt it, it scared them. When I began to bang his head on the rail, I remember thinking of white space, a very beautiful white space that got bigger and bigger. Very far away I could hear myself thinking that I might hurt him more than he deserved (that is, more than *they* deserved), that what I was doing wasn't good, that everyone (that is, my family) might think badly of me, that I would get in terrible trouble with someone like a teacher or a scoutmaster. In that order —the arguments got weaker and weaker."

"Why did you stop?"

"I thought I'd killed him."

"How did—what *had* happened to him?"

"He was out cold—he had a concussion. He was still out when they took him to the hospital. An ambulance came for him. The schoolteachers thought I was crazy. I was suspended, and I had to go talk to the school district psychologist and take a lot of tests. An odd thing came out of it—the psychologist's conclusion was that I was smarter than anyone thought. To the schoolteachers I'd been a dumb kid—a pint-sized jock—sullen—shying rocks at pigeons and squirrels. Disappearing a lot."

"How old were you?"

"Twelve. The whole thing hung on till I was eighteen—a lot of the kids in my class went on from that junior high to the same senior high. It was never quite forgotten. It kept me outside the gang. And of course I never forgot it, but *I* only thought of it as having to do with everyone else's thoughts.

"When I played hockey—there was good hockey even around there—the other kids were scared of me. I was never a dirty player, not even a mean player, but I could feel guys slow up rather than skate into the corner with me.

"What was strange was that in the place I thought of as home—my mother's family's place in Canada, where we went Christmas, Easter, and all summer—a third of the year in all—I spoke the language badly. I was a linguistic foreigner. The Greek notion of barbarian. *Bar-bar-bar*.

"But at least, I thought, my relations with the people in that family were permanent. It seemed to me that they had all the skills and knowledge necessary to civilization—there was a doctor, a restaurant owner, a plumber, a seafood wholesaler. The thing I noticed was that they had fewer anxieties than their American counterparts. There was less movement, or at least less restlessness in their manner. It was a cross section of the lower and middle bourgeoisie—just getting along. But that didn't mean hustle, not there, it meant piety, family, well-arranged comforts and pleasures. More attachment than ambition. It seemed to me, too, that their houses, their occupations, their feelings could only change glacially. Everything was slower, smoother than in Schenectady, but much more alive. For all the sharp edges, for all the tearing up and building in Schenectady, for all the threat I felt there, it all seemed lifeless. I didn't believe that real feelings could exist in our life in Schenectady—I didn't believe my father's friends were anything more than men from work. It was willful blindness on my part because actually he had good friends. My mother did, too.

"But I was suspicious there, and the kids I knew were suspicious of me. To give you an idea of how unhappy I must have been—when I went in the army after high school, I felt no increase in anxiety. In fact I was pleased at the imposition of order on the other men."

Mac paused and said to Raftery, "I told you about my trouble in the army. That was like banging that kid's head on the rail—I don't mean my knocking the sergeant down but afterwards, the wish to get some magic way out, away from that lifeless place—where dead things moved at high speed. At that time it seemed to me that a barbarian was someone who was bound to fuck up in civilization because he would keep triggering mechanisms. It was not a question of intelligence or skill—I was good at all the training. I liked it—but I couldn't retract my presence. I kept doing things or just being someone who set off alarms in the institutional wiring. But I was a great admirer of the institution. Even a romanticizer of it. Much later I realized that—"

Raftery said, "—but hitting a sergeant is sort of a crude way to object to the army."

Mac said, "You don't get it—I *liked* the army. As I hit him, the first impulse was personal. But there was a secondary impulse which was that this sergeant should be corrected, should be made a better sergeant. In fact, I had in mind several sergeants he should be like. *As* I hit him.

"I was extracted from all this by two JAG lawyers from South Philadelphia. They were very funny. Sharp dead-end kids who made a pet of me. It was their delight to get me off. And to instruct me. They both seemed to know right off what I was. That calmed me. And they knew what I could be made to appear to be. That got me off. They were both that nifty kind of middle man who can change the appearance of something to make it fit into an institutional category so that it will not cause confusion. They did this partly out of sympathy for me, for which I loved them. It was that—I longed for their visits like a dog in a kennel. I was ready to jump and lick their faces. It was the strongest feeling I had for anyone outside my family. It was stronger in a way because it was a surprise. And the other reason they did it was that it amused them, a very civilized amusement which I didn't understand. I mean, I understood amusement, but not that kind—where real life became a film they could run back and edit. They kept my feelings for them at a distance with wisecracks. I don't know what they felt.

"But I never recovered from the feeling that they had painted a mask for me. They even fiddled around with the guard schedule so that my MP escort into the courtroom was six feet three with an eighteen-inch neck. I looked like a midget. And my hand in a cast. Barber-shaved so I had a baby face."

Anya said, "I never thought of this before—they were putting on *Billy Budd*."

Mac didn't seem to hear. Raftery looked at Mac and said, "Yes—'the handsome sailor'!"

Mac said, "What upset me was that I wasn't really standing trial. It wasn't really me who was innocent—it was this creature they'd made up—smaller, sweeter, more injured. And what *I* really was was locked up in my brain. That was the frightening part—because I was so confined—I couldn't talk to anyone except those two lawyers, and of course I couldn't go anywhere—I began to imagine infinite spaces inside my brain. That it was possible for my real person to disappear into my own feelings, and be lost. I'll tell you what the feeling was like—where one of those astronauts is dangling out in space held by one line—that physical terror. Seeing that picture makes me grab hold of something. That same physical terror—but also an urge, a thirst—to drink in space—through your eyes—no, directly with your brain. To drink it *all*."

Mac was looking only at Raftery. Anya looked at Raftery, and she saw that skinny Raftery was sitting like a placid, fat abbot, hot and bright behind his glasses.

Mac said, "The important thing was to find the center of this space and breathe deeply because I was sure if I became angry, or self-pitying, or *any* partial way of feeling, I would be whirled away forever.

"Particularly if I became so angry that the space became white."

Mac stopped with a click as though he'd made it all clear. The others at the table, although not talking, had stopped listening closely, and looked around at each other now that Raftery and Mac had finished. Through the scattered attentions Anya felt the pulse of Mac's seriousness. She thought he felt tired, but immediately she felt a clear energy rise up in him. And she felt a third mental operation—her own energy rising toward his. She recognized that that involuntary movement toward him was a stronger symptom of a bond than she'd felt before. Especially as it came at a time when she felt no aesthetic interest in him, was in fact annoyed with him. She held back for an intant, curious. She thought, It's like watching yourself fall asleep. She thought, The only way out is all the way through to the other side.

Now that she knew she wanted him, Mac suddenly appeared to recede. She'd thought all fall that she'd only have to stop avoiding him. Only stand still to meet him. But his current no longer seemed to be pressing toward her.

*   *   *

As it happened he was physically apart, too. While Sigurd was in the hospital getting his cobalt treatments, Mac spent a six-hour morning at Sigurd's. Ergenbright took over during the afternoon.

Mac worked on the *Alchemist* set all afternoon. He ate supper, read for an hour, then fell asleep.

Mac and Anya had a quarrel over borrowing some of Sigurd's barn space heaters for the theater. Mac didn't even want to ask Sigurd or Selma. Anya thought it wasn't much of a favor considering how much Mac was doing. They finally settled it—borrowed one from Ergenbright and bought one.

Anya found herself impossibly jealous. Mac's feelings had rooted all about—Dulcie, Hugh, Raftery, Sigurd . . . Lying in bed at night, Mac wanted to talk about Sigurd's farm, Ergenbright's farm—kinds of farmers.

Anya was afraid that she would have to *ask* him to pay attention to her feelings.

After a few days she was no longer afraid she would have to ask. She would do anything. As soon as she entered their bedroom she felt willowy and strangely light-headed. She forgot the whole day, the next day, the next week. She wanted to tease him. She wanted to lure his attention into silly froth, start him fooling around. She felt

294

that only after a scene of foolish wooing would they be alone.

The third night she went upstairs, lit the candles, the kerosene lamp, the small kerosene heater. The heater threw a rose-window pattern on the ceiling.

One of the problems was that the room was so cold. She'd liked the effect at first—their cold bodies stretched out together, the feverish penetration. An unreal heat. No longer what she had in mind.

She wanted to make love, but not just to make love—to draw him to her out of new curiosity and delight. Then she herself could let go, not so much for the pleasure, which she foresaw rather coolly, but because she would have his whole attention, all the way into the dark fall into sleep.

But it didn't work that way. He came in, worried about the candles, the wicks in the lamp and the heater. He was restless or wary. She danced around in her bathrobe and wool knee socks and sang, " 'Oh, he's a deep-sea diver an' he don't come up for air.' " He was too puzzled to be any fun. He seemed to prefer her plain.

She finally said, "I sometimes worry about your puritan lack of imagination."

He didn't get mad, he was surprised at the phrase. "Is that what makes a puritan—lack of imagination?" He thought for a while.

He said, "But maybe it's not *lack* of imagination but shying away from it."

He took off his boots and his outer layer of socks.

He said, "I suppose it amounts to the same thing. I can think of a dozen things I'd rather not imagine because I can imagine them so clearly." He sat on the bed. "Of course a lot of puritans spend time imagining the pains of hell." Mac laughed. "—For other people. Maybe *that's* a puritan." He looked up at her. "That's not me."

He thought awhile. Anya knew she'd started him thinking about what he was. She thought, Three evenings in a row of Raftery's attention has gone to his head.

He took off his inner socks and wiggled his toes.

She said, "I want to save you from a life of rural idiocy."

He said, "Where'd you get that idea?" He was about to get mad.

She said, "That's just what Lenin said to the Russian peasants."

Mac said, "Hey, look here. Ergenbright and I are doing something tomorrow—you might want to watch a little rural idiocy. We're going to castrate pigs."

Anya thought she might as well give up her idea of an elegant screw.

After a moment she laughed. She still wanted him. In fact his self-absorption and his irritation attracted her—she could approach while he wasn't looking. A bawdy imp came to life in her. She decided to act like Annabelle—he probably wouldn't even notice. She stood by the kesosene heater brushing her hair, feeling her own heat. She tried to feel the spirit of Annabelle's teddy-bear tricks, Annabelle's talent of making her flesh seem in need of being touched.

She didn't succeed in feeling like Annabelle. She settled for feeling like a dirty little schoolgirl, hoisting the skirt of her nightgown but leaving her knee socks on. She contrived to attract him from behind, thinking, Oh, we didn't do *this* in ninth grade. Oh, Mr. MacKenzie, is this part of gym?

She stood by the bed, Mac on tiptoe on account of her long legs. She sank to her knees on the quilt and finally she was pressed flat, tipping her rump up in the last bit of doggy pleasure.

But the very fact that this was just the sort of interlude she'd imagined for herself left her adrift after Mac had gone to sleep. It reminded her that she used to live in scenes. Scenes where substance was drawn off from other people's situation but whose form was her invention. She had been successful as a parasite, even happy as an adventurous parasite. She thought, Now I'm becoming a host animal. I don't enter situations anymore. I am a situation.

She tried to imagine leaving the theater group. She couldn't. She couldn't imagine herself as the thin adventurous spirit she'd been. Even after she used her imagination to expel members of the troupe (Alice and Babette off to a nomad dance group, Annabelle off to model tennis dresses, Dulcie back to rock on her front porch in Kansas, Peewee back to Mercks' Iowa City underground), even after she got rid of them one by one, she couldn't get rid of the group as a whole.

She'd grown larger, she couldn't just pull away. She

would have to absorb her connection to these people in order to dissolve it.

* * *

Ergenbright said to Mac, "Sigurd let them get too big. You ought to cut them when they're under thirty pounds. These here are fifty, sixty, some of them a little more."

Mac said, "Does that make it harder?"

Ergenbright said, "For you. Not for me. You got to pick them up."

Mac said, "I'll be all right."

Ergenbright laughed. "You're going to be wore out, I guarantee you." He pronounced *guarantee* to rhyme with *warranty*. "I'm going to let you catch them, too. I'll catch the first one and show you how to grab hold."

Ergenbright and Mac were standing in the midst of the pigs in a pen in Sigurd's pig shed. The pigs were squeezing against the far side of the pen. On a chest-high shelf on the wall near the men's corner were two scalpels, a pot of tarlike disinfectant with a swab. The low gate to the next empty pen was behind Mac. Beside his left foot there was an empty pail for the pigs' balls.

Ergenbright advanced on the squealing crowd, caught a pig by the hind legs and walked over to Mac, the pig's head hanging down. He handed the rear legs to Mac so that the pig's belly was exposed.

Ergenbright said, "Now hoist him up so that the feet are up to your shoulders. That's it. Now lean back against the gate. You got to take the weight off your back and arms and onto the gate—okay, now clamp your knees on his head."

Mac did. The pig's squealing went down in pitch from a bleat to a rippling grunt.

Ergenbright said, "Now pull his legs apart to get that skin pulled tight. It cuts easier if it's real tight."

Mac stretched the pig's feet apart and looked down. A half-foot from Mac's face Ergenbright touched the scalpel to the pig's taut, delicate skin. The pig didn't move at all. Mac felt the heat of the pig's back against his stomach, the pig's shoulders in his own groin.

Ergenbright reached in and pulled out one testicle and a loop of the *vas deferens*. He reached in with his forefinger and hooked the other testicle out. He flicked them into the pail.

Ergenbright said, "It's important you get them both. If you don't get the upper one, then later on he starts acting like a boar. Fighting and raising hell. So you better be sure to get both."

Ergenbright slapped some of the disinfectant over the cut, and said, "That's all there is to it."

Mac let the pig down forefeet first in the empty pen. The pig started squealing high again, the two first notes of a whinny, over and over.

Mac caught the second pig and Ergenbright castrated him, working a little faster. Mac swung him over the gate, and the pig ran across the pen, squealing wildly until he bumped into the first pig. They both stopped squealing when they touched. They stood shoulder to shoulder, grunting. Mac was amazed and oddly relieved.

Ergenbright continued to instruct Mac as he cut, narrating any problem he had. There was almost no blood.

Mac could hear him over the squeals and grunts because their heads were close together over the pig's underbelly, but he found his main attention was on the feel of the pig against his body. It was an enjoyable feeling, more enjoyable now that it was part of a rhythm and now that he was sweaty and his body was worked over—not bruised, just worked over.

He asked Ergenbright why the pigs didn't bite.

Ergenbright said, "I don't know. Boars and sows'll bite you if you don't know them. If you go at them wrong." He laughed. "Maybe these ones like you."

After an hour Mac's forearms began to tremble. He said he had to rest. Ergenbright said, "Your back'll feel it this evening, I guarantee you." The pigs sensed the lull and quieted down.

Anya, Babette, and Raftery came in.

Raftery surveyed the pigs and recited grandly, " 'Qué piensa el cerdo de la aurora? / No cantan pero la sostienen / con sus grandes cuerpos rosados, / con sus pequeñ patas duras / . . . Quiero conversar con los cerdos.' " He turned back to Ergenbright and Mac and translated, "What do pigs think of the dawn? They do not sing but bear it up with their huge pink bodies, with their small hard hoofs. I want to talk to the pigs.' "

Ergenbright said, "I didn't know you knew how to talk Spanish."

Raftery said, *"Si, señor."*

Babette discovered the pail of testicles. She peered in and said, "Are these things—" and then she turned away.

Ergenbright said, "Hey, Babs, I'll show you how to cook them."

Babette said, "Don't be disgusting."

Mac said to Raftery, "These aren't pink, they're Chester Whites."

Anya said to him, "You really are a farmer when you get your gum boots on."

Ergenbright saw no offense in the remark. He said to Anya, "Yeah, Mac's picking it up." He turned to Mac. "You want to cut these last ones?"

Mac said, "No. I'll hold."

Anya said, "I'll cut them."

Ergenbright said, "You know how?"

Anya said, "Yes."

Ergenbright said, "Okay."

Mac caught a pig, twisted it around, and spread it out. Ergenbright traced a line on the pig's skin with the disinfectant. Anya said, "Right." She made the incision and plucked out the testicles and the *vas deferens*. Mac dumped the pig over the gate.

Raftery said to Anya, "Where did you pick that up?"

Anya said, "They kept some pigs at Putney one year."

Ergenbright said, "Well, well, well."

Anya said she'd let Ergenbright finish the last four. Ergenbright asked Babette if she'd like to try. Babette said, "No."

After Mac dumped the last one over the gate, Ergenbright scooped out a can of testicles for himself. He said to Mac, "Now, here's how you fix them." He picked one up and cut into it. "You open up along the cut then you just turn it inside out." As he peeled back the casing and squeezed, an elongated olive of pale, hard flesh popped out. Ergenbright said, "Now, that's the part you eat. You don't need to clean it, it's as clean as anything in the world. Then you just roll it in a little flour and fry it up. Only thing is they're rich. You don't want to eat but a dozen or so." Ergenbright sighed. "It's the sweetest meat in the world. Except maybe tom-turkey nuts. Pardon me, ladies."

Mac regretted the change in atmosphere. He knew if he served them for supper Og and Tagh would carry on the same way. Maybe he wouldn't tell them. He'd cook them, all right; he didn't want to waste a bucket of good meat.

On the road on the way back home for lunch Raftery linked his arm through Mac's.

Raftery said, "Everything doesn't have to be perfect. You don't have to be perfect. Have you ever seen a careful person who was happy?"

Mac said, "I've seen lots of careless people who are unhappy." Raftery dropped his arm and jumped up and down in mock rage. "'A false conclusion! I hate a false conclusion as I hate an unfilled can!'"

Raftery took Mac's arm again.

Mac said, "I wish you wouldn't quote all the time."

Raftery said, "And you carry service too far. I know myself what a pleasure it is to bring you your cup of tea in bed in the morning, but I don't imagine I can do more. Helping Sigurd—? You have a terrible pride. I may have a cockerel vanity but you have deep, gnarled roots of pride. That you sustain the earth. That you hold it all together with your roots."

Mac felt himself moving Raftery to a distance in his mind. He was willing to listen at a distance.

Mac admitted to himself that in helping Sigurd he was trying to rearrange elements of their life, trying to stitch himself into this place bounded by the river and oak trees on one side, the fields rising gently to a low, straight line against the sky on the other. But he preferred not to think about his feelings. It *was* superstitious, romantic—but he didn't have to think about it because the question was simple—Sigurd had asked him to do some work and he said yes. That was all anyone—that was all he himself needed to know.

Mac thought, Ergenbright uses neighbor as a verb. He said he was glad to neighbor for Sig.

Mac looked at Anya. If she had a complaint about what he owed her, she could say so. He thought there was a winter stillness and simplicity to the day, their talk disappeared as fast as their breath or their body heat. What he was up to was simple. He saw Selma's unspoken point now, you did what there was to do properly, and then it didn't matter what was said. Or thought or felt.

Raftery stopped talking. Mac shifted the bucket to his other hand. There was no wind, just the solid cold. Mac saw with satisfaction that the gray clay of the road was so hard their boot treads didn't leave a mark.

CHAPTER

||||||||||||||||||||||||||||||||||||||

18

Anya thought that *The Alchemist* was in good shape. She decided that next year their major efforts should be during what had been their vacations. They'd survived as a parasite on the University of Iowa. Now what Anya wanted was an independent life—to do a show in Chicago over Thanksgiving. A Christmas run in another big city—bigger than Des Moines—St. Louis or Detroit. Somewhere they could drive with their sets and costumes. And maybe go to New Orleans for Mardi Gras. They might get lost in the shuffle —didn't the crowds just want parades and booze? Maybe she should aim for Dallas-Fort Worth or Houston. Some rich, culturally-anxious Texas backers. She'd heard that Rice had money to burn for their theater program.

The summer ahead. New York—they'd get lost. Unless they had a new show, a novel show.

She decided they could use a booking agent. She wanted an ally in her practical ambition. She was tired of being the only one to think with shrewdness and venality.

And by now she had to line something up. If the group stayed right there, she guessed that the University theater department would swallow them. Make an offer that Og's and Annabelle's fathers would give in to. Perhaps the University would offer her a job—assistant professor in charge of the workshop theater. And Andrew. Ray's half-year leave would be up, and he'd be back on their payroll. And he'd probably marry Bangs or get her a job, too. The rest of them would drift away.

And then she'd never move up. Her life would be com-

mittee meetings, the college theater convention, a Chicago
NET show once a year, worrying about tenure.

There was just enough temptation in the prospect to
make her writhe. She'd rather get chiseled by businessmen
producers than smothered by a department chairman.

That was the problem with the Midwest. The University
was where everything went on. *Real* life was farming and
trucking and banking—commodities and money. All the
arts were taken care of at the University—there was
enough Germanic and Scandinavian concern, mixed with
just enough fear of being uncultured, for the state legis-
lature to put up money. They would rather have had a
football team like Nebraska's or a basketball team like
UCLA's, but the arts were as good as, say, a gymnastics
team.

The student symphony was as good as any small city's.
The faculty string quartet was almost up to the Budapest
or the Juilliard. The drama department was technically as
good as Yale's. There were as many poets and novelists
hired or subsidized as lived on, say, Cape Cod. The music
department put on an opera once a month—as good as
what had been standard fifties or sixties performances in
Washington, Richmond, Louisville, Baltimore. Puccini, Ros-
sini, Bizet all unevenly acted, no big voices, church-choir
soloists—in tone thin and pious, but well schooled.

Enough painting on view in the art department to stock
a block of New York galleries. Where, in fact, it went if it
didn't fall short at Chicago.

Iowa City was undoubtedly a cultural center. Or at least
a training camp. What depressed her was the feeling that
the whole town had—exile and native alike—that real life
(if it wasn't farming and trucking and banking, and it
wasn't), that *real* life was going on somewhere else.

She had to confess she had her own idea of where real
life was—a sticky collage of Uncle Timmy and the *New
York Times* and Cambridge and Manhattan and national
acclaim. The idea suddenly depressed her, it was so common. Raftery at least thought real real life was in the
clouds. Mercks thought it was speeding into or out of
Mexico. Peewee didn't think—Peewee just knew it wasn't
where she was.

Anya tried again—real life, civilized life. Somewhere.
Somewhere there was a group of people who each put as

much effort into pleasing the others in private as most successful people put into a public career. Was that Bloomsbury? Thinking itself the psychological center of the world, the most civilized moment so far in history? And yet they'd missed so much—D. H. Lawrence was right, seeing them as water bugs skimming only on the surface.

All right then, what did she dream of? Her brains in Tassie's situation? It was undreamable—her orphan wit couldn't have grown in Tassie's house.

Anya thought, There is no point in dreaming of the comforts of family any more than the comforts of friends. Temporary custodies and temporary alliances were all there were, and if you allowed yourself to think that wasn't so, you became a stunted parasite.

The last time she had steeled herself with such tough talk was when Henry Sewall died. This time she wasn't so sure what she was scared of.

*   *   *

At supper Mac suddenly became talkative. He said, "I remember from summers in Canada, way off in the woods with my mother's family—that by the end of two months of living pretty much in the wild, everyone divided up pretty clearly into plants and animals."

"What on earth are you talking about?"

"I mean everyone finally came under the influence of the wildness—the water, the sky, the woods. The cabins and the lodge seemed unimportant after a while. The plant people settled in—their rhythm was connected to sunlight. They bloomed and were fairly happy. The animal people were more excited than happy—restless, always poking around, moving toward someone or away from someone."

"What were you?"

"I was an animal. But that's why I notice it here. Here I'm a plant."

"I suppose you think the plant is the higher form—contrary to the usual evolutionary notion."

Mac said, "It's not a question of higher and lower, better or worse. It's just something . . . I've noticed."

Raftery said, "There are days I feel like a plant."

Dulcie said, "Yes, a weak reed."

Anya was surprised. Raftery laughed.

304

Andrew said, "If I'm a plant, I hope I'm a house plant."

Mac said, "It has to do with how steep and jagged your pleasures are. If you seize and devour them. And then have to start all over again."

Peewee started to speak. "I'll say one thing, there's—"

Raftery said, "It's a slower death being a plant. That's all."

Peewee said, "There's a big difference between the way Mercks and his group live and living here. They really were a pack of monkeys. They were always ending up bored, just bored of everything."

Raftery said, "Aren't you bored here?"

Peewee said, "Sure. But it's not so bad. *Some*one's usually having a good time."

Raftery said, "I thought monkeys had fun. 'More fun than a barrel of monkeys.' "

Peewee said, "Maybe he should call his movie that."

They all looked up. Andrew said, "I thought that was just a lot of talk."

Peewee said, "No. Ryan paid for it and bought it, and he won't let Mercks show it. But now Mercks wants to show it this spring—at the big festival this spring. Ryan's scared that if Mercks gets busted for it, it'll come out he paid for it."

Anya said, "What's this festival?"

Raftery said, "Oh, it's one of those synthetic events. For the animals, not for us plants."

Anya said, "Will everyone be stoned or can we sell them tickets to a show?" Anya was irritated no one had told her. "Who's in charge?"

No one knew.

She thought it might just be student rinky-dink. They should stay clear of that. But then it might be what she was looking for.

She said, "It's not just a rock concert?"

Raftery and Peewee said, "No."

Peewee said, "Mercks says it's going to be an underground World's Fair. He's fixing up a barn to show movies in. There's going to be a parade from in town out to the grounds—up north of town out the Prairie du Chien Road. That's where his barn is. He figures he's going to make a lot of money."

Anya said, "What else are they going to do? Who else is working on it?"

Peewee said, "A bunch of guys, I don't know who. You ought to ask Mercks. He said he'd come out here, but he feels bad about last time, you know, the sheriff and all. He says he's been straight ever since."

Raftery said, "The only good thing I've heard is that some guys from the art school are putting up domes. A life-sized catalog of domes. One of them is for a soup kitchen. Maybe Dulcie and Mac ought to run a restaurant."

Mac said, "I don't want to do anything with Mercks."

Anya said, "But Mercks isn't in charge, is he?" As she spoke she felt that she didn't want Dulcie and Mac to work together by themselves—she also didn't want them to fritter themselves away on a small enterprise. She also realized that she had a fear of the rock-concert mentality. The situation would be too raw for the civilized attention she wanted in an audience. But she also wanted to be in on this festival if it was going to be the event that lit the place up, that attracted coverage in the *Village Voice, Rolling Stone, Playboy, Time, New Times, The New York Times.*

She imagined what Mac would think of what she was thinking, and she was furious with him.

*   *   *

Over the next month Anya had two changes of heart. The first was that her desire to succeed in a more important arena was settled. There was no more question. It was part of her.

The second was that she was suddenly pierced by sympathy for Mac's life. She was no longer antagonistic or puzzled or analytical. Her harshest notions of him dissolved—or at least softened—into a single sympathy. Strangely enough this happened just before the night she found him sleeplessly padding through the dark house.

She imagined his weekly visits to Sigurd, his allegiance to him. His affection for Raftery, for Dulcie. His physical attachment to Hugh—it had previously vaguely repelled her that he couldn't keep his hands off Hugh, kissed him on the temple, check, even the mouth, on the stomach, deliberately parted Hugh's fine hair and kissed him in the deep hollow between the back of his neck and his skull.

Dulcie stirring with pleasure across the room as he did it. But now Anya suddenly sympathized with this thoughtless, sensual affection. It was as much a part of Mac as the heat he gave off at night.

She also found herself suddenly patient with his occasional sullenness. It was much more than a surface disturbance. She had counted it as on the same level as his love of order in the kitchen, the larder, the toolroom. She realized he often allowed that order to be upset, he even laughed at certain disruptions, or at worst complained loudly but briefly. Small flares. But his sullenness was for her, and was much deeper. He himself didn't understand the depths. He was afflicted by—ultimately confused by— her fucking him, depending on him and yet maneuvering herself coolly with his feelings.

The night after all this occurred to her—after she shortened the comic distance at which she'd kept so much of his life—she woke up and noticed he wasn't there. She put on her boots and wrapped herself in the quilt over her nightgown. She started down the stairs, heard him move in the kitchen. She stood still for a moment, heard him pacing around the kitchen. He was checking the pilot light in the oven in the gas stove, splashing water as he primed the pump and ran some water to keep the pipes clear of ice, putting another chunk of hardwood in the wood stove, banking the fire. It took her a moment to realize that he was crying. She heard him pull a chair to the table and set the lamp down. She heard him control his breathing.

She didn't know whether to sneak back up or go down. She decided to go down. She might finally see through the loosened mesh. At the same time she thought that her curiosity didn't have to be kept clear of her affection.

It struck her that that was how she'd missed understanding Tassie—she'd only advanced experimentally, although she'd had real feeling. What a foolish mistake—of *course* there had only been sharp jolts and flashes, only fingertip electricity and nerves, even when they'd been crushed together, even dreaming about each other.

Mac stood up and turned away as she stepped off the bottom step. She didn't want to go closer without his seeing her. Her patience filled her with pleasure. His embarrassment seemed very small compared to what she wanted.

Even as it became clear to her that her good feelings

were unreceived, they continued to make her happy. She felt herself a ghost drifting toward him. She wouldn't learn anything, but she wasn't disappointed.

He came back to the table and turned the lamp down. He sat in the chair again, staring at the small humped line of flame.

She finally suspected herself, that her exhilaration was too triumphant.

She couldn't escape it, it was funny, her hovering as the spirit of wifely comfort. Both of them were at a distance again.

She said sharply, "What were you thinking about?"

Mac drew a long breath.

She said, "Sigurd? Dulcie and Raftery?"

Mac said, "I'm just sad."

She said, "You and me?"

Mac said, "It would take too long—no, it's not you and me."

Anya said, "Are you worried about your life, that you have no life of your own?"

Mac looked surprised. He said, "Where did you get that idea? No. This place has everything."

The word *place* surprised her.

Mac said, "I've been waking up a lot lately about this time. I get up and walk around. I usually like it—the house full of people in the dark, all disconnected until morning. I imagine that the light coming up over the ridge starts up the way they feel, the way they think. Folds their dreams in. It seems simple and in order. Tonight it suddenly seemed impossible—not that it wouldn't happen, but that it wouldn't be simple and in order. That we might all just as well be going on mechanically, that it didn't matter what we felt, that there was no connection between feeling and eating, feeling and seeing each other, feeling and being awake. That we could as easily be disconnected as connected to anyone else or anything else. What got me"— Mac looked up at her from the light—"was the idea that Hugh could simply be misplaced, that he wouldn't have a hold on anyone or anyone have a hold on him." Mac paused. He said, "It's passed now. It's not what I believe most of the time. I suppose you're right, it had something to do with Sigurd, too. I feel strongly about Sigurd—the same kind of protective feeling I have for Hugh. The same

kind of admiration, too. For both of them. For how perfect
and full they are. It's like pulling the husk off a perfect ear
of corn. It's just the reverse of a flower. What's perfect is
growing in secret—"

Anya bit her lip but laughed anyway.

She said, "I'm sorry—it was the perfect ear of corn
that—"

Mac said, "Yeah, yeah."

She said, "I do know what you mean."

Mac's neck was still tight and flushed. He said, "Yeah,
it's a corny idea."

She said, "I do know, I sometimes feel that way about
you."

Mac said, "Yeah, fine. I believe you do. Your problem
is that your taste is way ahead of your feelings."

Anya said, "They're not such different things."

Mac said, "There you are. What I meant by taste is when
you say 'amusing,' 'just perfect,' 'it's really quite wonderful.' All that shit is from high position . . . Let me ask you
something. Can you honestly say you think I'm your equal?"

Anya said, "Yes."

Mac said, "I don't believe you."

Anya knew she could be hurt and silent and win the
argument.

. She said, "But it's true. If there are times you think I'm
watching you—looking down at you—I do the same thing
to myself. I look at myself through a lens, too." She
laughed. "And *I*'m certainly my equal."

Mac said, "But you *know* you're trying to get better. You
don't know it about me. You worry that I've stopped.
You're worried about how I'll stand in the life you're *going*
to have."

Anya was startled. She said, "The other day Andrew
asked me if I'm completely heartless. What's going on
around here? I'm not sentimental, but I'm not *heartless*. Is
that going to be the line on me now? All of you preening
yourselves on your beautiful feelings—"

Anya realized she was just arguing.

She said, "It wasn't so long ago you were worried about
my being jealous. You thought I had feelings then."

Mac didn't argue back.

They went up to bed. As he fell asleep, she said, "I'm only
heartless about the theater. About what's not real."

She was left awake, arguing both sides.

And then she was left wondering whether she really did know his feelings. She was pretty sure she knew them at the stage just before he spoke: as his feelings entered his civilized mind, as they became nameable parts of nameable feelings. But she wanted his feelings before then. She wanted to feel his feelings *become* feelings. To feel him blank and level and *then* to feel the gathering swell—to rise with him to the crest of his feeling—to ride it while it plunged forward—until it broke into words like surf.

Without doing that, how would she know what he meant?

He'd tried to tell her something about his feelings. And how had that been? She'd understood what he said about his feelings for Sigurd and Hugh, about his fear of things not connecting—but she couldn't imagine where his feeling started.

His words that she could trace back to their original far-off storm force were "You don't think I'm your equal."

She wondered if he could understand any answer she could give. She was superior in clear-sightedness, in reason, in shrewdness, in self-knowledge, in self-appreciation.

She smiled at herself.

But what he saw, what he touched, what he tasted—the energy of his senses astonished her, no matter what strange superstitions veiled his talking about what he sensed.

And his attention to her. His sudden brutal attention. Innocent dark heat. That was his feeling that she understood the least in its origin.

She was sure that he himself was often surprised by it.

She drifted away from her clear thoughts toward sleep. She was warm under the quilt, Mac was sunk like a sash weight in his half of the mattress. She thought, I'm an old-fashioned girl, I don't mind being adored by someone who can't help himself.

*   *   *

Mac was going to see Sigurd in the hospital, so Anya drove into town with him. The road was glazed with ice all the way to the macadam where the town school-bus route ended.

She dropped Mac on the other side of town at the hospital. She went to see Mercks.

Mercks now lived in a one-story bungalow on the north side of town. There were four square rooms, all connected with double glass doors. Anya could see all four rooms through the front-door window. It struck Anya as a bizarre way to plan a house. Each room had a bed or a day bed in it, even the kitchen. There was also an attic, which was where Mercks was when she rang the bell. She saw a ladder swing down and Mercks descend.

At first Mercks was coy about the festival. He pretended he didn't know much about it. Then he put on a mysterious air, trying to imply that Anya had made a lucky guess, penetrated his disguise—Hey, you've got me, I'm really in charge.

He said simply, "What do you want to know?"

Anya asked him what his job was. Mercks laughed and said that he was the landlord. It turned out there had been a smaller festival the year before in a small valley just north of town. The people showing movies had used an old barn, and several other groups had put up tents. There had been a balloon ascension and a small band. Mercks called it a thousand arts-and-crafters at a picnic. Everyone had thought it was a one-shot deal. Mercks thought not and had formed a corporation with his lawyer which leased the whole valley and the barn.

Mercks showed Anya a map of the twenty-acre site on which he'd marked out small plots for tents and domes. He'd already sublet a half dozen. There was a committee made up, in Mercks' phrase, of the big-deal arts-and-crafters around the University. They were going to run contests for the best experimental dance group, best film, best poetry reading. They hoped to get their costs back from entry fees. They were also screening applicants for the other sites. They might have a dome to exhibit pieces of sculpture, and they were considering having a tent for amateur magic acts. Mercks pointed out that he didn't have to lift a finger. All he had to do was sit back and collect rent.

Mercks asked Anya if she wanted to rent some space for the theater group to do a number.

Anya said she thought that they did their shows best in their own theater, but that she wouldn't mind being listed as part of the festival, and hiring an extra bus or so. She and Mercks might even work out a discount on tickets to extra performances.

Mercks then asked her if she'd like to show any of the five-minute films she'd made during the fall and winter.

Anya said that those were just exercises for herself. But she was impressed that Mercks found out about everything she did.

Mercks suddenly said, "Hey, you want to see a piece of my dirty movie?"

Anya said, "Okay."

They climbed the ladder to the attic where Mercks had his projector and screen set up.

The movie was short. It had a low-budget, black-and-white late-forties quality. Three guys made up remarkably like the Three Stooges were established in a prison yard in striped convict suits, two of them with striped pillbox hats over their fright wigs. The bald one had a glued-on rubber pate with tufts over the ears. The first two and a half minutes were devoted to the old dirty joke "Now it's your turn in the barrel." There was a lot of the standard Three Stooges eye gouging, slapping, kicking in the ass, nose twisting.

Anya said, "It's not quite a parody, is it."

Mercks said, "No. I love the Three Stooges. They used to run every day on TV when I was a kid. Wait—here comes a quick part."

Interior of a bakery kitchen. There was a mix-up between two enormous cakes. One concocted for the Three Stooges filled with hacksaws, files, and a jackhammer. The other on its way to a stag party with a girl inside. Switch on the loading platform. The cake with girl goes to the prison. Some low-comedy contortions as a prison guard pokes the cake with a two-foot hatpin and the girl twists to avoid it. Anya saw that the girl was Peewee. She was surprised at how limber Peewee was.

The Three Stooges hide the cake in the barrel. Anya saw the next twist coming, but she was still startled.

The girl eats her way out of the cake. Can't get lid off barrel. Three Stooges come back, they can't get lid off barrel either. Dumbest one sticks his prick in through a knothole. Interior shot of long, blue-veined prick with a visible pulse on the near lower side. Girl gives tentative lick. Cut to face of Stooge. Lit up. Moe bops him. Face alternates between pleasure and pain, as Moe bops and girl licks. Other two Stooges finally believe him. Speeded up shots of pushing and pulling between the three to plug in. Nose twisting, head bopping of three of them alternating with shots of now naked girl contorting to deal with the entries. Squatting. Curled up, one foot behind her ear. Standing on her hand. Both hands clasped around prick to pull her head up to it.

Exterior shot of two Stooges trying to pull third Stooge out. They pull him six feet away—he's still connected by an attenuated elastic dummy prick. Barrel suddenly snaps to him. Three Stooges pratfall, each in lap of one behind. Barrel on top. Interior shot of girl's face—lit up for first time after stony deadpan.

Exterior. Huge fat guard comes up. Hey, what's going on? Garbled three-way simultaneous explanation. Guard— Well, we'll just see about this. Inserts prick. It's puny. Girl bites. Guard flaps hands. Help! Help! Three Stooges grab guard's key ring. They open prison yard gate. Dance and caper out. Guard finally plucks barrel off, heaves it over wall. Obviously dummied footage of barrel flying through air, slide-whistle sound effect. Three Stooges catch it and dance off at jerky high speed. Frantic final theme as they disappear carrying the barrel. The End.

Anya said, "Jesus."

Mercks said, "What do you think? Neat, huh?"

Anya said, "It's horrible."

Mercks said, "Yeah. It gets you. What's good is you can take any old TV show or old movie short and just undo their flies and you got a built-in zap. What you always really wanted to see. I've got a Pete Smith-voice one—remember *Behind the Eight Ball?* I've got the voice narrating a sex scene. 'Oh! Oh! Look out, Joe! That's not the way . . .' I got a guy who does that voice just perfect.

"And I'm thinking of a Lone Ranger bit. Maybe some Batman and Robin. See, with masks it's good, you don't have to worry about look-alikes and the actors get into it better."

Anya said, "How'd you get the prison gate and wall?"

Mercks said, "It's where they're building the annex to the art building. That's the nice thing about low-quality black-and-white, the backgrounds can be rough. The rock pile is real, though. Now, the actual gate opening is stock footage. You couldn't tell, could you? The barrel that the guard throws is cardboard.

"Hey, you want to see my sewing-machine bit? It's only ten minutes. Not much plot to it, just a wild idea. We got an old-fashioned Singer with treadle action—the kind you pump your feet to make it go. We made in into a fucking machine."

Anya said, "No."

Mercks said, "It's my science fiction number. Only one character and this big machine." He began to change reels.

Anya felt a real shock that she couldn't quite place—it was a kind of sympathy for Peewee. What got her into this? How thick was her numbness? That was what horrified Anya—that Peewee seemed to be deprived of her senses. Not by floating her in a pool of warm water, blindfolded and earmuffed, but by cutting off her external senses from any feeling she might have. Snipping all connections just beneath the skin. Anya wondered if Mercks understood that.

But Anya was also impressed in a strange way by the hard varnish of sophomoric talent with which the film was coated. And by another nagging notion—the film was also a put-down of the stag audience. You fools, you're just watching the Three Stooges. You don't know how dumb you are.

The next film started.

Interior. A figure in a space suit entered a white chamber. Faced a huge panel of dials. Turned some of them, consulted a plastic-coated instruction card, and turned some more. Removed helmet. Peewee again. Removed rubber suit. She had on a white togalike outfit. Lay down in a drawer that popped out. She pushed a button and the drawer closed.

Interior of machine. Peewee on a conveyor belt. Robot pincers held hem of gown which was peeled off as conveyor moved. Close-up of dial which said, "Foreplay." Her hand set dial to three. Steel tube descended. A huge tongue lolled out.

Anya said, "What is *that?*"

Mercks said, "We had to buy a beef tongue."

The body kept moving—the tongue lapped the sole of one foot and up the leg and over one breast. Another tube, another tongue up the other foot, leg, breast. A third up the middle—under the chin, up the cheek, over the brow.

A shot down the dim corridor in the direction the conveyor was moving. The sound effect of chugging was audible before the phallic machine was visible. A white ghost of a prick.

Anya said, "If you're trying to keep a tension between the gruesome and the erotic, you've lost your balance."

Mercks said, "Wait."

She said crossly, "Wait for what?" She was angry on behalf of Peewee. And angry that she was affected at all, that she was prickled with erotic feeling. Unpleasantly. A mental heat rash.

But more than that, she felt some admiration for Mercks' ability, that he'd really got something done. Her admiration was surrounded by her own stuffy virtue, which she found as unpleasant and as difficult to move as the erotic prickling. She found herself thinking phrases like "prostitution of your talent," "easy cartoons," "sophomoric." There was some jealousy, but the jealousy was not as important or as upsetting to her as her righteousness.

She could feel herself filling up with advice to Mercks. She was pretty sure that he would listen to her and that, in fact, he hoped she would become an adviser to him. Lick off his cub callowness.

All her feelings fused and stopped. She watched from a great distance as Peewee reached the phallus.

She said, "I suppose this is your remake of *The Perils of Pauline*. Going into the buzz saw."

Mercks said, "But this Pauline loves it."

She said, "It doesn't make much difference."

Mercks said, "She really does."

The conveyor stopped and Peewee began to hunch the object. Anya was suddenly sad, close to tears. There was a shot of the thing slithering through Peewee's hands as it moved back up into its piston waggle. The camera moved up and then moved with the thing so the audience could read the printing on the seam of the covering—"Made in Japan."

Anya said, "That's not funny. That is just dumb."

Mercks said, "Yeah, you're right. No one laughs. I'll cut it."

Anya turned away. She looked back when she saw a change in brightness.

It was a shot of the machine's exterior panel short-circuiting—sparking and smoking. There was a close-up of a bolt of electricity playing between two poles.

Anya said, "What's this?"

Mercks said, "A Tesla coil. Like in a Frankenstein movie."

Anya said, "No, I mean what's it supposed to mean?" She realized she was being slow.

Mercks said, "Hey—it's the—"

She said, "—Oh, yeah. Woman checkmates machine."

Mercks said, "Well, sort of. The machine comes."

The reel ended. Mercks turned on the overhead light and stopped the projector.

Anya said, "I've got to pick Mac up." She had a sudden thought of Mac's reaction to the movies. Was she right? Would he be angry? He might go numb.

She said, "Look—I'll talk to you again about that festival. About your movies—I suppose there's no point in saying anything to you if you actually peddle them somewhere."

Mercks said, "No. I can always make money. I want to get good at it, too."

On the drive back to the hospital Anya thought of a movie Mercks should make. His trip to Mexico to buy grass. The story as Peewee had told it. Peewee a real character, Mercks a real character.

Raftery was right about the Midwest in a way—people now growing up in the Midwest could do anything. There was no high art, no high society, so you started out unintimidated. Was that right? Surely the old story still held for some people. She'd seen boys from the Midwest arrive at Harvard and change in a half year—from two-button suits with a burlap weave so coarse you could stick a pencil through it to three-piece pin-striped suits, double-breasted blazers with silver buttons, hacking jackets with slash pockets. And their voices grew lush and smooth as their clothes. Cashmere elocution. Of course, that was six or seven years ago. Henniker must have been like that. Moving on to Oxford after Harvard. When he finally got back to Chicago the more innocent ears of his students heard him as English.

The voice change was certainly part of the old story, the wish to be born again by going East, by learning the shadowy intricacies of eastern big-city life, the frozen ethnic stances, the Anglophilia. The urge to rise on a magic carpet of cosmopolitanism.

Even then, six years ago, there had been Midwesterners who ignored it—simply kept on as themselves until with a mysterious twirl of the wheel of fashion it was wonderful to be a farm boy from Wisconsin, to be a proletarian from Gary.

But more amazing to Anya was the lack of shadow in Iowa. Maybe Raftery was right—real freedom could be here. Even a short way east the University of Chicago had its lingering second-to-Harvard complex, the analogue of Chicago's second-city suspicion of itself. But the real Midwest was blissfully ignorant. The shadow of doubt didn't get darker west of Chicago, it vanished.

She remembered hearing a discussion a half year before at the art department, where she'd gone to find a set designer. A girl had said to a boy, "He thinks he's the best sculptor in Iowa City, but he's nowhere." Anya had laughed. She knew now she'd been wrong. There were fifty sculptors in town—thirty *were* nowhere, but the other twenty were good. And a dozen of them sold to museums and through galleries all over the country. New York was just another market. Not paradise.

The student musicians were better than any Anya had heard around Boston or New York. They would just as soon be hired in Atlanta or Denver or Minneapolis or Seattle or Baltimore. She thought, Maybe that's going too far. But it's certainly not New York or die.

She herself still had some of that feeling—New York or die. Everything else a steppingstone. That was her infection.

But, she thought, if Raftery and Mercks were vigorous growths of the Midwest, what was Peewee? What shadow of what belief was she a victim of? Anya had an idea that there existed in Peewee the dark side of the brilliant, unpopulated expanse of Raftery's Midwest mind. Peewee was numb, and because Peewee had no feeling that the cogs of her life meshed with the cogs of any other life, she had no sense of time. Having no sense of time left her lonely. She could stop feeling numb only by calling out too loudly, opening herself too widely and deeply, submitting too fully. And once Mercks wounded her (Mercks or the cousin who came before Mercks), she had to numb herself as deeply as she had been pierced. And feeling numb again, she called out . . .

Anya thought again that Peewee in Mexico was the story for Mercks. There were problems in making her character visible, but, Anya thought, starting with the story in which her cousin tied her shoelaces together—and then perhaps raped her?—it was more visible than, say, the story of Tassie's cousin Jeannie. Anya began to see the scenes of Peewee's home life—the enormous empty sky, the straight dirt road rising over the swell of land like the wake of a vanished boat. Would the audience be able to see? To see how vehement and desperate she had to become in the emptiness—like a solitary lightning bug flaring her loneliness for miles around?

Anya drove up to the hospital lobby. She couldn't stop the idea.

Mac said Sigurd was better, the cobalt treatment worked, he would be coming home in ten days. She couldn't talk. She nodded. She felt Mac subside, disappointed in her.

She thought: Peewee by a farm pond, calling after her cousin. Howling his name. The cousin and another two boys seeing her—everything at a great distance. Perhaps at dusk—the hollows of land filled with darkness, the sky smoldering the endless summer sunset. Peewee carrying a flashlight which she blinked on and off, nervous and lonely.

Anya looked quickly at Mac. She thought of his farm work—farm work would come in to it—Peewee mastering huge machines and animals—driving a tractor with five-foot-high rear wheels, driving a boar into a pen with a two-by-four. But herself mastered by the hand of her cousin. Anya thought, But Peewee would be the heroine, her yearning dwarfing the house and the people as much as the sky dwarfed her. No need to go to Mexico, telescope Mercks into the cousin. Would the cousin come to the University at Iowa City? Make him a year older, Peewee could still be his slave. And then Peewee triumphs. Grows past him.

The technical problem was how to film a thirteen-year-old Peewee and an eighteen-year-old Peewee. Use Peewee herself for the thirteen-year-old—cut her hair even shorter. Sure. Make her fourteen, she could pass for fourteen, that would still work.

Anya thought she would once again have to look closely at Peewee's face.

She looked over at Mac and thought that some of her own feelings about the landscape and sky came from him.

With a sharp jolt Anya realized that she herself should make the movie.

Part Four

IOWA
GIRL

CHAPTER

19

The day Sigurd was released the county roads were bad, so Mac picked him up at the hospital and drove him home.

Selma and Sigurd's daughter, Sigrid, were waiting for him. Selma had been in to see him every day except when the roads were iced, so she wasn't surprised at how bad he looked. The daughter was stunned. She drew back from her father. Mac recognized the fear, had felt it himself, but still held it against her. Selma moved to help Sigurd when he stood by the car. Sigurd said, "I can walk. I'm just looking around for a minute."

No one introduced Mac to the daughter. She was a plain, fair girl whose looks were spoiled by her blue plastic eyeglass frames. She wore a skirt and sweater. Around her waist was a very wide black patent leather belt. It hit her hipbone on the bottom and her rib cage on top. Mac was surprised to see she was wearing nylon stockings and shoes with heels. Then he noticed that both mother and daughter had set their hair in tight waves. Mac wished he'd dressed up for the homecoming, too.

They put Sigurd to bed and asked Mac to stay for lunch.

They sat down. Sigrid reached for a dish before Selma said grace. Her mother pushed it out of reach and began grace. Sigrid looked at Mac with interest. The blue of her eyes matched the blue of her eyeglass frames. It was a terrible idea. Mac thought the mistake was the kind of bad taste he himself used to have. Before Anya.

From where he sat at the table Mac could see the trees on this side of Raftery's yard and the smoke from the two

323

chimneys and from the stovepipe out Hugh's window, three lines rising straight and then abruptly blurred by the slow-moving air above tree level.

He said, "It's nice there's no wind."

They ate in silence until another thought occurred to Mac as he finished his ham steak and raisin sauce, mashed sweet potato with marshmallow crust, cole slaw with diced pineapple, stewed tomatoes thickened with flour and sugar —a farmer's lunch. He said, "Did the doctor give you a diet for Sigurd?"

Selma said, "He told me a lot of things he shouldn't have. I think it's more important for him to get his strength back."

Sigrid started to speak but stopped.

Selma noticed her daughter's movement and said, "We'll see what he wants when he gets his appetite."

When Mac got up to go out, Selma got his mackinaw and held it for him. Mac felt this act of courtesy. It was fragile, quaint, and binding.

The next three days Mac had lunch with the Olsons. Sigurd was up around the house, but he didn't eat with them.

It turned out Sigrid worked for the mining survey company that had sent the expedition to Labrador that Mac had gone on.

Mac took Sigrid to see the last performance of *Thieves' Carnival* at the theater. He took her backstage afterwards and introduced her to everyone. She remembered playing in that barn as a little girl.

When Mac took her home, Sigurd was still up. He couldn't sleep. Sigrid went to bed and Sigurd asked Mac to sit with him awhile.

Sigurd said, "I got an offer on the farm. I told the fellow to wait. I didn't like his coming round like that, pretending he didn't know I'd been sick. He knew all right, just like a buzzard. But it was a good offer."

Mac said, "You'll be working again by spring."

Sigurd said, "Maybe. But they can't be sure I won't be sick again. Cancer can come back."

Sigurd opened his bathrobe and pulled up his pajama top. He pointed out the postcard-size purple rectangle on his stomach. "That's the scar they made with that treatment."

He pulled his bathrobe back around him. "I'll tell you something, I was looking death right in the eye."

Mac forced himself to hold Sigurd's gaze. Mac was ashamed that he was embarrassed at Sigurd's phrase.

After a moment Sigurd said, "I got to thinking what would be left of me when they put me in that box and put the lid on. Most people don't think about it much until they're just about there. I want to do something while I'm here. The first thing is I'm going to build a building in town. I own a piece of land right where all that building's going on. I've got some money, and the bank would lend me some. That building's the first thing I thought of. It would give me a lot of satisfaction to build a building that would be there for quite a while after they put me in that box.

"The second thing I thought of is this farm here. Selma and me have got Sigrid and that's all—we're lucky to have her what with what having her did to Selma.

"This is a big enough farm to be one of the farms in the county that will keep on. That's not true of most family farms. I wouldn't tell anybody to take up farming now. You can't start a farm anymore. But this farm can make it. The land's in good shape. There's two hundred acres on the other side of the road that gave over a hundred and fifty bushels. You saw that. You didn't see that those acres weren't pushed all the way. Some of that other land I'm going to plant next year could give two hundred bushels. I'm not saying that's a good idea, I'm just saying that there's land over there as good as any of them experimental farms near Cedar Rapids. And *they* push *theirs* all the way.

"There's the pasture on this side—nobody knows just how good that is. They're sorry for me that it floods so I can't grow corn. But every farm should have some land that's good pasture and can't be taxed as though it could be growing corn."

Sigurd paused. He was tired. He sank back in his chair. He added, "So long as you've got enough land on the other side to rotate."

Mac had been impatient at first. Now he sensed there was going to be a point.

Sigurd rested awhile and then said, "You could learn to run this farm. Even if I was dead, you could learn. Now here's the second thing I thought of. I want you to take a good look at Sigrid."

Mac hadn't thought Sigurd would go that far. After a long ten seconds of blankness Mac began to think of objections so fast he couldn't say them.

Sigurd said, "This is over the next year I'm talking about. Just take a look. She's a smart girl. She's not just a secretary for that company, she's an assistant vice-president. She'll be twenty-eight this June. That's a little old, but she's Swedish on both sides—her looks won't change till she's fifty. And you wouldn't get any foolishness. That's a good part of it—you'd both of you be done with foolishness. By the time a year's up, you'll be all through sowing your wild oats.

"Now I'm only bringing this up because the only thing wrong with you I can see is you're likely to let things stay the way they are. I just want to stir your thinking up some. Once you turn your mind to something, I figure you're smart enough. How old are you now?"

Mac said, "Twenty-seven."

Sigurd said, "Well, it's time you figured out what you're going to be doing when you're forty."

After a short while Sigurd got up. He said, "I meant to have a talk about how things are going. Time enough tomorrow. That's about all I can do now is talk."

Mac said, "Oh, come on. Don't be impatient. It's not so long till spring."

As Mac got out of the car in his yard, he thought that he shouldn't have been so surprised. Sigurd had such enormous energy that he had to do something, even if it was awkward. Mac sympathized with the push of Sigurd's physical energy diverted into his mind, the sudden disproportion in Sigurd's life.

Mac wondered if Sigurd was going to talk to Sigrid. He supposed so. The thought of Sigrid and him looking each other over while Sigurd watched them made him laugh.

He stopped laughing. He was suddenly more affected than he'd thought—the other thing he couldn't help taking a look at was the farm. He didn't think he could imagine the farm as his, himself as the farmer, but he felt a dark pull—a shapeless force beyond his picturable imagining, much stronger than he dared to let rise in him.

He had thought he could deal with the problem of

Sigurd's proposal in a small, deft way. That was a mistake.

The next morning Mac drove a truckload of pigs to Clinton. When he got back he had lunch with Selma and Sigrid and then went in to talk to Sigurd. Mac wanted to tell Sigurd right away that Sigurd's idea was impossible. No matter what.

But Sigurd talked about a number of small problems in a way that made Mac think that Sigurd didn't want to talk about the proposal, that perhaps he even hadn't meant it in such a definite way, that it was just a passing idea.

Mac had trouble remembering what Sigurd had said exactly, he remembered only his own reactions with clarity. He began to think he'd exaggerated it.

Sigurd was sure it was going to thaw soon, and he wanted Mac to help Ergenbright move Ergenbright's cows away from the riverside. Ergenbright had put a small herd in one of Sigurd's pastures in exchange for the help he'd given over the past month.

Sigurd explained Ergenbright's difficulties. Ergenbright ran a small breeding operation, but the price for calves had been low so he'd been holding on to them. But the price of feed had just gone up. So he'd asked Sigurd to let his breed cows into the corner pasture near the woods and riverbank to pick over the junk that was still sticking up through the old snow.

Sigurd said, "Now we have to move them, he'll take some hay. What I *was* going to ask was the pick of his calves. He's got a pretty sorry lot there but there're a few passable ones. Now I think I'll get some more plowing from him. The problem with Ergenbright is when he's in a hole, he'll promise a lot. When it comes time for him to do it, he'll make you feel like you're sticking him too hard. There's no point in squeezing him or the work won't get done right. He sometimes'll go and do something extra about a year later. He doesn't take into account the waiting, but there could be worse neighbors.

"I'll tell you something, the only time to squeeze someone is when he's going all the way under, because then you either have to get what's owed you or the bank gets the whole thing and then nobody gets any use of it. Most times, with most people, you might just as well not be pushy, even with stupid people. You just make them crazy. You got to find something you want and that they can part with so as they don't feel it."

Mac was interested in Ergenbright's problems but not in Sigurd's principles. He was afraid that being sick would make Sigurd talk about principles. The real principle was that all the farmers thought each other crazy. If a farmer was rich, he owed it to luck. If a farmer was poor, he wasn't a go-getter. Just working hard didn't make a go-getter. They all admitted their neighbors worked hard. There weren't any lazy farmers left. That was the only virtue that bound them.

Beyond the borders of the county there might be model farmers—industrious and kind and wise, blending old common sense with the latest advice from Iowa State, blending go-getting with good neighboring. But immediate neighbors were always defective. Of the dozen farmers Mac had dealt with in the last two months, almost all had warned him about two or three of the others. Not enough of a go-getter, too much of a go-getter, too old-fashioned, too addicted to advice from college professors, too politically cozy with the agent who set the value on soil-bank land . . . But the most common complaint was craziness. "I'll tell you something about him, boy, he's crazy. Why one time I saw him . . ."

Sigurd was considered defective in his methods because he did too many different things, particularly sheep. Four farmers thought he was crazy. Mac didn't find out why, he'd cut them off. All the farmers thought Sigurd's success was precarious good luck, both in farming and in real estate.

The only person who admired them all was the man who drove the propane delivery truck. As he drove from farm to farm listening to the weather reports and farm prices on his truck radio, he didn't see how they could stand the tension. He'd told Mac that the only time he felt relaxed about them was during a good spring when he saw the fields black and shiny as coal and the first shoots of corn coming up, the top four leaves laying themselves out flat, the whole field a fat black quilt sewn with perfect green clusters.

After that he worried about drought, flood, tornadoes, hail, grass fires. The farmers thought he was crazy. One of them said you could tell he was crazy because he'd lost his teeth before he was thirty-five.

Mac got Ergenbright on the phone. Ergenbright couldn't get away so they planned to meet first thing in the morning. Sigurd told Mac to look at the outside thermometer. It was up to thirty. The sky was a soft, deep gray. Mac said even if it thawed it would freeze again at night. Sigurd said that might be true where Mac came from.

Mac left to look after the sheep.

It rained that night. The ditch beside the road to Sigurd's had a foot of slush in it.

Ergenbright wasn't at Sigurd's. Sigurd got Sigrid to drive him in the pickup. He told Mac to follow in the tractor. Selma told Sigurd he was crazy. Sigurd said he might as well sit in the pickup cab as in an armchair.

When they got to the bottom field the herd was in the one high corner. There was water over three-quarters of the field. In the middle of it there was a cow. Mac waded out and saw there was a calf behind her. When he got close he saw the cow's hind legs were sunk in a hole. He spoke to her to coax her out. She strained her head up, but couldn't move. He reached into the water and found her forelegs. He pulled the feet out front so she could pull herself with them. She tried, but she seemed weak. Mac went around and touched the calf. The calf started away and fell down.

Mac picked the calf up and began to carry him to the pickup. He hoped the cow would follow the calf. Halfway to the pickup he looked back. The cow was moaning at him but not even moving her forelegs.

Sigrid got out and opened the gate. The herd all started down from the high ground toward the gate. Mac came through and put the calf down. Sigurd stuck his head out the window and said, "Jesus, that goddamn fool." His eyes were watery red, his face seemed to be withering in the cold. He said, "Put that one in the back. Take the tractor in and pull that cow out."

Mac stood still. He said to Sigurd, "Maybe you should go on back."

Sigurd put both hands on top of the rolled-down window edge and shook it. He shouted, "Don't you tell me what to do!" His spit fell on his hands.

Mac stepped back and said, "All right." He went around

and lowered the tailgate, picked up the calf, and heaved him in. The calf struggled to his feet. Sigurd yelled, "Tie his feet! Tie his feet!"

Sigrid came back with some cord, tied the calf's feet, and patted it.

Mac backed up the tractor to let Sigrid get the truck out of his way. The cows were pushing against the gate which had swung shut. Mac shoved the gate against them and yelled. They backed away. Sigrid came and held the gate open for him, yelling at the cows and waving them away with one arm.

Mac drove in and backed the tractor near the cow's head. He unwrapped a length of chain, ran it around the clevis pin, and hooked it. He took the free end and stood for a moment. He couldn't tell where to attach it to the cow.

The truck came through the gate. Sigrid closed the gate and drove through the water. She pulled up so Sigurd's window was near Mac. Mac saw him pointing and pushing Sigrid's hands. Mac ran the chain under the cow's forelegs.

Sigurd said, "No! You'll break her legs."

Mac pulled the chain loose again.

Sigurd said, "Go round her neck and up around her horns."

The cow had flopped on her side, felt the water on her cheek and heaved her head up again, bugling through her nose. Mac ran the chain around as Sigurd had told him. He had some trouble fitting the point of the hook through a link. Sigurd banged on the dashboard and told Sigrid to drive the tractor.

Mac got the six-foot spike out of the back of the pickup. Sigurd said, "What good is that?"

Mac said, "I'm going to try to raise her hind end."

Sigurd said, "Well, don't go in under her tits."

Mac said, "No, her hind end's twisted to one side. That's why she can't use her hind legs. I'll get the rod—"

Sigurd interrupted. "She can't use her hind legs 'cause they're paralyzed from calving."

Mac poked in beside the cow's bottom hip. The tip of the rod didn't hit bottom. He tried pushing his end down using the lip of the hole as a fulcrum. The rod bit into the mud sideways. It was useless.

Sigrid started pulling with the tractor. Mac watched the cow's neck stretch. She bellowed one long note. The cow's neck was pulled out twice as long as it had been. It looked five feet long. The body wasn't moving at all. Her eyes were popping out. Mac reached in with his arms, trying to get under the cow's hip.

Sigurd yelled at him, "Get out of there!"

Mac realized he wasn't doing any good. There was an enormous heave of water, slush, and mud, then the cow's hip appeared, and then a belch of air broke around her. The cow's body slid across the lip of the hole. Her hind legs trailed after, flabby in the hip sockets but stiff down the shank. Sigrid stopped the tractor, the chain went slack, and the cow's head dunked under water.

Sigurd yelled at Sigrid to keep going. The tractor stalled. Mac took the rod and pried her head out of the water.

Mac said to Sigurd, "You can't drag her all the way back like this." Mac waited for Sigurd to get mad.

Sigurd was suddenly exhausted. He said, "She'll die in the water for sure." Mac could barely hear him.

Mac said, "We should put her in the pickup."

Sigurd said, "How're you going to get her up?"

Mac said, "We can use the gate. We can put her on the gate and pull her."

Sigurd said, "Okay. You get the gate over here."

Sigrid held the cow's head up and Mac drove the pickup over to the gate, lifted it off its hinges, and ran a chain through it.

He had to stop to drive away the cows who pressed toward the gate opening.

Sigurd handed him a pair of wire cutters from the glove compartment. Mac cut the middle strand of barbed wire from the fence, pulled it across the gap, and twisted it around the gatepost.

Mac pulled another wire across and pushed a cow who'd backed onto the gate. When he drove into the water the gate floated just under the surface.

It took Sigrid and him another ten minutes to get the cow pulled onto the gate. Mac held her hind legs up while Sigrid pulled her with the tractor. Mac slipped to his knees once and filled his rubber boots with water. By the time they were ready to pull the gate to the barn, sweat was pouring down Mac's cheeks, but his feet were freezing.

Mac wiped the sweat out of his eyes. He saw blood floating in the water. He couldn't tell where the cow was

331

AN AMERICAN ROMANCE

bleeding. Or what it was that had cut her—a bolt end or a sliver.

Mac drove the tractor with the gate now chained to it. The cow was belted on, with spare chain hooked around her horns, her neck, and behind her forelegs.

Sigrid drove her father and the calf ahead in the pickup.

It took Mac twenty minutes to haul the gate to the barn. Even after he reached the upper fields that still had a crust of snow to slide the gate on, he couldn't go much faster than a walk.

Sigrid had left some of the gates open for him, but he still had to climb down to close them. He'd emptied the water out of his boots and put on his leather mittens, but he was getting colder. He stomped his feet and banged his hands on the steering wheel.

He met Ergenbright outside Sigurd's.

Ergenbright said, "Sig's gone crazy."

Mac said, "What'll we do with the cow?"

Ergenbright's eyes were shining with anger; Mac could sense the heat behind them.

Ergenbright wanted to drag the cow back to his place.

Mac said, "I don't know. I'm afraid another mile and a half will kill her."

Ergenbright said, "Well then, the son of a bitch can buy me another."

Mac persuaded Ergenbright to let him put the cow in Sigurd's best barn. Sigrid had already put the calf in a pen there and turned on a propane heater.

He and Ergenbright were talking about whether to call the vet when Sigrid came out. Sigrid asked them both to stay for lunch after they moved the other cows. She said that Sigurd was afraid he might have said something he didn't mean.

Ergenbright snorted.

Sigrid said, "He says to go ahead and bring your cows up from that field. They can stay in the barn overnight." She touched Ergenbright's arm. "You go on ahead, I'll feed your calf."

Ergenbright was soothed. He waved to Mac to come on. Mac wanted to change his socks and boots, but he knew if he slowed Ergenbright down, Ergenbright might turn sour again.

After Mac and Ergenbright walked the cows from the

flooded pasture to the barn, Ergenbright said he had to go phone his wife to hold his lunch. Ergenbright added, "And then you watch old Sigurd skin me. By the time we're through eating we'll all be budddies again and he'll own as much of me as the bank."

Ergenbright left.

Mac took off his rubber boots and wrung his socks out. He put the socks near the heater, and dried the inside of his boots with straw.

He sat down beside the cow. She rolled her head to look at him. He put his feet under the blanket and rubbed them on her hip. He stretched his leg out and touched her udder with his toes. It was hot and tight. He wondered if they should get her up with a sling so the calf could get some milk out. He also thought he could still feel her terror—a sweet heat now just underneath her hide, in the steady seeping of blood through her muscles.

He lay down along her spine and patted her neck. He said, "I'll bet we stretched it a foot for good." He handled her ear. "It's a good thing they left your horns on."

He thought it wasn't just an urge to efficiency that made Sigurd violent. American farming wasn't really an efficient process—making grass and corn grow to feed cows to make them grow to feed people. It was the violence itself that Sigurd liked—starting forces in motion and then struggling to connect them. Mac thought of the force in a field of corn. Every grass but this giant one killed by powders or fire. The corn pulled up the water, the stalks creaking up higher than the farmer could reach. In a single acre the movement of water up the stalks was as powerful as a river. And then the stalks snapped in two as the eight-row picker rolled through, ripping off the ears, the stalks all bent in one direction, a vast square window.

It was all as violent as pulling the cow out of the bog hole. A cow—flesh on four stalks. In this case breeding more flesh. The picker tore up miles of field corn (cows' flesh beforehand), another machine augered it up into silos, funneled it out into the steers, who went in rows to the slaughterhouse—the cow picker. As though the stalks of corn started walking on their prop roots toward the picker.

One of Sigurd's favorite statistics was that Iowa produced one-tenth of all the foodstuff consumed in the United States.

Mac felt the shoulder muscle of the cow, ran his hand under her throat, felt the artery. She seemed bigger suddenly; he could just see the blackness of her side moving in the dim light.

It occurred to him that Sigurd, all the farmers, were like bargehands, their farms heaving over the swells, their houses deckhouses, dots of light in the corners of their black barges, riding out the storm of growth. The whole state a raft of barges barely afloat between the Mississippi and the Missouri, wallowing under the loads of feed and meat.

Mac touched the corner of the cow's mouth. She rolled her head back toward him, and he put his hand on her horn to keep his forehead away from it. He was rolled onto his back. He got up and went around her and touched her muzzle. Did she recognize him?

The barn door rolled open. Gray daylight lit the stall. Mac looked at the doorway, the thin figure. He said, "Sigrid?"

He saw now it was Anya.

Anya laughed. She said, "Sigrid? Did I just meet Sigrid? Sigurd's daughter. Sort of a nonvegetarian Dulcie? I mean Sigrid is meatier."

Mac said, "Yes." On his knees now, he'd moved away from the cow.

Anya asked what was wrong with the cow; Mac told her about the morning.

Anya said, "I can see why it appeals to you."

Mac said, "I must have left something out."

Anya said, "But here you are—the Royal Canadian Mounted Police always get their cow."

Mac said, "What brings you over here?"

Anya said, "How's Sigurd?—I want to ask him a favor."

Mac said, "Not today."

Anya said, "Remember the story Peewee told about getting dope in Mexico? And the one about her cousin knotting up her shoelaces?"

Mac said, "Yes."

Anya said, "I want to make a movie about those stories. About Peewee. About Iowa. I want to use Sigurd's farm for the farm near Rock River where she starts out."

Mac said, "I can't see why he'd mind. Unless you do her cousin raping her on his front porch."

Anya said, "What do you think—*did* her cousin rape her? Or was her mother telling some kind of hysterical lie? Maybe her mother said it was rape to make it better than it was. I'll bet it was worse. I'll bet it was crueler than rape. Her cousin was like a boy playing with an animal. I'll bet he guessed how hungry she was for him. For anything."

Mac thought hungry was right. Peewee was as nervous as an athlete in training.

Anya said, "The story is about what it's like to be as hungry and lonely as she was in the middle of a place as empty as this. To be as open as she was, as full of ungrounded energy. A lot of the people out here are like unpainted weathered wood—tough, gray, finished. But she managed to stay raw. Innocent in spite of experience. Just the opposite of Rousseau—you know the thing he says in his confessions, that he'd read so much as a kid that he knew every passion secondhand by the time he was thirteen. Peewee is just the opposite—talking in that flat voice of hers, saying 'Doing one thing was just like doing any other, smoking dope, having the trots, giving head.' You remember that?"

Mac said, "Yes, I remember that."

Anya said, "You think I'm going to make fun of her. Look down on her. I'm not. Both Peewee and Mercks are more like me than you think. If I'd been shipped out here in 1942, I might have been one or the other. I can't say which. I think I prefer her. But what I like is that she can be done in pictures, the way she is really has to do with what it *looks* like out here." She paused. She said, "Mac. I really want to do it. Let me do it."

Mac knew what she meant—that she'd come across him in her thoughts and she would have trouble going on if he said no, or even maybe. He regretted having seemed to object before he knew what she wanted. But he still wasn't sure.

Anya said, "The people I knew, the first thing they learned was to coat their rawness. Later on in college you could see people trying to strip off their first coverings. It got to be very complicated how terrible a college sophomore could feel about the way he'd *been*—frantic rewriting of his childhood—inventing significant early cosmopolitan experience, pretending to have been all sorts of things: privileged, underprivileged, sophisticated, innocent. I figured

out one time that the ideal boyhood for a Harvard sophomore in 1960 would have been to be born the son of a
French Communist aristocrat who was shot saving Jews
and have the mother remarry a dockworker who became
an artist whom the son lived with in Brooklyn playing stick-
ball but spending the summers receiving tutoring at the hands
of his European degenerate relatives. You'd be amazed
at the attempts I heard to bend the truth toward this—and
of course it all changed in the next three years. But the
superstition persisted—that there were origins that made
you wonderful. Having been some place, having known
someone. And so many people were working on the same
material it got to be done implicitly, with neat, small gestures. Like crossing your sevens. Little tics like that.

"The pretense was laid on coat after coat. Of course I'm
not saying pretense is terrible, not if it makes you try things.
That's how you get good, isn't it? By trying to live up to
your pretensions. The problem was that a lot of these people were frightened off from doing a lot of things that it
seemed you had to have grown up doing. That included a
lot of the arts—there were enough people around who had
had summers at the Neighborhood Playhouse or ballet lessons from the age of seven to make you think you'd always
be trying to catch up. And of course there was the real
thing to be seen so that doing something well enough to
score with it appeared hopeless."

Anya caught her breath. Mac felt Anya's urgency as
clearly as he had the cow's pulse in its neck. And he recognized that Anya's urgency was beyond what he'd been doing
and that once again his morning, the beat of blood in his
morning, was being swept off the past edge of the present.
He nodded to show he was listening.

"But look around here. Look at Raftery. He thinks he
can do anything. Mercks is the same way, I mean he's that
same way in a different way. And it's not that they're
stupid, they just don't think you have to *be* something before you *do* something. The people I knew in college spent
almost all their energy worrying about whether they *were*
something—a poet or an artist, or whatever—before they
could even move. And then a lot of time after that was
spent maneuvering around to keep on *being*. They would
pick up mannerisms, even vices, of poets or actors—they
would go to *the* place to drink, *the* place to spend the sum-

mer, *the* place to have a breakdown. It was like reverse method acting—if you assume the right pose, make the right gesture, perhaps the emotion will come to you. Maybe it was less calculated than that, more superstitious—you probably could have sold Robert Lowell's toenail clippings for their magical properties—except it wouldn't have worked unless you knew to call him 'Cal.'

"There was a negative side, too. People feared terrifically that something bad could be said of them. 'Oh, he's just a————.' Fill in the blank—mindless preppie, a wonk, a dumb jock, greasy grind, social climber. Just the hint would weigh on people heavily. It was worse for girls in a way, more complicated by the question of sexual reputation. You might suddenly be a slut or a prig. And where was the higher court of appeal?—you could see a lot of people thought that this was it, they'd reached the highest plateau. Curiously enough, the people freest from any kind of hobbles were the rich kids who were just playing around before they entered their prepared world. They were also dangerous because they might suddenly vanish—whoops, Daddy's arranged for me to join the firm, everything's off. *Their* real world was to them a looming *force majeure,* no matter how old-fashioned or despicable or even invisible it seemed to their ordinary friends who thought that everyone was really there. For the poor kid on a scholarship it was like being one of the crowd in Wonderland when Alice wakes up and goes home. 'You're nothing but a pack of cards!'

"Now Peewee—in a way she's even more interesting than Raftery or Mercks in their freedom because she's not just unvarnished, she's transparent right back to her beginning. You can see right into her. You can see back for years. I didn't think so at first, but now I do."

Mac said, "I don't know."

Anya said, "Maybe you don't want to look. I've thought about it a lot. Her sort of stupefied submission is really stronger than it seems. In spite of her having been hurt, she still has ambition. Maybe ambition is the wrong word —a huge, wordless wanting. It was never social or intellectual—it was just her trying to fill up the space. There is something wonderful about her, she still—I can't really say what it is. It's terrible, too. That's what makes it worth seeing."

Anya stopped for a moment. Then she said, "You're worried I'm being heartless about her."

Mac said, "Well, what are you going to do? Restage her cousin tying knots in her shoelaces? Mercks fucking her mouth? She's going to do it all while you take her picture?"

Anya said, "But she comes through, she wins, she ends up better off—not happy, that's not the point, but stronger and wilder. Oh, why can't you—" Anya stopped. "Look, you'll see what I mean when you see the movie. But I want you to help me."

Mac knew he should say yes.

Anya said, "I am going to use her as herself. I think I can from the movies I've seen of her—"

Mac said, "What movies?"

Anya said, "Mercks'. A couple of short movies."

Mac said, "You mean his dirty movie? What was she doing?"

Anya said, "The usual—actually not the usual, there's no straight balling. They're more like comic strips. I've thought of using them. Show that the Mercks character is making them, show her off-camera. The point would be she keeps on going, she's used. Okay, fine, but so what? In her case, so what? It's the guy, the cousin, the Mercks character who gets more stuck by it all than she does."

Mac hoped that was so.

Anya said, "What would be good, incidentally, is the effect on the audience. Here is a girl, and by now you know her and you're for her, and then you see this strip of junk she's in, and you realize that the reaction you're having is entirely different from what you'd feel if you were just watching the little dirty movie—you get a chance to observe yourself begin to turn on but you can't just turn on, because you know the girl. Do you see . . . ?

"What I want now is to *try* this. I've been getting good at a certain line, getting a certain effect out of this group, a certain effect out of myself, out of my taste. In all the plays, almost everything was done to set up the words. Now I want to do this story with the way things look. I want to have all the things I can't have on stage—sky, clouds, fields, dust in the wind, real distance. And what's small, too— eyes, teeth, toes. Pigs' faces, flies, those clouds of yellow butterflies that crud up the windshield. And Peewee's voice, you couldn't do that on stage. Imagine that voice, small, hard, flat—taped close so it comes out with all the breath . . . right in the audience's ear. At the same time you're seeing the sky and fields and the straight dirt road. What she says, the way she talks—that and the countryside connected to each other . . ."

Mac wasn't sure then what convinced him, he wasn't sure whether he just gave up or whether he saw splashes of what Anya was talking about. Later on he thought he must have thought of himself walking back to Lac Gros Caillou, the huge, windy northern sky touching him in a way he hadn't been touched since, the tinfoil packet of rubbers in his pocket, all his senses wonderfully alarmed, almost tasting the wind coming through the close-set pines, his guilt and expectation connected to the woods and sky.

Whatever he thought faded. He wondered again what Anya had in mind. He said, "Okay."

He put his socks and boots back on. He looked at Anya. Anya's eyes were focused past him, past the wall.

He thought of Sigurd, how like his uncles. That was what he'd found; Anya had found Peewee and Mercks. He thought, Is that right? You keep on finding earlier parts of your life over and over? There was no such thing as a new world. He and Anya were colonies of themselves.

He remembered Anya had asked him early on, part of her questionnaire, "How long have you been the way you are now?" He was surprised at how easily he agreed that he'd changed.

And he'd thought they would change again in Iowa. Their composition—the saturations, encrustations—would be leached away. Anything you wanted to get rid of could be leached away by the new space.

But he'd thought it was more for her.

It seemed to him this was the first time he'd considered what they were really doing.

And here she was, taking the whole sky and earth of this place—was she just turning it into a set for an idea?

Of course they'd grown closer, their recent growth all entwined, but she still could keep herself back, knowing now how little it took to avoid him. What drew him to her was unchanged, the surprise of her pale skin below her dark hair and eyes, her long back plated with muscles, her high-arched feet . . . No, those were details that were too light and clear, only signals bordering the hot darkness in which he moved senselessly now, without deep pleasure or pain, sometimes drawn with a rush by her attention, sometimes suddenly slack and muddled at her inattention.

He touched her arm to say he was going in to lunch.

Anya said, "See if you can sound out Sigurd for me."

She touched his chest in a friendly way. It made him forget to tell her about Sigurd's proposal. He remembered only when he got to the lunch table.

CHAPTER

‖‖‖‖‖‖‖‖‖‖‖‖‖‖‖‖‖‖‖‖‖‖‖‖‖‖‖‖‖

20

Anya felt herself get wired.

She wrote a thirty-page treatment of the movie and sent a copy to Mr. Danziger, her old boss at Ikon Films. She put in a list of her credits and reviews. She sent another copy to Ryan in Des Moines and then drove up to see him. Ryan went for it, said if Ikon went for it, he'd go in for half. Seventy-five thousand.

They went back to his apartment, he made a tentative pass at her. She didn't even have to say anything—he put his hands on her hips, she looked thoughtful, he quit.

They talked about his paintings. He liked what she said about the one of the dead bull. The talk about paintings led to Mercks. She said she'd seen some of Mercks' movies. She was careful to refer to them as Mercks'. She told Ryan that she wanted to include some of them in *Iowa Girl*. Ryan said he could easily arrange that with Mercks, Mercks would probably do it as much for the credit as for the money. Ryan was confident he would have no problem. He didn't say he'd backed them.

Anya liked what he said about *The House of Bernarda Alba* he'd helped sponsor.

As she was leaving he said, "It should be worth it. You're almost as good as a pro, and I think you're about to get lucky."

Anya was stunned. Ryan was still smiling pleasantly. It struck her as such a wrong thing to say she couldn't think of what to say back. She wanted to flatten his face. Before she thought of what to say, she thought of the seventy-five

341

thousand dollars. She thought he could be as cute as he
wanted. She said as pleasantly as he was smiling, "I'm even
better than you think."

But as she drove back along Interstate 80 she felt
rankled, and then tired, and then suddenly frightened. She
had to pull into the breakdown lane to catch her breath.

All she told the group was that she was setting up a film
project to be shot nearby. But there was a whiff of something that stirred them. The extra phone calls, her trips,
her withdrawal.

Her next problem was with Raftery. He kept telling her
amusing things she ought to get into her film. Twenty miles
down the Iowa River from them was a town called Fre-
donia. She thought a minute. He said, "It's the name of the
country in *Duck Soup*. You ought to get the signpost in."

He'd been to see the house Dvorak lived in in Iowa. He
said, "When you open the door there's a life-size dummy
of Dvorak that turns and looks up at you from his desk
where he's writing the *New World Symphony*."

He thought she should get that in.

He wanted her to get in auction day at Kalona, the
parking lot filled with Amish horses and buggies.

Dulcie would chime in from time to time saying that
yes, that really *was* wonderful. Dulcie didn't get it any
more than Raftery got it. Anya got it—Raftery was jealous
and this constant suggesting was the pleasantest form jealousy could take.

He was filled with praise that she could work in two
writing sessions a day. She said she didn't think it was like
writing poetry or stories—she didn't have to wait for something perfect. It was quick drafts, models of scenes that
would get broken up again and again. She said, "Words
aren't the end product."

Raftery wanted to have a long talk about that. Anya
wanted to be left alone.

Anya was greatly relieved when Raftery was invited to
read some poems at Coe College along with ten other young
Midwestern poets. He was to be paid seventy-five dollars.

Dulcie sewed him a new shirt for his reading.

Andrew read the treatment, and the parts of the script
she'd completed. He told her it was a wonderful idea. He

also said he could take over her direction of *Exit the King,* one of the two new plays they were preparing for the spring.

Anya thought she would need only a little time from the actors in the group. Ray for Peewee's father—that would only be a few days. She did want Tagh for Peewee's cousin, which was a longer part.

Andrew said he would be glad to help with the casting. He had some idea of what was available from the drama department at Iowa, and even what was going on in the Midwest generally.

Anya realized that Andrew's helpfulness was as much a movement toward the project as Raftery's suggestions. She softened her feelings toward both Raftery and Andrew, but hardened the isolation in which she conceived what she wanted.

Peewee was perfectly happy about the whole thing. She was willing to answer Anya's questions, and, when Anya borrowed a camera and sound equipment from her acquaintances at the University of Iowa studio, Peewee was as happy being filmed as she was having to work for Dulcie.

Anya wanted to get the winter scenes in the Rock River prelude done before she took time off to write the long Iowa City sequences. She wasn't sure when she'd have a good snow again. She needed only a few shots of Peewee's farm life in winter—she included a pig-castrating scene, and a dehorning of a steer, which Mac and Ergenbright set up for Peewee. Peewee knew what she was doing. Ergenbright had to show Tagh how to hold a pig.

Anya solved the problem of Peewee's looking fourteen in the winter exteriors by putting all Peewee's hair up into an ugly wool stocking cap. Peewee's neck looked as frail as a baby's. The cold air marbled the skin on her face in childish pink and white, and seemed to flatten her features, at least in the long shots.

Mac was the one who surprised her most about her new project. One night in bed while she was reading he suddenly said, "You know, I didn't believe you when you said there was a lot of you in your idea of what Peewee's like, but I can guess how you meant that now. She's not like you, but you think she's a way you might have been. And in a way

343

you're more tender with her than you are with yourself. You're sometimes very hard on your own feelings."

Anya said, "Why do you say that?"

Mac said, "I was just remembering the way you were when you used to act during the fall when you were still doing improvisations with the others. You used to turn everything you brought up into tough comic touches. It used to break my heart."

Anya said, "I thought I was pretty good."

Mac said, "I guess you were. But it made me nervous. And sad. I liked it better watching you dance, and you aren't as good at dancing as you are at acting. I suppose I thought I could tell where you got your gestures of tenderness and then it upset me to see you turn them into something ridiculous. And you would do it so fast, I imagined it must have been painful. I felt as though you were picking out a real feeling and yanking it out by the root. There was no pity. Now Andrew can be funny, he can show a feeling to be laughed at without hitting a nerve."

Anya said, "Without hitting whose nerve?"

Mac said, "Well, when you get as good as you and Andrew are, the actor's nervous system seems to be held in common by someone watching."

Anya said, "I wish someone had said that in a review." She wasn't sure she wanted to pursue the subject.

Mac said, "I'll tell you what it felt like for me. The goalie on our hockey team in college was a friend of mine." Anya looked bemused. Mac held up a hand to show her he wouldn't take long. "In general, when you play on a hockey team, you have tender feelings about your goalie, but I liked this guy somewhat more than that. He was lighthearted and cheerful, and physically nimble and rubbery, but when he got in a game, I could feel him concentrate on the puck. I had the feeling he'd go after it with his teeth if he had to.

"One time he had to play with two broken bones in his hand, his stick hand. It wasn't his *pain* that bothered me so much, I don't think he felt the hand, it was shot full of Novocain. His hand *worked* all right, each broken finger taped to a good one. I couldn't see his face, he had his mask on. But each time he used his stick, or took a shot on the back of his glove, I had a picture in my mind, like an X-ray, a motion picture X-ray of a piece of bone moving inside his finger. It drove me crazy. I used to get pitched pretty high for a game, and this guy's hand took away that lift, that extra nerve that I usually wanted, that usually was a physical joy that came shooting up and made the game large—desirable. The extra nerve that ate up fear. But that whole feeling turned back and—that hand was all I could see and it brought everything back, the fear, the suspicion that it was all ridiculous, that the game was a pinball machine, that we'd made a terrible mistake in agreeing to dismantle that hand, because it was now clear that it was attached to his brain."

Anya could picture him suddenly struck dumb and still; she was herself struck by the jaggedness of his feelings. She hadn't considered this rhythm of his life—that he was so subject not only to the surge of his energy but to its sudden reversal.

She also thought that it was remarkable how he managed to confuse other people's welfare with his own.

She said, "Tell me the dream you were telling Dulcie. The one about Hugh."

Mac looked surprised but said, "About Hugh? About Hugh on that other planet?"

Anya said, "Yes, I think that's it."

Mac said, "I've been taken off to another planet as a prisoner, no, a specimen—you know, this is really old science-fiction, I don't know how it gets in here along with the good stuff—I'm a specimen but they're interested in talking to me and I like them, they're asking me wonderful questions about life on earth, questions about how we feel about each other, about animals and trees. I couldn't hear what I said back, but the sensation was that I was suddenly saying wonderful things, getting it just right, and they were hovering around and loving it. Then they asked me about pain, and I was suddenly terrified. My fear drove them back from me. They shrank away, a curtain opened, and at the bottom of an amphitheater I saw a large green turtle in a tank wired up to a child. Someone explained that the turtle was going to be put in pain, but that the child could will the pain away from the turtle into his own body. The child understood that he and the turtle were both creatures from earth and that the turtle might die unless he shared the pain. It started before I had a chance to say anything. I put my hands against a glass wall and watched the turtle begin to curl up and the child immediately take the pain away. The child, who was Hugh, was crying, but kept on taking away the turtle's pain. What was odd was that for a while then I was outside my body and I was able to *see* the feeling in Hugh's mind that was behaving so well. It looked like an arrangement of crystals. My first reaction was a kind of joy. Pride. I thought, Good, he's perfect. He knows to do the right thing. Then I was back in my body, and I could see the terrible surprise of his body, each time he felt one of these pulses, he would look down at his body and try to back away from it. I began to tear down the glass, there was layer after layer until finally I was wading through the water toward Hugh. The creatures running the experiment could feel my hate, which interested them. They began to record it. They also realized I was helpless in the dark, and it all ended with me looking for Hugh in the water, my legs couldn't move because of the dark, and even though my arms were very long I still couldn't find him. I woke up.

"And then lying here awake I couldn't help seeing parts of it all over again—the first conversation when I liked them, the feeling that Hugh was perfect—unflawed right to the core, and then my helplessness. When I first woke up it was a nightmare, but then the parts became more mysterious—I didn't hate those creatures—they really didn't know what they were doing, they were doing the best they could. And the part that stayed with me clearly for the longest time was Hugh's mind. That's gone now, too. I've just given you an outline."

Mac paused. He said, "Why do you ask?"

Anya said, "I should be flattered—I've made it into the same league with a hockey player and with Hugh. It's funny, though—acting *doesn't* cause me any pain."

Mac said, "Oh—I think the goalie story is about harm, not pain. Harm without pain is more frightening—the Hugh story is about something else. The pain was in there, but it wasn't the real point there either. I remember, one of the odd things was that these creatures had no bodies, just force fields—so they couldn't feel pain, but they could measure it. There were graduated beakers beside Hugh and the green turtle that were filling up with liquid—the liquid was used-up pain. So the creatures could keep track." Mac laughed. "A green turtle, for God's sake."

Anya was suddenly content. She lay still for a moment. She considered filling a beaker or two with used-up pleasure. She thought Mac would like her little joke. He was asleep. She didn't mind. She was content that Mac made his imagination available to her. At the moment it was as far from her, as useless in a pleasant way, as the larger part of recorded history. His rounds of chores and thoughts and pleasures in his own day were as vague to her as the rise of the Dutch Republic or the fall of Cracow, but she was pleased by the echo of what he did, the telling of it in the slow intimacy of their square bed.

Now that she had a fast part to her day—the fast part, somewhat surprisingly, was when she was at work on the script alone, not when she had to make a dozen phone calls or explain things to Peewee, Tagh, or Ray. It was when she began to imagine what she wanted in the movie, and the electrons of her thoughts moved to their outermost orbits, rearranged their allegiances, the bonding of nuclei, so fast that she could not be sure of what she was doing or losing or whether she was going to approve. But she was sure she had to let it happen, had to risk her planned moves of each morning in this experimental disruption, so that when the time finally came to compose a picture, to ask an actor to utter words, her wishes would emerge both calm and urgent—calm because she had rehearsed them in her imagination, and urgent because they were not finished.

But after that excitement—even now the thought of what she was doing and would have to do made her go rigid in bed—she welcomed the busywork of the afternoon, and then the slower shrewdness of looking at her work for a little while after supper, and then this comfortable blunt nuzzling and bedding down under the horse-blanket canopy with her stablemate.

CHAPTER

||||||||||||||||||||||||||||||||||||||||

21

Anya used the big front room for work in the mornings. There was a week of warm, sunny days when the sky was a deep blue, and melting snow and ice running off the roof made a comfortable blurred sound outside the double windows.

Only Dulcie and Hugh were at home. With Mac working longer for Sigurd, Dulcie had more kitchen work to do. The big evening meal for the group was all Dulcie's.

Raftery had disappeared again. His first seventy-five-dollar reading had led to another and then another. He came back once for three days. He'd told Anya that he was now giving his lectures on the Midwest as well as reading his poems. He left off a hundred dollars with Dulcie, packed his duffel bag with clean clothes and some of his notebooks, and got Mac to drive him to the Interstate. He was thumbing up to Grinnell.

Mac told Anya that Raftery had said he was at last entering his public ministry. Anya wanted to know more, but Mac had only asked enough to satisfy himself that Raftery wasn't getting into trouble.

Anya barely knew Dulcie was in the house. When Anya took a break they would sometimes have tea together in the kitchen or step outside for a short stroll. Hugh tagging along behind. Anya felt the fluffed-up comfort of Dulcie's gestures toward her—it was like finding the bed turned down at night. Dulcie made the tea for them both, and made elegant little lunches, mysteriously ready when Anya was—a miniature quiche, an omelette, a green pepper-onion-cheese sofrito, with country sausage in Anya's half.

Anya was grateful for the quiet; occasionally she would hear Hugh start to cry and Dulcie swoop him upstairs out of earshot. Dulcie was treating her far better than she treated Raftery, and Anya decided there was a puritan work ethic in Dulcie which worked in Anya's favor as Dulcie heard Anya typing away in the front room. Dulcie's silent good will was in direct proportion to Anya's sustained workmanlike noise. Even though Dulcie was cooking from midmorning on in the kitchen, there wasn't any of the usual clatter—the pan ringing on the stove, the oven door thudding shut. When Raftery had used to sit talking at the kitchen table, the noise had grown louder and louder: Dulcie would start plopping down bowls of rising dough or colanders of vegetables by his elbow.

Anya's feeling about Dulcie gave a sympathetic reson-ance to her feelings about Peewee. Dulcie interested her less, excited her less. Peewee had qualities that were more crudely marked, more highly contrasted to each other. Dulcie was layer after layer of silk, she was never really there and never really not there. Peewee was either nakedly and even unpleasantly present, or a blank. Once Anya thought that perhaps if Peewee spun her feelings finer for ten years . . . No, Anya thought, Dulcie is Raftery's wife, in many ways like his early poems, his best finished work, it's downhill for him since he began to grasp at the whole world and failed to sustain her.

But it all reminded her how Peewee would come across.

Anya now shared Dulcie's relief when Mac would come clomping into the house for a spare half hour in the early afternoon. She was surprised that Mac didn't talk to Dulcie much during the day. Anya watched closely and was sure this was the way it usually was. Hugh went for Mac im-mediately, he tried to climb Mac's leg, grabbed the skirt of Mac's coat to be picked up, thrown around, hung by his feet. The two of them would usually go outside. Mac would pull Hugh on the box sled to the woodshed and they would fill it with logs. Hugh would climb on top and get pulled back. He would stagger up the steps pulling at a split log half as big as he was.

The next event in Hugh's day was Peewee. Hugh was warier with her. Sometimes she would pick him up, kiss him, take him up to her room. Other times she would pat him once and have nothing to do with him. He would try to charm her, and once in a while it worked—she would pull off her boots and let Hugh tickle her feet. Other times she would speak crossly to him, equal to equal—"Fuck off, Hugh. I'm tired."

If he failed with Peewee, Hugh could see that Dulcie had no time now that supper was only an hour off. Hugh would then look for Anya. He never went in the front room, but if she was through working and was in her bedroom or taking a bath he would walk up to her and carefully pronounce one of his long sentences—"Dussie is making bread." Or "Daddy reads books." Or "The road has mud."

If she was in bed he would stare at her face. If she was in the bath he would stare at her bosom. The same blankly childish stare. Although she knew she should be grateful for his formal social effort, she found it impossible to think of anything to say.

One day she reached out her hand to touch his face. He stepped back and stared at her hand, his face for once a miniature of a complicated adult expression: "Madam, I fear you have mistaken the purpose of my visit."

*　　*　　*

Anya completed a draft of the script, mailed copies to Mr. Danziger at Ikon Films and to Ryan. She then spent a week going over to Sigurd's with Mac and following him around the farm, looking for different effects of the landscape and buildings.

She drove around to the small towns—River Junction, Downey, Lone Tree, Riverside, Hills, Kalona. They all had pieces of what she wanted. A ghostly quality. They were all shrinking now that most commerce was carried on by truck and not by railroad.

She also confirmed her feeling that no matter how beautiful she found the countryside it was because she could move freely through it—the roads, the roll of the land, the full streams pouring into the Iowa River all suggested movement to her. She decided she would have to convey both the size and the peculiar beauty, and at the same time Peewee's being held prisoner by it—bound and oppressed by it because Peewee's spirit was too undefined, too unseparated from it. Her chains and her own existence were one substance.

But Peewee also derived some freedom from her prelyric underdevelopment—she had a peculiar ability to say fuck you to anyone. Her only notion of moral restraints was that they restrained others; they had no weight with her. She did fear some people, and she seemed to have some affections that were not abnormally short-lived, possibly because of inertia.

She gave up shoplifting groceries when Mac asked her not to, but only because there had been a scene.

Her collapse before she'd come to live in Raftery's house was not because Mercks had stripped her of her dignity—it was the increasing coldness of Mercks (and Mercks' buddies). Peewee had also been impatient with the too coolly gentle concern of her Spanish teacher, who was, from what Anya could tell from Peewee's account, a sweet, old-fashioned, self-tortured lesbian. Peewee did want physical contact—whether it was sexual or not wasn't all that important. Although she did get turned on from time to time, she had only a primitive idea of what in her turned other people on. Her lack of this knowledge made sustained sexual drama impossible. In fact, she was put off by any notion of mutually sustained theater in which the orchestration of feelings between two people became the end.

The most intense experiences in her life were, one, being filled by her surroundings—she said she sometimes had the sensation of being melted into by clouds or sky or earth— and, two, being occupied by a hard alien force, usually some person, with clear sharp edges, usually defined by some cruelty, as in the cases of her cousin and Mercks.

The rest of her relations seemed tepid and unimportant to her.

During this period of reflection Anya rarely spoke to Peewee, but she grew closer and closer to her, or at least to the projected character, as the scenes arranged themselves in new orders and in more detail.

Anya thought of the notes she had from her conversations with Peewee that were not yet fully embodied in the script:

Peewee's father, crazed from fourteen straight hours at the wheel of the tractor during spring plowing, trying to finish the fields the next day, hallucinating a brass band playing outside the tractor cab—not alarmed by it but distracted into letting the diesel run dry so that there was an airlock in the fuel line. Peewee watching her father's hands tremble so badly he couldn't fix the line—he held the light and told her what to do. The tractors on the farm across the road continuing to plow after nightfall, their headlights surrounded by halos of spring mist. The noise—the noise of the special tractor radios designed to cut through the engine noise, the two noises not blending—not like the brass band and tractor.

Peewee herself said she didn't leave the farm because her father treated her all that bad, she left because he was a loser. Her cousin called her father "Uncle Shakey."

Peewee didn't give a backward glance to any of them.

She walked for miles to the nearest hard-top road, stuck out her thumb twice—once to the Interstate and the second time all the way east to Iowa City.

Anya had a hard time with Iowa City—there was so much that was physically loathsome. What had been charming about the parts of town built in the first quarter of the century was being eaten into by the usual commercial fungus. But Peewee was enchanted—the threads of people tangling before her eyes, the possibility of the thousand people she saw at one time being available to her . . .

Peewee said, "When I got to Iowa City the first thing I thought was, My life isn't too long."

Anya felt Peewee's nervous ferocity. Her gushing democratic eroticism—no barriers of contempt or envy. Peewee was Walt Whitman in her skin. The people she saw there were an element to her, like the sky, the earth, the wind.

Anya asked her why the people were different from the people back in Rock River. Peewee said, "They aren't sealed up."

Peewee found the freak element quickly. But what interested Anya was that Peewee didn't join the freak fringe by default, not as Peewee saw it. Peewee didn't feel any discrimination against her. She felt invisible, but that it was *possible* for her to become as visible as any of the people she saw. Peewee saw a sorority ceremony—all the pledges standing on the sidewalk being sung to by the sisters standing by the windows inside the darkened house, each sister holding a lighted candle.

Peewee saw the Miss University of Iowa homecoming queen contest.

Peewee saw the University of Iowa Highlanders, an all-girl bagpipe band.

Anya herself had seen these things and had laughed at all those things with a delight she now found a little shrill. Peewee had thought very simply that to enter any of those groups all she had to do was put on the costume.

Peewee had no impatience with the University bureaucracy. She'd gone to the registrar's office and someone had told her everything she had to do. She'd done it all—tests, forms. She listed her parents as deceased, her uncle as her guardian. She called her uncle up and told him she was pregnant by her cousin but that she'd never come home if he would send her a thousand dollars for an abortion and keep his mouth shut. He did. Her only regret was she hadn't asked him for more. She had no idea of the risk of telling these lies.

She took freshman rhetoric, life drawing, Spanish, hygiene, and earth science.

She lived in a rooming house with a freak landlord. She never quite got it straight who lived there and who didn't. She had no room of her own—she drifted from room to room as she'd drifted into the house, blind but drawn to heat, like a tick. She said she balled some of the guys and one couple, but a lot of the time she just slept across the end of someone's bed or on a couch.

People fed her and gave her things. She stole food for the house from supermarkets. She was sick for the first time since she was a child.

The house was sold. They were all evicted. She moved into a one-room bungalow with two guys. It was a two-mile walk to school. It got cold. She stole a fur coat from Good Will. She walked back home and the bungalow was gone. She asked in the furniture store across the street and found out the bungalow had been hauled away because the furniture store had bought the land and was clearing the lot to build an annex. Peewee found the bungalow on the back of a flat-bed trailer in a junk yard.

Mercks had just bought the bungalow from the junk dealer. He took her along, too.

Anya had notes from Mercks, too. Anya was interested that Mercks had caught on to Peewee right away. He understood that what was fiercest about her was not her sexuality. Mercks had said to Anya, "Peewee would do the whole slave thing, but she never like got *under* it. Some chicks are there kind of caving in and thinking, 'Far out! I'm really into this.' But Peewee was so far out already. You know the tutors at the freshman writing clinic—Peewee got sent there 'cause she wrote so bad. One of those tutors correcting a paper of hers—just the paper, he hadn't seen her—he wanted to send her to the English-as-a-foreign-language class. You see? He thought she was a foreigner, Lucinda Nadl from the old country. It wasn't *bad*, you dig, it was just you couldn't understand it. If you get her to explain what she means you sometimes get a clue of something weird, something rock hard about what she feels strongest. She's not crazy, she's not dumb, and she's not bullshit. What else is there for a chick to be? Normal, I guess, and she's not that. I'll tell you something, she doesn't turn me on anymore, but usually when I'm not turned on by a chick anymore I forget what it was that turned me on. I've got a picture of Peewee—it's just from the mouth to the eyes, not the whole head. It's that pad of an upper lip with that scar you can hardly see.

"Right now I'm into sort of chubby, soft sorority chicks. They think I'm awful. They dig how nasty I am. You know, they're lavaliered to a guy in civil engineering at Iowa State, they wear plaid jumpers and white knee socks, Daddy bought them a Camaro or a Le Mans, and they have real thin mouths. They say, 'If you think you can get anywhere with me, you're just crazy.' I really dig it, that cold, dishonest fat."

Anya said, "You fuck these girls?"

Mercks said, "That's not the point—I mean once in a while, sure, but what I like is when I say, 'I bet you and your boyfriend always do it from the front,' and the chick says, 'That's none of your beeswax.' I love it.

"But it's not real. It's all bullshit. I mean to them, I'm like a banana split while they're on a diet. Gobble it up. They don't even taste it. They say, 'Oh, what have I done?' But Peewee went for something in me I wasn't sure was there—the only way I could keep her in balance was to scare her. She's scared of being shut up, she's scared of deep water, and she's scared of fire. But she loves storms—windstorms, electric storms, rainstorms, snowstorms. I'll tell you another thing—what she really could go for is taking care of some dude who like once in a while would do something to her, I don't mean balling. Who would just . . . get into her . . . with some kind of . . ."

Anya knew what Mercks was floundering after. She had a sudden fear that Peewee would aim for Mac. His willingness to enter and be entered. Then she thought, No, that's wrong—Mac is too busy amassing order, building the perfect city in himself. Even the final form of Peewee was an outlaw force.

Then Anya realized with surprise that the final form of Peewee existed only in the script, in the imagination attached to the script. That everything in the script that Peewee did would be more or less what happened, but that the final reactions that Anya wanted Peewee to have were still to be constructed. Anya was sure that Peewee had become free, but Anya couldn't think of how to portray it. In the script she'd sent Mr. Danziger Peewee simply left to go to the West Coast. Riding back past Rock River, across the Missouri River, leaving Iowa for the first time. Anya wasn't happy. She was just following a rule: Stories end when people die or go away.

Mercks said, "Her Spanish teacher almost got into Peewee but she blew it, she was too—too possessive and too scared. It made her—I mean the Spanish teacher—grabby and shy. You ought to get Peewee to imitate her teacher grabbing her and then running off to make sure the shades are down, the whole time explaining how that what they were doing was very beautiful. Peewee's very funny."

Anya was tempted to play the Spanish teacher herself. She knew she could be very funny at it—the coy indirection —gushing, "You poor child, you are unhappy!"—Peewee, voice-over, saying, "I knew she wanted to ball, I mean it was drooling out of her. Why couldn't she just say, 'Let's go, Peewee'?"

The Spanish teacher twisted into a pretzel, her fingers stiff, overcome with a sense of danger at her good luck. Taking a deep breath to steady herself, coming on again with muted, throbbing voice, a heavy eye contact: "Miss Nadl . . . Lucinda . . . Cindy . . . believe me . . ." *Sforzando* on "Cindy," *diminuendo* on "believe me."

Anya backed away from it—an Elaine May cameo satire of an Iowa dyke schoolteacher. Squirmingly funny. Wickedly funny. The wrong kind of laughter. Anya wanted it to be funny, but also difficult, uneasy. Some sympathetic sense of the woman's pain.

As complicated as Peewee's mother helplessly saying in her slow prairie voice, "Cindy honey, don't feel bad, he raped you, you didn't do anything wrong." Peewee not knowing what on earth she was talking about, not helping her at all.

It occurred to Anya that one of Peewee's difficulties was that all the people who embraced her, including Mercks, were finally afraid of her. Anya added that thought to her notes. And Peewee was bewildered; she didn't understand what they felt, they just weren't doing it right anymore. Anya was sure Peewee had said just that—"I don't know why I leave people. They just stop doing it right." Anya found the index card. She couldn't think where it would go in.

Anya and Mercks went out to look at locations in Iowa City. Mercks marched into the different boardinghouses and communes as though he were a field marshal reviewing the troops. Magic words—"We're looking over locations for a movie." Anya was embarrassed. Only one person recognized her. A girl in a boardinghouse said, "Hey—I saw you in that play. Hey, it's weird, you were so much older." Mercks knew someone everywhere.

They finally found a place Anya liked—an extravagant turn-of-the-century house badly used, some windows still carrying the original glass, some covered with plastic sheeting. The loft of the carriage house was the only clean room. Three outside iron fire escapes spoiled the lines of the house.

Mercks said, "I thought you'd like this one. The landlord's a son of a bitch, but that's good—for a little money he'll throw a couple of roomers out of the rooms we want."

Anya looked uneasy.

Mercks said, "It's okay. I'll put them up. The landlord'll be grateful—he loves a chance to be a son of a bitch as much as he loves money."

Anya realized she'd hired Mercks.

The weather turned bright and raw. Mac started putting in all day and part of the evening at spring plowing. Anya still liked the pleasant sexless comradeship as they climbed up to their room together yawning at nine thirty. They were asleep by nine forty. One night Anya was sure they'd had a longer conversation. She'd asked how long the all-day plowing went on. Mac had mumbled, "First we'll plow, then we'll disc. You want the discer? I can't tell. We'll certainly still be discing for your movie."

Anya had the impression it was a long conversation because she included her own calculations:

She wanted to start filming before the plowing was over. Ray, in his capacity of assistant professor of drama, had arranged to lease the University's 35-mm. camera and Mr. Danziger had set up the film project's legal status (a partnership of small corporations), but Ryan's lawyer was checking it out before Ryan set up her checking account. Mr. Danziger was waiting for Ryan. Anya imagined she was explaining all this to Mac. She wanted to ask what the discer looked like, but Mac was asleep. She realized that she herself was halfway to sleep. She turned into it.

For a week she fell asleep like that—sleep loomed up below her and she could dive down into it at will with a deliberate flex of her whole body. She had distinct impressions of her feet dangling loosely behind her in the ragged light of the trailing edge of her mind as she slid into the blackness, felt it smoothly closing over her.

After a week of that, she spent a night during which she kept waking up rigid with fear. She was being betrayed—not by anyone's malice but by the way things worked—by leaves sprouting on a tree she wanted bare. By a face closing over with contentment so that she could no longer see into it. By the very air thickening so she couldn't see.

This anxiety didn't stop when the money started coming into a bank account in the film's name. She could still fall into a sleep, but it was shallow and troubled—she woke up every time Mac moved.

She and Peewee went in to the drama department's sound studio and made some tapes of the voice-overs.

Anya had written the voice-overs so that they were answers to questions. She wasn't sure if she should leave the questions in or not. She asked the questions herself. She made a tape with just the answers. She liked it. Peewee's voice had the prod of the question in it.

The first cameraman from Ikon arrived. Anya put him up at the theater house. He was glad to pocket his *per diem*. He didn't say whether he liked the script, but when Mercks set up the shop-lifting sequences in a supermarket, the cameraman caught on, worked very fast. He was happy to spend a half hour with Anya in the evening explaining why some things were impossible (but he'd always try), suggesting variations, helping to set up the next day's schedule in more detail.

The only time the cameraman gave her any comment apart from the possibility or impossibility of a particular shot was when they discussed the end. He said, "I can do it, but it won't be strong."

The end Anya now planned was a lyric reprise of farm scenes alternating with Peewee riding the bus west—each shot of a field by the side of the bus would be swept forward and seem to melt in the sun. The scenes seen from the bus included Peewee so that she was apparently seeing herself.

Anya could talk herself into it, but she wasn't happy.

Anya said out loud, "Real life stories end when somebody dies or goes away. I'm not going to have her kill herself."

The cameraman said, "Well, it's good to there. You'll think of something. This going to California idea—dreaming dreamy dreams. She isn't that bullshit. But you're dynamite up to there."

Anya decided Peewee should stay in Iowa. But that was no advance, only a good retreat.

They went ahead with the dope-dealing sequences.

CHAPTER

████████████████████████

22

Raftery came back. He was driven by a newspaper reporter from Des Moines who was doing a story on him. A boy and a girl from Grinnell were along. It became clear they were his followers. The newspaperman told Anya that Raftery had drawn a crowd of five hundred students at Grinnell.

He said, "That's about as good as Norman Mailer or Margaret Mead did there. Of course *they* charged two and a half bucks a head and Raftery just left a bushel basket by each door."

Anya said, "How much did he make?"

The reporter said, "I don't know. He says *he* doesn't know. It was a good show. A lot of kids left a dollar."

Anya said, "What's he do?"

The reporter said, "He talks. In ten words or less what he's saying is that you can be ecstatic if you just pay attention to what you're doing. And Iowa is the perfect place because you can start from scratch. That sound familiar?"

Anya said, "But what got people to come?"

The reporter said, "Well, he was hanging around in dorm rooms for a while, I guess he was reciting poems and giving the same rap. I couldn't find whoever it was that started him in the first place. I sat in one room for a while. He was asking people when they were happy, and then why aren't they still doing whatever it was that made them happy. Then someone said something and then he topped it and off they went. He's pretty funny. How long have you known him?"

Anya said, "A while. You going to stay for supper?"

"I don't know. If it's okay with whoever lives here."

Anya said, "I live here." She was surprised she was being so pissy. Of course she wasn't ready for a newspaper story, especially a newspaper story starring Raftery. Who might say anything.

She said, "I'm sorry. I've had a long day. There're different things going on here. We'll have a talk after supper. I'll try to help you."

"Who are you?"

Anya said, "I'm the director of the theater."

The reporter said, "I'm sorry—I'm getting confused. This is my first Sunday feature. I've been covering straight news, the double-hitch trucking bill in the State House."

Anya said, "That's okay, we'll get it straight."

Mac came in, was delighted to see Raftery, asked Raftery if he wanted a sauna, went out to light the fire. Raftery went with him.

Anya took the reporter by the arm in to the front room to look through the theater scrapbooks.

Dulcie was clanging the two stew pots around, her back rigid. Hugh had gone off with Raftery and Mac.

Peewee came down and helped Dulcie.

The rest of the group began to trickle in from the theater. Bangs went into the little back room off the kitchen, in a huff. Ray stood by the door, not sure whether to follow her.

The reporter came back in with a picture of Raftery from *The Alchemist* scrapbook.

The rest of the group heard that Raftery was out in the sauna and headed out through the larder to see him.

Andrew stayed behind to talk to Anya and the reporter. The reporter asked, "You mean Raftery's an actor?"

Andrew said, "Well, he was amazingly good in that. But he's also a poet." Andrew pointed to the picture. "He played Sir Epicure Mammon. Do you know the play?"

The reporter said, "No. But do you think his acting has anything to do with what he's doing now?"

Andrew asked what that was. The reporter told him. Andrew was amused. Andrew said, "You know, I think that's mostly his wife's idea. One night she said, 'You know, what you say when you're talking is so much better than what you write.' A lesser man might have shriveled. But you see, the aspiring man rises."

The reporter took out his notepad. Anya gave up.

Andrew said, "Of course it was Anya who realized what a lovely—an extraordin*arily* lovely, rich voice he has. It's the first really musical Midwestern voice I've heard. His *r*— have you heard him say 'war'?—or 'yard'? 'When lilacs last in the dooryard bloomed'? Of course he's a lovely, lovely man."

The reporter was baffled again. Anya kept herself from laughing. Then she was ashamed of her own sour bullying beside Andrew's appreciative sweetness.

Mercks and the cameraman from Ikon came in, and they and Anya went in to the front room to talk until supper was ready.

During the next week Anya felt her patience and concentration increase. She couldn't imagine what would have happened to her if they hadn't, because at the same time she felt a terrible increase in the weight of the work she had still to do. A pull inside her eyes, as though her brain were becoming denser.

Raftery had moved out again—this time only to the other side of Iowa City. Dulcie and Hugh had gone with him, along with his two followers from Grinnell and some new ones whose house he'd gone to, just outside town on the north. Raftery was holding meetings in their barn.

Dulcie came back with Hugh. She looked forlorn. Andrew explained to Anya that Dulcie had hurt feelings because of Raftery's latest talk. Raftery had said (Andrew reported) that the greatest danger in his life, in anyone's life, was constancy. That you had to face each day like Adam, each day receive life new through your fingertips.

He'd said that you must feel which of the virtues you had learned were giving you strength and which were inert. He'd said you should stay away from inert people while you were still struggling with your own inertia.

Andrew, who was sitting in the back with Dulcie, said she'd begun to wilt at the phrase "inert people."

Afterward Dulcie had asked Raftery how long he was going to be on his lecture tour. Raftery had said, "Until it becomes inert."

Dulcie had said, "I'm not comfortable in someone else's house. I'll be at home."

Anya noticed during the days that followed Dulcie's return that Dulcie's face was mottled. The skin under the wings of her nose began to flake. She bit one of her fingernails, all of which were already bitten short, so that it uncovered the quick, which bled. She kept sucking it, and it wouldn't heal.

Anya found the outward and visible signs of Dulcie's depression irritating. She was glad the schedule now took the movie company in town to the rooming house all day and into the evening. There were Tagh, Anya, Alice, Babette, Peewee, Mercks, and the cameraman, along with the several bit players Anya had picked up, and some of Mercks' crew from his movie efforts. They all ate at a steak house where Mercks had arranged a discount.

When Anya got home she could sense the ashes of a dreary evening. Andrew would drop in on her about ten to confirm the worst. Bangs was having a terrible time as Queen Marguerite; Ray, who was having a good time as king, finally lost patience with her. Dulcie kept her back to everyone while she moped and cooked at the stove. Mac would sag in from his day at the farm, still having two or three more hours to face that evening. Hugh would start to cry in his room upstairs. Dulcie would begin to weep. Mac would go up with Dulcie to comfort Hugh and her.

Og was once again being tortured by Annabelle. Andrew said Annabelle was jealous because Mac and Ray were paying what was left of their gray, dutiful attention to Dulcie and Bangs.

Anya asked how Annabelle was doing as Queen Marie. Andrew said she was terrific. She was also perfectly good as the girl with two noses in *Jacques,* the show that was currently playing on a double bill with another one-act play, O'Casey's *Bedtime Story*.

Anya discovered what it was that was bothering Og.

One night Anya stopped by the theater after the performance of *Jacques.* Annabelle was receiving admirers in the green room. The rest of the cast were, as usual, back in the theater house taking their makeup off. Annabelle sat in her sleeveless smock, the gardenia-petal skin of her bare arms and legs smoothed by a blast of warmth from a portable heater she had turned up to high.

Anya announced she was closing up the theater, and the half dozen young men left obediently. Annabelle laughed.

362

She said to Anya, "They want me to be the guest of honor at their fraternity party. I'm the sweetheart of Sigma Chi!"

Anya said, "When the show is over you're supposed to turn off all the lights and all the heat in the theater. I don't give a shit what you do with Og or what you do in town, but I wish you'd go clean your face in the house. It's sloppy as hell to sit around with the audience in your makeup. And it costs money to have you sitting around sunning yourself in front of a heater."

Annabelle picked up her hairbrush and comb. She said, "Andrew is directing this show. So I think—"

Anya said, "Okay, fine, I'll have Andrew tell you."

Annabelle's face changed from cool, pursed lips and thin nostril-breathing to a pout and full panting. No tears, but a shakiness that was close to sobbing.

Anya found herself studying Annabelle's face, registering the effects with an interest that was both absent-mindedly carnal and reflective. The absent-minded interest was that she wanted to touch Annabelle's face but without any more feeling in her hand than would be necessary to find the hard and soft spots. Anya's reflective interest was in what a prisoner of the clichés of dramatic expression Annabelle was. It occurred to Anya that the life in Annabelle's face was not constant. It came in pulses—the face was of interest only when it was resolved into a finished expression. The passage from one expression to the next was blurred and slack.

Peewee's face, Anya thought, was much less various. But it was denser. There was less creaminess. Anya imagined that feeling Annabelle's change of expression through one's fingers would be like feeling a shifting of fluids. Feeling Peewee's would be like feeling a hum through a rock.

Peewee had no set vocabulary of expressions, so she couldn't use her face to send a valentine or a get-well card or a cute reminder to come see her sometime soon. Peewee's face was just the more nervously complex end of her body. Annabelle's was a screen for her idea of herself.

If Annabelle wanted to attract someone her face would flow through several semaphores of attraction, although only about one frame in ten was actually filled with the energy of a complete unit of meaning. You had to look closely to see the illusion.

If Peewee wanted to attract—probably that wasn't a possible strategy for her . . . If Peewee wanted someone, she became a beacon of energy, began to move toward him, or her, emitting and receiving physical (as opposed to psychic) vibrations.

Anya thought of her old word for Peewee's face—"reptilian." It wasn't quite right. Reptilian in that the range of expression was limited, reptilian in that the skin was close-grained and tight. But reptiles seemed ancient, torpid, and malevolent. Peewee was raw and young, her skin and teeth milk-blue. She was attracted to blood and sun heat, but she had her own. And yet Anya thought of how abstractly Peewee had dealt with the prick in the barrel. As unemotionally and sinuously as a lovely five-foot python arranging to swallow a speckled frog.

In fact one of Peewee's cool voluptuousnesses (unknown to Peewee) was her mouth—the full, hard upper lip delicately nicked with the diagonal line of her scar. That mouth an instrument with which she was unconsciously adroit—no useless grimaces or poses of the lips, no backing away, no puckering, no preparatory licking. Direct.

Anya realized that while she'd been thinking she'd taken a step closer to Annabelle, who was now puzzled.

Anya said, "I'm sorry," to excuse her absent-mindedness. She saw that she might as well apologize in general and said, "I'm sorry" again.

Annabelle's face swirled through a few empty frames and then coagulated in shining-eyed relief.

Annabelle said, "I'm so glad!" and hugged Anya. Anya was interested that Annabelle's breasts and arms felt so light—like a spongy mushroom—in spite of the fact that she looked big-boned and heavy as custard.

Annabelle said, "When you're angry I feel it"—Annabelle stepped back and put her palm on her solar plexus—"so painfully." Annabelle's face squashed down a little to show pain. Anya remembered Annabelle's flirting with Mac, how much more alarmingly concrete Annabelle had seemed then, her flesh like unsalted butter.

Anya said, "Andrew says you've been terrific the last three shows."

Annabelle re-embraced Anya. Their hipbones touched on one side. Anya thought of baboons, the submitter presenting his ass, the dominant baboon giving it a polite hump or two, more social than sexual.

Annabelle left. Anya turned out the lights, sat in the dark. She thought she had made her life a nightmare of imaginary baboons. She was alarmed at how jumpy and pictorial all her thoughts were—it was worst at the end of the day.

She thought it was a bad sign too that she was counting the days of shooting, believing that the film was only allowed to weigh on her for a set term, that if she just endured she'd be okay. She tried to tell herself that she had created it all, it was all up to her; getting what she wanted, getting it right had almost nothing to do with brownie points for endurance. It was too painful to believe for more than a moment that effort alone might fail. She reverted to promising herself that it was almost over, if she could just hang on everything would be fine.

She looked at her watch and was sad to see that Mac would be sound asleep by the time she got home.

*   *   *

Anya listened to the first of the voice-over tapes, decided she'd been right, that most of what Peewee said on the tape, even when it was in answer to a question, was clear by itself. There was no need for another narrative voice.

Peewee said, "After I tried to kill myself, the dean of women wrote me a letter to tell me I was on social probation. She said if I tried it again I'd be expelled."

Later Anya asked, "But you were trying to get someone's attention?"

Peewee said. "Sure, I was trying to get attention. But not from any of the guys *I* knew. I wanted some kind of new attention." Peewee laughed. "Boy, some attention."

Anya was glad she'd had her thoughts about the density of Peewee's face. There was an analogue to that density of her flesh and bones in her voice. During the taping sessions Anya began to explore how Peewee's voice could be made more or less dense, more or less hard, by the way Anya asked a question, whether or not what Peewee answered was in the script. Anya also discovered a less theatrical method of altering Peewee's voice. Anya could make her almost purr by giving her a neck and shoulder massage as she spoke. By sitting Peewee in a chair and holding her hands on the chair arms, Anya could make

Peewee sound as slow and forlorn as if she were taking a lie-detector test.

The two of them spent six evenings in town at the student radio station sound studio. Anya would have a word or two with the sound engineer up in his booth and then she and Peewee would settle down in the middle of the empty cubicle and start talking. Anya would steer the conversation toward the section of narration she wanted. Peewee was mysteriously natural in making the transition. She responded to Anya's voice and touch, but, Anya realized, Peewee used them more as promptings than as absolute controls. Peewee had never had any barrier in her own mind between truth and construction, and she was capable of doing her part more or less as written, doing it again with variations, and even a third time, without losing interest.

Anya was impressed by Peewee's endurance. Peewee even asked if she could start going to Andrew's improvisation hour in the morning. Anya said no, not until they were through filming. But she let Peewee go to Alice and Babette's dance sessions.

Anya devised a new end and got that in the can. She now had to prepare Peewee for the last part of the shooting schedule—the fourteen-year-old summer sequences in Rock River. Anya had a dentist make a fake set of braces and a retainer for Peewee. She had Peewee's hair hacked short again. Her costume was a hooded sweat shirt, oversize jeans, and high-top sneakers.

Anya realized that Peewee had suddenly bloomed—she was the only person in the whole troupe to put on any good flesh during the long winter. She looked healthier, sleeker, less urchinlike. It made the end of the film make sense, but Anya had to disguise it for the early scenes.

Luckily the most important scene was at dusk. They set the picnic at the pond on the neighboring farm, the picnic at which Peewee's cousin seemed to be fondling her feet but turned out to have tied her shoelaces together in knots. It was still too cold at dusk to shoot exteriors comfortably, but Anya was more distressed by the quality of light. The sunsets were still pale—not the rich summer glow that smoldered on and on for an hour after the sun went down. Anya finally found a patch of ground by the pond that caught reflected light from the water when the sun was low. She also thickened the texture of the light by using blond, highly varnished wood panels as reflectors just off camera.

Finally they were down to the last scheduled shot: Pee-wee woke up, heard her cousin call "Pee-weee . . . ," tried to go to her cousin, fell—half in the mud, half in the water. Close-up of the feet—all four loose ends of the laces tied in knot after knot. Pull back. All of Peewee now visible as she sat where she was, tugging at the wet knots.

Anya signaled to the cameraman to stop the lens down slowly so that—she hoped—all that would be visible in the end against the dark bank and the muddy water would be Peewee's face, her dirty white sneakers, and her pale fingers working at the laces.

CHAPTER

23

Sigurd was in a much better mood. He was worrying about there being too much rain just as they were about to plant the corn. But his worrying was boisterous, optimistic.

"Now if that rain'll just hold off, we'll be all set. That's why we planted that lower field first, to get it sprouted before it rains. If that seed just sits in water it'll rot, it'll just peel apart like wet paper. But if that seed gets a shoot up—boy, it'll take right off. You see, corn is mostly water when it's young, same as grass. Now up on the higher ground, we have a different type problem, there's a runoff. I want the water up there not down here, that's why I got mad that time you plowed right through the grass in that draw. Of course, that was my fault, too, letting you go up there in the dark."

Sigurd would go on like that, stomping around the tractor shed, checking the oil, the water in the batteries, making sure the various hydraulic arms were retracted into their sleeves so they wouldn't rust, patting the machinery and Mac with the same affection.

He was worried about Mac's health, said Mac looked thin. He sent Mac home before dark now.

Mac loved the half-mile walk home in the dusk, the huge oaks by the river dark against the pale spring sky.

For the time that he was walking, nothing he thought of bothered him. He didn't worry about Dulcie or Raftery, or Sigurd's proposal, or Sigrid, or Anya's movie.

He thought of all these people with pleasure and tenderness and at a distance. He had some idea that this mood was related to the period of his late-night melancholia, the print of that negative, because this was clear and bright and lighthearted, like the beginning of a fairy tale in which the youngest son sets out into the world to seek his fortune and at first his way leads him past sunlit fields and into a beautiful green forest.

In the ten minutes it took to walk between the farmhouses he was as happy and as filled with a taste for the physical world as he had ever been. And he felt detached but without any ironic or even comic thoughts. In fact there weren't even any wishes or regrets. He thought of Mireille, and she appeared to him to be happy, pleased with her marriage (he imagined her to be married), her life, her large family (although she looked as young as when he last saw her). But above all she seemed to him wise and good. Her smile was approving. Her husband's voice said, *"Et Mac—il va toujours bien?"* Mireille said yes. Mac felt that there was no need to put into words his pleasure at seeing her.

He thought of skating with his father.

He thought of a canoe—thin, varnished cedar ribs, dark-blue canvas reflected a shade darker in the flat black water over which it rode.

Birch, pine, aspen, maple, and beech shone in the water near the shore—the branches of the hardwood trees were brighter as he moved closer because then it was the pale undersides of their leaves that he saw reflected, the birch and aspen leaves twirling and fluttering on the single plane of black, bright water.

All of these thoughts left him as he reached the driveway. They left smoothly but with finality, like the last bubble of air from the neck of a sunken bottle now settling on its side in the feathery silt of the lake bed.

He stepped into the kitchen and shut the door. He felt rehardened from crossing the dark yard. Still cheerful, but wary. The kitchen was an awful mess. Everyone was holding on tight to something—the handle of the frying pan, a clipboard, a door knob, their other hand.

Two days later, the weather changed. It had been clear, a winter sky of stars at night but well above freezing, during the day warm enough to work without gloves.

Then suddenly a low dense sky moved in, the air thickened and held still, and then rain began to fall in heavy, fat drops. Mac was out in Sigurd's feed lot when it broke. He took off his jacket. The rain felt warm on his neck, through his shirt.

Sigurd gave him a ride back home.

He ran up the porch steps and into the kitchen. The kitchen was empty and he suddenly felt alarmed. He felt foolish and walked upstairs. On the stairs he smelled a heavy stench. The hallway was dark so he knocked on Dulcie's door before he realized it was smoke. He shoved the door open. The room was filled with smoke. He backed out. He shouted for Dulcie. Peewee yelled from her room. Mac didn't understand her. She opened her door and said, "Hugh's asleep," and ran past Mac into Dulcie's room. Mac took a breath and followed her. He ran into her as she was coming back. He held onto her and they ended up in the hall. Mac felt Hugh in her arms.

They went down the stairs and ran out the kitchen door.

Sigurd's truck had just turned onto the road. Mac ran after it. Sigurd stopped the truck.

Mac said, "The room's on fire."

While Sigurd backed the truck to turn into the yard, Mac ran back to Peewee. Peewee was holding Hugh under the arms, staring at his face. Mac took him back onto the porch, laid him down, and began to breathe into Hugh's mouth. At first Mac tried to fit his mouth over Hugh's, then he remembered to cover Hugh's nose, too. Mac felt giddy, he was afraid he wasn't breathing hard enough.

Dulcie appeared. She'd been in the garden and gone into the tool shed when it began to rain.

She put her hands on Hugh. Mac suddenly could hear her voice at the same time that he heard Sigurd's.

Sigurd told Mac to get in the truck with Hugh. He told Peewee to call the fire house. Dulcie got in beside Mac. She held Hugh's body on her lap. Mac had Hugh's head in his hands and kept on trying to breathe air into him.

Sigurd drove them to the hospital.

A doctor took Hugh away from Dulcie, who was holding him while Mac was still breathing into him.

Sigurd said, "It's smoke." He took Mac by the shoulders and said to him, "Was it smoke?"

Mac said, "Yes."

Dulcie followed the doctor down the hall. A nurse put

her arms around her, tried to stop her, and then walked with her, holding her around the waist. Mac started to follow them but he passed out.

When he came to he was on his feet again. Someone was holding him around the waist, someone else was holding his head.

He sat down in a chair. He said, "Where are they?"

The intern standing in front of him said, "They're with the doctor. It's okay."

Sigurd came back and sat down beside him. Sigurd said, "I talked to Selma, the fire company got there. It wasn't a real fire, they sent somebody to get me, and he said it wasn't but the bedclothes and an oil heater and some of the flooring."

After a long time the doctor came back. Sigurd and Mac stood up. The doctor asked Mac if he was the father. Mac said no. The doctor looked relieved and said they would keep the mother at the hospital. The child was dead. They'd told the mother.

The doctor paused. Mac twisted away from him. Sigurd held Mac. Then Mac thought it might not be true and turned back to the doctor.

The doctor said, "I'm sorry."

Mac believed him that Hugh was dead. Then Mac was terrified.

The terror was so entire that the pain and grief he felt next came as a relief.

Then he became confused. He thought about Dulcie and Raftery, wondered where they were.

CHAPTER

|||||||||||||||||||||||||||||||||||

24

Raftery came back. Mac was alarmed at his appearance. He was even thinner. His face appeared ragged and inflamed—there was in fact no physical sore, only the redness of his eyes, and a heightened contrast between the white over his cheeks and the fleshy red of his lower lip. But his face gave Mac the impression of a wound.

Mac begged Anya not to go to New York.

Anya had put off her trip to Ikon for three days. It was she who had been able to persuade Raftery to let Dulcie have a Catholic funeral service. She had also had a long talk with Dulcie in which she asked Dulcie to get back to work right away and not to be so harsh with Raftery. Dulcie told Mac that Anya made her feel better. Anya cleaned out Hugh's room. It was because Anya was doing so much better day to day with everyone that Mac wanted her to stay longer. Anya said she would be as quick as she could but she had to go.

Mac asked if New York was more important than the place they were living in. He didn't say the people they were living with.

Anya was exasperated that he kept fumbling around with what he took to be helpful inexactitude.

She said, "I've got to go. I can't do anything else here."

Dulcie wouldn't take the sleeping pills the doctor gave her. Raftery did. He'd smoked a joint late the first night and felt terrible—he woke up and they walked up and down the road in front of the house for an hour and a half. They were silent for a while and then Raftery talked about Ben Jonson. He recited Jonson's poem—"Slow, slow fresh fount, keep time with my salt tears."

Mac couldn't talk with him. He had to stop Raftery from going on to recite Jonson's poem on the death of his son. It was not because all this poetry struck Mac as false in any way, but as painfully frantic—Raftery like a caught bird trying to flap loose, and doing himself harm.

Mac felt glad, of course, that Raftery had come to him, but he was afraid of what Raftery might say or ask. Mac was glad that Raftery held his arm while they walked.

Raftery finally said he thought he might go on another long walk. Perhaps west, perhaps to New Mexico or Colorado.

Mac understood that wish. It would be a relief, being tired and seeing new landscapes. Mac said, "And Dulcie?"

Raftery said he hoped Dulcie would go with him part of the way, or at least take a bus out to be with him.

They talked about what states he'd go through.

The thought of walking got Raftery tired enough to go back to bed.

The next night he took one of Dulcie's sleeping pills.

The night after that Mac woke up. He went downstairs and found Dulcie making bread.

Before Anya left for New York, Mac had told her that it frightened him that Dulcie could speak so freely to him about details of Hugh's death. Dulcie had talked to the doctor a lot before she came home, and told Mac what she could remember of what the doctor had done. She was able to describe what the doctor did, the resuscitator, and Hugh's body in technically clear detail.

Anya had told Mac that that was probably good for her. Mac wasn't sure. He was amazed that Dulcie could focus her memory so clearly and for so long. Her language was calm and expository. It made him wince, as though she were sewing her own numb flesh with a needle.

The night Mac found her making bread, she sat down across the table from Mac and said, "I didn't really understand what you were doing to Hugh while we were driving to the hospital. The doctor explained it to me later. I know you were trying to do it right because I can remember feeling Hugh's stomach move. I had my hand on his stomach, and I felt it puff out when you breathed into him. I knew it wasn't him breathing though. But his skin wasn't cold so I didn't think he was dead . . . He *was* dead. His soul had left."

Mac couldn't say anything. He looked at her face and was shocked to find himself stirred by thinking of her beauty, by the heat of her face in shadow. He said, "Do you want to go for a walk? It'll get you tired enough to sleep."

Dulcie said, "No." She picked up his hand and held it to the side of her head. Mac felt her hair slide under his palm.

She put his hand down and smiled. She said, "No. Raftery's the one who likes to walk. I like to dig in the garden, but I can't do that in the dark.

"You know, if Raftery stays here it'll be more on account of you than anything else. He likes you a lot. He likes the way you take him. He gets nervous with most people, he thinks if they take him seriously then he's not free to change, I mean that then they don't want him to be free to change.

"And of course there're a lot of other people who *don't* take him seriously.

"But he likes the way you take him. He thinks as long as he feels good about what he's trying to do, you'll sympathize with him."

Mac said, "I guess that's right."

Dulcie said, "He wants to leave here."

Mac said, "You mean go on his walk?"

Dulcie said, "That's just the start of it. When he gets out there he'll start giving talks again—and I'll bet he won't stop till he gets to California. You know, he didn't smoke at all while he was giving those talks. That shows how it affected him. It gets him high."

Mac said, "Oh, come on."

Dulcie said "California!" again, with contempt.

Mac said, "Why don't you go with him?"

Dulcie said, "Oh, if you can't see that! He likes being with those people because they drift up to him and he can get them excited. But they can get excited because they don't stand to lose anything."

Mac said, "*They. They* aren't all the same."

Dulcie said, "The ones *he* goes to are."

Mac felt more comfortable now that he was disagreeing

with her. Mac said, "You're making it sound like some kind of vice."

Dulcie said, "I used to have patience. But I guess it was easy because I thought I knew where the center of his life was. Now I don't know. I used to think he really was finding out things, but I don't think that anymore. Just a month ago he used to say that right here in the Midwest was the place to be. Remember his going on about 'omphalos of the world'?—'between the Mississippi and the Missouri, the new fertile crescent.' Now he wants to go to California."

Mac said, "He told me New Mexico or Colorado."

Dulcie said, "I don't believe that." Then she said, "What's the difference?" She got up and covered the bowls of dough with cloths and set them on the side of the stove.

Mac felt helpless, as though Dulcie and Raftery were storms, far away and above, discharging lightning down on the people watching from the bare earth.

Dulcie said, "He used to come back full of where he'd been, it just poured out of him. He'd go out and charm the world and come back as if every step he'd taken was to come home."

Dulcie began to cry.

Mac thought, It'll be all right, she still wants him.

But then the sound of her crying changed, as though it were a rotary saw that finally cut through her flesh and hit the bone. From that sound Mac guessed she'd thought about Hugh again.

She turned back to face the table, sagged to her knees, and held onto the edge with her hands. Her head rolled to one side against her upper arm.

Mac got up, tried to pick her up from behind. Her forehead hit the edge of the table. He knelt beside her. She turned and grabbed his arm. He got her up and made her sit on the bench. She leaned forward over his arm, still holding on with both hands to his forearm, pressing the arm between her breastbone and thighs, rocking back and forth.

She slowly stopped moving, her cheek came to rest against her knee.

After a short while she said she was tired, and she went up to bed.

Mac stoked the fire in the stove, closed the damper down, and stepped outside. There was a ground fog. He couldn't see Sigurd's yard light across the field. He sat on the porch steps mourning a little—an echo of Dulcie and Raftery and even Peewee (who blamed herself for having been asleep when the bedcovers caught fire). He didn't feel his own mourning clearly. He also thought that all their nerves lay across each other's and that was why some of his feelings seemed blocked while other feelings seemed forced into an excitement that was unfamiliar. The cool close darkness of the yard rested him, but he knew he would feel his underlying worry again the next day.

It was not because Anya was off in New York. Or because of the falling apart in the house. Or in the theater.

He thought perhaps his usefulness to these people was a habit for him—a waning of strength now. He had lost some independent power and felt he was drifting internally toward his flaw again.

The nights stayed cool and foggy. During the day the sun burned off the visible fog, and the weather was steamy and warm. Sigurd said they needed warmer nights, that it was warm nights that really got corn to grow. Mac liked the lingering fog.

Raftery left.

Anya was still away. It was ten days now.

The schedule of their lives went on at the theater, in the costume room, and the carpentry workshop. In fact, Dulcie held herself to a stricter schedule, making sure she was always busy. She preferred tasks that required repetition—kneading dough four hundred times, taking the hooked rugs outside and beating them a hundred times. Mac noticed that Dulcie counted everything—he could see her lips move. It was as though she was learning a new piece of music and was counting time.

Mac thought this was probably a healthy craziness.

But what struck him as horrible was that no one spoke freely or easily at meals. For a while he thought that it was because Anya and Raftery were missing. Then he thought that perhaps they'd always sounded this inconsequential and he'd only noticed it now. He finally thought that they might have sounded stupid but that they used to get *some*where finally. Now they didn't talk at any length out of fear that they might come near the subject of Hugh.

And now there was the subject of Raftery that had to be

avoided. Mac didn't blame him for leaving, even after Andrew, who'd seen him last, told Mac that he'd left in a VW bus with a girl from town. Not walking after all. Andrew had seen her around—a large jolly girl who'd been in one of his dance classes the year before. Mac was only sorry that Raftery wasn't walking.

Andrew couldn't quite forgive Raftery for not facing Dulcie to say good-by. The note Raftery had left didn't make it clear what he meant by leaving.

Peewee moved in with Dulcie to keep her company at night. Mac thought that was probably a good idea. Peewee was the only one who dared to joke with her—Peewee asked her to go cruise some bars with her, and Dulcie laughed.

Dulcie asked Peewee to cut her long hair as short as Peewee's. Mac found this alarming. Dulcie's feelings were hurt by the expression on Mac's face when he saw her shorn.

Mac felt bad about that, so he was glad to be distracted by what happened at Sigurd's. Sigrid came down from Minnesota to visit, and Sigurd asked Mac over for supper.

After supper Sigurd and Selma left to go to a church meeting. As he was leaving, Sigurd showed Mac the porch glider he'd stored in the cellar for the winter; he asked Sigrid and Mac to hang it.

They did. Sigrid sat down and Mac sat beside her after a second of hesitation.

Sigrid laughed and then said, "I'm sorry; I'm just laughing. I'm not laughing *at* you."

Mac said, "I guess Sigurd has told you about his idea."

Sigrid laughed again. She said, "There we are. I guess we'd better talk about it."

Mac said, "I've come to like Sigurd a lot but this idea of his is—pretty old-fashioned."

Sigrid said, "Well, I was a little *worried* about you!" She had a nice big voice now. She'd been feeling her way softly, only her laugh had been loud. "See, I asked Dad when it was he told you his idea, and he said it was when he got home from the hospital. And it was just last night he came out and told *me*. So I just didn't know. For all I knew you and Dad had it all settled." Sigrid laughed. "You know, all the grandchildren's names picked out."

Mac said, "To be fair to your father, it wasn't exactly—"

Sigrid said, "I know, I know. But you should have heard Mom talk about your health. That's always the first thing she wants to know about my friends. But here she was saying you had such good health, so I knew she was in on it, too." Sigrid started laughing again. "Mom's ideas about men are just this. Is he healthy? Does he get places on time? Does he save? She says, 'I don't care how much money a man makes so long as he puts part of everything he gets into the bank.' Dad couldn't ever talk to her about taking a loan or a mortgage without her complaining. The only thing she holds against you is the theater. She thinks they take advantage of you. I was about to say Dad was getting a bigger hunk out of you than anybody."

Mac said, "It's all voluntary."

Sigrid said, "Well now, I'll bet he didn't forget he's the landlord. I'll bet he said, 'It's no use my renting you a house when I can't get any help.'

"I won't say Dad has a fault, but if he does have a fault it's just that he wants *more*. He can't help it. He doesn't want money, he just wants to take care of more, to run more, because he thinks he can do it better—get more use out of things.

"It's going to be awful hard for him to give it up. To even think about it.

"There are some days when he thinks I'm doing fine. I'm making a good salary, I like the company I work for, and he seems pleased with me. But then you came along and he saw a way to have more. It's hard for him to see it comes out of that same part of him that gets more land, or more leverage at the bank. That part of him that puts a deal together.

"But don't you worry. I'll tell him just before I go back that it doesn't look like it'll work out. I'm not going to give up my job. That's the reason, he'll understand that."

Mac thought she was a sensible, kind girl, and it was a great relief to deal with someone who wasn't worried about anything, who seemed to have a lot of time.

Mac took out a cigar, and Sigrid got up and made him change places so he'd be downwind.

Mac said, "I don't have to smoke."

Sigrid said, "No, I like it fine when it's not blowing at me."

They sat in silence a moment and then Sigrid began to

laugh again. Mac smiled. Their feet scuffed the floor of the porch, the chains holding the glider squeaked. Mac felt comfortable. She was handsome in a plain, cheerful way. Her body was solid and strong, but there was a delicacy to her face—the fine line of her chin which ran deep to the back of her jaw made her cheeks and throat and eyes seem soft and precise. There wasn't a cloud in the deep blue sky of her expression.

But what at first had irritated Mac (as he'd come to realize what it was) was that Sigrid could not rock the glider rhythmically. Not only not in time with Mac—Mac had tried to adjust to her foot scuffings and shifts of weight —but simply without rhythm. It relieved him of all temptation. Completely.

Sigrid said, "You've been a lot of help to Dad, though." She shook her head. "I don't know, he'll just have to face up to what's up to him and what's up to other people." She paused and then laughed again. "Of course there's a sweet side to his trying to poke into this."

Mac put his feet up on the porch rail to hold the glider still. He still liked her.

Sigrid asked him about the survey he'd been on in Labrador. It turned out she knew the chief geologist. She started to put her feet on the rail but her legs were too short.

She asked him what they were putting on at the theater. He told her the story of *Jacques*. She laughed at the girl with two noses. She put her hand on the back of Mac's wrist and swung her ankles up onto his shins.

She said, "I can't reach the railing."

She asked about the filming that had gone on around the farm, and Mac told her. She began to talk about her growing up on the farm.

Mac's feet fell asleep. But he was filled with plain comfort.

He finished his cigar and Sigrid offered to drive him home. He said he'd walk, and she decided to walk with him.

When they got to the gate to the yard, Sigrid patted him on the shoulder, laughed, and hugged him. She said she'd let him know about Sigurd's state of mind.

Mac sat on the porch step. After a moment Dulcie glided out of the haze by the garden. Mac was startled.

Dulcie pulled her shawl tight around her shoulders. She said, "Where have *you* been?" and walked by him up the steps and into the kitchen.

The next day was Saturday, and Mac was able to spend the whole morning on the set for *Exit the King*. He helped Dulcie feed everyone and then went back for an hour to deal with the peculiar problems of lighting *Exit the King*—the king finally dissolving into gray mist was only the most obvious. He hadn't solved the problem when it was time to set up for *Jacques*.

Sigrid arrived in her car. She'd stopped by the house, and Dulcie had told her Mac was at the theater. She told Mac she'd talked a little with Sigurd, who was in a good mood. She'd told him her job was the most important thing in her life and he'd said he knew that, he just wanted her to get to know Mac since Mac had been such a help. Sigrid said, "Of course, he may be just putting on a poker face now. But he's in a real good mood. That's all I'm worried about, he has a worse time than anybody when he's in a bad mood."

Mac asked Sigrid if she'd like to watch the show. She said yes. Mac set up a seat for Sigrid in the lighting booth.

He felt too tired to stay. Sigrid said she'd drop by the next afternoon on her way back to Minnesota.

Mac walked along the road, instead of cutting through the oatfield. He was walking with a lightheaded stumble, as though he were drunk. He felt nervous and fine.

When he reached the house, Dulcie was going around the corner of the house toward the garden. He said, "What are you going to do? It's dark."

She stared at him for a second and then said, "I'm going to be by myself."

He said, "Okay. I'm sorry."

He added, "I'll be upstairs."

Dulcie said, "I'm thinking of going back home to Kansas." She disappeared.

Mac sat on the porch steps.

After a while Dulcie came back, walked by him, and turned out the yellow porch light. She walked back down the steps. After a few steps she stopped to look back at him, took a deep breath, and walked past the corner of the house toward the garden shed.

Mac thought, This is the worst thing I've ever done.

But it was physically difficult for him to reach the garden. He had to stop beside a maple tree to rest, his hands on the trunk. He thought, I'm meant to repent here.

But his hands moving on the bark roused him again. He walked down a furrow, unable to see where he was going.

He heard Dulcie move.

His mind began to jump with a queer, light abruptness—at first he thought, It's all right, nothing's happened. He kept moving, it seemed to him he was gliding on forever. Then he thought, I was wrong, she didn't say anything, she didn't mean anything, she'll stop me. He thought, I feel as if it's over, maybe I've already come, and it'll be all right.

He was surprised to find himself back in what seemed the past when he reached Dulcie and she took his hand. As though it were the second time.

He was surprised to find her hands smaller than last time.

Her skin felt cold—as strange and wonderful as ice.

Dulcie said, "Did you feel it or did you just guess?"

Mac didn't say anything. He was sure this was another moment in which he was meant to repent.

Dulcie said, "I'm not sure myself, I may be making it up, but maybe it doesn't matter. I really felt something come close to me. And this is where I was when it began to rain."

Mac felt as if his head split open all the way to the stars. He realized she was talking about Hugh.

She held Mac's hands tighter. Then she said, "I don't think I'm supposed to do anything. It's gone now."

Mac repented. It washed over him, numbing the surface of his skin.

He said, "Let's go back in. I think Peewee's up in your room."

Dulcie said, "Stay here."

Mac walked toward her. He was certain they were going back in to the house, that he was calm. He put his hands on her waist. She said, "You don't like my hair, do you?"

Mac touched her hair. He said, "I like the way it feels. I can feel the ends."

She pushed his hand away from her head, but she trailed her fingers along his as she did it—a piece of flirtation that annoyed him superficially—he thought it was beneath her.

But at a deeper level it made his feelings grind together, closing off his thoughts from his body.

He held her arms and began to kiss her. And it was suddenly once more as though it were happening a second time. Her mouth—her lips small, cool and rough, like crusts of snow.

She seemed lighter and lighter, her shoulders and back smaller and bonier every minute. Mac stepped away, holding her hands. He felt calm, he was about to say something pleasant, and then they would go back to the kitchen.

But they lay down in the tall grass beside the edge of the garden. He undid the buttons on the front of her dress and put his hand in over her breast. He thought it was a stupid thing to do, it was not a gesture that was worthy of her.

Dulcie got up on her knees. She pulled her dress off. Mac was shocked at how calm she was, how calm her movements were. He reached and felt her bare back. And then her long underwear bottoms, her knee socks and work shoes. He tried to unlace the work shoes. Dulcie said, "That's sweet. Wait." She stood up, put her hand on his shoulder while she slipped her shoes off and pulled the rest of her clothes past her feet.

Mac felt a slightly brutish and curious impulse. He could barely see her pale legs—he'd never seen them—he put his hands on her knees and carefully examined her upper legs with his mouth, licking, smelling, gnawing with his lips.

He stopped. Everything was suddenly clear. He thought, I can stop now. I can go back to the theater.

But he had taken his clothes off and laid them out over hers. He sat back on his heels.

Still standing, she put her hands in his hair and pulled his face to her stomach. She knelt quickly and kissed him. She felt his shoulders, chest, stomach, legs. She cradled his balls in her hands.

She said, "This is wonderful. I wish I could see you."

Mac couldn't believe she could have spoken so lightly. He put it out of his mind.

She lay back on the clothes.

He began to make love to her. All his sensations were very distinct and small until he began to hear her sweet, clear soprano whine. He felt a surge of despair lift him as she sang just behind his ear, higher and more staccato. As he'd once heard her noise coming through the heating vent, mixed with the sound of bedsprings.

He was almost unconscious of his body, more aware of her small bones. He came after her—a sharp, quick splinter.

She seemed much more alive than he. He knew he was in a state of shock, both right afterwards and later when they got up, put their clothes on, and walked toward the river in the dark. She was cheerful and solicitous.

She said several times, "Don't feel bad," and hugged him around the waist.

She said, "I'll be lonely enough back in Kansas."

He was aware of the dominant feeling which was about to surround him: a terrible gloom which was enormous, but for the moment was still sluggish and undescended.

There was also a present time taking place—strange and miniature.

The pressure of her body, warmer now and stronger, her skin damp. She couldn't keep still. She kissed him from time to time—short, gay smacks—as though they were entering a bright new romance.

His sensations were clearer and clearer. Every touch, smell, and sound. Perhaps because they were doomed he felt them clearly—crackling radiations of the final stages of decay.

She held his hands to her face. She said, "Can you feel my smile?"

It occurred to him that Anya was right, Dulcie was corny, and he quickly flung that thought back up into the gloom where it belonged.

They reached a warm pocket of air between the trees and the riverbank. Mac could not believe it was Dulcie's body—not her arm through his. Her voice sounded different, too. Yet all his sensations were so precise. He felt her face again with his fingers. She put down her shawl in which she'd bundled her underwear and socks.

She said, "I feel wonderfully silly."

She was so cheerful, so easy. He admired her for being bright and corny. He thought they should have a calm talk about how it was going to be all right.

But part of him was suddenly an energetic automaton marching toward her out of curiosity and desire. His fingers touched her collarbone, the side of her neck, her ear. He hurried to catch up to this automaton.

They lay down. The old grass crumpled under them. She put her head on her bundle.

Lying on her back with her ankles crossed, she began to make jokes. She said, "Cheer up! Cheer up!" making it sound like a comic birdcall. She laughed. She plucked some grass and let it float onto him.

He caught up with the automaton, and he bent down and began to kiss Dulcie's legs. The hair on her calf felt as long and soft as a cat's.

He put his hands up to her hips over her dress. He kissed her bare knees. There was a small patch of short fine bristles below her kneecap.

He was sure he could feel her bones spread out against the ground.

He began to gather up the skirt of her dress inch by inch between his thumbs and her hip bones. He licked the top of her thigh, her matted pubic hair, the line joining her leg to her pelvis. He kissed her kneecap again.

He heard Dulcie's voice begin to pipe. He knew it was Dulcie's voice and her dress and her fingers touching the backs of his hands, but as his face moved higher between her legs, his forehead, cheeks, and mouth touching the relaxed flesh of her inner thighs, he imagined her effigy on top of a tomb, and then below, the skeleton of a female saint, the shroud decayed but intact, like the mantle of a gas lamp. It was the bones of a female saint still alive, spread out in the glowing dust. Only the bones were bearable. Her good works and parched flesh were dead during her life.

That thought flew up by itself into the still lowering gloom. The gloom now seemed to protect him.

Then he thought he and Dulcie were really just cute little animals, as soft-boned as currents of water. What he smelled was a hot summer smell, as rich and sweet as his own skin.

He thought, Poor banished children of Eve. They got up on their knees and twisted around getting their clothes off once more.

Now he felt that they were both enveloped in the same cocoon of sentiment. But within it they were both a little numb; their own bodies were coarse and more coarsely motioned—not butterflies after all. White grubs. Not models of delicacy anymore, or of airy sweetness. Just damp hard motion.

The lay together and kissed prolonged rubbery kisses. Her small mouth blurred larger. He noticed the enormous calluses on her fingertips floating, then pressing on his back, her hips working. It excited him that she and he were thrashing out of their cocoon, that *she* was, that *she* could do this.

His own clambering blanked his mind. Motion became clearer and sharper than any notion of his skin, all his flesh vanished into the fog across the ground.

Dulcie was exhausted and without a word climbed the stairs ahead of him. She went to her room. She went to sleep as soon as she got in her bed. Peewee was already asleep on the far side of the bed.

Mac lay awake reading. He had a hard time focusing, but was glad he was reading.

Later, Peewee poked her head in.

She said, "I saw the light." She paused. "I guess you two got it on."

Mac didn't answer, looking hard at his book again.

Peewee laughed. She said, "You're so fucking serious." She laughed some more and then went back to bed.

Mac fell asleep with the open book under his face.

He half woke up when Peewee came in again; she blew out the lamp, put the book on the floor, and pulled the quilt over his shoulders.

*   *   *

Mac decided he should drive by himself to the Cedar Rapids airport thirty miles away to meet Anya's plane.

Andrew asked him if he wanted company. Andrew (along with Peewee, Ray, Bangs, Babette, Alice, and Tagh) seemed to know what had gone on.

Ray and Bangs looked at him with what he was sure was fear. As though when he left they would shake their heads and say, "Oh my God, what's going to happen to us all?" Mac despised them.

Babette, Alice, and Tagh seemed silently, guardedly curious.

Annabelle and Og had some feeling of unease, but they couldn't figure out where it came from.

Peewee and Andrew went out of their way to spend time with Dulcie, Andrew amiably talking, Peewee helping with chores.

Mac wondered what Dulcie was going to do about leaving for Kansas, but he didn't dare ask. He was ashamed of his moving back from her to think that. He was alarmed at how false her spurt of gaiety now seemed. And ashamed of himself for being alarmed.

He tried at first to be friendly to her. They went for a walk down the road. They didn't say a word. When they got near Sigurd's, Mac took her arm to turn her around. She took both his hands and stared into his eyes. Mac had no idea what she felt—her eyes meant nothing, the clutch of her hands meant nothing.

As he drove to the airport in the green Volkswagen, Mac realized what Dulcie had been feeling—it was clumsy, witless terror. For which he had done nothing.

He'd been stalled. His feelings weren't shattered as Dulcie's were, but congealed, impacted.

He realized that he was waiting for Anya to break apart his impacted feelings.

It was not a position he would have chosen to put himself in. Not even a position he had ever imagined anyone being in.

He didn't have a very clear idea of what form the blow would take—anger or pain or contempt. Or some feeling or combination of feelings that he could not now picture. He realized he had confidence that Anya would make her feelings clear and penetrating. That was what he was waiting for.

He was, of course, afraid. But he found that his fear was subordinate to his desire to resume the full movement of his feelings.

There was also a small, alert piece of his mind that saw the situation from far away. Every so often it made him laugh to see himself as a very stupid cow trotting east along a railroad track (looking perplexed but confident) toward the Silver Chief coming west.

Anya got off the plane. She was wearing her chocolate

velvet suit. She was carrying her briefcase, her knapsack, and packages of film held together with web straps.

She put down all her baggage and ran to him. They embraced. She kissed him again just under one eye, and then led him back to her bags. She was laughing and filled with talk.

They got in the car, and she said again that it all looked good. Not just that *they* said it looked good but that *she* thought it looked good.

She apologized for being so high. She said, "I'm tired but I feel good. There are still snarls, but not bad. The movie is finished. The Ikon people have been fine, they pushed me around some, and we had a fight about some stuff, but all in all—" She undid the waist button of her skirt. She laughed. "I gained five pounds. All those Italian restaurants on the expense account."

She stopped. He couldn't talk.

She said, "Have things been bad here?"

Mac said, "I have something to tell you."

She listened.

Mac said, "I slept with Dulcie. I . . ."

Anya turned away. The rest of the ride home she looked out the side window. His unfinished "I" hung in the air for thirty miles.

Mac stopped the car just before turning in to the yard. He started to speak.

Anya said, "Go on. Go on in."

Anya picked up her bags from the back seat. Mac opened the kitchen door. Dulcie looked up from the table as Anya came in. Anya looked at Dulcie's face and held her stare until Dulcie looked away toward Mac. Anya went upstairs.

Mac went over to Dulcie. He couldn't say anything, and he was relieved when he heard voices upstairs.

Peewee came down and said to Dulcie, "Let's go over to the theater. There's some stuff to do."

Mac walked upstairs. Anya looked out the window. Mac stood beside her until he noticed she was watching Dulcie and Peewee walk along the road. He turned away.

Anya said, "Come here." She pointed at Dulcie and Peewee climbing the fence to get on the path to the theater through the oatfield. She said, "Tell me about it."

Mac said, "One night I came back from Sigurd's. No, I was at the theater. I came back—"

Anya said, "When was it? What night did you fuck her?"

Mac said, "Saturday."

Anya said, "Saturday night you fucked her."

Mac said, "Yes. I fucked her Saturday night."

Anya said, "You know, I thought at first you weren't talking in the car because you were scared I'd been fucking around in New York."

Anya looked at him. Mac realized he was meant to ask. He said, "Did you?"

Anya screamed, "No! You stupid cunt! No!" She said, "You are so dumb. You and your fat asshole prick." She laughed at her own words. It made her madder. She said, "Even if I had, it wouldn't have been as boring and stupid as that. Pathetic! You are pathetic!"

After several minutes of silence Mac started to leave. Anya said, "Where are you going?"

Mac said, "Over to Sigurd's."

Anya said, "There's more work to do at the theater."

Mac said, "Okay."

Later in the evening Mac made a bed for himself out of some blankets and quilts in the front room.

Anya came in and asked him to tell her what happened. She said, "Tell me everything you said to each other from the time I left."

Mac tried to tell her.

Anya said, "Which night was it she was out in the garden—Friday or Saturday?"

Mac said, "Both."

Anya said, "Where were you Friday night?"

Mac said, "I was at Sigurd's for supper. Sigrid walked back with me, and Dulcie came around from the garden when Sigrid left."

Anya said, "Sigrid? Sigrid? What is that all about?"

Mac told her.

Anya said, "And you were so pleased with yourself at resisting this corn-fed farmer's daughter—Jesus! In a porch swing!—you were so pleased with yourself as a rustic swain, you came home— No, she walked you home. By the light of the silvery moon. But you were so taken with your rustic charm you just had to take it out to the vegetable garden."

Mac said, "No. That was Saturday. Sigrid was on Friday."

Anya said, "You are a busy little bee."

Mac said, "You think you have it all straight now?" He couldn't help his irritation.

Anya said, "Well, there's one good thing—this little act of piety we've had to put up with is all over. This Catholic first-communion spiritual necking. You two finally unzipped it. Only people like you could get a thrill out of that holy little bony fuck."

Mac said, "She was helpless. She was completely alone—"

Anya said, "Don't you tell me how good she is, don't you puke out one word of that shit!"

Mac said, "—she—"

Anya said, "—Not one fucking word! No! I'll tell you. What is disgusting about what you're trying to do now is you're trying to crawl back to being the only dumb goodness around here. That is bullshit. Your bullshit about Mercks, your bullshit about Peewee, pulling your fucking shotgun. And your bullshit about Sigurd—helping the poor old man, the holy farmer trying to get the hired help to fuck his pig-daughter! Go on, fuck her! Get paid for it! And then tell me the fucking truth about yourself!"

Anya began to sob. She stepped back from him, glaring at him. He thought she was going to hit him but she turned away and lay across her desk.

She cried for a long time.

Mac didn't dare touch her, but he felt a terrible bright triumph. He couldn't believe he felt it. Then he resisted it. He tried to return to his feeling of shame. His shame had been like a chill on exposed rot in his nerves through his whole body. But he couldn't look away from Anya. Her hands holding the far edge of the desk, her toes digging at the floor, her feet twisting against each other, her face rolling from one cheek to the other on the flat surface.

*   *   *

When Anya began to wake up the next morning she'd slept almost eleven hours. She felt calm and slow. Her thoughts swam past her, stirring her feelings only enough so that she knew she was still in bed. The daylight glowed

through the window curtains and the partly lowered bed
curtains. Sunlight shone through the gaps in the window
curtains in clean pieces. The bare room seemed to have
been scrubbed with light.

In the part of her that was still dark there was some
subdued but comic narration going on—a half-dream—
network news announcers were reporting about her and
Mac and Dulcie. They were having difficulty filling the
time. She recognized the irritation and slightly blasphemous
amusement she'd felt at TV announcers during the days
following the Kennedy assassination—dredging up reactions
from family retainers, framing every piece of news with
careful clichés, showing off a manly effort to *carry on*.

She thought her half-dream was in some way their revenge on her; she nevertheless found their attention pleasantly sustaining.

A historical bulletin—it was, to the best of the on-the-
scene correspondent's recollection, the first time Mac had
ever seen Anya cry. This statistic was checked and immediately confirmed by the anchorman. The global correspon-
dents were heard from, reporting—amid static breathiness
and a background noise of air traffic—the official deplor-
ings of adultery by Western European heads of state.

She didn't laugh, but she thought it might be a funny bit
sometime, she would have to remember it. She woke up
some more, tried to add to it—a Vatican spokesman—no
good.

She woke up completely. She thought of Dulcie. Helpless. The way Dulcie twitched away from Mac at the theater, around the house.

It was too obviously sexual—even if it was now negatively charged. Magnetic Scottie dogs pushing each other's
noses away. One whirling around to present its hind-
quarters . . .

Anya felt some contempt for this behavior of Dulcie's,
but she couldn't hate her. Mac had been all that was left
in Dulcie's life, so of course she'd tried . . . Raftery had
abandoned her without even a satisfactory scene. Quietly
slipped his mooring.

Anya had gathered pieces of the story from Mercks and
Andrew. Mercks was more amazed that Raftery had abandoned his following—according to Mercks, the barn where
he'd set up on the other side of Iowa City had turned into

"the weird high place," people wandering in to see Raftery, asking for advice, Raftery quirky as ever, referring some of the boring ones to the shrinks at Student Health ("my esteemed colleagues"). Raftery used to laugh at the thought of a student answering the file-card question, "Who referred you to this service?" Answer; "My holy man." He sent others off to donate blood, to gather a gunny sack of litter, to live a month in perfect chastity. A few he talked to endlessly.

Raftery had given three lectures in all. Mercks thought he could have kept on. Anya had suddenly seen Mercks' blindness.

Andrew had been to see Raftery at his barn the day he left. Raftery had been packing his clothes in a white laundry bag. He had two lab coats, his two homemade shirts, a pair of green wool pants and suspenders that Mac had loaned him, and a pair of Andrew's socks. Andrew had burst into tears. He and Raftery had gone outside to wait by the mailbox.

A girl showed up in a Volkswagen bus with California plates. She was a large, blond girl with a baby face and a pug nose. Andrew recognized her from a dance class he'd given in town.

Anya had asked Andrew if she was any good. Andrew had said—suddenly switching back to professional appraisal so smoothly that Anya had laughed—"Well, amazingly strong and athletic and even a little graceful, without being any good at all."

Andrew, without missing a beat, returned to his story. "She recognized me, and she appeared to think I'd come to stop Raftery. I hadn't at all. I'd come to wish him God-speed. I did ask when he'd be back, and he said he couldn't bear the thought of the place. I may have looked hurt, because then he hugged me rather sweetly. I said I knew he meant the *place* and that we all loved him. The reason it was so sad is that he was one of the most attractive *people* here in a situation where there are, at most, ten bearable people within an hour's drive, and that is why it is heartbreaking to see some of you at odds with each other."

Anya said, "There's nothing we can do about Raftery."

Andrew said, "Perhaps not. But we can manage to keep Dulcie."

Anya had met his eyes. She had realized then that

391

AN AMERICAN ROMANCE

Andrew was strong enough to run the theater—which made
her both wary and relieved.

Anya had said, "Well, that's up to her, she's the one
that wants to go back to Kansas."

Andrew had said, "You are being willfully obtuse."

Anya wondered if she was being heartless. She had seen
the half-size coffin. She had felt—horror more than grief.
She had cringed away so badly that she had retreated to
thinking of how to manage and arrange.

Raftery—Dulcie—Peewee—Mac. All separate figures.
She had not wished to be near their numb, slow inner
workings.

Even now she thought, They buried *it*, the coffin.

She had looked away. She hadn't seen the crumbling of
the remaining link between Raftery and Dulcie.

Now she missed Raftery.

Fat lot of good that did him.

But at least—lying in her curtained bed—she was not unhappy at the slow revolution of events in her mind, the
unplanned shifting of weights, the shortening and lengthen-
ing of distances.

She felt convalescent. She supposed she forgave Mac.
She was still mad at him, but her anger was like the itch
around a healing sore.

CHAPTER

||||||||||||||||||||||||||||||||

25

Anya went over to the theater and returned a call from Mr. Danziger. She had some difficulty focusing on the question—it was a matter of the proper presentation of her New York expenses to the corporation. She finally realized she couldn't just say, "Fine, do it the way you think best," and she had to have him explain it again so she could do what he wanted.

Before they hung up he told her that the people who'd seen the film so far split about as expected—a few people loved it, really loved it, and some others liked it, thought it had enough of a new twist to show it as arty exploitation (Anya said, "Je-*sus!*" He said, "Look, don't worry about *why*"), and there were the others who thought it was too slow, too literary. Mr. Danziger said, "Don't worry, it's good that people are arguing—that's as good as advertising. It may help with the reviews, too—it makes critics want to rise to the occasion, you know, write the definitive word on an issue. That's what we want, is to be an issue. You sound like you could use a vacation. Don't worry, I'm on this all the way. You can start thinking what next."

Anya said good-by and had the strange thought that the Ikon Film side of her life was dangerous to her because it felt so buoyant and uncontrolled. Without it she knew she

393

would be miserably enmired, but she had the queer feeling that she needed to damp the velocity of that energy before she was shot into isolation.

* * *

The weather turned hot and sunny. Spring had been two weeks of warm rain and steam, and now in May it was an early summer.

Mac looked from the road up to the ridge—the whole slope a black quilt of earth decorated with the first brilliant green, sharp-edged corn leaves, hypnotically regular across the field, four to a plant, pointing north, east, south, west, lying flat on the glossy lumps of soil.

Back toward the theater the oats were ankle high.

Toward the woods by the river there was no contrast between black and green as in the cornfield—the trees were green, every green from dark to pale. All sizes and shapes and shades of green, from the few dark scrub pines on the near edge to the maples, beeches, and, behind them, the huge oaks. Some feathery pale weeds. All blurred by overlapping colors. Later each tree would take shape, but now there was still a haze of buds and leaves making the green waver the length of the river.

Mac thought his own thoughts about Hugh for the first time. Slow and dull.

He thought he could have taught Hugh how to swim in the river. Hold him around the belly in the muddy water. Use the current to help get him floating. He was strong and well knit for his age. Good zany nerve, like his father.

Go down river in the little double-ended duckboat he meant to build. Paddle down, pole back. Let Hugh troll some live bait, nothing in the river big enough to pull him in.

It wasn't painful to think about, in fact there was a dumb calm. The pictures passed through Mac's mind softly —they were not vivid or beautiful. More like the river; all of the suspended mud and water moving all at once, its motion visible but not its force, its flat tree-shadowed sun-splotched surface moving as evenly as deep sleep, covering shapes in every stage of growth and decay.

* * *

Late at night Anya went downstairs and stood by the sliding doors to the front room. She saw that the light was on. She heard Mac move on his bedroll and turn a page. She knew she was being frivolous.

She slid the doors apart, sauntered in, and stood over him. He was embarrassed. She was still pissed off.

She said, "Seeking solace in the printed word."

She flipped his book shut with her toe and read the title. He was reading *Exit the King* in French—*Le Roi Se Meurt.*

She said, "I've come to see if your will power has improved."

She said, "Maybe you should sleep on the bare floor like a monk."

She knelt on the corner of his pile of quilts. She said, "Perhaps I repel you." She laughed. "That would make it too easy for you." She peeled the top blanket down to his knees. He was weearing an old practice jersey. It came down just over his ass.

She said, "Have you thought about leaving?"

Mac rolled over on his other side so his back was to her. He said, "Yes."

She said, "But it was just a daydream."

He said, "Yes."

She put her foot on his hip. She said, "It doesn't feel the same, does it?"

He said, "The same as what?"

She got angry again. She didn't want him to rise up. She said, "The same as if I didn't think you're a fool."

At the same time she couldn't help seeing what was funny—she'd come down to him after all.

She took off her bathrobe and got under the blanket. She said, "This is a test. To see if you're still putty in the hands of women."

Even after they began to make love she could feel that her anger and desire were uneasily mixed, like globules of oil and vinegar. She rather enjoyed the way this arrangement of her feelings qualified her first sensations, made them splintered and penetrating, full of surprises.

Afterwards she found she was full of delicious self-reproach. For having fucked Mac before she was through being mad at him, or for being a bitch. She liked the way her self-reproach and anger spiraled down the channels of her nerves, scraping the edges with a flutter of sensual contradiction.

Mac lay still beside her. Apparently subdued.

She was right. It didn't feel the same. It hadn't felt the same.

Their bodies were smaller now, cooler and more intimate.

She remembered how, long before, their bodies had seemed enormous to her—both of them hacking at each other's hot parts, skin and motion, a muscular large-boned gluttony. Their dizzy ghosts fainting on top of each other, rattled half-blind, relieved to be out of the way of the gorging—her arms and legs cramming him in whole, into her hollow center, the whole cavity from pelvis to collarbone. She laughed—like stuffing a bird.

It now seemed sweet, unnecessarily energetic, and comic.

She thought of lying in the noon sun by the lake in Ontario—joined and motionless on the flat rock. Even that lying still had been just as ravenous and flailing.

She was still angry at him, but no longer pained.

She would make him suffer a little more, but only formally.

She guessed that he must have been relieved by her sobbing the other night. Yet, could he have known whether it was the end or not? She wished she could have seen and heard herself—she herself hadn't been able to tell at the time what she'd meant. She was surprised she had no contempt for the public baby act. It seemed instead a completed statement satisfyingly repeated until it drowned out every other noise in her brain and his. And then that was that, the act closed into a sphere—Anya's distress—orbiting in the system they shared.

And Mac's fucking Dulcie?—a pale little heavenly body, cooled out of a dark, gaseous cloud.

Anya looked at Mac. One hand under his head.

So now they lay on their backs, two lovers again, staring up at their system of created planets. Why did she think this was the final creation?

A new silent distress.

Each new play-production an experimental system, disassembled on closing night. Uncle Timmy, Henniker had been a play each, an interesting experimental model. She hadn't seen any infinity—they had all played against the backdrop of her own small space.

But now there was a terrible intimation of permanence. After a moment she was able to think about it.

It wasn't Mac. Not just Mac. And it wasn't only her desire to make something permanent, a movie in a can instead of play after play vanishing into the memories of the season-ticket holders. (Mac was wrong about one thing he'd thought about her movie—the landscape wasn't a backdrop for the Peewee plot. Other way around—the plot shoved into the foreground the real size of the space. What was beautiful, the occasional perfectly beautiful picture, was arresting because it came onto the screen slowly, the elements composed themselves, the proportions weren't held, the picture moved from marred to beautiful to marred with only the rhythm of the take to help the audience, no sustained chorus of faces, or skies, or bodies, or houses, or roads.)

But there was Mac. There was the picture. There was the theater itself. There was her distress at Raftery's leaving. And Hugh dying to her through Mac, Raftery, Peewee, Dulcie—she could now hold Dulcie grieving steady in her mind for wave after wave of sympathetic awe.

Her feelings of permanence had all those elements—and another occurred to her: This time New York had been interchangeable offices, restaurants, talk. . . . She had been there only as a representative of herself. Her ambassador had been there, not her.

New York was now a closed world. Before, she'd had it the other way around. New York had been the only picture in her life with a receding horizon, with a vanishing point.

New York had lost nothing concrete—she still wanted it all, but her designs on it were now *only* concrete. Pleasures, opportunities, services, occasions. But the disappearing point to infinity was gone from her idea of New York. It was not re-established in this darker, larger life she found herself in, which didn't just run to her first triumph but all the way to her death.

She saw that it was funny—her permanence containing her vanishing point—that her new permanence was a mortal wound.

Mac had fallen asleep on his back.

CHAPTER

||||||||||||||||||||||||||||||||||

26

A few days before the festival all the roads to town had a few hitchhikers—tote bags, knapsacks, sleeping bags, and guitars. Interstate 80, old U.S. 6, 1, 218.

Anya was pleased with the posters for *Iowa Girl*.

Mac repainted the road signs to the theater.

He had to move his half-built duckboat out of the sauna where he'd been steaming and bending the planks. The sauna benches were now beds for the troupe's friends from out of town. Peewee moved back in with Dulcie to leave her room free for guests. A small group moved into the barn across the yard. Some friends of Alice's arrived in a van that popped a tent out from its side doors.

All these people seemed to expect free tickets, a never-ending meal, and hot water. The house next to the theater had six visitors.

Mac finally rounded up a dozen of the twenty-seven guests and made them help build a shower out of a huge cow trough on a platform. They filled buckets from the pump and passed them hand-to-hand across the yard and up a stepladder. One of the guests laid a dark tarp over it and by midafternoon the water was up to body-temperature. There was a mass frolic of white bodies under the shower which Anya found attractive and comic.

Mac became more amiable with the gang after that effort. Anya was all for them—her own claque for the theater and for the movie house in town.

She passed through town on her way to Mercks' festival grounds. She parked and got out at Ryan's movie theater to look at the marquee and the posters. The shows were that evening at five, seven, nine, and eleven.

As she turned away from the theater, she thought she saw Tassie in the passenger seat of a car going by.

She watched the car recede. Iowa plates, the sloping rear window reflecting the sky.

She thought about what she'd seen. The closed passenger window. A vent window? Bare hands rising as though scooping up water. Tassie used to do that when she was explaining. A string of pearls. The face had turned toward the driver too soon for her to examine it. The driver looked a little like Henniker. And then the car was gone. It could be an Iowa girl, a sorority princess, one of Mercks' fantasies. The Iowa plates made Anya think she was hallucinating. But the neck and chin were so fine and tense. Of course you could put Dulcie in pearls and she'd look like that.

Anya was surprised at how shaken she was.

She drove to Mercks' house. No one home. She drove out to the festival grounds.

The idea of Mercks' festival suddenly made her laugh. She thought she and Mac should take an afternoon off to catch it all.

The broad hollow was well filled with the three barns (one large, two small), two small circus tents, two domes (one dome with translucent panels—presumably where the paintings and sculture were to be exhibited. The other dome had a few tinted plexiglas panels—rose and blue).

There was a band platform at the bottom of a natural fold between two slopes, some guys carrying pieces of sound equipment out of the back of a truck.

Anya was of two minds—she was touched by the industry, the physical exertion. She liked seeing Mercks' troops—bare-to-the-waist boys, their jeans low on their hips, drooping to one side from the weight of a wrench or a hammer. Nice, hard stomachs, spines sheathed in long pads of muscle, their ponytails swishing on their sweaty backs. Young cocky Verrocchio Davids, their balls pouched tight in their worn-thin jeans.

She thought of the theory that women's breasts were front-end adumbrations of the rear-end attraction of women's buttocks. She decided that a male ass jutting out in tight worn jeans might as well be an adumbration of a well-filled pouch.

She liked the domes, the tents pulled taut, the ambition to build a good time.

But she also couldn't help thinking of the oily side of Mercks, the sly go-getter. Of course he was struggling to get his taste up from the local comradely norm of deaf-rock music, a jug of beer, big tits . . . There was also Mercks on his own, Mercks the connoisseur of grass, of Mexican art, of his own harsh view of life. He half-understood Peewee. He half-understood Raftery. He wanted a playboy penthouse, she'd wanted Timmy's apartment. Let him be. Let him make enough money to wonder what to do with it.

Anya thought she preferred Mercks to Henniker. It surprised her to think this. Surely Henniker operated on a more sophisticated level—quick charm, cleverness, intricate appreciations, love of luxury, social nerve. She certainly knew other people with his faults whom she continued to like: Timmy had the same plump self-indulgence; Ryan, the same glib contempt for everyone he imagined beneath him; Mercks, the same quick selfishness; Raftery, the same insane insistence of his gifts.

It was Henniker's desperation, she decided, that made him a shit. He was insatiable not because of a large healthy appetite but out of desperate fear—there was a terror in him that kept him a secret vacuum. He didn't have either of the ordinary dirty secrets. Not the old dirty-little-secret of sex, not the new dirty-little-secret of success. He was as open about his snobbisms as about his sex life—as eager to recite his list of nobodies, to fawn on successes, as he was to exhibit his interesting liaisons. But where did his fear come from? What made him so insistent, made his maneuverings and intrigues at last tedious—a single droning note? It was not his unfulfilled yearning for his own success that was so awful for him, although other people's successes did turn to acid in him. But it must be something beyond envy that tightened his nerves to that shrill pitch.

She thought of Mercks again—was there a Henniker in Mercks? Was Mercks his country cousin? No—Mercks' scurrying was in response to something different from envy. Mercks moved more quickly and directly in the physical world—out of a simpler greed. Anya wondered if perhaps Henniker's problems had to do with the physical world. There was his insistence on his discrimination in art, his fine tastes—and yet the physical world seemed to affect him painfully. As painfully as his envy.

She thought perhaps that was why there was always a stream of new people in his life—his feast of spoiled meat: the unhappily promiscuous wives of graduate students, recent divorcées, careless undergraduate heroes about to crash. It was the positive charge of other people's disintegration he needed to ease the pain of his own.

Was that it? Certainly his soothing his envy by working up the careful little triumph of a snob wasn't his whole plot. That alone couldn't account for that much shrill pain. But an envy of anyone who could receive the physical world completely, without distaste or a twinge of fear. Was that it?

Anya thought that theory would explain the stream of people—an easing of pain by adopting someone else's senses.

Anya then found the theory more interesting than Henniker. The problem became abstract; and then the problem became how to show it. Would it be possible to set up a character on film for whom the sensation of the physical world was painful, menacing—diminishing his existence?

Through the character's eyes?

She tried to think of filmed delusions, hallucinations. All those camera tilts, wide-angle lenses. Okay for brief moments of terror. But not for a longer, slower affliction of the senses . . .

The difficulty was to establish a normal, pleasant vision of what would then be threatening when seen through the impinged senses of the character.

And the further difficulty of representing the relief of moving into yet another set of senses.

She thought, No. The physical world wouldn't serve as a Rorschach blot.

But she shied off for a different reason. It would be like trying to film intestinal worms. She'd had enough trouble with the cousin/Mercks character—a much more lively, boisterous, visible bullying (for a moment she thought of *Iowa Girl* with pleasure), a bullying that finally ended up at a loss, baffled by the Peewee character's tough blooming.

Anya thought again she'd been lucky. It was growth—Peewee finally just getting bigger, strong enough to be careless—that made the movie full enough to come to an end. Anya was pretty sure she would have worked it out by herself—she hadn't been in love with the first ending. But it was good luck to have caught Peewee in a reckless good mood one day—just farting around for the camera. Tagh had caught on right away and played down—asked Peewee not to leave him. Anya had to talk to Peewee without spoiling her gaiety. "Say you don't care, say that you're not mad at him."

Peewee did better than that. Tagh kept mumbling at her, finally said, "I don't know why you feel so good."

Peewee said, "I don't know why you feel so bad." Almost cruel—her face bright and full, her legs and hips tight in her old jeans. Careless with him—her freeness afflicting him.

Tagh mumbled on, "I got you set up, you know, you'd be in tough shape, you know, I mean all that stuff I've been just giving you, I was giving you—"

Peewee laughed. She said, "That's *on*fair!"—the way she used to make fun of her own Iowa pronunciation for Raftery. She laughed, amused at the sound. She said again, "That's just *on*true and *on*fair!" It came out on film self-absorbed, self-amused. The cameraman knew it was the end before Anya did. He said later, "If you end with this, you don't need that hokey bus trip to California." Anya had agreed, but she still wanted some reprise of the countryside. A lyrical end after the dramatic one—they shot picture after picture—a lot of pretty footage but not right. Anya finally added a shot that filled the screen with just sky, a blue so intense it seemed to come in waves—and then the reprise pictures came—a series of twelve pictures from dawn to dawn. They didn't use any of the pretty pictures, they were all cuts from her own exercises in composition that made a book of hours. They ran through all the colors of the Iowa landscape from spring to spring. The only one that lingered at all was one winter field—it looked like a zebra, the snow white in the endless furrows, the ridges between the furrows black. A black Angus browsing across the vertical stripes through the weathered colorless broken cornstalks against a colorless sky—shot in color so that for a second or two it seemed that the picture was black and white, and in another second there emerged the hidden color in the pearl sky, in the black, shaggy coat of the Angus, the bruised toenail color of its hooves, the old yellow left in the bleached, broken cornstalks.

Anya had only a moment of pleasure and then she went dead on it all.

She began to wonder about delusions again—perhaps film a character's vision in short focus, everything blurred beyond ten feet.

She didn't think so. It would drive you nuts after a minute. She thought she should have shot some of the dope-dealing in short focus. Maybe she had, she couldn't remember anymore.

She thought of a scene in the film version of *A View from the Bridge:* Morris Carnovsky picking up a chair by one leg with one hand—the Raf Vallone character couldn't do it—suddenly the top of the chairback hits the ceiling. You feel how small the room is, how enclosed they all are. But that was it—it was for all of them—it wasn't a delusion, it was their situation.

She ticked her tongue against the back of her front teeth.

She thought of her notebook idea to film *Twelfth Night*. To film not only the action on stage but also the figures of speech. To film the mind's eye of each major character in the midst of a soliloquy. Different film quality for the different characters' fancies—lovely gooey bleeding Sov-Kino color for the Duke's hyped-up lovesickness. Malvolio's notion of himself adored by Olivia in grainy black and white —with his yellow cross-gaiters tinted in.

She ticked her tongue again. Not that the idea wasn't appealing. It was the fast turnover of her thinking that struck her as a bad symptom. She wondered if there was such a thing as a brain spasm—like a muscle spasm. All the old ideas came jerking out. She shouldn't have started.

She was suddenly horrified at the ambiguity of film. Of filmed images.

She thought she could put more meaning in the screen of Annabelle's face. The mind behind the face filled with the whole play, with direction, with subtext, until slow Annabelle herself filled with an intention that burned through the skin of her face. Annabelle's intentions held in place by the other players—all of them full of intentions that either burned clear or were nothing. There was nothing else. No help from the world. No natural excuse for being. Nothing but performance.

Anya felt she could be responsible for meaning in her theater, on her stage jutting into the dark audience. But now she was afraid of the careless people about to wander in to *Iowa Girl*. Wander in off the street. The movie house was theirs. She was the visitor. They could loll back chewing on the waxy rims of their Coca-Cola cups, hands up to the wrist in oily popcorn; they could touch each other.

There was no fear. No sympathetic fear for the actor, no straining toward poor, pretty Annabelle, brave and alone in front of us. No fear that the voice from the stage might fail. Or suddenly speak to them—"You!"

In the movie house there was no way to get in touch with that leaning forward—the hypnosis was in the image, not in the seduction by performance with its lovely implied reassurance: yes, believe, it's going fine, we won't do anything to you. Not if you know how. And of course you do.

If they saw a beautiful place in a movie they could always think, There's another place I'd like to go to. What was beautiful to see on stage was only there right then. The live space between the actors would last only while they played—it was more made of intentions than of the dusty floor (why was it always so dusty? They swept, wet-mopped, dry-mopped . . .), than of the backdrops, the scrims, the bath of light. Anya remembered her own complaint to herself that it all vanished. That was the other good element of fear in the audience. Would the place they'd heard about appear? They couldn't just watch; they must conspire.

Anya saw her theater in her imagination. She saw Mac appear on stage by day, the sun streaming through the dirty skylights as he folded up his six-foot rule, surveyed the disassembled junk, leaned to walk up the now visible rake of the stage.

How odd, she thought. Mac on stage by day was really the antithesis of theater, of performance. But he was one of the hidden forces that gave it shape. It was a neat reversal—as though Vulcan were not hidden by the dark, but by the daylight. She had put his fair midday darkness to work. She thought of him hauling in whole doors and frames, whole sides of disused sheds, pens, and cribs—fitting them onto the stage, into ramps and platforms and partitions. And although she saw him working by the cold bright daylight, muffled up in the empty, half-heated theater, it seemed that he was working with a blacksmith's heat—the heat of his concentration—exact measurements, tight scarf joints. The point of his hammering, drilling, sawing, and rasping was, oddly enough, complete quiet. Even Og, crossing, trotting up a level and flinging himself off through a door, didn't set off creaks or echoes. The set was like a piano with a damper pedal, each footfall exactly finished.

Anya found herself strangely comforted by thinking of this small point. Her instrument, her theater.

She watched another van arrive in the valley, and another half-dozen people clamber out and set to work on their site. The whole enterprise of Mercks' valley struck her again as comic. She admired Mercks' hustle—there was a vast amount of aimless physical energy in the crowd of students and hangers-around in town, and Mercks was a grown-up Tom Sawyer getting them all out here to whitewash his fence—but even her admiration made her laugh.

The car she'd seen in town outside the movie theater pulled off the hard-top road and through the gate and crossed the field on the rutted lane, jouncing on its soft springs. It came to a stop down the hill from her. Mercks got out the back door. Henniker got out the driver's door. Tassie got out the passenger's door and started waving at her.

Tassie started up the hill toward Anya but her high heels made it hard. Anya went down to her and Tassie hugged her.

"Anya, you look terrific! I love it!"

Anya was still too surprised to say anything. Tassie looked older, but Anya thought it might be her clothes, her wool suit and silk blouse.

Tassie held her at arm's length and said, "You look like a cowgirl!" Tassie laughed and squeezed Anya's hands. Tassie said, " 'Come-a ti yi yippee yippee yea,' honey." Anya laughed—it was such an old-pal, schoolgirl thing to say, and Tassie's voice—the same as ever—sounded strange. Tassie explained that they'd flown out, rented a car. Henniker was doing a magazine article.

After a moment Henniker spoke. His voice sounded even stranger. "Anya. How very convenient, we were afraid we'd have to spend days finding your—uh, spread. Lost in the corn." He laughed. "Like lost in the stars, what."

Anya had forgot that careful ironic tone.

Henniker said, "We've heard about your great successes from your friend Mr. Mercks."

Mercks piped up, "He's here doing a magazine story on my festival. Not bad, hey."

Henniker smiled. He said, "You know, I don't think my editor in New York really knows the difference between Iowa and Idaho and Ohio."

Tassie laughed. "He's been this way all day. Asking where he can change his money."

Anya looked puzzled.

Tassie said, "You know, which bank has the best exchange rates, like a foreign country . . ."

Anya said, "Oh, I see." She said to Henniker, "You're traveling on your New York passport, I gather. What happened to your job in Chicago?"

Henniker said, "That was only a two-year contract. My sentence was up a year ago."

Anya said, "Didn't you get renewed?"

Henniker cleared his throat. "I wasn't on the regular academic treadmill, just filling in as a lecturer." He looked at her. "Now I've got a much more amusing job. I'm here to bring back the report—Is there life on Mars?"

Mercks laughed loudly, and said, "Wild, that's wild."

Henniker said, "To see if anything flourishes here except corn."

Mercks laughed.

Tassie said, "You said that at breakfast."

Henniker said, "Then that should be one of our little secrets, shouldn't it?"

Tassie looked away. She rearranged her blouse collar and the sashes attached to it that were tied in a loose bow.

Anya asked Tassie if she would come have lunch.

Tassie looked to Henniker. Henniker nodded. He said, "After I see what friend Mercks is up to, I'll come get you. How do I find your *rancho grande*, Anya?"

Anya said she'd bring Tassie back.

Henniker said, "I had hoped to have a look in at your theater. Mercks here tells me it's not to be missed."

Anya said she'd give Tassie two tickets to the show. She

asked if Henniker had tickets to the movie theater to see *Iowa Girl*. Henniker looked at Mercks.

Mercks said to him, "Oh yeah, that's part of the program. And then we all go back to Ryan's party. He's staying right next to you at the Old Gold Motel. He's bringing in a whole truckload of food and stuff."

Henniker said, "I thought your Canadian friend was the head cook."

Anya said, "I see you've been busy with your research."

Henniker said, "Anya, you know how it is—I just smile and people tell me the most amazing things."

Mercks said, "Hey—you've got your ear to the ground."

Anya stopped herself. She'd been about to add, "And your eye to the keyhole." She couldn't tell if she didn't want to make bitchy remarks because that was to join his style, or whether it was because she still thought he might write something good about *Iowa Girl*.

She and Tassie walked to Anya's Volkswagen. Henniker waved good-by, maintaining his watchful smile.

Driving back to the theater, Anya asked how long Tassie had been with Henniker.

Tassie said, "Well, I've been separated from Paul for two months. And then this trip came up, and I really wanted to get out of New York, and I didn't want to just go back to Boston."

Anya thought it was an uneasy answer.

Tassie said, "It seems just what I had in mind for the moment. I mean, it's no fun—the usual affair in New York. No one has the time. Married or not, they're always on their way somewhere. I even tried to seduce my psychiatrist. I mean, at least I'd have had fifty minutes. You'd think it would have been easy. I mean from all you hear."

Tassie paused. She said, "When you were in Chicago you and Henniker . . ."

Anya said, "Yes."

After a moment Anya said, "But he must have told you."

Tassie laughed. "Yes, he did."

After a moment Tassie said, "He said he was very interested in you. But you were scared off by the rumors about him."

Anya said, "Is that what he said?"

Tassie laughed.

Anya slowed down for the narrow wooden bridge.

Tassie asked what the little sheds in the field were for. Anya said, "Pigs. I think they're called farrow pens. You'll have to ask Mac."

Tassie said, "I thought they might be jumps. You know, for horses. They look just like chicken-coop jumps."

After a moment Tassie said, "Who's Mac?"

Anya said, "You'll meet the whole group in just a minute."

Tassie said, "Oh, *I* know who Mac is."

Anya pulled into the yard and looked at the crowd of strangers. Mac and Og were carrying a kettle of soup hanging from a broom handle.

Anya could hardly believe she lived here. It was as hard to believe as her having roomed with Tassie.

Tassie got out. She went a little rigid as everyone stared at her outfit. Anya looped her arm through Tassie's and walked into the house with her.

Anya took her upstairs. She wanted to have her off by herself for a while—it wasn't attraction (although Anya felt a disembodied affection) as much as curiosity, intensified by Tassie's complete contrast to the healthy, coarse-skinned, supple women in the group. Tassie had none of her old baby fat—she was now even too thin in the face and arms. A blue tint to her face (all around the eyes, the forehead and temples, and all along the tight throat) under a wonderfully fine powder. Beautifully applied lip gloss. She moved awkwardly and abruptly. She talked fast, but her sentences quickly lost energy and volume, slouched at the end.

Anya took her up to see the view from her turret study, which was once again warmed enough by the sun to be comfortable.

Tassie looked out toward the theater barn, and then along the ridge until she was looking past Sigurd's. She said, "Now *this* is pretty. You know, I think my grandfather owned a railroad that came through Iowa."

Anya thought, Now *that's* the kind of remark that I used to adore.

But Tassie began to talk about her troubles.

The smell of Tassie's face powder, clean hair, and old perfume filled the close sunlit space. Tassie called Henniker by his first name—Norman. He was only the most recent trouble. It all was very abstract to Tassie; she saw herself the victim of anxieties—as though anxieties were ghosts roaming New York looking for her. The details of her life were harrowing enough—loneliness, Paul's coldness, her separation, more loneliness, various quick boyfriends' meannesses. But they were boring—Tassie didn't tell them very well. Until the odd weekend affair with an Egyptian member of a delegation to the U.N. who'd thought she was somebody else. Terrible confusion on a Sunday morning. His disappointment, blunt and naked. What had sent her home, however, shaken with a fear she couldn't deal with, was that he wouldn't tell her who he'd thought she was.

For the rest of that Sunday she couldn't even formulate the problem in her mind; she couldn't start to think of how it all came about, because she couldn't imagine that it was physically possible for her to have been with the man (from Friday night to Sunday noon) if she was the wrong person.

She'd tried counting the times they'd fucked—she'd thought if she could remember that she would be able to remember who she was meant to be. Tassie also said she'd felt sure that she couldn't be herself again until she knew who she wasn't.

Anya was interested in this. She asked, with a half laugh, if Tassie could explain how she untied this queer mental knot.

Tassie looked blank.

Anya said, "Well, there you are, on a dismal Sunday afternoon, trying to unravel this nonsense . . ."

Tassie said, "No. You really are . . . I can't imagine why you ask that kind of question—*that way.*"

Anya was surprised at how upset Tassie suddenly became, as though her fear recurred. Anya felt stupid, and then slightly cross at Tassie.

Anya said, "I'm sorry. I didn't mean to be unsympathetic."

Tassie said, "Well, if you're just interested in it for your amusement . . ."

Tassie lit a cigarette, and after two or three puffs the whole fishbowl space of the little turret room was filled with smoke. Tassie waved her hand at it, and then they both began to laugh and cough. Tassie opened a window, but the storm window outside it was nailed on, so they had to clamber out through the attic and down the ladder into the hall.

Anya asked Tassie if she'd like to eat lunch. Tassie said not just yet, so they went into Anya's bedroom. Tassie admired the homemade bed and canopy.

Tassie said, "Well, tell me about what you've been doing. I guess you're never lonely—it's like summer here—a couple of big houses full of people. I always liked summer best. You could always find *some*one. I even liked talking to Mummy, she could be quite funny about everyone after they'd all gone off sailing and just the two of us were sitting around."

Anya said, "How is your mother?"

Tassie said, "Oh, she's furious with me."

Anya said, "—I've always liked her. For being nice to me then. I can't imagine where her sympathy came from. But it—"

Tassie said, "Well, *every*one was nice to you as far as I could see."

Anya realized how difficult it was for Tassie to arrive here at a busy time in her (Anya's) life, a time when she was apparently successful—the theater busy—the movie about to come out. And here was Tassie—at first apparently blithe, but unable to be interested in anything but her own area of pain. And who could blame her? It was annoying, but Anya found that her annoyance passed quickly and lightly—just ripples.

Of course she couldn't say to Tassie what struck her— how the tension of rivalry and attraction that had existed between them now seemed broken for good. Anya felt the loss—she'd had fantasies of her success finally bringing her back to Tassie's admiration.

Anya said, "I suppose they were nice, but I felt it more from your mother, and you."

Tassie said, "She *can* be a sweet old bird. Of course she looks like hell now. She thought you were dangerous, you know. She thought you might do anything. But she did *like* you. She looks a little whacky now—a sort of a caricature of a gaga Boston lady trudging through the snow to get to the symphony. When did you see her last?"

Anya said, "Oh—Jeannie's wedding, I guess. My awful New York year. She looked beautiful then."

Tassie said, "You should see *Jeannie*—she has two children. She had one on the way, you know, when she got married, but she just kept at it. As though she wanted to show it wasn't a mistake. She's so earnest—she talks on and on about politics. They live in Washington and she has a new voice for discussing things, she sounds like a news commentator. Uncle Timmy took me to some do there and I stayed with her."

Tassie sat up, apparently realizing she'd brought up Uncle Timmy.

Anya said, "And how is Timmy?"

Tassie said, "Mmm—same as ever." She looked at Anya with a little glitter of pleasurable superiority. She said, "Did you ever get your dress back?"

Anya said, "Was it very difficult for him?"

Tassie said, "Well, you weren't the first, you weren't even the first she found out about. I guess he was a little squashed for a while. I'll tell you, though, she never forgave *me*. And I didn't even know for quite a while. She was frosty, but that wasn't unusual for her. But then when I was about to get married she asked me who the bridesmaids were going to be and when I got to *you*, she just came out and asked me not to invite you. So of course I guessed why. I may say, Mother asked me about you. She was sorry you couldn't come. I can't remember what I said your excuse was. I must say, Anya, you did indulge yourself a little bit close to home. I mean to say, I've managed to do a few things that weren't altogether attractive but . . ." Tassie laughed and added, "I suppose it *was* bad luck, I mean you didn't *want* anybody to know, did you . . ."

Anya recognized that Tassie's last remark contained a barb, but she doubted that Tassie meant to be shitty. Tassie seemed to have picked up the New York reflex of making fast remarks that were unsettling because they implied a certainty about real (necessarily base) motives. But in Tassie this reflex was clearly traceable to its teen-age antecedent in which a sexual implication was always good for a snort of laughter (—"What were you two doing?"—"Just talking."— "That kind of talk can get you in trouble"). Anya realized that a lot of Henniker's chat was the same kind of pouncing, except Henniker was better at it, dealt in longer and more sinuous implications.

Anya thought that the wariness necessary to that kind

of conversation would be very draining. She also thought that she would be just as bored by the antidote—sluggishly sincere metastatements ("Come on—" heavy eye contact—"Why are you being hostile?").

She realized she was tired and worried. She asked Tassie again to go down and have lunch.

When they got to the kitchen, Anya felt Tassie flinch from the crowd in the yard. She set places for the two of them at the kitchen table, and explained to Tassie who all the people were. Tassie appeared to have thought they all worked for Anya. Mac came in and sat down.

As all three of them sat and talked, Anya had the feeling that she had a lens to her eye which could diminish or enlarge Tassie, depending on which end she used.

Mac got up to cook some eggs for them. Anya thought he looked deformed. Part of it was the clothes he was wearing. With the sleeves of his old fatigue shirt rolled up, his forearms and hands appeared overdeveloped. It gave them a clumsy, monkey look. He was wearing cut-off khaki pants, crudely hemmed across his thighs. He wore his high-top work shoes with old stretched-out wool socks hanging over the leather like sagging flower petals. The pants and shirt were both so baggy and wrinkled there was no way to guess the whole lines and proportions of his body —just the stubs, the kneecaps rising out of heavy muscle like apricot halves decorating pork. Mac turned back to the gas stove. Anya watched his calf muscles divide as he stooped to look at the flame under the pan. He flicked in a drop of water from a cup to see if the pan was hot enough to make the drop bounce. Anya knew if Tassie hadn't been there he would have spit.

Mac poured in the eggs, picked the pan up at arm's length, stepped back and then forward—a two-step shuffle —and rolled it around to make the liquid spread out. She and Tassie watched.

Anya said, "Mac's omelettes seem to depend on footwork."

Mac presented the first omelette to Tassie. She said, "Oh, it's lovely—just a little *baveuse*." She turned to keep talking to Mac, who was back at the stove. "Were you in fact a boxer?"

Mac said, "No."

Tassie said, "Well, there is an air about you. What was Anya talking about? Footwork. You *did* break your nose?"

"Yes."

Anya smiled to herself. She thought, of all the unlikely times to flirt with Mac. While he was still wearing a hair shirt from his fall with Dulcie.

Tassie said, "Well, you have an athletic look I don't recognize. I mean I usually recognize, say, squash players. And there's a kind of stringy look to people who hunt—I mean, all the time—they begin to look like their horses. What *did* you do?"

Mac said, "Hockey."

Tassie said, "Oh, I *love* hockey!—you mean *ice* hockey."

"Yes."

"Oh, I *adore* it. Were you any good?" Tassie smiled at her charming impertinence.

Anya said, "He was all-American."

Tassie said, "Oh, well—my gracious—"

Mac slid Anya's omelette in front of her.

Tassie said, "I used to go to all the Harvard games, did you ever play against Harvard?"

"Yes."

"Oh, I must have seen you! Well, I must say you certainly keep in shape."

Anya could see that Mac was embarrassed and slightly irritated. Irritated that Tassie wasn't eating her omelette and that she was speaking to him as though to a strange being, a foreigner or a servant—fingering her pearls and over-enunciating.

Tassie said, "Well, and here you are now—you're one of the actors?"

Mac said, "I'm the cook."

Tassie laughed with polite gaiety. Mac didn't laugh. Tassie was at a loss. She took a bite of her omelette. She said, "Well, it's absolutely delicious!"

Anya broke out laughing.

Dulcie came in and stood waiting for a chance to get Anya's attention.

Anya tried to think of some way of soothing Tassie's hurt feelings. She said, "Mac, why don't you come along with us and show Tassie around the theater. You know the way it's set up for this show better than I do."

Dulcie said, "I'm sorry, but the dry cleaner's truck came

this morning, and he's mad because there was personal laundry mixed in with the costumes. He says that's not part of the deal he gave you and he wants to talk to you."

Anya said, "How could he tell? What was in that batch? Did you look it over?"

Dulcie said, "Yes. It's a bunch of sweaters and blankets, I think they're Og's and Annabelle's."

Anya said, "Well, you tell him you're the costume mistress and you're in charge, and it won't happen again. It's just as much in our interest to keep it straight. You can do that. Is he still there?"

Dulcie said, "No. He asked for you to call him up."

Anya said, "You can do that, you're the one to keep it straight. You talk to Og and Annabelle and get them to pay up."

Dulcie nodded and left, and Anya got up and followed her onto the porch and stopped her by touching her arm.

Anya said, "I'm sorry. This is such a chaotic weekend."

Dulcie said, "I feel such shame. Toward you."

Anya shuddered—she remembered the coil of self-loathing she'd felt after she'd faced Timmy's wife. She had a sharp memory of that basilisk look.

Dulcie and Mac seemed now to Anya to be far in the past. Across an ice age. Anya thought this feeling probably came from having seen them every day. Anya's strongest feeling for Dulcie was a pity that swung back and forth between contempt and awe. Dulcie had lost (in descending order) her child, her husband, and her best friend by fucking him. Anya thought both of them silly and self-serious for their air of wearing ashes on their foreheads, but at least it drew a clean line.

Anya held on to Dulcie's arm and walked to the road with her, and then down the road a few steps. They stopped.

Anya thought, This is a way I could never be, I could never feel the way she feels or do what she's doing.

Anya tried again to imagine herself as Dulcie at that moment. The closest she could come was to imagine how she appeared to Dulcie. So Anya only succeeded in feeling scared of herself, which struck her as funny. And then not quite right—Dulcie wasn't scared of *her* the way she'd been scared by Timmy's wife.

Anya said, "Well, don't worry, it's not so bad. It seems a long time ago."

It occurred to Anya that perhaps Dulcie was still struggling with some desire, or echoes of desire, for Mac.

Anya knew she couldn't ask Dulcie.

She became irritated at them both for their blindness toward their own feelings.

Dulcie said, "I don't think I could be as forgiving as you."

Anya was irritated further—a formal irritation. She thought that Dulcie was assuming that the declaration of forgiveness had been spoken. Anya thought this was so unlike herself as to be funny, too.

Anya said, "It's not a matter of my good heart—it's just the way it's happened."

Dulcie said in a drowsy, dreamy way, "Anya, you're so practical."

Anya finally laughed out loud.

Dulcie blushed. She opened her mouth to explain, closed it, and blushed more fiercely. Her fair skin seemed to grow dark in the bright light surrounding them. Light falling from the pale spring sky and the unripe sun, reflected up from the chalky surface of the road.

Anya said, "No, it's okay." They let go of each other's hands.

Walking back to Raftery's house, Anya thought again of her new feeling of weight—it *did* make her *practical*. It absorbed a lot of the variation that used to make her bounce around, skitter. She and Dulcie had moved closer to each other—it had nothing to do with Mac.

She thought, Dulcie has the courage of her weaknesses. But there was no one to whom she could repeat the remark.

Anya wondered how Dulcie had felt, how she'd felt herself tempted. Probably not much fun. Probably all in a state of shock.

But Anya realized she wasn't concentrating on it. She'd been afraid at first that she wouldn't be able to keep from thinking about it. Now she was surprised at how unconcentrated her thoughts were. Perhaps *that* was forgiving.

She supposed she was happy—pleased with her pace, her momentum, her connection to the movement around her.

CHAPTER

██████████████████████

27

Her happiness persisted during the next day. She and Mac
went over to the festival. She hung on his arm. They both
laughed at some of the events. Bacchanalia #2—four modern dancers flinging themselves about and bursting little bags
of animal blood over themselves and smearing it around
with their fingers. The costumes were fur loincloths and
sheepskins held over the girls' fronts with thongs which
came loose, apparently by design. When the four dancers
all collapsed in a heap with their half-attached furs and
blood-smeared skin, they looked, as Mac said, like a pile
of badly skinned rabbits.

Anya and Mac ran into Henniker and Tassie on their
way out of the dome. Tassie introduced Henniker to Mac.
Mac said, "We've met." Henniker looked surprised and
said, "Really?" He lowered his sunglasses and peered over
them. Anya thought the gesture didn't quite come off and
was embarrassed for Tassie. Tassie said brightly, "What
did you think of all that? Maybe they should have called
it corpse de ballet."

Anya laughed helpfully, and said to her that Mac had
said they looked like skinned rabbits.

Tassie said, "Oh, Mac! How gruesome! You're awful!"

Henniker said, "Oh, I'm sure he didn't mean to be."

Mac cocked his head and looked puzzled. Anya saw the
base of his neck thicken. She thought it would be satisfying
to see Mac take a swing at Henniker, but only momentarily.

Anya looped her arm through Mac's and said, "Mac and
I have to do some things."

Anya and Mac walked up to the barn where *Hail Holy Queen* was about to be shown. Anya had heard of this film. It had been an underground item, part of it had been filmed at the festival the year before.

Anya asked Mac if he'd been thinking of punching Henniker. Mac said, "No." He was surprised. He said, "Disgust is not a good reason to hit someone like that. If he'd come right out—but it's all furtive and halfway. Like the time he nailed your shoes to the floor." Mac snorted. "He's like some crazy burglar who breaks in at night and shits on the rug."

Anya said, "Well, you can't expect him to act like a defenseman for the Boston Bruins. Why should he? He has no reason to have an interest in physical courage. Or any old-fashioned notion for that matter—everything is subordinate to his working on his own sensibility. If someone said to you you're a coward you'd get furious. Or if someone called you a liar. Or lazy. Now that I think of it, there are a thousand ways to insult you. But for him there's only his sensibility, and even that is—as you say—never completely exposed. If someone said to him you're a cowardly, lying, lazy parasite I doubt if he'd even say no. I guess he'd think you were a clod for not knowing everything is justified by his artistic sensibility." Anya laughed. "Which nobody can deny. All he has to do is show some symptoms. It's a way of being Byron without actually writing poetry. Or actually going to Greece."

Mac was looking at the stills from *Hail Holy Queen* on the side of the barn. He said, "Look. That's Ergenbright's. That's his barn with the balloon flying over it."

Anya looked. She wasn't sure.

Mac said, "Sure it is. It's the north side. That's why you can't tell."

Anya thought with a twinge that Mac was good at remembering what he saw—if he saw Dulcie's foot ten years from now he'd know it. But, she thought, he has to pay for it—it would break his heart to leave Iowa, it would break his heart to leave Raftery's house. It suddenly occurred to Anya that perhaps part of the reason Mac had given in to Dulcie (Anya preferred that formulation) was that he shared Dulcie's loss of Hugh and therefore Dulcie's need to be comforted. A blind need. For all his acuteness in seeing the physical world, Mac was often blind to his feelings. No, she thought. He's blind to the beginnings of his feelings. When they arrive, he sees nothing else.

She herself could see the slightest stirring in herself. She had to rely on other people for surprises. She looked at Mac's hand against the board beside the photograph. She remembered thinking, He can't keep his hands off Hugh. It had been an expression of her irritation then.

She tried to imagine what it would be like to have Mac's hands, that sense of touch. She succeeded only in *seeing* his hands—she pictured them paddling a canoe—the long pull ending with a short flicked J-stroke, an unconscious habit, the canoe gliding straight. A kind of tactile perfect pitch.

She admired it now. It used to irritate her to watch his hands at work on a set—the regular tempo, the habitual tug or shove to test a fastened joint. She'd wanted to whip him along, to scream, "Just get the fucking thing up! You're not building *furniture*, for Chrissake!" But it had annoyed her as much to see him reach for his hammer without looking at it. Set the nail with a delicate tap, then whack it in with two shots. It had been the same annoyance she'd felt watching a blind man set his cup carefully on the table edge, return to it later slipping his finger neatly through the handle.

But now she was in sympathy with his hands. She couldn't imagine how she'd been offended by his hands that morning—dangling from his sleeves. Apelike, she'd thought. No, the grain of the skin was too fine. Even along the top of the palm where the grain was obliterated, the color was attractive—each callus a circle of amber with white shreds where the skin had begun to wear away.

She felt comfortable with her sentiment. She'd concentrated so hard on her movie that now there was a backwash of vague sappiness. Her own habit of concentration, without the control now, kept surprising her—the play of light on almost any object brought her close to tears.

She hung on Mac's arm again when they went into the movie. She watched it happily, uncritically. *Hail Holy Queen*—blasphemous farce, a little sophomoric, zany. Parts of it beautifully shot. The twelve apostles in robes chasing after Mary—or was it Mary Magdalene? Through the swamp near the Coralville Reservoir (that favorite locale of her film class), through fields, through an old stone and plaster house. Mary—suddenly topless—ascending harnessed to a balloon, flapping a set of preposterous wings, swooping away downwind. Lovely shots of the river, the oak forest along it, and then a long, slow pictorial ode to the Iowa landscape, which at first made Anya wince with jealous possessiveness, but then filled her with a puff of relief: She hadn't exaggerated what she'd done, someone else had seen it too—the crazy precision of sections and right-angle roads imposed on the swells of the earth, across the intricate fern patterns of rivulets, creeks, branches, rivers. The upright frame houses flung a half mile or a mile apart in the blanks of black earth. Visible democracy.

Ten miles of wire to divide a square mile into forty-acre fields. How many miles of furrows? This linear regularity set off by the more intricate regularity of running water. And by the slow wandering figures of pigs, cows, people— and machines. The bottled-gas delivery truck crawling ahead of its plume of dust. And the covert life that wasn't subject to the rule—a cock pheasant just squeezing through a mesh of the wire and then rocketing into the air with an ugly squawk—red-combed and wattled, its short head feathers iridescent green, ring-necked in pure white, trailing its ornamental tail feathers. Cousin to the peacock, it was too exotic for the weathered stalks, grass, or snowdrifts it burst from. Imported from China. Mac had told her— where had Mac learned that? His six-volume bird book. Not a migratory bird, transported by man. She'd believed the Chinese part right away—the birds had all the disconcerting beauty of a Chinese junk: fierce eyes framed in enamel red.

And feral cats and starlings—more imports. Everything that couldn't fit through the six-inch squares of hog wire had moved on. No—a few deer in what was left of the woods. Mac had showed her the snow-cast hoofprints of a deer who had jumped the shoulder-high wire. At least thirty feet through the air. Mac said he'd seen longer. But he also said that deer weren't any wilder than rabbits, squirrels, pigeons. Back-yard animals he called them. He admired their adaptability, but not their wildness.

She'd been interested in all those signs of life up to a point, and then she'd resisted his layers of information. It had made her feel restless. She didn't want to be familiar with the whole place the way Mac did. She'd loved it for completely different reasons. Now, she thought, she was

420

bound to leave. Making the movie had been like shedding a skin—not just slithering out of the impressions the place had marked on her, but out of all she'd seen in Peewee that was her own past.

She was tired, and a new appetite seemed the only thing that would revive her.

What she couldn't get straight was why she suddenly felt so ravenously tender toward Mac. She hung on his arm again as they left the movie barn. She could see the difficulty, but she didn't feel it at all, only as easy brimming generosity, and not just toward Mac, but to all of the group. It was much more than the thin electric affection of being backstage together.

Mac said, "Do you want to go all the way home to eat? Or shall we wait till Ryan's? We're going to the nine o'clock show, right?"

Anya said, "Let's go for a walk. We can get popcorn at the movies." She laughed, thinking of herself as her own bad audience.

Mac said, "Shouldn't we change clothes?"

Anya said, "It's not Grauman's Chinese. It's just going into town to see another movie." She felt she ought to feel that.

Mac said, "What about for Ryan's party?"

Anya said, "I don't know. I guess we should go back to help drive the troops in to Ryan's . . . I don't know why I'm resisting seeing you dressed up in a coat and tie. I can't tell if it's superstitious compulsion to be casual or a feeling we can do no wrong."

Mac said, "I don't care about that—I'm just worried that you're too nervous to eat."

Anya said, "I like being nervous. I've *seen* the movie. What fun would I have if I *wasn't* nervous?"

* * *

But when the house lights went down in Ryan's movie theater, Anya had a moment of panic. She was suddenly certain that there was a terrible flaw in the movie that was so exactly like a flaw in her own intelligence that she had been unable to see it—a terrible flaw that would be laughably clear to everyone sitting around her.

She thought if she laughed first no one would know who she was.

She looked around to see where the exits were.

The credits came on and her panic stopped. She felt wonderful. She didn't care. She loved being this nervous. There was no other way to be.

The noise of the tractor came out of the predawn fog. Then the pale headlights. Anya thought it was splendid.

Mac said, "I remember this day."

The person next to him said, "Shh."

Anya sank down in her seat, suddenly and unaccountably bored.

The film rolled through her like a dream. A morning dream she was almost able to edit, but which slipped on to new scenes before she could quite make up her mind.

She tried to keep track of the noises she heard the audience make. It was like a bad sound track—words and noises blurred and overlapping, the background full of choppy crests in which the crucial whisperings were drowned.

She was even more baffled by the laughter. There were some comic scenes—the Mercks character's helter-skelter shooting of *his* scenes for the porn movie. The Mercks character and Peewee at the meat counter of the supermarket casting the beef tongue. Tagh asking the butcher to unwrap the tongue, as though it were a showgirl's legs. They leave the supermarket. The store is part of the sudden growth of the town; the parking lot is right on the edge of a cornfield. The laughter continued through the exterior long shot—which Anya had always thought was one of the most beautiful pictures—the fluorescent supermarket sign and parking-lot lights reduced and precise against the huge, violet sky. The black asphalt giving way to the blacker earth. Anya had thought it was an eerie picture, as mysterious and full as a Hopper painting.

Who was laughing? Were they all laughing? Was it just the men? The boys in varsity windbreakers? Couldn't they see while they were laughing?

These questions recurred—but Anya had given up—when Peewee was taken in by her Spanish teacher/lover. Peewee read aloud to the Spanish teacher the letter from the dean in which the dean wrote that Peewee was on probation for having tried to commit suicide—and that if she tried it again she would be expelled. Laugh. But it wasn't meant to get these hoots of glee and easy antiuniversity applause.

Anya realized that a dean of women was always good for a laugh. Like nuns, policemen on foot, or men in top hats used to be. She should have known.

Anya had to force herself to keep watching.

It occurred to her that there was a great deal in her work that was perverse and antagonistic. She often brought scenes close to farce or close to sentimentality, and then reversed the flow. She'd always thought of these reversals as attempts to pry out the feelings that lay in the seams between the categories—attempts to find some other way of moving from comic to pathetic than the stock pause that telegraphed a change in tempo.

But her quick zigzag through some of these scenes struck her as an attempt to lose the dumb half of the audience, to make the bright half try harder.

She hoped she was only accusing herself of this because she was sliding into a trough after her elation at the beginning.

Anya stopped watching the picture, but she heard Peewee's long voice-over. Sitting on the window sill looking at her bare feet hanging in the air above the ugly, mottled branches of a sycamore.

Tagh and his gang passed by, saw Peewee, and yelled up at her. The voice-over went on.

"I knew they were going to do just one more dumb thing, I don't know, put speed in the cat's food, some dumb thing. Say something dumb—they weren't really that dumb, it was just that they didn't *mind* being dumb. You know, being dumb was part of their style. If you're cool and dumb, then nothing bad can happen. But it bothered me just then, I'd been just about to feel good, so I didn't say anything."

One of the gang—"Is she stoned?"

—"Hey, Peewee!"

—"Peeee-wee!"

Tagh stood by the tree and sang a Mexican song to her.

Peewee's voice-over—"I could feel his singing—it was one of those Mexican songs from our trip—I could feel his singing right through my feet, as if his mouth was that close to my feet. But—I don't know. He wasn't alone. He was just screwing around with his buddies. I *knew* for sure I was more interested in what I'd been about to think, not even think, just feel, all by myself. His coming by made me feel like balling, of course. That was the same."

The gang moved on.

"But when I was alone again"—Peewee laughed—"I thought, Shit, I'd just as soon wait. I thought, Maybe I'm getting a flashback. But it was just me."

Anya looked up to watch Peewee touch her ankles, then her legs. She rubbed her knee with her thumb and then rolled forward, jumped out the window, and grabbed a branch. She pulled herself up and lay across the branch on her stomach.

Her voice said, "That was just one more dumb thing, too. But it made me laugh. No. It made me feel like it was next week."

The boy next to Anya said, "What the hell . . ."

Anya thought, That was a bit that really happened to Peewee—but it doesn't make any difference that it really happened.

Then came the short period of Peewee's wandering about Iowa City watching groups.

The boy next to Anya laughed a lot through the shots of the sorority singsong—the windows of the sorority house suddenly lit by the sisters, each wearing a "formal" and each holding a candle—singing out to the pledges huddled on the sidewalk "For you belong to Alpha Kappa, and Alpha Kappa belongs to you."

And the rehearsal of the University of Iowa all-girl bagpipe band. Looking very sweet and earnest, puffing away on their pipes—which, as Mac had pointed out, were not full-size.

Reappearance of Tagh's group.

Rehearsal of the Berlioz *Requiem* by the Iowa Chorus and Orchestra. *Lacrymosa* segment. Peewee outside the rehearsal hall in the sun, at first peering in the window at the faces of the singers, the orchestra, the trombone player shaking the spit out of her mouthpiece. Then Peewee lying in the sun trickling dirt from one hand to the other.

Anya noticed the sound was at last up to full on this theater's speaker system. She had a sudden flutter of panic —she couldn't remember whether Ikon had paid the royalty for the use of the recording, or even whether she'd remembered to tell them.

The music stopped.

For some reason Peewee's voice calmed Anya.

"I had no idea what any of this was—what that music was—what all the people around me were doing. I knew I was ignorant, I'd known I was ignorant before, but for the first time since I knew it, I didn't think it was my fault. It was because I lived in the middle—so far from the edge of anything. Even if my family was no great shakes at doing anything, we were never near the edge of anything, of starving or anything."

Peewee walked to her Spanish teacher's house.

"But I began to pay attention to all the things going on in Iowa City, and I couldn't see what they had to do with each other."

The Spanish teacher began to fuss over her. Brought her a glass of lemonade. Peewee accepted it, let the woman hover, shyly sit next to her. Peewee rolled back on the sofa.

"My Spanish teached laughed at me and then got mad because I said to her once when she was getting worked up about something and said it was as bad as Hitler—and I said to her, 'What's so bad about Hitler? You think you know everything but maybe there's something worse you just haven't heard of.'

"She just jumped down my throat.

"So I said to her where did she get off knowing anything for sure. And then I thought I should get the dumb bitch to really freak out so I said—'Hitler was just doing his thing.' "

The Spanish teacher kissed the palm of Peewee's hand.

Peewee's voice-over finished: "But all she did then was cry."

Anya realized where that scene came from—it was one she'd cooked up out of fragments of Peewee's talk, but it was also an old scene between Tassie and her—Tassie as Peewee, herself as the Spanish teacher. She was surprised she hadn't seen that before. Tassie dumb but wily, accepting foolish adoration.

There were a few people laughing in the theater. Anya couldn't tell whether they were laughing at the voice-over or the silently smitten, awkward teacher. But Anya thought the edge of Peewee's most cruel and terrifying side had glittered for a second. As it had to before she used that edge on Mercks.

Anya thought it had been very lucky—it made sense to her only now to have the Spanish teacher be so much more than the caricature she'd started as. She was the victim who kept Peewee from being the victim.

When it was over a few people applauded. Mac took it up, but the houselights came on, and it died of the futility of applauding a blank screen.

She went out the side door with Mac. She was excited, but she found it hard to walk—she felt sore, as though she'd strained all her muscles.

*   *   *

In the car, Anya said to Mac, "That was sweet, your clapping. Your claque-work. Your claque-work orange . . . You're really getting to be show-biz, honey."

Mac looked straight ahead. He said, "It's very good." He paused. "If you're not too tired, I'll talk to you later on."

"I'm too tired already. What I need now is—do you remember when we used to be driving along—the first time we drove out here from Chicago—and we couldn't keep our hands off each other . . ."

Anya saw that she'd made Mac uneasy. She wasn't sure why—that he'd failed to preserve that exact excitement? It was a despondent side of him that she found most curious —his hating to see anything disappear. Or was it only that he grew restless when she spoke carelessly of their feelings? (But she wasn't careless, only tired.)

Everyone was dressed up and waiting when they got to the theater after they'd changed. It was a very odd sight, all of them in their best clothes. Andrew had brought Dulcie up from the other house. She was wearing a long, Madonna-blue dress Andrew had bought her at a boutique in town. She looked very young and fragile, her short hair brushed straight back.

Annabelle, Alice, Babette, and Peewee looked shiny, leggy, and hard, their eyes drawn wide and pointed with liner. Peewee was no longer a stray. One of the actresses now.

Andrew and Dulcie got in the back of Anya's car; the rest of them piled into the Wagoneer.

Anya caught a glimpse of Dulcie's face in the rear-view

mirror as the turning Wagoneer's lights swept through the Volkswagen. And again, when they reached the lights at the level crossing at the end of town, and again in the middle of town. The theater district, Anya thought, and laughed. Then glanced again in the mirror.

Dulcie's was the only soft face left among the women, the only one not lined with—acting? control? Dulcie's face was taut, all the lines thin and clear, but the expression was soft as a wandering child's. Was it ground soft by sorrow?

When they reached the lobby, Anya looked in a mirror. Her own face was impenetrable, set.

They all made a great hit when they arrived in Ryan's suite. He'd invited a gang of his business friends down from Des Moines—they were openly, wonderfully, curious to meet the troupe. They were not disappointed—they were visibly struck by the bright tension, the element of pose—as though the lights had come up on the floor show.

Andrew held a cornerful of Ryan's friends with a story—warming to his audience, his hands blooming with gestures. It was the overdramatic trilled charm they expected. The three men facing him laughed. Their politeness and warmness half-melted. She could imagine them thinking, Hey, this little fella's all right.

Henniker entered into a conversation with Ray. Anya could see Henniker getting furious; Ray was giving him the standard gracious-actor routine.

Ray said, "Did you have good seats?—Could you hear all right?—It's a wonderful, wonderful play, I'm happy you came to see it."

Henniker said, "I'm afraid it's a very difficult play to do in translation."

Their two balding heads separated.

Anya watched Mac standing by the bar. She hadn't ever seen him in a white shirt—he looked like Sigurd going to church, his face and hands too fierce for his clothes.

The manager of the Des Moines NET station recognized her, came over and asked her about one-acts that would fit into half-hour time slots. She told him *Jacques* would go, and they could do O'Casey's *Bedtime Story*—she said he should speak to Andrew.

Anya's heart wasn't in it.

The man said he'd heard the review of *Iowa Girl* in the *Des Moines Register* was going to be good.

Anya said, "Good."

The man said, "It's very lucky, they generally avoid movies with explicit sex."

Anya said, "Oh, a lot of that was cut. Besides, the point was more antisex, wasn't it? I suppose that's a hard point to make in Des Moines."

The man said, "I understand, I understand."

Anya knew she'd spoken too sharply. She couldn't help it.

She drifted back near Andrew. Andrew was still holding his audience.

Andrew said, "Sigurd wanted to see the film that was shot on his place and we sent him a ticket, but he came to the barn theater instead of the movie house in town. So he saw the play. Just as well in some ways—he would have been upset by the film." The three men stirred uneasily. But Anya guessed that Andrew's flattery of their sophistication would take. Andrew said, "Sigurd pronounces it 'fil-um,' as in 'all my el-ums died of Dutch el-um disease.' "

Polite laughter. The Des Moines businessmen knew they weren't farmers.

"I *wish* you could see the play. Anytime you want the house seats, just let me know. In a word, the play is about a king who is told he is dying. At first he doesn't believe it. 'Why me? I'm not ready!' He rages and cringes and blusters . . . It's actually funny in a way, and then in that brilliant way that Ionesco has it moves from that comic phase—a sort of Braque or Picasso painting of a Feydeau farce—into something even richer . . . The whole stage becomes the sensate mind of the poor king.

"Anyway— Sigurd Olson has never seen a play in his life and—having spent, as I said, six weeks in the hospital with stomach cancer—in he walks on this. Wham!"

Andrew screwed his fingertips into his forehead and spun around. He ended up facing his audience again, his knees sagging, his arms dangling, head to one side.

He held the pose for a beat. Then he straightened up and said, "Believe me—he got every . . . single . . . word. I mean every *syllable* of meaning. When I talked to him afterwards he wasn't worried about what country it was supposed to be, why the king had two wives—not bothered at all by the hyperbole, surrealism. What he had was *fusion*.

428

Ionesco and Sigurd Olson. Sigurd just plain got it. He didn't have to say, 'That could be me and my farm.' He just got it. Now *that* is success."

The three men loved it. Anya herself thought Andrew was laying it on thick, but there was no question that the three men were pleased to get a story they could take home.

It occurred to Anya that Andrew was leading up to getting these men to back *Exit the King* in Des Moines. She thought that would be fine. But when had Andrew got back his will? his authority? his directorship? There was no question but that he had, and she was surprised she was so pleased. It even gave her pleasure to think of Andrew as the cultural darling of Ryan's gang. He would be much better for them—and *with* them—than she could be.

Of *course* she was happy about Andrew. She would be less embarrassed now to strike out on her own.

Had Andrew *really* needed her in the first place? Had the troupe really needed her?

She thought with a sudden weight that she had certainly needed them. She had needed Iowa. The space and time to enlarge herself, to shed her constricting shell of being eastern—of being a courtier. Of being part of the high-speed jockeying for temporary small advantage. Of tuning her taste to the shrill exaggeration of concert pitch. Of wasting time and energy on the alarms that necessarily afflicted her when she'd been one of the dependents of someone else's enterprise.

She supposed there were a lot of circumstances that would have served her as well—any colony of easterners in any state west of the Mississippi. Provided, of course, the colony mixed in, rooted in. She'd needed Peewee, Mercks, Raftery, Ryan, Iowa City as much as she'd needed the troupe.

And Mac.

And had Mac found anything? Had he found anything that he wanted, that he needed, that was good for him? Or had she brought him here and turned him into a specialist in her affairs who would be useless to anyone else?

It was odd—she could only sense him in balance with herself. It was *absurd*—she knew that Raftery and Andrew loved him (and Mac himself told her he loved Sigurd, Sigurd's farm . . .), but in her feelings she held him alone,

429

away from other people and things. And at arm's length from herself.

Was Mac going to be a piece of Iowa? She guessed that Mac had guessed that she was bound to leave Iowa.

For the first time she was afraid of her own hardheartedness, not only because it made her ashamed, but also because it might harm her in a way she couldn't foresee. None of her measurements reached far enough.

She was surprised at what the absence of measurement revealed to her—about her. She'd always thought she was shrewd. She realized now that even when she couldn't predict the risk she wanted to try the next step. She *didn't* know why. She'd thought she'd know why. It terrified her to think that her ambition was uncontrollable. That her ambition was not, after all, part of her intelligence, her talent, or her craft—that it was deep-rooted, childish, possibly crazy—that it might even betray her.

She felt as though her flesh was preparing to leave her bones.

But almost instantly she felt herself contract, click back together.

Something made her feel like laughing. What it was became clear to her. Although she was terrified at the picture of herself she'd just seen, she realized she also admired it. A part of her was a mad alpinist. It was not any specific desire that made her ambitious. It was an almost physical impulse to make the next move, to add one more astounding maneuver. The safe part of her life was roped to this alpinist. Good. She found the idea deeply, physically gratifying.

She thought that it was even possible that she would be happier now that her ambition could have a medium other than her own life.

*   *   *

The party was a success for Ryan. When Anya talked to him near the end, he was filled with princely sentiment.

He said, "Anya, I want to give something to you. Not to the theater. To you. I think you know what it is, but I want you to tell me."

Anya knew what he meant, but she thought of the small

430

statue of Leda and the Swan in Timmy's apartment in New York.

She said, "If I was sure you'd forget it by the morning, I'd tell you."

He said, "Well, I know what it is. It's the painting of the dead bull." He laughed. "I'm right. I know I'm right."

Anya said, "That's too much——"

Ryan said, "Well, look here now——our Mr. Danziger tells me I'm going to make a little something, so I'm feeling pretty good. I thought I was just having fun and it turns out I've done some business . . ."

Anya said, "No more fun, huh?" She didn't want to talk to him at this time.

Ryan said, "No——now you get to the real fun. What we're going to do next."

Anya said, "Yes, that's the spirit." He was right, but she didn't feel ready for his idea of what next before she'd thought of her own.

Tassie came over to her and drew her aside. She said, "Will you kindly do something about that redheaded bitch of yours." Anya was startled.

Tassie said in a less vehement tone, "Norman is very upset about his work, and traveling makes him nervous, and he really can't help the way he is, so I hope you're going to take your gang out of here soon."

Anya said, "You mean Annabelle? Where are they?"

Tassie said, "In the next room. At the moment."

Anya said, "Well, okay. I mean, if it really bothers you." She knew that was a dumb thing to say. She was distressed for Tassie, found it pathetic and embarrassing that Tassie turned to her. She was of course also annoyed that Tassie implied that she, Anya, was somehow to blame. And annoyed that Tassie assumed that the rest of the party should be ordered to deal with her problem.

Anya found them and told Annabelle that Ryan wanted to meet her.

When Anya brought Annabelle to Ryan, Og veered over to her and stood sullenly by.

But Tassie didn't want to be with Henniker. She took Anya into the bathroom and began to tell her the second installment of her troubles.

Anya listened with some effort. Tassie was, although

more frantic, also more lucid than she'd been the day before. What Tassie was saying made perfect sense, Tassie grasped the direction of her own life, the drain of her energy, the reasons for her apathy and depression. Tassie argued with intelligence from her givens, drew the hard conclusion that there was very little hope.

Anya, now numb with fatigue, sat on the edge of the washbasin while Tassie sat on the closed toilet lid. From premise to Q.E.D. Tassie knew the subject well; it was a subject she took seriously; she presented it forcefully. Anya found it funny and sad that Tassie's brightest moment was so narrowly walled in.

Tassie waited for Anya to reply. Anya thought about what Tassie said.

Get rid of Henniker? It was no use. Tassie disliked loneliness more than Henniker, and everyone else she knew found her too demanding or boring. Henniker took an interest in her.

There was also a money problem. Tassie's father paid her psychiatrist's bills, but he wouldn't give her any other money. The income from her trust wasn't enough to support herself and Henniker in New York. It was less than eight thousand a year. The alimony she got from Paul was fifteen thousand. Henniker had got a grant for six thousand dollars, but that had disappeared, Tassie didn't know how. If he didn't sell the article he was writing, Tassie didn't know what he'd do. She couldn't touch capital till she was thirty. She couldn't bear to sell the house. Where would they live? Trust income, grant, alimony—all gone.

Anya knew it wouldn't do any good to point out that twenty-three thousand dollars was a lot. That what Tassie spent on restaurants alone was equal to Anya's personal income.

Tassie said, "I envy you your knack with money. I suppose it goes with your knack for work . . ."

Anya was not offended. It was part of Tassie's brilliant insensitivity. Anya wished to do something for Tassie. She couldn't think of anything.

Anya looked at Tassie's face. Tassie's eyes met hers— Anya felt the shock of Tassie's gaze—a helpless, nervous excitement. Tassie's eyes seemed filled with motion and power, seemed to be sucking particles of light into the crystal of her irises. Dizzying . . . It was like watching a green winter river through a break in the ice—the water seeming to hold still, shimmering with small delicacy, only the larger movement of shadow beneath the green light gave away the enormous rush in darkness.

Tassie said, "What should I do?" A faint prompting.

Anya looked at Tassie's face again. The bones seemed to have tightened. She was beautiful. But all this intense beauty seemed unconnected—unconnected to Anya, unconnected to what Tassie had been saying, unconnected to Tassie herself—as though Tassie's beauty had fed on the feelings of Tassie's life, had absorbed the energy of her feelings and wishes and rendered them into these moments of beauty, signals of itself, that flashed out through her.

For an instant Anya suspected that Tassie knew what she was doing, knew her own beauty as well as she knew her misery.

The suspicion was swept away.

Certainly Tassie knew what she was doing—but she was helpless in her own motion and what she knew did not reach beyond herself.

The signal of Tassie's beauty stopped.

Tassie stood up and kissed Anya.

Anya felt sorry for Tassie. Anya imagined she could smell the harsh, chilled gloom in Tassie's life—the small, elaborate house which her husband had abandoned to her, the waiting rooms of her lawyer, her psychiatrist, the front hall of her parents' summer house where she was uneasily received.

It was a tentative kiss—Tassie's lips parted slightly after they touched Anya's—Anya felt the small movement of her own lips being brushed apart. That was all. The sensation was blocked by a general numbness.

Anya thought that this second interview—more powerful and evocative than the one in her workroom—had roused all the feelings of the past, only to reduce them. Tassie hurtled back into the past, vanished, and reappeared in a miniature Cambridge, a miniature Boston, a miniature New York.

Tassie sat down again. She folded her arms, her hands tucked under her armpits. She seemed to Anya to be in fact chilled, as though her storytelling and then the uncontrollable occurrence of her beauty had passed through her and drained her of heat.

After a while, they heard a noise outside the door, someone clearing his throat. Tassie said, "Just a minute," and they left.

As the troupe gathered to leave the party, Tassie came up to Anya again. Tassie said, "I'm sorry—I didn't say—I thought your movie was well done." She said this carefully. Then she added, "I'm sorry—but it was also very cold."

CHAPTER

||||||||||||||||||||||||||||||||||

28

Anya got a message to call Mr. Danziger. She drove to a pay phone in town rather than use the phone at the theater.

Mr. Danziger had some details to chat about, but Anya guessed he was leading up to something.

He told her about a review in a trade journal that compared *Iowa Girl* to *The Savage Eye,* a semidocumentary of a distraught woman's life in Los Angeles. Anya remembered seeing it her first year at Radcliffe. She hadn't loved it, thought it was a little slow. She thought, What did I know then? Would I have liked *Iowa Girl?*

Distribution, Mr. Danziger said, was okay. Anya was interested that the movie was scheduled for the Brattle Theater in Cambridge—it would have seemed wonderful to her some time ago (she could still picture the tiny marquee, and the old-fashioned green awning jutting out to the curb, the line of students along the uneven brick sidewalk), but she'd uncorked the hope too long before the event—now it was a little flat.

Mr. Danziger said, "I'll tell you, Anya, I was sorry to see you leave—when was it? two years ago? I thought you were a clever girl and I liked you. What'd I say I'd do then?—give you a raise? How could I know how serious you were? You probably didn't know yourself. You seemed a little sad.

"But I took a chance on your proposal this winter, and I'm very, very happy about it. Not rich, but happy. Now I'd like to talk to you, I'd like you to read some of the

435

scripts we've got, I'd like to hear what you're thinking about. I'm not going to give you your head, you understand—I'm not going to give you a blank check. But I'd like to set something up. And maybe you should get an agent. I'll tell you what I know and what I've heard. It's less important than you think, if you get a decent one, but it's bad if you get a bad one. So you should do it right.

"Can you come for a few days? We'll pay for the ticket. You can stay with Mrs. Danziger and me. Now that you know what you're doing, you probably want to make sure I still know what I'm doing. We'll have a nice time, nothing fancy, just us."

Anya said she'd go. She felt good about Mr. Danziger. It was odd—for the time she'd worked for Ikon, why hadn't she valued what he was. Only two years ago she'd resented his deliberately weary attention to business, perhaps even attached the blame for her own good-gray-ladyness to him.

She thought, Come back, Dick Whittington, thrice Lord Mayor of London—she really had hoped for that. Was it necessary for her to have been dazzled before she could come to her own senses? Tassie, Timmy, and Henniker had dazzled her. It was a little sad to think of Tassie and Henniker as they were now. Anya wasn't sure whether she had produced the magic lighting, or whether they'd had a real charm which had burned away. It didn't matter, they now were sad. Henniker's precise and talented malice had seemed more impressive when it was an aura, a kind of St. Elmo's fire, dancing around his own ideas. Now the aura was all that was left.

But it was Tassie who seemed worse off . . . Tassie's contempt for her life as a princess, a contempt that had been blithe when they were college girls, now seemed a form of self-despising because Tassie had still not let go of that life. She hadn't let go because there was no new life for her to take hold of.

Anya thought it was no virtue of her own that had saved her. She hadn't been a beautiful princess or a bright young man with promise, and so she'd had nothing to cling to. Her own hope had been as decorated with romance— *Come back, Dick Whittington, thrice Lord Mayor of London.* It was her own good luck that it hadn't turned sour— it had turned ordinary. *Dear Dick, Work available. Hock what you can and come soonest.*

Anya thought that if this was the postpartum depression after *Iowa Girl,* it wasn't too bad.

Late that night Anya went looking for Mac. She finally found him in the sauna room working on his duckboat. It was almost finished. Anya noticed for the first time that it was a pretty little thing, all its curves tucked in, like a quarter wedge of an apple. It was sturdy and compact, but it was the most delicate work Anya had seen Mac do—as though it were designed by a Dutch elf.

Mac quit, and they went and sat on the porch steps. It was a soft June night, but Mac seemed restless.

Anya said, "I thought it calmed you down to work on that thing."

Mac shrugged. He said, "I've been thinking about your work."

Anya laughed and said, "And it makes you nervous?" She didn't want him to get serious.

Mac said, "No. But I've been thinking about this year and how I was wrong to want to have you easy to get to. As easy to get to as I am for you." Before Anya could speak, he continued, "And another thing I've been thinking is this—I have some skills, and I can pick up how to do certain things. I was pleased with some of the contraptions I made—the *Wozzeck* set, for one thing. That was pretty good, for what you had in mind."

Anya nodded.

Mac said, "But in general the things I admire most are things that take a long time. I used to wish that I could find something to do that would take a long time. But lately I've had to think that I may not. That I may not have a life's work."

Anya said, "That must come as a relief."

She regretted her remark until she saw Mac was patiently overlooking her interruption, as though he was chairman of the conversation, wisely restraining his use of the gavel while a little frivolity ran its course.

Mac said, "Then I thought about *Iowa Girl* some more. You see, I didn't think it was going to be as good as it is. I think now you could make a really wonderful movie."

Anya said, "I remember you saying something like that."

Mac said, "I had no idea when we came out here that you knew what you were doing. I didn't really understand how you directed the shows—I liked them, but I didn't *think* about them—I knew I couldn't have done what you were doing, but I thought there were a lot of people who could. Sometime during the winter I changed my mind, but I still didn't really *think* about it. But now I've thought about it, and I think you could have a life's work."

Anya clicked her tongue. She had just chucked out her old Dick-Whittington romance. What was Mac doing with it?

Mac took a breath and said, "And so what I've been thinking is . . . If you think I could be useful to what you plan to do . . ." He took another breath and said, "I will serve you."

Anya was embarrassed she'd been making fun of him.

But she was in a deeper way horrified.

She wasn't sure how it had come to this, but it was all wrong.

For an instant she thought it was like the time in college when Tassie offered her money, trying to help out her poor roommate.

Then she thought it was beyond that—Tassie had only annoyed her—Mac was doing something desperate.

Anya couldn't speak. She felt a terrible panic fluttering in her.

How could he come to her in this strange way? He was a stranger who suddenly had power over her. It was her fault somehow. She felt herself giving up. It was like the time in the motel . . .

Mac abruptly said, "I didn't do this right." He shook his head. "I can't explain what . . . I see I've done it wrong."

Mac went into the house. The screen door swung shut, but not the heavy kitchen door, so Anya could hear his footsteps on the stairs up to their bedroom.

Her panic passed. She now began to wonder sadly what brought him to say what he'd said, what was in it that had upset her.

She supposed he'd been brought to it because she'd kept him away for so long. So now he came to her with a contract. No—worse than that—a vow. She had felt that this was an attempt to reach deeper into her.

Anya tried hard to imagine what he wanted, how it felt to want something from her.

She could imagine that she seemed to him to be moving

away. And she could imagine why he gathered his energy and lurched into the pitiful clumsiness of his proposal.

She sympathized more now with what he intended, but still it was all wrong. All least he'd realized that. Or had he only seen her reaction?

Swearing fealty. It was romance again. She thought he must feel the way he had in the army when he'd been in trouble, he must feel that unsettled. Wanting to throw himself on the mercy of the court.

She then thought, To be fair, how should he do it right? Was she going to be more and more difficult? There was a point, after all, where wanting something done the right way became heartlessness.

She tried again to imagine Mac's state of mind. She had accepted as a piece of peculiar good luck that he adored her body. She had never figured out completely how he felt about her. He'd certainly had to modify some of his principles to follow her as he had.

She suddenly saw that Mac was perfectly capable of changing direction by sheer will. If she were to leave him now, he was capable of tearing out everything he'd felt for her, of walking down to Sigurd's and saying he would run the farm, take the daughter—all with a whole-heartedness that would be like rage. Sigrid would never know what hit her. The perfect city would be built and populated with their muscular children before she blinked.

Anya imagined another script. If she were to leave him, he would linger in a wounded state of dumb bereavement, furiously working about the house and theater until one day he realized that Dulcie was waiting for him in the garden. And then, moved by a deep tender pity that he would by his will make permanent, he would set about building Dulcie a rustic bower, bordered with sunflowers and sweet corn. Another perfect city, this one looking like a needlepoint of the Peaceable Kingdom.

Anya doubted that Mac had imagined either of these possibilities. At least not the way she had. Then it occurred to her that she'd set out to imagine them mockingly, but having imagined them, she now found herself admiring Mac for being capable of such furious, dangerous changes.

Anya went upstairs. The kerosene lamp was still burning, but Mac was asleep. It was warm enough now in June so that he slept naked under a single sheet. She thought,

No wonder he's tired, wanting to mend so many things. She understood more clearly his thirst for wholeness and the size of his willingness.

Beside those qualities, her own wish for him to have an easier style, to approach her with more fluid courtliness, seemed shriveled.

And yet she knew that she would insist on something else, like the spoiled princess she'd never been able to be before, sending the suitor on another intricate quest for something small. Anya wasn't sure if she wanted Mac to give up a part of the way he was, or acquire part of the way she was. Or just approach her from a new side.

She thought, That last isn't so unfair. I don't want him to give up anything important, just surprise me.

Then she could give up having to surprise herself.

She got into bed and thought she was going to have to give up surprising herself anyway.

* * *

Sigurd told Mac that he'd signed an agreement to sell the farm.

They were standing inside the tractor shed.

Sigurd said, "I'll tell you, there's only so long you can worry about a thing, and then you'd better just go and do it. I've got ten acres of land right on the north edge of town. I'm going to build two big towers there—just like those corncob-looking towers in Chicago. It's up on a hill, so you'll be able to see the whole of Iowa City. The old capitol dome lit up at night, the river, all the way across to the law college up on the bluff.

"Some people told me I should just take the money and go south." Sigurd laughed. "I know how old I am—I'm fifty-eight. I started to work when I was eighteen. I got this farm when I was twenty-eight. I worked it for thirty years. I'll admit there was a time there when I felt awful about leaving it—I was out here yesterday walking around saying good-by to all this—I went round and touched every one of these machines. I was like a kid giving up his toys. But I'm better off now. I'm handing this farm over in prime order. Everything works perfect. I'm not going to have no auction. The farm goes all of one piece. They're going to come in here and just push any starter button, and she'll turn right over. This whole farm won't miss a stroke."

Mac had thought he would feel terrible when the farm was sold. He felt instead a sympathy for Sigurd's energy.

Sigurd showed him the architect's drawing at lunch. Sigurd explained how he reduced the capital gains tax by starting right in on a new enterprise; he had whole new chapters of lore on taxes, building materials, zoning codes, his corporate structure, his general contractor, his subcontractors. He had a list of the salaries of the University, the Purina food factory, the Procter & Gamble plant. A list of what students paid for off-campus apartments.

Sigurd said, "You know, I still feel bad about that little boy—I know accidents happen, but for example if you'd been living in a place like I'm going to build, that wouldn't have happened. That place over there is fine for someone like you, but I always worried about that family. The wife's still there?"

Mac said, "Yes."

Sigurd said, "But Raftery just went off."

Mac said, "Yes, he left."

Sigurd said, "That's just wrong."

Mac said, "No—"

Sigurd said, "I know he's your friend. I know that. But you tell me if that's a decent way to act."

Mac said, "He'd been drifting away before that—when Hugh died, they either had to get stronger or split up. Raftery couldn't stand to stay here anymore. Dulcie couldn't stand to go away."

Sigurd said, "I'm sorry to hear you think that way. It seems to me there was one thing for him to do and that's all.

"I've never asked about what goes on over there. I think young people should live a little wild. But then when you get married you ought to make a home. Now, don't you think that?"

Mac didn't want to argue. He felt the angle between his affection for Sigurd and his love for Raftery gape open.

Mac didn't blame Raftery at all—but he felt the pull of Sigurd's surprise and disapproval that he, Mac, failed to blame Raftery. It was a sensation—even though he could think of arguments—that left him helpless.

Later in the day when Sigurd and he were up on the

ridge looking down on the fields and houses, Mac found it hard to reconcile his view of the farm with the change in ownership. It was as though he expected some cast of shadow.

The corn was as high as the fence posts now.

He asked Sigurd if Sigurd would consider asking the buyer to leave out Raftery's house, and maybe ten acres or twenty, just a strip back to the river.

Sigurd pointed to the adjoining farm toward town. The impounded pond shone in the middle of its nearest field.

Sigurd said, "They've bought that farm. They've bought Ergenbright's. Their fields will run straight from there"— he moved his arm in a sweep past Raftery's house, his own, and beyond—"to way down there. You can't expect them to leave out a strip.

"Besides—I don't think I could do it. Even that little bit you're asking about. What would you do? You'd grow your snap beans and sweet corn and sunflower seeds, and you'd feed a dozen people. That's not enough. That part of a big farm will feed a hundred people or more. This isn't hard-scrabble land like back east. Iowa produces ten percent of all—"

Mac said, "Yes, I know."

Sigurd, "Well then, you know. If you want to have a garden up by your theater, I'm sure they'll lend you a tractor and plow as easy as I do."

Mac said, "What'll happen to the house we're in?"

Sigurd said, "I don't know. I don't think their help'll want to live there. They'll want a modern house. I expect they'll just run the field straight from the pond all the way down past my place. Put the manager in my house. The assistant manager in Ergenbright's. It's not worth trying to move those sheds. I think the sills are too old, they'd just give way. They're going to farm it a little different—a little bigger scale. Those furrows there'll run straight for nearly a mile."

Mac said, "You mean they'll tear the house down?"

Sigurd said, "Yes. I'll tell you what I can do is to find out how soon after the closing they're going to start rear-ranging things. Maybe they'll let you stay on for a bit."

Sigurd added, "You know, they may be going to do what you said to me back last year—bulldoze that dike back nearer the river. Maybe right up against that little creek.

442

They have the money to do things like that that take a few years to pay off. Maybe put in some drainage tiles down in those wet fields. That'd pay off in ten years."

Mac said, "I'm not sure I would get along with them."

Sigurd said, "Maybe not. But you're working for them now."

Mac said, "What do you mean?"

Sigurd said, "This crop is going to be theirs. Most farms change over in winter, but their company wanted it sooner, and they paid enough. It suits me fine."

Mac said, "When is the closing date?"

Sigurd said, "Six weeks."

Mac said, "I'll work for *you* for six weeks."

Sigurd said, "Well, I'm glad to hear it. I guessed I was paying you more than they do at the theater."

Mac said, "That's not why."

Sigurd said, "I know. I guess I shouldn't have said that . . . I'll tell you why I am glad, though. When they take this crop in and then work their own crop next year, with all their crew, and their new eight-row picker—and they look at those two years side by side, they're going to have to wonder. That new manager may just have to talk fast. And if someone comes down to my new office and says, 'Sigurd, I wonder if you could tell me something'—then I'll just have to say, 'Sorry, boys. Don't ask me about farming. I'm a builder now. Anything you want to know about building, just ask.' "

Sigurd laughed.

Mac thought, I don't blame him, either. Not Sigurd's thirty years here feeding ten percent of the country. Or Raftery's bounding from group to group, getting tossed in a blanket, persisting in his folly.

Then why, if he set them free—wished them their wishes —did he wish to bind Anya?

CHAPTER

||||||||||||||||||||||||||||||||||||

29

They began to move the furniture, the icebox, the wood stove, the gas stove, Dulcie's sewing machine, books, the wheelbarrow, and even the doors with the oval windows. Sigurd had asked his buyer if the group could pick the house bare and the company had said yes.

There weren't enough bedrooms in the house by the theater. Peewee and Dulcie had to sleep in the main room on mattresses on the floor.

Andrew gave Anya and Mac his room, and he slept in town.

Mac launched his duckboat in a shallow part of the creek and left it there to swell tight. He'd hoped to spend a day fishing but he thought he should start to wall in the side porch to add a room to the house. He, Og, and Tagh tore out the cedar planking from the sauna.

Anya went to New York for five days.

Andrew arranged a Fourth of July booking in Chicago. *Captain Jinks of the Horse Marines,* a bit of turn-of-the-century Americana that Andrew had had his eye on for some time. Gibson girls and clean young men. Og got to sing, "I'm Captain Jinks of the Horse Marines." There were some groans over the script, but the money was better than they'd ever had before. They voted themselves a vacation after the Fourth of July weekend.

Mac began to wall in the side porch.

*   *   *

Everyone but Mac got into the Wagoneer. Andrew was already in Chicago. The costumes and props were in a trailer behind the Wagoneer. Mac helped them load and said good-by to them in the yard. Dulcie was strangely nervous. Mac was afraid she'd suddenly decide to stay behind—and he was supposed to meet Anya at the airport. He asked her if anything was wrong. She said, "No. It's just nervousness. I've never stayed at a hotel before."

Mac took the VW and picked Anya up at the Cedar Rapids airport. He absent-mindedly drove by the turn to the theater. He had to go all the way to the driveway at Raftery's house to turn around.

The day cooled off by the time they ate supper. They sat on the half-enclosed porch. The sunset lingered until nine. The bales of hay in the field to the north of Sigurd's oats threw long, neat shadows. The air was still and heavy but very clear. It made the bales look unreal, like pictures through a stereopticon.

Mac said, "I should put in some more of those studs." It was clear from his tone that he wasn't going to move.

Anya said, "They won't be back till Tuesday. This is wonderful." She took his head in her lap. She was awed how pleased she was by the four days of doing nothing. Her skin felt scrubbed and ticklish. Her bones felt heavy, slow, and sweet, as if the marrow were compressed honey.

It became dark.

They went for a walk through the fields. Mac wanted to see if they could hear the corn grow.

Anya said, "I thought that was a joke."

Mac said, "I don't know. Sigurd says you can hear the joints pop if it's a hot night."

They climbed a fence and lay down in the grass beside the corn.

Mac said, "There. You hear it?"

Anya said, "I think it's the leaves moving."

Mac said, "There's no wind."

Anya said, "I saw one move."

They never were sure—there were small animals moving in the grass. An owl flew by. The moon came up.

Anya spent the next day reading.

Mac came back from Sigurd's at four, filled with furious

445

energy. Anya helped him set studs between the top of the waist-high porch railing and the bottom edge of the roof.

As suddenly as he started, he stopped. Tossed his hammer into the toolbox, went into the main room, and lay down on the floor. Anya stood over him. He reached for her legs. She stepped back but let him have one leg. He said, "I can't stand it." He kissed her ankle.

Anya worried that this second honeymoon of dumb, restful pleasure and sentiment was a flare that would burn out —end in a fight—or worse, lead them back into their stalemate. But she couldn't resist it.

Sunday Mac didn't go to Sigurd's. They weeded Andrew's flower garden, Dulcie's vegetable garden, bailed out Mac's duckboat, walked into the woods, went swimming in the river.

Monday Anya went along to Sigurd's. The livestock was all gone. They stayed for supper with Sigurd and Selma. They finished eating by five thirty, stayed until six, and then walked slowly back along the road.

Anya said, "I didn't intend to feel this way—I feel like I'm just visiting here."

Mac said, "It's a good time. It felt like this once in January during a thaw. Completely still. The middle of the flat world. A filled bowl."

Anya said, "I meant our vacation."

Farther down the road she said, "Do you think we could live like this? My coming to visit you?"

Mac said, "I don't know."

They turned up the road to the theater.

Mac said, "It couldn't just go on, I guess."

They were uneasy in the twilight, so they called Andrew in Chicago. They got him at the hotel just before he left for the theater. He said that they were all exhausted but it had gone okay. The theater manager had said, "It's not much of a play, but it's a *show*." Andrew said, "Out of the mouths of managers . . ."

Andrew said he had to go, they'd be back for a late lunch tomorrow.

Anya felt better. She didn't mind their coming back.

She and Mac went out and sat on the lawn. She said, "Where's the moon?"

Mac said, "Not up yet . . . You know, the only thing I miss out here is the sea."

Anya said, "You want everything."

Mac said, "Not anymore. Raftery wants everything. I want less and less.

"I still think of things I want to talk to him about. I was thinking today that I used to have a state of mind that was like his. When I used to receive communion as a kid I would think—for just a while—that the world was a perfect place, and therefore I was ready to die—I'd think, Right now, God. Because I knew I'd be out of a state of grace by Sunday lunch." Mac laughed.

"And after that—that was over by the time I was fifteen, though there were traces that lasted through college—after that the only time I was happy was playing hockey. Even hating to lose was wonderful. There seemed to be a road that went on and on, improvement after improvement. It was still a form of Catholic self-improvement—examination of conscience, performing set exercises in the hope of grace.

"I suppose the next thing was romance—the idea of a rebel grace. The whole thing with Mireille—it came later than it might have so I made more of it. I wrapped much more around it. I only realized the other day that she may not have known what I thought about her. I was filled with superstition that she had no way of knowing about. I tried to cram everything I'd ever felt before into it. I have no idea what she thought."

He said, "But I guess I had some sense that there was a pattern of less and less—I mean, from a state of grace and harmony with heaven, down to playing hockey, down to romance. You see, I knew that whatever happened with Mireille, whatever secret we set up, it wouldn't include everything. In fact it would *only* include us.

"And then I thought I should know how to do things. That was another step down. Just being accomplished. When I ran into you—"

Anya laughed and said, "Don't tell me that was another step down."

Mac said, "No. It wasn't. But it wasn't a step up either. I mean this year has had its good parts . . . but I realize

447

now why you couldn't give in to the way I was. You had a lot to do. You did a lot. And all the ways I was drawn—and all the ways things ended badly—were just part of me. Dulcie was my fault. I ruined that affection—"

Anya said, "You can say love."

Mac said, "All right . . . I really was dumb. I didn't bear that weight right."

Anya was touched by the phrase; it was the kind of idea Mac would have—that failure was a loss of strength. But it also annoyed her. That he was the tree at the center of the earth that held up everything . . . that was a romantic notion of such weight that it kept him from moving easily to her. He moved, but carrying too much.

She wished she knew whether she wanted him free, or free to move easily to her . . .

Mac said, "And Raftery. I miss Raftery."

Anya said, "And Hugh."

Mac said, "Yes."

Mac thought awhile. He said, "I wouldn't have mentioned him. I suppose because *missing* isn't the right word. You only miss what you might reach."

After a moment, Mac said, "I'll miss Sigurd. It's not so awful what he's done. I felt a little bad about his farm. I learned a lot working for him, but now that's done."

Mac paused. He said, "The fact that I'm left with nothing from what I've done is right. I'm left free. I was worse off when we got here. For one thing, I still had the superstition that making things that would last had some magic. But what I made in the theater and then tore apart again turns out to be just as good as anything I put in at Sigurd's. It's all gone, and I'm a blank."

Anya felt a twinge of fear. For an instant she thought he meant to say he didn't feel anything anymore.

She had turned her face away when he spoke. Now she looked back at his face and he appeared too calm to have meant that.

She was sure he didn't just mean that he'd lost what he'd made—he did mean he'd lost what he'd felt for the people he'd adopted. But not her?

Her fear didn't leave her, it turned in her slightly. She couldn't bring herself to say that she could make it right for him, that she was ready to stand in the center of his feelings.

But she felt he was approaching her once more. In spite of what he'd said about bearing weight, Anya guessed that he meant that he was now empty, but that he would be full again. She thought he was very close to approaching her the right way this time. Her fear turned another way. She feared that this was as close as he would ever come. And that it was a lack of courage in her that was what was missing.

For the first time in as long as she could remember she wasn't sure what she wanted. She resented not knowing, and had to make an effort not to blame Mac.

Then she thought that he was changing too in this slack time. She simply hadn't noticed. It was plain enough. As soon as she stilled her own worries, she could feel the difference in him. Something was moving in him. She thought she could sense it, as though she were discovering the slight but growing turbulence in the air as she came nearer and nearer to a river whose current was the major movement causing the minor movement of the air against her skin whenever she stood still.

* * *

The next day Anya got a letter from Tassie. It was almost incoherent. Henniker had left to go to England. It wasn't clear from what Tassie said whether he was leaving her for good or not.

Tassie wrote, "You shouldn't feel badly about what Norman wrote in his article. If you knew how desperately he's been working this last year and how terrible people have been to him. He's tried and tried and tried and that piece he wrote about you isn't personal, it's a professional effort. He really meant it when he said—I tried to stop him and he said it was how he felt about art that was more important."

Anya thought, Shit.

Andrew showed her the reviews of *Iowa Girl* he'd clipped in Chicago. The Sunday *Times* wasn't due until Wednesday in Iowa City. The others were from weekly magazines and the Chicago papers.

Anya looked through them. She asked Andrew if he'd seen the one Henniker wrote. Andrew pulled it out. He

449

said, "I wasn't going to show it to you. You'd probably have missed it."

Anya read it. It was slick and nasty but not quite as well written as she'd thought it would be. It still angered her.

Andrew said, "It's hateful. But it seems clear to me that anyone reading it would guess that your work is pretty good and that's what's making him froth at the mouth."

Anya wasn't ready for that line yet.

It took her until after supper to calm down.

She showed the piece to Mac. She was surprised that Mac didn't seem to get mad.

Mac said, "What did you expect? It's a cupful of spit he spent a month salivating. 'It is too painfully obvious that *Iowa Girl* is more a record of the bizarre relations of the directress and actress than an evocation of Iowa—for whatever *that* would be worth.' When you think of his cultivating Mercks to get bits of gossip for his column—his wheedling around doing research. He was more effective when he nailed your shoe to the floor. He ran some risk there. He was at the door for a second before he ran off. This is just spit."

Anya thought that was probably right.

Mac said, "Make another movie and he'll choke to death."

Mac looked the piece over again. He said, "I'll tell you what is a pain is that he puts down everything else—*Hail Holy Queen*, Ryan—and he's shitty about Andrew's directing *Exit the King*. 'This rustic Iowa theater company makes a sow's ear out of a silk purse'."

Mac finally said, "He wanted to really lay you out for good. He tried his best shot, and it's just this . . ."

But Anya found it more difficult than that. She felt terrible for Tassie—that was part of it. But she felt a horror too—not because of what Henniker said but because his tone was so desperate, like the flailing and grabbing of a drowning man.

Anya had not set a definite date to move to New York. She still hadn't read the film scripts that Mr. Danziger had asked her to read. As for her own ideas, she had none that stayed with her longer than it took them to puff up and burst.

Mr. Danziger also wanted her to work on some of the

promotional short films for various industries that were still part of Ikon's bread and butter.

She envied the group their chores. Mac had finished up the porch room, and was now helping Andrew oversee the heating company install three fans in the roof of the barn to blow the hot air back down during the winter and out during the summer. Dulcie and Peewee started making the costumes for the September production of *The White Devil*. Ray was teaching an acting class in the summer school and casting some of the *White Devil* bit parts from his students. Bangs was already learning her lines—Isabella, the wronged wife. That made Anya laugh. Tagh was going to play Flamingo.

Anya mentioned to Andrew that she'd played Vittoria Corombona—the White Devil—in college.

Andrew said that she must have been terrific. But he spoke absent-mindedly. She realized she'd wanted him to ask her to stay for one more play.

Anya couldn't figure out why she was mooning around.

Then it occurred to her in her idleness that she hadn't really understood Henniker's piece. It was two things: It was in many ways a portrait of himself—in its accusations of private sexual theater, manipulation, ambition born of curiosity.

And secondly, it was a curse. His intention, his subtext, was to say, "You will fail the same way I did, you will enter the same hell of pretense, disconnection, weightlessness."

His piece was an invitation to rejoin him.

He wished her to take back her rejection. In his world it was possible. He himself constantly had to forget the terrible things his friends said about him. He probably imagined he and she were alike. She thought then that for all his research he'd missed the point. She had changed beyond what he could imagine since Chicago. She continued to worry about Tassie, but she stopped thinking about Henniker.

She started reading the scripts and treatments Mr. Danziger had given her.

In the industrial/promotional file she found a GE proposal. They wanted a film showing off their "world of the future." There were, among other things, electric prosthetic devices. There was an inflatable suit for shriveled old people that supported them and magnified every movement of their limbs. There were artificial arms and legs that took the real body's nervous impulses and transformed them into electrically operated movement. She showed the proposal to Mac.

She said, "Think what Mercks could do with these. Senior citizens going at it in their inflatable suits."

Mac pointed to the diagram of the electronic artificial arm. He said, "I saw one of the earlier models of this—they made it for my father. He got so he could use it to paddle a canoe—even reel in a bait-casting reel. He can't use a fly rod, though."

Anya couldn't tell if he brushed past the slight embarrassment she felt on purpose or not. But her chief reaction was how odd that even as objects—not just ideas—flew at the two of them, their separate magnetisms sorted them out into their separate styles.

Mac's magnetic hand attracted blunt usefulness. He raised his hand and cast iron flew to it—Dutch oven, skillet, a spring-loaded double-pronged fork for the wood stove lids.

Even his ingenuities had been so large and simple as to seem homely. The backstage arrangement of pulleys, wooden cleats, and rope (all the ends whipped with linen thread) looked functional but cumbersome—half hand-me-down hardware from Sigurd's barn junk, half homemade nautical, as though the scene changers were going to lift a ton of hay or lower a longboat.

He held up his hand—he attracted Sigurd and Sigrid, Dulcie, Hugh. She drew Peewee, Mercks, Ryan. They'd both drawn Raftery. And the theater—she realized that in an odd way it seemed to lie in both their magnetic spheres.

What did it mean that he was changing?

She'd seen Raftery change—Peewee—Andrew— Wasn't Mac still trying to build the perfect city in himself?

She closed the folder.

She didn't dare ask him if he was coming to New York. She still, though, could not help thinking that he must approach her in some way that was just right.

She wished he would come to New York without her raising *her* practical cast-iron hand. She decided she would explain the practical side of her wishes. Perhaps that would draw him.

She said, "I may do this GE short. Just to get something done while I wait for an idea for a movie that I like. What I *am* going to do anyway is go to New York. I liked being here, but it's almost safe now. I want to go on. Without a net. The reason I'm going is that I still want the feeling of taking a next step, of taking a dare. As much that as the noble uplift of a life's work."

She was speaking more harshly and dramatically than she wished. What she said was what she felt, but she was leaving out the four days they'd spent alone, her uncertainty about what to do with that dark pull of sweetness.

Later that evening in bed in their borrowed room, she said, "For a long time you thought of me as your weakness. You didn't blame me for anything, but you had a feeling that I was some sort of Delilah to you. I mean you were honest enough about it—you knew you liked the idea enough to keep on with its sinful delights. But then the other day when you said you thought I might eventually make a good movie"—Anya held up her hand to keep him from interrupting—"I suddenly got promoted from your weakness to some kind of heroine, a sort of plaster saint you could burn candles to." She added, "You can see the difficulties."

Mac lay on his back and put his hands under his head. She couldn't see his mouth, but she guessed it was puffed out while he wondered.

She regretted that they weren't going to have a fight.

He finally said, "I can't leave just yet."

Anya said, "I have to."

*　　*　　*

The next day they all walked down to see Raftery's house wrecked. Mac was surprised at how little he felt. His only twinge came when he thought of the built-in drawers in the upstairs hall. They were very well made. And then he thought of the homely awkwardness of the two doors out of his and Anya's bedroom: The door to the hall and the door to Peewee's room were built so close to the corner of the room that the corners of their lintels just touched. Mac thought, Not for long.

But he found he felt less now for that detail than he'd

felt during the odd moments he'd noticed it all during the year.

Dulcie seemed almost satisfied when the first wall caved in.

They all left before it was over, though they could hear the whine of the caterpillar engines and occasional splinterings and collapsings all the way back to the theater.

When the sun was down to the tops of the oak trees lining the river, Mac walked past the rubble and on to Sigurd's house. The new manager and his wife were sitting on the porch in the glider.

Mac introduced himself and stayed to smoke a cigar on their porch steps.

The man asked Mac about the duckboat tied up in the creek. Mac was pleased the man had bothered to walk back into the woods. Mac told the man he'd just put it in to swell the planking tight. The man admired the boat. It began to occur to Mac that a new mood was on him. Mac said, "I haven't a use for it. Do you want it?"

The man wouldn't take it for free. He said he'd buy it. Mac said a hundred. The man said it was too little, but finally agreed. The man made out a bill of sale.

Mac thought that was a detail as homely as the awkward lintels—the man's belief in the necessary magic of fair dealing, that it was bad luck to take too much advantage of someone else's folly or hardship. A few of the farmers still felt that.

Mac walked farther down the road flanked by shoulder-high corn rising up to the ridge on one side, stretching flat to the low, wet pasture and the oak trees on the other. The greens were all darker and more intense now—as though the black earth was radiating its darkness out through the full leaves.

He'd been washed up here and he'd burrowed in, like some slow sea creature.

The land still reminded him of the sea. And what was changing was like a change in the sea—a small change in the mixture of dissolved oxygen and salt in the water, not a toxic or even a threatening change, but one that signaled to him that this was no longer the place to hold on to and be nourished.

He walked to the theater the long way around the section,

and by the time he got back it was dark, and Anya had left for New York in the green Volkswagen.

He thought of New York—treeless, earthless, skyless, childless.

He gave his things away. Left Sigrid's shotgun for Og. His stew pot and frying pan to Dulcie, his tools to Andrew. Bedclothes to everyone. Andrew said not to worry, he'd store what was left. Andrew said he'd write to Mac about his money, not to worry. Mac could tell that Andrew saw the new pull of energy in him.

Mac started thinking of Raftery. The Raftery whimsical walk from—where? Missouri? The Mississippi? The Midwest. From wherever he happened to be. He couldn't remember if Raftery had actually got to New York.

He thought, This is a last superstitious gesture. He would be different in New York, it would be much more practical.

As Mac stepped onto the dirt road the thick summer air around him billowed up as light as his senses. His left arm nestled on his fishing sack slung from his shoulder.

It struck him how amused Raftery would be to go through his sack. The practical pilgrim—a change of socks and a poncho. A screw-top jar of water, a pocketknife. Fly reel, hooks and line, three-section rod. Raftery, none of your poems mimeographed in purple ink, none of your spiral-bound pages of tiny script, your notes on the universe. Not your striped umbrella.

But it *is* your gift of carelessness that has made me lighter. Not as careless as you, but for the moment less afraid to be a fool. There are quick short truths as well as slow enduring ones. There's no need to be afraid of lightness when it lifts you up.

It was a momentary gift, but it was crucial—lighthearted passage to New York.

Bestselling
Novels
From
POCKET BOOKS